I0748114

LEGACY OF ROSES

KINGDOMS OF LEGACY WORLD

KINGDOMS OF LEGACY

Legacy of Roses: A Beauty and the Beast Tale (Book One)

Legacy of Glass: A Cinderella Tale (Book Two)

Legacy of Thorns: A Sleeping Beauty Tale (Book Three)

Legacy of Gold: A Rumpelstiltskin Tale (Book Four)

Legacy of Locks: A Rapunzel Tale (Book Five)

Legacy of Ice: A Snow Queen Tale (Book Six)

TETHERED HEARTS

Ties of Legacy: A Companion Novel

LEGACY OF ROSES

A BEAUTY AND THE BEAST TALE

KINGDOMS OF LEGACY BOOK 1

MELANIE CELLIER

LUMINANT PUBLICATIONS

For Angelica Rose,
who also shines more brightly than any flower

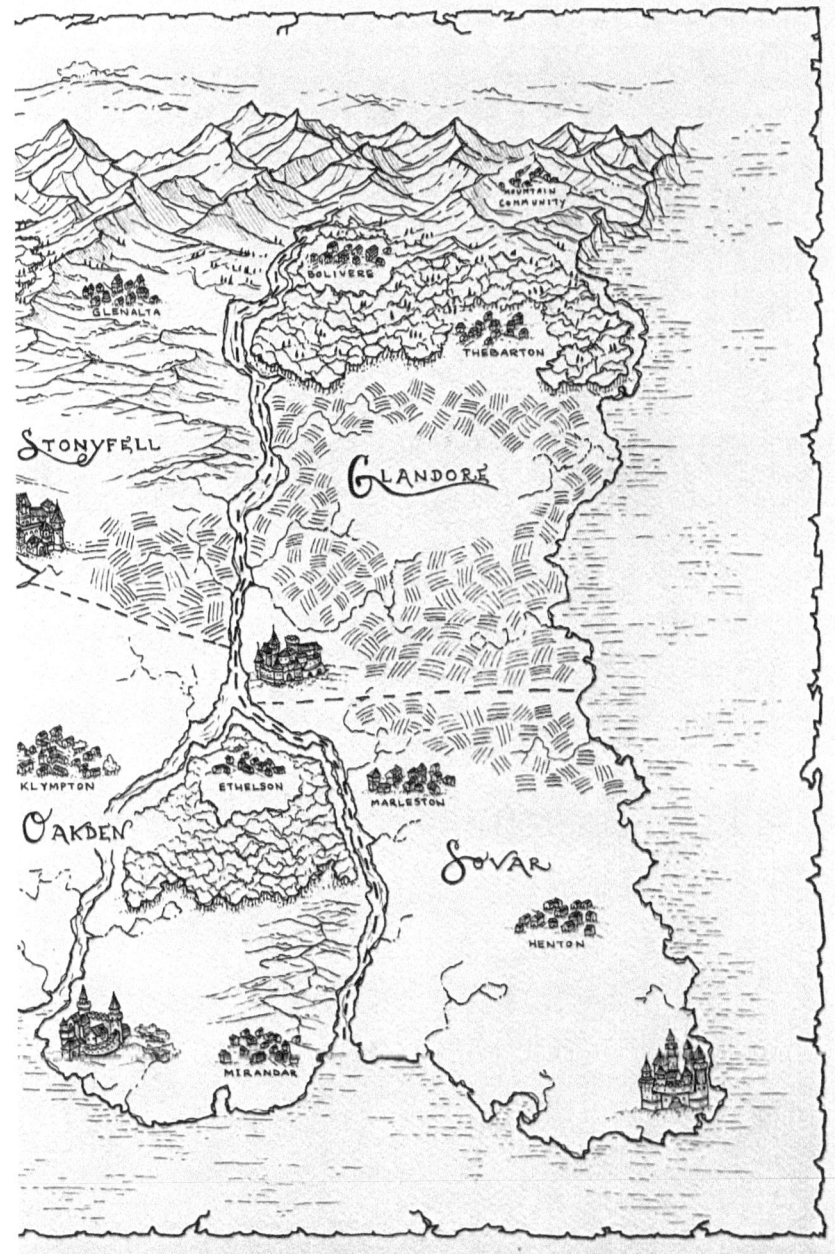

CHAPTER 1
ROSALIE

"Can't you go a little faster?" Rosalie gazed back at her friend, her hands on her hips.

Daphne sighed, her body visibly drooping and her steps slowing even further. Rosalie hurried back to her side, looping her arm through the other girl's and tugging her down the road. If they kept walking at Daphne's pace, it would be nightfall before they got anywhere.

"You were the one who said we should come out here to investigate in the first place!" Rosalie said as she tugged her friend along. "Can't you put in a little effort to stay awake?"

Daphne's eyes flew open at the accusation, her expression wounded. "I never suggested any such thing! I wouldn't be so foolhardy. I merely said I saw something strange. You're the one who dragged me out here."

"Anyone would think we'd come ten miles instead of

only one," Rosalie cried. "But we're nearly there. The castle is only a little further."

Daphne allowed herself to be tugged along, despite the doubt in her voice. "Does it really count as a castle? A manor house at most, surely?"

Rosalie shook her head stubbornly. "The size doesn't matter. It looks enough like a castle to count. Just think of all that gray stone—and it even has turrets! You can call it what you like, but as far as the Legacy is concerned, it's a castle."

"I don't care if the Legacy considers it a castle or a pigsty," Daphne said firmly. "We would both do better to stay far away from it. Especially you."

Rosalie's mouth set into lines of mulish determination. "Do you think I could sleep a wink with such a horrid specter hanging over me? The castle hasn't been inhabited in more than a generation, and I just turned eighteen a week ago." Her voice edged toward a despairing wail. "It can't be inhabited now, of all times!"

Daphne groaned as Rosalie dragged her around the final turn. Spying a fence post, she slipped free of her friend and flung both arms onto it, resting her head on top. Her eyes fluttered closed.

Rosalie ignored her, too busy staring at the building that had come into view. It was still a fair distance from them, separated from the road by a long stretch of overgrown garden. But from their current angle, she could see down the sweeping, tree-lined drive to the front of the castle-like stone structure. And just as Daphne had reported, the heavy wooden door stood partially open.

"There can't be a Beast here," Rosalie moaned. "I won't allow it!"

Daphne cracked one eye open. "Do you think you can prevent it through willpower alone?" Her curiosity sounded genuine.

Rosalie's eyes remained fixed on the distant door. "I know you said it looked as if someone was here, but I thought..."

Daphne raised her head, roused from sleepiness to indignation. "Just because I like to take the occasional nap doesn't mean I'm a fool. I can tell the difference between an open door and a closed one!"

Rosalie threw her a disbelieving look. "The occasional nap? If everyone from Oakden is as fond of sleeping as you are, I don't know how your kingdom functions at all!"

Daphne shrugged and yawned. "We can't all have as much energy as you, Rosalie. And you know I wasn't as bad before I came to Glandore. It isn't my fault the Legacies punish us for leaving our kingdoms."

Rosalie's eyes narrowed. It was true that the Legacies always inflicted discomfort on those who strayed beyond the bounds of their birth kingdom, and it was equally true that it was hard to predict what form that discomfort would take. It certainly wasn't Daphne's fault, but Rosalie did blame Daphne's parents. Glandorians by birth, they had chosen to move to Oakden and have a child there. And when they had eventually grown too uncomfortable living outside their own birth kingdom, they had moved home to Glandore, bringing their daughter with them. Now

Daphne, uprooted from her home kingdom, was the one suffering in their place.

Perhaps they thought it was acceptable because Daphne was merely sleepy, but Rosalie found it extremely trying. From what she had learned in school, the famous sleepiness of the Oakden Legacy wasn't supposed to be anywhere near as severe as what Daphne experienced. The Legacy had magnified the effect to excessive levels when she crossed the kingdom's border. But Rosalie also suspected her friend of taking advantage of the situation.

Daphne got noticeably more sleepy when she didn't want to do something. Such as being dragged down the road from their town in order to examine the nearby derelict manor house.

It was a good thing Rosalie had enough energy for both of them. She had acquired it young thanks to the combination of five siblings and the unwelcome attention of the Glandore Legacy.

"Do you think we should go closer and have a peek inside?" Rosalie asked, hearing the doubt in her voice. She believed in being proactive, but there was a fine line between staying ahead of the Legacy and provoking it.

She expected horrified disagreement from her closest friend but received only silence instead. Glancing over at Daphne, she sighed.

Daphne was asleep. Of course she was.

Rosalie worried at her lower lip as she gazed again at the small castle. Actually stepping onto the grounds did seem like a foolhardy move. But the longer she gazed at the lush garden, the more the roses that covered it seemed to glow as if lit from within. If she plucked a bouquet of them to take home for her mother—

She froze, horrified. What was she thinking? She didn't even like roses. She would be happy if she never saw another one again.

Rosalie growled, directing her ire at the faceless, mindless Legacy. The door of the castle was open and already it was trying to lure her in! But even the dimmest inhabitant of Glandore knew not to pick someone else's roses. And Rosalie knew it better than most.

If she hadn't been so worried about the door, she would have noticed the garden straight away. When she had walked past two days ago, it had been derelict and overgrown, as it had been every day of her life. But now it was bright and lush with fresh growth. It wasn't just the door that had changed.

Movement drew her eye to one side of the drive. Her mouth dropped open as she saw a tall young man bend toward the closest rose bush, his hand extending toward the brightest of the blooms. Apparently there was someone in Glandore foolish enough to pick the castle's roses.

But if the Legacy had anything to say about the matter, it wouldn't only be him embroiled in whatever mess followed. Which meant Rosalie had to act and act fast. She was going to have to step onto the castle grounds after all.

CHAPTER 2
DIMITRI

"Stop!"

Dimitri froze with his hand on the rose's stem. The voice called again, sounding even more desperate, and he straightened. He had stepped outside for a moment of fresh air and couldn't even remember what had drawn him to pluck a rose. He had no use for one.

He scanned the surrounding garden. The cry had come from a young female, and she had sounded distressed. He hadn't seen another soul in the building or grounds since his arrival that morning, but he had been on edge the whole time. An abandoned manor seemed like an open invitation to rogues and misdeeds.

He turned toward the drive, his eyes still searching for the owner of the voice. His hand strayed to his waist, but he hadn't strapped on his sword when he stepped outside, intending to only go a few steps. He would have to attempt assistance without a weapon.

A young woman appeared, dark hair flying and fire in her eyes as she slid to a stop in front of him. He glanced behind her for pursuers, but there was no one else in sight.

When he refocused on her, his words of reassurance died on his lips. The force of her outraged expression was almost enough to send him staggering backward. He had caught a glimpse of surprise there as well—as if she were taken aback to see him—but it had been immediately swallowed by her ire.

The girl's chest heaved as she struggled to regain her breath and talk at the same time.

"What are you doing? Are you out of your senses?" She glared at him as if expecting an answer, but all coherent words had deserted him.

He glanced from side to side, looking for something that might explain the girl's indignation. But there was still no one else in sight, and the grounds looked just as they had moments before.

"I'm...sorry?" he said when the silence stretched out, her glare continuing full force.

He could have turned the question back on her. She was the one trespassing on his lands, after all. But he had only just arrived in Glandore to claim possession of his unexpected inheritance, and he didn't want to antagonize the locals.

On first arrival, he had been concerned that they might be justifiably resentful of him for leaving the building so long abandoned. His family had clearly failed in their duties when they allowed the large grounds to become a wilderness and the building itself to sit empty. It had been an invitation to those who operated in the shadows.

But thankfully, a closer inspection had revealed that neither the building nor the grounds were half as dilapidated as they had appeared at first sight. He was even starting to wonder if his initial impression of long abandonment was wrong. So surely that could not be the cause of this girl's indignation.

The girl's head tipped slightly to the side, her expression softening into one of confusion. He watched her expressive countenance with fascination. As much as he wanted a positive connection with the locals, his response to her was more than neighborly goodwill. The flash in the girl's gray-blue eyes reminded him of a lightning storm, and he couldn't look away. He had been momentarily struck by the beauty of the roses, but they were nothing to the living, burning beauty of this girl.

"Were you really about to pluck a rose?" she asked at last, disbelief in her voice.

He frowned. She was worried about a flower? From his own garden? Did Glandorians hold plants to be so precious?

He couldn't believe it—not when greenery in Glandore grew the moment it was planted. The kingdom fed not only their own populace but half the surrounding kingdoms as well. They must harvest their plants many times a year.

But the girl was still staring at him, clearly waiting for an answer.

"They just looked so beautiful," he said with a note of apology.

He added his most charming smile, hoping to coax her into a better mood. He had seen several expressions from her, but not yet a smile. A girl who looked so captivating when angry had to be breathtaking when those eyes were filled with laughter instead.

But the girl shook her head in response to his effort, pity filling her eyes instead of the smile he had hoped for.

She patted his arm, almost as if he were a child. "It's a good thing I was here, then. The unwary can easily fall prey to the Legacy without even realizing. Next time you should ask yourself why these roses look so particularly bright. They're trying to lure you in."

"Lure me in?" he repeated, his original confusion back in full force. The girl was treating him as if he was simple, but was she the one addled in the brain?

Looking at her eyes again, he couldn't believe it. And yet her words made little sense.

The girl continued, unheeding of his confusion. "You must be from a distant part of the kingdom if you don't know about this place. It's been empty for more years than I've been alive, you know. But look."

She pointed dramatically at the manor's front door which he had left open in an attempt to air out the large entryway. He blinked at the unmoving door for a moment before looking back at the girl.

She seemed to think she had made her point effectively because she seized his arm and dragged him toward the drive. He allowed her to tug him along, his protest silenced by the combination of confusion and fascination that she evoked in him.

"Since I stopped you in time, we should be able to escape the grounds before the Beast appears," she said over her shoulder.

He stiffened, his mind flashing to the sword he hadn't brought along. He was never leaving the manor house without it again.

"What sort of beast?" he asked.

She rolled her eyes. "How should I know? It isn't as if the Legacy is entirely predictable. Life would be a lot easier if it were." She grumbled the last line under her breath, still towing him along with more energy and strength than he'd expected from her small frame.

"I just feel sorry for the poor soul," she added. "They must have bungled things badly for it to get that far. There hasn't been a Beast in this region for several generations."

"You feel sorry for...the beast?" Dimitri asked tentatively, feeling more and more as if he had strayed into a dream.

The girl pulled him over the boundary of the manor grounds onto the public road and immediately released him. She didn't leave, however, her eyes fixing on him and her brow creasing.

"Of course I feel sorry for the man. Would you like to be cursed to take the form of a terrifying animal?"

"No?" he said tentatively. Was the beast she kept referring to a cursed man? He had seen no sign of such an unfortunate individual since his arrival.

The girl shook her head and spoke slowly, as if it was

his understanding that was lacking rather than her own nonsensical words. "Now that the Legacy has found a Beast for the castle, the roses are back in the garden and trying to lure unwary passersby into plucking them. Even if you didn't realize the castle was inhabited again, you should know better than to pluck someone else's rose! The presence of both a castle and a Beast will make the Legacy incredibly potent right here, but that doesn't mean there's no danger elsewhere. It can still find a way to trap you with a flower from a different garden."

Dimitri finally gathered his wits enough to intervene. "I think there's been a misunderstanding. I've only newly arrived in Glandore, and—"

He had intended to claim ownership of the castle, but the girl cut him off with a dramatic gasp. He'd already gathered that travelers from beyond the kingdom's borders were rare, but it seemed an excessive reaction.

"Don't tell me you came into Glandore without researching our Legacy!?" She shook her head. "You really must be a fool."

He flushed and straightened. He had been raised in a remote area, but that didn't make him deficient in understanding. He opened his mouth to repudiate the accusation, but she spoke again.

"Where are you from? You haven't shown any inclination to nap so far, so I'm guessing it isn't Oakden."

His earlier protests dissipated in the face of fresh confusion. Half of the girl's sentences made no sense.

"Are you from Sovar then?" She scanned him up and down as if looking for something. "Do you have anything made from glass? One of the girls in town has the most useful pair of glass gloves that her father bought for her from a peddler. I've been waiting and waiting for the peddler to come around again." She wilted. "Not that I could afford something like that now, even if she does reappear." Her voice lowered, her eyes clouding over. "Not after him."

The combination of anger, sadness, and resignation on her face shook Dimitri. He was seized with the unfamiliar desire to seek out a man he'd never met and squeeze restitution out of him. He bit his tongue on the hot words that wanted to pour out, reminding himself they were complete strangers. Instead, he tried to distract her.

"Glass *gloves*?"

As he had hoped, the girl's expression changed completely yet again, her eyes lighting up. "Avery is one of the few peddlers who actually travels between the kingdoms herself instead of exchanging goods at the border like most merchant trains. She acquires the most amazing items. Last time she visited, she had just been in Sovar. Her cart was full of useful items made from glass." She sighed. "But she doesn't come through often."

Dimitri still didn't know how you could possibly make gloves out of glass, but at least the girl no longer looked as if all her fire had been extinguished.

"Daphne isn't from Glandore, either," the girl continued. "But she's not just traveling through like you. She actually lives here." She peered up at him. "What discomfort are you afflicted with? Is it very terrible?" Sudden understanding illuminated her face. "Has it clouded your mind? Is that why you fell prey to the Legacy so easily?"

"Ah…" Dimitri had no idea how to answer her question, instead seizing on one of his own. "Who's Daphne?"

"My friend." The girl gestured to the side of the road, and he started, not having realized they weren't alone.

But as he took in the second girl's appearance, his brow slowly creased. She was propped on her arms on a fence post, which was already strange enough in the circumstances. But more remarkable still was that she looked utterly at peace, her eyes closed and her breaths rhythmic and slow despite the conversation taking place right beside her.

"Is she…asleep?" he asked.

The first girl giggled at the obvious wonder in his voice, and he forgot all about the sleeping girl. The teasing twinkle in the first girl's eyes was just as charming as he had imagined.

"Daphne can sleep anywhere," she said. "It's the Oakden Legacy's punishment for leaving her kingdom. You know what it's like over there."

Dimitri didn't know. He knew almost nothing about Oakden. Just like he knew nothing about these Legacies she kept mentioning. He knew he should tell her as much and request an explanation, but he couldn't bring himself to say anything that might drive away the amusement lighting her face.

"I'm Dimitri, by the way," he said instead.

"Rosalie," she replied, and he smiled involuntarily. It was a fitting name given his first impression of her.

She misunderstood his expression however, her mouth twisting. "I know. I still don't understand what my mother was thinking! It's like she *wanted* to provoke the Legacy."

A loud yawn prevented him from answering, drawing his eyes to the girl on the post. She straightened, regarding the two of them from half-lidded eyes.

"Who is this?" she asked.

"Dimitri," Rosalie said promptly, as if she had known his name for years. "He's from out of kingdom like you."

Hearing his name on her lips sent a thrill through him, and in its wake, he felt the first stirring of unease. His mother had warned him countless times that Glandore and the other kingdoms were strange places full of deception and treachery. And even Rosalie herself kept uttering cryptic warnings about fantastical happenings.

Could he trust the instinct that had drawn him to Rosalie the moment he'd seen her? Or did the strength of that pull mean he should distrust it?

He shifted, uncomfortable with where his thoughts were leading. He didn't want to view his new acquaintance with doubt and mistrust. But a charming rogue was of necessity charming and appealing—wasn't she?

Not for the first time, he wished he had someone to advise him. But the remote mountain community that had been his home until recently was full of those who had fled the easier life of the kingdoms. They had each possessed a reason for leaving that made them reluctant to speak of their past homes. The mutual silence had been like an unspoken agreement between them—one that had frequently frustrated a youthful Dimitri. But his mother had hated mention of the kingdoms most of all, so there had been no point pressing her for answers.

When she had died, he had come into possession of her private papers. He had been curious, in an idle way. He certainly hadn't expected to find a master key, the deed to a manor—and a whole host of further questions. But there had been no point seeking clarification from his neighbors —his mother would never have confided in them. And though they had offered assistance during her long illness and sympathy after her passing, no one had tried to stop him packing up and leaving. No one had even asked his destination, so they were still in ignorance of the inheritance waiting for him. Not asking questions about each other's business was a foundation of the mountain community.

Dimitri had been braced to find Glandore a dark place, but so far it seemed the opposite. From the beginning his steps had been lighter, as if his whole body weighed less in Glandore than it had in the mountains. And his fears about what he would find at the manor had so far proven unfounded. He had feared his arrival would instigate a property dispute over the manor's true ownership, but instead he had found the building and grounds deserted.

His concern had then switched to the burden of how to restore the house and grounds. And yet every moment seemed to render the once derelict building more habitable rather than less. With the building in much better shape than he'd feared, he was left only with the reality of loneliness and isolation—a possibility that had barely formed in his mind when a young woman catapulted into his day, bringing more brightness than the cloudy sky.

It was a wonder he hadn't been more suspicious from the beginning. Everything had been too easy so far. Had he already fallen prey to the enchantment his mother used to hint at? Was Rosalie luring him in for some fell purpose?

Daphne sidled up to Rosalie, lowering her voice although Dimitri could still clearly hear her words.

"He looks just like—"

"Don't talk nonsense." Rosalie cut her off, her nose raised at a suspicious angle.

Whichever unknown person Daphne was referring to, Rosalie didn't want to talk about him.

"He's just a traveler who failed to sufficiently educate himself before entering Glandore," she said. "I had to stop him just as he was about to pluck a rose!"

Given the severity of Rosalie's earlier reaction, Dimitri expected a dramatic response from Daphne. But she merely raised her eyebrows before glancing at the lush garden and wincing.

Dimitri followed her gaze and frowned. Did the garden look even more abundant than it had an hour ago? He knew plants grew unnaturally well in Glandore, even out of season. But he hadn't expected anything so impressive.

"Is this garden...special?" he asked, unsure how to phrase his question.

Rosalie rolled her eyes. "Now he catches on." She slipped her arm through Daphne's and nodded down the road. "You really shouldn't travel any further into Glandore without properly educating yourself on our kingdom's history. We can see you as far as the edge of Thebarton and give you directions from there into town. The record keeper's office is on the central square."

Dimitri wanted to ask what Glandore's history had to do with anything, but Rosalie and Daphne immediately started walking, clearly expecting him to fall into step beside them.

He hesitated for a moment, glancing back at the manor. He should tell them he wasn't a traveler—not anymore. He could even reassure them about his access to information. The large library inside the manor—complete with a history section—made a visit to the record keepers' unnecessary.

But if he did that, he would have to farewell Rosalie and Daphne immediately.

Dimitri launched into motion, his long legs easily covering the small distance that had grown between them. When he caught up, he modified his stride to keep pace with Rosalie. Glancing down at her, he smiled at the air of suppressed energy that radiated from her. She might be on the shorter side, but he suspected it was only her reluctant friend that was slowing her down.

As they walked, his eyes caught on roses growing along the side of the road. Roses made sense in the garden of a manor house, but he was surprised to see wild ones along the verge of a remote country road. And when the first scattered homes came into view, their gardens were full of roses as well.

Apparently the people of this region really loved the flower. He couldn't see a sign of any other kind of flower.

Rosalie had mentioned roses several times as well. He frowned, trying to remember the roads he had passed on his journey from the mountains to the manor. He could vaguely remember seeing roses there too, but his mind had been too full—of grief over the past and tension over the future—to pay detailed attention to the plants he was passing.

"There seems to be a lot of roses." He glanced sideways at Rosalie.

She shook her head, but her lips were curved upward. "That is an understatement." When he opened his mouth to respond, she quickly cut him off. "And don't even think about making a comment that relates to me and my name. Believe me, I've already heard them all."

Dimitri's lips quivered, but he didn't dare laugh in case he offended her further.

"And don't bother asking me any questions either," she added. "Since you don't know anything, it's better for you to get the whole picture in one go from the record keeper."

Once again, Dimitri wanted to protest her assessment of his education. But since he had felt hopelessly ignorant since the moment of their meeting, he kept his mouth closed.

The two girls stopped in front of a neat cottage with a bordering garden—full of roses, of course. There was no fence, but the garden ended in such an abrupt line that it was easy to tell where their land ended. And it was equally obvious that someone cared for it meticulously.

He glanced again at Rosalie? Was it her? Somehow he

couldn't imagine it—not given the barely repressed energy that poured out of her and her obvious scorn for roses. She didn't seem like she had the patience for careful gardening.

Dimitri only wished her house had been further into Thebarton so he could have more time with her. Would she reject questions about herself the same way she had about the flowers?

His thoughts were still occupied with her when she launched into a precise and detailed set of instructions for how to find the record keeper's office.

"Once you reach the center of town," she concluded, "look for the largest house with the most elaborate frontage. It's two buildings to the left of that."

"If the house is still there," Daphne said mildly.

Rosalie gave her an impatient look. "We aren't that far out of town! We would have heard if there was a fire—or smelled it, at least. Plus the boys would already be out here telling us all about it."

Dimitri wasn't sure about the cause of his sudden tension—the casual suggestion that Thebarton was full of arsonists or the equally casual reference to boys. He would have liked to question both things, but the two girls' conversation continued too quickly for him to interject.

"I suppose you're right," Daphne conceded. "Those terrors would be delighted at having such dramatic news. As if your family isn't traumatized enough."

Some of Dimitri's tension eased at the obvious indication that the boys in question were children. Rosalie, on the other hand, took offense at Daphne's words, dropping her friend's arm as her hands flew to her hips.

"They aren't terrors, they're children. Even if they like to think of themselves as youths." She rolled her eyes. "And if the Fosters' home burns down, it will be no one's fault but their own. They've been making it more and more fancy ever since—" She broke off, glancing at her family's cottage.

Dimitri frowned, once again feeling as if he was missing most of the story.

"Don't bother trying to pick a fight with me," Daphne said without heat. "You know I can't be bothered arguing with you. Your brothers can be angels if you insist, and I quite agree about the Fosters. They should forget about their new elevated status and consider the dangers instead." She shrugged. "But it's no business of mine. Or yours, for that matter." She added the last part as if she didn't think there was much point in trying to direct Rosalie toward disinterest.

Rosalie giggled in response, her momentary heat passed. "My brothers are far from angels as we both know. And since all three of them are smitten with you, I can understand why you think them terrors."

Daphne shuddered—the most animated reaction Dimitri had yet seen from her.

"Please don't remind me."

"But how could they help it?" Rosalie said loyally. "You're so beautiful."

Daphne rolled her eyes. "If you start up, too, I really won't come to visit anymore."

Rosalie grinned, the secure expression of someone who knew her friend would never abandon her. Dimitri smiled as well, unable to help his face mirroring Rosalie's expressive one.

But a moment later, his good humor dropped away as he remembered his upcoming solitary walk back to an abandoned house. He had never possessed a close friend in the mountain community—the inhabitants kept too much distance for that, and his mother had never encouraged it. He hadn't felt the lack, though. When he had wanted company, there had always been someone to be found, and when he had wanted solitude, no one had bothered him. It had seemed ideal. But suddenly he found himself wishing for a friend he could rely on in everything. It was a novel concept.

"Farewell!" Rosalie said abruptly, piercing his thoughts. He blinked at her as she dragged Daphne up the path toward the cottage's door. "Just continue down the road, remember." She waved toward where the houses grew closer together. "And don't forget it's the second building on the left."

Dimitri didn't even have time to thank her before the two girls disappeared inside the house, the door closing firmly behind them. He stood for a long moment staring at it and wondering what sort of family and home lay on the other side.

But at last he shook himself and turned back toward the manor. Thanks to Rosalie he now knew the name and location of the closest town, and it appeared to be a decent size as well. When he was ready to visit a store and meet the local leaders, he would know where to go.

He wasn't in a hurry to do so, however. He had watched plenty of newcomers join the mountain community over the years, and those who sought out the unofficial leaders usually fared the best. But he wanted to do some reading in the manor library to check that matters were conducted the same way in Glandore. He didn't want to miss some essential step out of ignorance.

But as he walked away, his thoughts strayed from Thebarton and its leaders. He glanced back at the cottage. His path into the town would bring him past her door every time. Surely he would run into her again?

Before he came back, though, he had study of a different sort before him. Rosalie had shown him that he had a lot to learn about Glandore—and something called a Legacy. And while he was at it, he would look for answers about his mother's family and why they had left her large and apparently prosperous estate abandoned for twenty years.

CHAPTER 3

ROSALIE

Rosalie dragged Daphne inside and shut the door behind them. She looked warily around, but apparently her brothers weren't home. If they were, they would already have converged on her friend. Ever since Rosalie's family had been forced to move from the center of town into the tiny cottage, it had been impossible to conceal Daphne's presence on any of her visits.

"I think we're safe," Rosalie said warily, afraid that speaking too loudly might summon them from the forest that crept close to the rear of the cottage.

Daphne gave a sigh of relief and sank into the threadbare sofa. Rosalie still had too much pent-up energy to sit, however. She paced instead, a difficult feat given the size of the room.

"I didn't see any sign of the Beast," she muttered as she strode up and down. "But then I managed to stop Dimitri from plucking a rose, so it makes sense he didn't appear." She paused for a moment to shake her head. "Can you believe Dimitri was lured in so easily? He had no wariness of roses at all! Who travels between kingdoms without learning the details of all the Legacies before setting out? Didn't he attend school as a child? He didn't even seem to know what the Sovaran Legacy does to glass!"

"He seemed remarkably ignorant," Daphne agreed in an indifferent voice. But her eyes sharpened as she looked up at Rosalie. "But his looks were interesting. Very interesting."

Rosalie abruptly swung around to pace in the other direction, obscuring her face from her friend.

"What do his looks have to do with anything?"

She bit her lip, aware she hadn't managed the carefree tone she had been aiming for. But she pushed on regardless. "Are you interested in him or something? I'll admit he was attractive, but considering he's only traveling through, we'll probably never see him again."

"Attractive? I suppose he was," Daphne said as if considering the matter for the first time. "Of course you would have found him so." She said the words without judgment. "He looks remarkably like Jace."

"Like Jace?" Rosalie attempted unaffected surprise, but again failed. "I suppose they are both fair."

"It was more than just that." Daphne pursed her lips consideringly. "Although he was...more than Jace. Definitely more."

Rosalie didn't have to ask what Daphne meant by that. She had noticed it too.

Although she didn't want to admit it to her friend, she had been shocked by Dimitri's appearance—nearly shocked enough to forget her urgent mission of separating him from the rose. He did look remarkably like Jace. But the longer she had looked at him, the less she had seen it. With his golden hair, dark brows, and strong, sculpted features, Dimitri had made Jace seem like a weak echo—an inexpert attempt to copy a master's work. But that thought only made her more ashamed, so she pushed it aside.

"More or less, what does it matter?" she said firmly. "As I said, we're never seeing him again."

Silence fell briefly before Daphne spoke in a hesitant voice. "Did you want to talk about him?"

Rosalie turned to face her, her brow creasing. "Talk about Dimitri? Whatever for?"

Daphne shook her head. "I mean Jace. You never mention him, but you've been different ever since..." She trailed off.

Rosalie glanced at the small house around them. It wasn't her that was different since Jace, it was everything else. But there was no point trying to explain that to Daphne, who persisted in believing Rosalie must be hiding a broken heart.

"I don't want to talk about him," she said with finality. "I want—" But as usual whatever she wanted was drowned out by the boisterous arrival of three long-limbed and raucous boys.

"We didn't know you were here, Rosalie," Vernon said, but his eyes were on Daphne. All of theirs were.

"Daphne's staying the night," Rosalie announced to universal male cries of delight.

Daphne, on the other hand, directed a wounded look at Rosalie. Rosalie just grinned back at her. Now that the boys were present, there would be no opportunity for Daphne to bring up Jace again. Besides, Daphne had promised only a week ago that she would come for a longer visit soon.

After Daphne's arrival in Thebarton at the age of seven, the two girls had been almost inseparable, flowing freely between Daphne's house and Rosalie's. But it wasn't the same now that they no longer lived only a few doors apart. Rosalie's whole family missed Daphne, and with Daphne's parents traveling, it was the perfect time for her to stay over.

"Don't worry," Rosalie murmured, dropping onto the sofa beside her friend. "We can escape to bed as soon as we've eaten. And you know Mother will be pleased. With you here, all three of them will volunteer to help prepare the meal. You won't have to lift a finger."

Sighing, Daphne capitulated at this final inducement.

"In that case," she said, shoving Rosalie off the seat and stretching out, "wake me when the food's ready."

As predicted, Rosalie had enthusiastic if unskilled assistance from Ralph, Vernon, and Oscar, who were all hoping Daphne would wake up and notice their contribution.

"How she can sleep through these three, I have no idea," Rosalie's mother said when she arrived from tending the cottage's garden. She surveyed her sons with an indulgent eye before embracing her youngest daughter.

"Practice." Rosalie gave the soup another stir. "Do you remember how loud they used to be when they were younger?" She shuddered dramatically, making her mother laugh.

Glancing sideways at her mother, Rosalie smiled. Every laugh she won from her seemed twice as valuable now. They had all been forced to work harder since the move, but her parents didn't have youth on their side like Rosalie and the boys.

"Don't look at me like that," her mother said softly, slipping her words beneath the boys' chatter. "I'm fine." She looked around the cramped kitchen which was part of the cottage's main room. "But thank you for this. You know we appreciate everything you do."

Rosalie flushed, leaning over to inspect the soup more closely. Her parents had been gracious from the beginning. Even when her father had been forced to transport his own merchant goods, leaving his family for long trip after long trip, no one had blamed Rosalie for the family's separation.

It only made her feel worse.

When the evening's tasks were finally done, and Rosalie lay in bed, Daphne already long gone to slumber, she couldn't get her mother's lined face from her thoughts. How long had she been working in the garden while Rosalie was off inspecting the manor?

Rosalie should have stayed behind and helped. But if she hadn't gone, Dimitri would have plucked that rose, and then they would all have been in trouble. Dimitri might have had no connection to Rosalie, but the Legacy would have sucked her and her family into the mess that followed somehow. She might have missed helping with the weeding, but at least she had averted disaster.

She scoffed quietly to herself in the darkness. It was no surprise that a young man with a face like Dimitri's would be causing trouble.

Objectively, Daphne was right about his good looks. He was even tall and broad-shouldered. Jace had caused enough of a stir among the local girls, and Dimitri far surpassed him. Young men as attractive as Dimitri were best avoided. Only someone with a face like his would have dared wander around an unfamiliar kingdom, getting himself and the innocent people in his orbit into trouble.

She was glad she would never see him again.

"You don't have to walk me home," Daphne said mildly. "I do know the way."

Rosalie grinned at her. "You know perfectly well I was itching to escape. The sun is shining far too beautifully to be cooped up inside—especially with those three."

Daphne grinned knowingly. "Do you think they'll actually clean to your mother's satisfaction this time? Or will they end up having to redo it all like usual?"

Rosalie's laughing rejoinder trailed off as she spotted a

small cluster of young people in front of the Fosters' elaborate home.

"What's going on over there?" She tugged Daphne toward the group, keeping her face carefully averted from the other side of the town's central square. It was still painful to see the charred ashes where her home had once stood.

"Is that Dimitri?" Daphne asked, making Rosalie forget all about the houses.

Dimitri should have been long gone. There had been enough time remaining the day before for him to complete the necessary research. Even if he'd stayed the night at one of Thebarton's inns, he should have been on his way first thing in the morning.

Unless his destination had been Thebarton. Her heart sank.

She wanted to deny it, but it was obviously Dimitri. His head stood tall among the young women who surrounded him, and she could clearly see his profile as he flashed them all a charming smile, chuckling at something one of them had just said. Rosalie's outrage grew as he gave the speaker a piercing look designed to set her heart fluttering. He was even worse than Jace had been.

Rosalie marched up to the collection of familiar faces. The five girls gathered around Dimitri had been Rosalie's friends once, even if they had never been as close as Daphne. And they were still friendly enough that Rosalie was greeted with an array of welcoming smiles.

But the welcome would have been far warmer a year ago. The group's dynamic had changed now that Rosalie was no longer the daughter of the most prosperous merchant in town. When Rosalie could no longer invite them to the largest house on the square, the invitations she received in return had dwindled considerably. And while she hadn't been totally excluded from her social circle, she had slid from its center to its fringe.

The experience had been more humiliating than if they had rejected her entirely. If faced with rejection, she could have blamed it on outside pressure or fear. As it was, she had been forced to accept that her old position hadn't been based on her value as a person and friend but on her parent's financial worth. It had been a sobering realization, and it colored backward to taint years of friendship.

Blythe—the Fosters' oldest daughter and new center of the social scene—gestured them into the circle.

"Rosalie! Daphne!" She looked pleased to have something interesting to share. "You must meet our newest neighbor."

Neighbor. Rosalie's heart sank the rest of the way from her belly to her toes. It was true, then. Dimitri was staying.

"Rosalie." Dimitri greeted her with visible pleasure, apparently oblivious to her reaction.

The single word was enough to send a frisson through the group. The eyes, which had already gravitated from the newcomers back to Dimitri, turned in Rosalie's direction again, their expressions now ranging from curious to sour.

Rosalie ignored them. These same girls had envied her Jace's attention once, and look at how that had turned out. She had been a fool then, but she refused to be one again. If the others hadn't learned from Jace that appearances could be deceiving, they were only setting themselves up for pain.

"You didn't tell us you were staying," she said to Dimitri, making no attempt to keep the accusation out of her voice.

His pleased expression faltered, replaced with a look of confusion. She might even have bought it if she hadn't just seen him playing to his audience, eating up the attention. Whatever game he was playing, he hadn't been honest the day before.

"I only arrived yesterday," he said carefully.

"I know that," she snapped. "I walked you part of the way, remember?"

"You met him outside the manor?" Blythe asked. "You must have been shocked." She giggled. "No one has lived there for twenty years," she added unnecessarily.

Rosalie frowned from Blythe to Dimitri. How had Blythe known they had met in the manor grounds?

"I walked him into town," she confirmed slowly, a horrifying possibility dawning on her.

A slight flush brushed Dimitri's cheeks, his face betraying him and giving away his guilt. He cleared his throat.

"Thank you for your directions," he said. "I was able to follow them this morning when I walked in to purchase supplies. Thebarton is a lovely town..." His voice faltered at her stony expression.

"You're the one who moved into the castle?" she asked, needing confirmation. "*You're* the Beast?"

Blythe snorted, and all four of the other girls giggled.

"Of course he's not a Beast, Rosalie," she said. "Obviously!" She flushed darker than Dimitri had, her gaze dropping shyly away from his handsome face.

"I don't know," Daphne said doubtfully. "The most terrifying creature I've yet encountered was a good-looking young man."

The other girls all cried out protests or rolled their eyes, but Rosalie squeezed her friend's hand. Daphne understood. Daphne knew that beneath Jace's pretty exterior had lurked a cold and heartless monster. Apparently the other girls had chosen to forget what he had done to Rosalie and her family under the guise of love. But Rosalie would never forget.

The love sometimes felt like the worst part of it. Her body still burned with humiliation when she thought of how easily she'd been deceived. Jace had been so obviously struck the first time they met, and she had soaked in his pretty words and flattery, had been so ready to believe he loved her. She had wanted to believe it because he represented an escape from the Legacy and the danger it represented for her—the youngest daughter of a merchant with three daughters and three sons. Once she was Jace's wife instead, the Legacy would have only the mildest interest in her. Jace was the key to a whole new life, and so she had thrown herself into their love with everything she had.

She had been so desperate for that future that she couldn't bear to wait as Jace said they had to until he found a proper position. It had seemed only natural for her to beg her father to give Jace the job he needed. And of course her loving father had given his daughter's beloved a trusted role within his thriving merchant empire. They were about to be family, after all.

But it had all been a lie. Just as Rosalie's friends hadn't really valued her for herself, Jace hadn't been struck by Rosalie's beauty or wit. He had been struck by her name and her family. He had seen an opportunity, and he had exploited it ruthlessly. With the Legacy to aid him, it had been child's play to embezzle a chunk of her father's fortune.

He couldn't get it all, of course. But his actions had been the spark, and the Legacy had fanned the flames that followed. Rosalie's eyes were drawn irresistibly to the place her childhood home had once stood. Not all the flames had been metaphorical, and when they had subsided, almost nothing had been left.

Jace had wielded his face like a weapon, taking what he wanted and not caring who was hurt in the process. And now here was Dimitri, just as careless of both the truth and the well-being of others. Her instincts had known it as soon as she saw his face, and she should have trusted them.

"I'm not a Beast." Dimitri watched her, his features twisted in false concern. "But I do live at the manor now. I'm sorry I didn't make that clear yesterday. I..." Words failed him. Clearly he couldn't think of an excuse fast enough.

"You told him not to ask you questions, but apparently

we should have asked him some," Daphne muttered beside her. Rosalie ignored her.

Sable, one of Blythe's closest friends, edged closer to Dimitri, looking up at him with admiration.

"We've all been so used to the manor being empty. I never thought we'd have our own prince in residence." She giggled.

Rosalie snorted. Dimitri was no prince—thankfully. She could only imagine how much the Legacy would love that.

Dimitri cleared his throat uncomfortably, and Rosalie's eyes snapped to his face. He was watching her, the others apparently forgotten, his expression rueful.

"Not a prince," he said. "I'm a more distant royal than that, I'm afraid."

Rosalie fell back a step, grasping at Daphne's arm in horror. He actually was a royal? Quibbling about exact titles was like insisting the castle was officially a manor. The Legacy didn't require such exactitude. It had a prince living alone in a castle, and she could already feel her life as she knew it crumbling around her.

Her fingers dug into Daphne's arm, making her friend squeak in protest.

"Sorry," Rosalie muttered, forcing her fingers to relax.

She didn't let go, though. Continuing backward, she dragged Daphne with her. They had to get away from Dimitri immediately, and she had to make sure she never ran into him again. She had thought she just needed to avoid the castle, but now there was a walking, talking prince she had to avoid as well. One who apparently felt at ease in her town, flirting with her friends. One who couldn't be trusted.

She groaned.

"Ahh...Where are we going?" Daphne asked, trying fruitlessly to free her arm.

"Away," Rosalie said shortly. "We will be avoiding Dimitri from now on."

Daphne raised an eyebrow, but it was Dimitri's voice that spoke. Rosalie had already dragged her friend halfway across the square, but Dimitri was striding after them, leaving the other girls behind.

"Wait!" he called. "I was wanting to speak with you."

"Well, I don't want to speak with you." Rosalie finally stopped walking backward and dropped Daphne's arm. Spinning, she strode forward instead, leaving Dimitri to address her back.

"I really am sorry," he said, sounding far too close. "To say I was confused yesterday is putting it mildly. I couldn't understand most of what you were saying."

Rosalie shook her head. So he was going to blame ignorance? Was she supposed to find that sympathetic?

He fell into silence, but she could still hear his steps, like a black cloud following her. Daphne had stuck to her side, and Rosalie could see her sneaking glances back at him. But Rosalie refused to do the same. She could hardly order him off—apparently his home lay in the same direction as hers—but she could ignore his presence. It was going to be her strategy from now on.

The houses thinned and grew more run-down, and the other traffic on the road lessened. When it was just the two of them walking with Dimitri's footsteps behind them, Rosalie couldn't hold herself back any longer.

She came to an abrupt stop, catching Daphne and their silent shadow by surprise. She whirled to face Dimitri just as he finally stopped as well, only inches from her.

Rosalie's breath caught. He was closer than she'd expected. Too close. She crossed her arms over her chest, unwilling to be the one to back away.

He froze, his body stilling. His gaze caught on her eyes and then dropped to her lips.

CHAPTER 4
DIMITRI

With an indrawn breath, Dimitri took two rapid steps backward. "Apologies, I didn't—" He wasn't entirely sure what he was going to say, but Rosalie cut him off before he could make the situation any worse by mangling another apology.

"Did you think about anything at all when you decided to come and live in Glandore—in an abandoned castle, no less?" She drew a horrified breath. "Did you know I live here? Is that why you're following me around?"

Panic crept in. It clearly wasn't a good idea to tell her the truth. He was following her because whenever she appeared, he couldn't look away—even if his presence seemed to make her spit fire. Or maybe it was that fire that so attracted him—making her glow from within. Whatever the cause, everyone else he'd met in the village seemed lifeless in comparison.

"I had no notion you existed until we met yesterday,"

he said truthfully, hoping that, at least, was unobjectionable.

Daphne gave a slow clap beside them, startling him. He'd forgotten she was there.

"Well done, Rose," she said without a trace of mockery. "You almost made it all the way through town!"

"Don't call me that!" Rosalie snapped, and Dimitri took note that she didn't like the nickname.

Daphne, however, seemed to know it wasn't the true source of Rosalie's irritation.

"You have many talents, dearest friend," she said sweetly. "But avoiding things is not one of them. May I remind you that as soon as I told you about the open manor door yesterday, you dragged me straight out there? I honestly didn't think you'd manage to ignore Dimitri for so long."

Rosalie glared at her friend, and Daphne smiled serenely back.

Dimitri bit down on a smile of his own. Apparently he didn't need to worry about Rosalie making good on her threat to avoid him. If she had insisted he keep his distance, he would have had to accept it, of course. But it would have been a blow. He had spent far too much of the previous evening thinking of her when he should have been focusing on the continuing mystery of his missing family and whatever threat had sent his mother fleeing the kingdom twenty years ago. But he had only walked into the village in the hope of seeing Rosalie.

"I have a library," he blurted out, reminded of his previous evening's task.

He immediately bit down on his tongue. He wasn't usually so witless. Despite his upbringing, he had some experience talking to women. Even in the small mountain community there had been a few girls who had shown interest. And even more had done so during his journey to the manor. Talking to them hadn't made him trip over his own tongue. His awkwardness around Rosalie was mortifying, but it still wasn't enough to make him walk away from the conversation.

"Congratulations," Rosalie said. "You also have a castle. And you're a prince." She glared up at him, clearly feeling none of the admiration for those facts that the girls in Thebarton had demonstrated.

He had spent the whole conversation with Blythe and her friends trying to think of a subtle way to bring up Rosalie and ask if she was likely to visit the town that day. But not even the biggest mountain recluse could have missed the way the group of girls had responded to his revelations.

"Not a prince," he clarified. "You know how big the Glandorian royal family is. There are useless cousins everywhere." He had learned that from his mother's papers, but he assumed it would be common knowledge for someone like Rosalie.

"Useless quibbling." Rosalie's eyes narrowed.

It didn't seem like a meaningless distinction to Dimitri. He still hadn't recovered from the shock of learning the truth of his heritage. He had been hoping the inhabitants of her manor might give him more information, but there had been no inhabitants, no long-lost family to greet him. Now he had nothing to go on but what he could find in the library—the library plus the enormous tapestry in the entryway which showed a family tree and included his name at the bottom.

He had always known he had been born in Glandore, but it had seemed an abstract fact given he had no memories of the kingdom. Seeing his name on the wall, as solid and immutable as the names of long-dead ancestors, had made it real in a way it hadn't been before.

But while he was now willing to acknowledge his origins, he couldn't accept someone classifying him as a prince. His mother had been far from the line of succession, and royalty was a reality too far removed from his. But Rosalie didn't seem like someone obsessed with rank, titles, or status. If she was bothered about his royal blood, it was for a different reason.

"I read as much as I could find on the Legacies last night," he said, guessing the Legacy was the source of her agitation. "So now I know why the Glandorian royal family is so large."

Rosalie's mouth twisted in impatience. "Yes, yes, the monarchs always have large families because they're afraid of the Legacy. Risking being left with only one child would be dangerous." Her expression soured even further. "Just like merchants usually have *small* families."

Dimitri winced. He still had a lot to learn about the Legacy, so he wasn't sure what had upset her in his words.

"I'm still learning," he said by way of apology. "I didn't know anything about the Legacies until yesterday."

Rosalie's mouth fell open, her earlier distaste wiped clean. "That can't possibly be true."

He winced. Did she think he was lying? She seemed determined to think the worst of him at every turn.

"Perhaps it might help my situation if I explain that up until very recently I lived in the mountains," he said.

"In the mountains?" Rosalie looked from him to Daphne. "Does anyone live in the mountains?"

He wasn't sure why she was looking to her friend for clarification when he was the one raised there, but he waited for Daphne to confirm his words.

"I think I've heard something about a few mountain communities," she said. "Some people flee the Legacies by leaving the kingdoms entirely. It's supposed to be a hard life in the mountains, but some find the escape worth it."

Dimitri nodded. It had been a hard life for many, although the community didn't let anyone starve. But Dimitri had been shielded from that reality by his mother. She had taken enough valuables with her when she fled to establish the two of them, and she had worked tirelessly every day after to ensure Dimitri had time for study and training. Once he had grown old enough, he had often hunted for them because she deemed hunting to be training of a sort, but most of his time had been spent learning from a handful of their neighbors.

If someone in the community possessed knowledge or skills his mother deemed useful, she had been quick to negotiate deals with them, offering laundry or cooking or child minding in exchange for their tutoring Dimitri. Whenever he had protested that she worked too hard, she had insisted that he could repay her by working equally hard at his study.

He had enjoyed learning to use a sword and bow, but while his other studies had been interesting, he had never understood why his mother thought he needed to know commerce, economics, mathematics, etiquette, or estate management. Such skills were of little use in the mountains.

Of course, it had all made sense after her death when he went through her papers. She had done her best to give him the same education she herself had received. And although she had always talked of Glandore with fear and distrust, he couldn't help but think her education was a tacit endorsement of the path he had chosen. She had educated him for his true status, so surely she had meant him to reclaim it?

"No one talks about the Legacies in the mountains," he said aloud, "but now that I've read about them, a lot of things make sense that didn't before. The Legacies might not be openly discussed, but they're still there, hidden in the cracks of every conversation."

Rosalie regarded him with a creased brow. She didn't seem to have softened, exactly, but at least confusion and uncertainty had replaced the outright condemnation in her eyes.

"So you were born in the mountains?" she asked.

He shook his head. "My mother left her home and moved there when I was very small. I don't remember it, but I was born in Glandore."

Her brow cleared slightly. "No wonder you wanted to

return, then. Was it very uncomfortable being away so long? Daphne's parents could only bear it for ten years, and you were gone for twenty."

"Uncomfortable?" He frowned. "I saw a mention of Legacies tying people to their birth kingdom, but I didn't really understand that part. I never noticed any discomfort."

"I suppose it's hard to document because it's different for everyone," Daphne said softly. "Part of it is the heart and emotions. Most people have no desire to leave. If they want to travel or move from their place of birth, they do so within the bounds of their own kingdom. But for those who do leave, the discomfort shows up differently for each person, so it would be impossible to make a comprehensive list."

"Daphne experiences the effects of the Legacy more strongly while in Glandore than she did back in Oakden," Rosalie added. "That's how moving affected her. Are you sure you didn't feel anything in the mountains? Nothing at all? I've never heard of someone not being affected."

Dimitri frowned, searching his memory for any forgotten pain or unusual happenings. He finally shrugged.

"I'll admit it's been more pleasant to return than I expected. I feel as if I could run for hours. The air here is so clear."

Rosalie's eyebrows rose. "More clear than in the mountains? But everyone always speaks of the high quality of mountain air."

Dimitri gave an apologetic smile. "I'm explaining it

badly. It's not the air, exactly. I just feel so..." He trailed off, his eyes widening.

Rosalie leaned toward him, although he suspected she didn't realize she was doing it. Her eyes were fixed on his face. "Feel so what?" she pressed.

"So light," he said slowly, fascinated by their conversation but also aware of Rosalie's nearness. "Is this how you feel all the time? Is this normal?"

"You'll have to be a little more specific," Daphne said with an amused look.

He grinned. "Now it's my turn not to make any sense." He thought for a moment, trying to find words to explain it. "I never thought anything was strange in the mountains, but then I'd never known anything else. When I crossed into Glandore, though, it felt like a weight had lifted off me, but I had no idea..." He paused, trying to sort out his thoughts. "I think maybe the discomfort of being out of the kingdom was like an extra weight, strapped to my shoulders and chest. A weight that was always there. And now feeling normal feels light by comparison."

"It could have been worse," Rosalie said matter-of-factly, and Dimitri suddenly wondered how the Legacy had affected his mother. What had she suffered in silence, never letting on to her young son? What could have driven her to such lengths?

"I knew there was some sort of enchantment at work in the kingdoms," he said. "There were enough hints dropped to pick up that much. But I always thought of it as a terrible curse that made the kingdoms into a monstrous place." He looked around at the trees which crept toward the road now that the town had ended and at the roses that lined the verge. "It doesn't look so monstrous to me."

"It is a curse!" Rosalie said explosively, startling him and pulling his attention back to her.

"Well, I suppose it started out as one," Daphne amended. "What we have left now—the Legacy—is more like the echo of a curse." She eyed the closest patch of roses. "A very odd echo."

"You must have read the history of each kingdom," Rosalie said. "About the first royal families?"

Dimitri nodded. He had focused most on Glandore, but he had at least skimmed the histories of the other kingdoms.

"So you know they founded beautiful kingdoms, unmarred by war or conflict. Except each of them fell prey to some sort of dark enchantment, and now the...*echoes*"— she glanced at Daphne—"of their stories have sunk into the fabric of their kingdoms. That's the Legacies. It was many generations ago, but we all experience the consequences of their mistakes and suffer alongside their suffering."

"And we get the benefit of their triumphs," Daphne added, seeming much less gloomy about the whole topic than Rosalie. "Personally I like roses. And the birds too."

Birds? Dimitri tried to remember any mention of birds in the histories he'd skimmed but couldn't. There had been a lot of material, and his mind had still been reeling from the day's experiences.

"Don't be ridiculous!" Rosalie gave a strangled sigh. "Who could like roses?"

"I like them." Dimitri looked down at her, wondering if his face gave away that it wasn't only the botanical kind he admired. "They don't grow in the mountains, and I think they're beautiful."

Rosalie rolled her eyes. "You would."

Daphne gave a strangled sound that might have been a suppressed laugh. But when they looked toward her, she was regarding them with her usual air of languor.

"We've gotten off topic," Rosalie said briskly, taking back control of the conversation. "Roses are beside the point." She frowned. "Or well, not entirely. But the crucial point is that you now know about the Legacy. So when are you going to leave?" She looked at him expectantly.

"Leave?" He stared at her blankly.

She propped her hands on her hips. "You can't possibly mean to stay! Do you want to end up a witless beast?"

"Err, no. Naturally not," he said. "But I can't leave. For one thing, I have nowhere else to go."

"You're part of the royal family, and you own an entire castle! Of course you must have somewhere else to go."

"My lineage might be descended from royalty, but the only relative I've ever met is my mother. And she recently died."

He hadn't meant to state it so baldly, but the information immediately dimmed Rosalie's indignation.

"Oh," she said softly. "I didn't realize. I'm sorry for your loss."

"Thank you," he replied. "It wasn't sudden, so we had time to say our goodbyes. But even so, she didn't tell me anything about my family or heritage. I only discovered it from her papers after her death. So if I did want to foist myself on the royal family, I don't have much in the way of proof. None of them will know me."

"There's the castle," Daphne said. "That supports your claim. Don't you think, Rosalie?" She glanced down the road in the direction of the manor.

"I'm not sure," Rosalie replied. "I'd have to see it again today to compare any differences, I think."

"Please!" Dimitri said promptly. "Be my guest."

Her eyes narrowed, her face closing off. "Don't think I'm setting foot in the grounds of that castle ever again!" Her eyes wandered down the road. "But maybe we could just walk past and have a look..."

Daphne grinned knowingly. "I told you that you can't leave anything alone."

Rosalie grinned back, apparently unoffended now that her earlier irritation had passed.

"It's all that extra energy I need to have to make up for you. Imagine if we both did nothing but nap all day!"

"I don't nap all day!" Daphne protested, but she was smiling.

For the second time, Dimitri fell into step on the other side of Rosalie, this time heading back toward his home instead of away. The lightness of Glandore buoyed his steps, but it was more than that. There was a warmness in his core that came from the company. Walking beside Rosalie and Daphne—feeling the familiarity of it—made him feel as if he had friends. As if he wasn't alone after all.

He hadn't realized how much his solitary journey had weighed him down—a sensation that had only grown when he found the manor abandoned. But now here he was, on only his second day, and he wasn't walking home alone.

He allowed himself to imagine for a moment that they were truly coming back with him. That the three of them would walk into the manor house together and sit down to the midday meal, laughing around the table and exchanging stories. He could show them the library and the books he'd found, and they could tell him which ones to read next. Perhaps Rosalie would—

He cut off his thoughts. He would be walking into a cold, lifeless manor alone, and such imaginings would only make the reality harder. He was greedy for more of Rosalie—he wanted to know her story and what fueled the fire inside her—but she wanted him to leave—to move to the capital or anywhere that wasn't near her.

Rosalie and Daphne stopped abruptly, simultaneous gasps dropping from both their lips. Instead of following their gazes, he watched them, amused by their reactions. He had been equally astonished when he had stepped out of the manor that morning and seen the changes that had appeared overnight. He still didn't understand what it had to do with his birthright, but there was no denying the startling transformation. On his first day, the garden had gone from overgrown and derelict to lush and glowing. But now it looked sculpted, as if it had been growing for years under the loving care of a team of gardeners. And as well as blooming flowers, the trees now bore ripe fruit, despite how little that made sense. It was easy to see why Glandore was the agricultural heart of six kingdoms.

"I've heard stories of how the manor used to look before I was born," Rosalie said, "but it wasn't anything like this! Look at that fruit!" She stared open-mouthed.

Daphne turned to Dimitri. "Here's your proof."

"Maybe," Rosalie said slowly, drawing out the word. She glanced toward her friend. "It's not just because he's a young man—any young man?"

Daphne shook her head firmly. "Yesterday might have been. But this?" She made a sweeping gesture toward the grounds. "In one day? I've only ever seen the Legacy use so much power once before."

She gave Rosalie a significant look, and Rosalie's mouth tightened, the same mixture of sadness and anger filling her eyes that he had seen before. What had the Legacy done to her?

"I'm not sure I follow," he said, wanting to distract her. "How does this admittedly impressive and bizarre garden prove my bloodline?"

"I thought you said you read all about Glandore's history and Legacy last night?" Rosalie exclaimed. "Surely you can't have missed the part about the poor prince who ended up alone in a castle? It's the center of the story! And all the descriptions I've read make his garden sound just like this."

Dimitri frowned. Perhaps he shouldn't have skipped

the long descriptions of the gardens. He did remember the castle, though.

"This isn't a castle," he said. "It's a manor house. And the young man in question may have been a prince, but wasn't he also a Beast at that stage?"

Rosalie waved her arms impatiently, as if brushing aside all his objections.

"Of course it's not going to fit *exactly*. If the Legacy was guaranteed to follow the original story exactly, we wouldn't have a problem. Not only would it be easy to avoid, but we'd at least be guaranteed a happy ending after all those troubles!"

Dimitri looked from Rosalie to Daphne. "Are we not? All the stories I read seemed to work out all right—more or less."

"That's because you were reading the original histories," Rosalie said. "You can't have had time for much else. But the Legacy isn't nearly as reliable. It has created plenty of tragedies in the generations since."

"The Legacy is happy to mimic elements from the story wherever it can," Daphne said. "No matter how disparate those elements might be. They don't have to be part of the greater narrative. Like the roses."

"Is it really true that every flower seed planted in Glandore grows into a rose?" Dimitri asked.

"Have you seen any other flowers since you crossed the border?" Rosalie watched him, clearly already knowing the answer. "And have you seen anyone pick a rose that wasn't from their own garden?"

He rubbed the back of his neck. "I wasn't paying much

attention, to be honest. But I haven't seen any other flowers around here. And I certainly haven't seen anyone picking any." He grimaced as he considered his own entrancement with the roses on his first day. He had felt the pull since, but it was easy to resist now he knew the dangers of plucking one.

"You won't see other flowers anywhere in Glandore," Daphne said, her voice turning wistful. "In Oakden we had roses, but so many other beautiful flowers besides."

"At least the trees have flowers," Rosalie said, a note of loyalty creeping into her voice despite her apparent aversion to Glandore's Legacy. "It's only flowers that grow in the ground that are affected."

"Except you don't have cherry blossoms around here," Daphne said on a sigh.

"That, at least, is not the Legacy's fault," Rosalie said in a spirit of fairness. "But the relevant point is that just because the Legacy works one element of the original story into your life, it doesn't mean you'll get all the other elements too. Sometimes that's useful—we use its power to grow our crops. They grow far faster and better here than other places. But we try to avoid it wreaking havoc in our lives."

"So you're saying that the Legacy is transforming the garden because I'm a young man of royal blood living alone in a castle-like building?" Dimitri asked, apprehension rising inside him. "Are you saying it's going to turn me into a Beast?"

"No," Rosalie said firmly, "it won't. Because you're going to leave."

Dimitri frowned. He couldn't dismiss her words as easily as he'd done earlier, but his reasons for staying still remained.

"I can't do that," he said slowly. "It's not just that I have nowhere to go. There are things I still need to discover—about my mother and myself. About my history. And this manor is the only place I know to look."

"And you're willing to risk turning into a Beast to get your answers?" Rosalie demanded. "Remember just because the Legacy turns you into a Beast doesn't mean it will ever turn you back into a prince again."

Dimitri considered reminding her that he wasn't a prince to start with but decided against the attempt.

"You said yourself that the Legacy isn't that predictable," he said. "So I'll just have to take my chances. With my mother gone, I have nothing and no one else. I'm not leaving without answers." He didn't add that even once he had the answers, he might not leave. This place was his heritage. It was where his mother had grown up. He belonged here, even if it didn't properly feel like it yet. His ancestors had managed to survive without all turning into Beasts. He would find a way, too.

"The problem," Rosalie said, "is that the Legacy gets stronger the more closely the situation aligns with the original tale. That's why Daphne said this garden could prove your royal blood. It transformed so quickly because the Legacy is pouring power into it. And it's doing that because it has a young, handsome prince living alone in a castle."

Despite himself, Dimitri's mouth curved upward at

hearing her call him handsome. From the glare she gave him, though, she knew exactly what he was thinking and was daring him to comment on it.

"There's no point looking so pleased with yourself," Daphne said, reminding him that he and Rosalie weren't the only two there. "I think Rosalie would treat you more kindly if you were hideous."

The two girls exchanged a look laden with meaning. While Dimitri now knew about the Legacy, there was clearly a great deal about Rosalie he still didn't understand.

"I suppose the manor house has become more livable too." Daphne gazed wistfully at the building at the end of the curved drive.

"Don't even think about it, Daph." Rosalie gave her a warning look. "We will not be going in just to rest our feet —or any other part of our persons. We're staying right here on the road."

Daphne gave her a pleading look, but she stood firm.

"In fact," she added, "we're not even going to stay here. We're going back."

"Already?" Dimitri asked before he could stop himself.

Rosalie gave him a quelling look. "Don't you start too. You should go inside and do some more reading and then do some reflecting. It's never too soon to start packing to go."

Dimitri remained silent. She was right about the research, but he wouldn't be leaving. Not now. Not yet.

Rosalie turned to leave before hesitating and turning

back. Her eyes skimmed over him, coming to rest on his empty hands.

"You said you went into Thebarton to get supplies, but you followed us out before you had a chance to buy anything." She hesitated again, clearly torn. "Will you be all right? Do you have what you need? You're not short on food or anything?"

Dimitri blinked, thrown off guard by her question. Despite her antagonism toward him, and her constant entreaties for him to leave, she was worried about him.

He smiled. "I'm fine. I won't be starving any time soon."

"Of course he won't be," Daphne said. "He has an enchanted castle."

Rosalie still hesitated for a moment before deciding that was a valid point.

"In that case," she said, "just remember why there's food appearing on your plate. Let it remind you why it's a bad idea to stay."

This time when she turned to leave, she didn't pause or look back, and all too soon, she had disappeared from sight.

Dimitri roused himself to walk slowly down the drive toward his new home. It was just as lonely a prospect as he had anticipated, so he didn't hurry. Instead, his thoughts remained full of Rosalie.

Daphne was right about her. For all Rosalie's attempts to be prickly and defensive, she couldn't help showing her true self. And her true self cared—she cared about what was happening around her, about her family, even about strangers she met on the road. Rosalie's true self saw a problem and wanted to fix it, without thought of the cost to herself.

It was no wonder she was so fascinating to him. He had spent his whole life surrounded by people who had run away from their problems. And up until a few days ago, he had allowed himself to be one of them. In the mountains he had known his place and his role. His life had been simple, and he had been content with that. Once he had left childhood behind, he had never pressed his mother to tell him why she left Glandore and her people behind.

He told himself he was keeping the peace, but in truth, he hadn't wanted to know. He hadn't wanted to take her burden on his shoulders. He understood her situation a little better now, and his past actions filled him with shame. She had silently borne the unknown pain of leaving her birth kingdom, and she could only have done it because of a pain that was deeper still. What sort of son would let his mother carry that alone?

Ever since he had left the mountains and stepped into Glandore, the past seemed more dreamlike than real. It was hard to remember why everything had felt so heavy and burdensome that he couldn't bear the thought of a further load.

Was that what Rosalie and Daphne had meant about the tie to your birth kingdom starting in your heart? It wasn't only his body that had been heavy in the mountains.

But even as he thought it, it felt like an excuse. He only

had to picture Rosalie in his place to know she wouldn't have given in to the sensation. As it was, she was clearly carrying a burden from something the Legacy had done, but it wasn't enough to extinguish her spark. She hadn't stopped caring.

It was that irrepressible spirit in her that drew him to her. But admiring her drive wasn't enough. He had to do better himself. He had to prove he wouldn't let the Legacy defeat him. He wouldn't be driven from his home by fear.

He would stay right where he was. He would discover what had haunted his mother, and what had happened to his family. And then he would find out what had happened to Rosalie. It was too late for him to lift his mother's weight, but it wasn't too late to help Rosalie.

CHAPTER 5
ROSALIE

Rosalie walked in silence, her mind consumed with worry. Why didn't Dimitri understand the seriousness of the situation? Why wouldn't he listen? He had royal blood. If he wanted to discover his family history, he should go to the capital. Did he have to stay here and torment her?

Her feet were moving as fast as her mind, and she quickly outpaced Daphne. When she finally noticed, she stopped dead.

How fast had she been going? She peered behind her and located Daphne, only just rounding the previous bend. Guilt washed over her. This was the second time she'd dragged Daphne out to the castle in as many days, and now she was abandoning her.

Rosalie retraced her steps, hurrying back toward her friend. Daphne looked like a wilting flower as she shuffled along, her head and shoulders drooping as if she was slipping into sleep while walking.

Sound exploded around Rosalie as three men erupted from the nearby trees with loud shouts, racing onto the road and toward Daphne. Rosalie faltered, her steps slowed by shock. But the first man reached for Daphne's arm, and Rosalie responded instinctively, flinging herself into a sprint.

She had never heard of bandits on this road, but the men were clearly after Daphne. She must have looked like an easy target walking alone. Rosalie shouldn't have left her behind.

There was no way for Rosalie to reach Daphne before the men, but the moment the first man's fingers closed around Daphne's upper arm, Daphne launched into movement. Gone was any appearance of sleepiness as she spun, wrenching her arm from his grip and driving it backward. Her elbow connected with his midriff, and he doubled over with a desperate wheeze.

His companions swore, assuming a more wary stance as they approached Daphne from either side. She lashed out, the toes of her sturdy boot catching one of them in the shin. He swore, his legs buckling for a moment. As he staggered, she smashed both of her palms against the sides of his face, flattening them against his ears. When she pulled them back, he howled, collapsing to the ground entirely.

Whatever Daphne's open-handed blows had done to his ears, the man was clearly in too much pain to continue his attack. But while dealing with him, the third man had come at Daphne from behind, seizing her around the middle and trapping both her arms at her sides.

She cried out in anger, kicking backward, but he lifted

her off the ground, taking the power out of her flailing efforts. Rosalie screamed as she threw herself at Daphne's captor. She lacked Daphne's smooth, confident grace, but she threw everything she had into the effort, kicking and striking him in a whirlwind of fury.

The surprise attack threw him off balance enough that Daphne managed to squirm out of his grip. Instead of attempting to recapture her, the man spun and lunged for Rosalie instead.

She screamed again, this time more in alarm than fury. She tried to fend him off, but without the element of surprise, she was less effectual. With a threatening growl, he managed to grab her arms, twisting them up and holding her so tightly she could barely breathe.

Daphne took two steps toward her, clearly ready to do battle on her friend's behalf. But behind her, the first man had recovered from the winding and was approaching again, this time with a knife.

Rosalie couldn't get enough breath to yell a warning, but she managed a strangled grunt, her eyes widening and her head straining toward the new threat. Daphne paused as she took in Rosalie's silent warning, glancing backward to see the new threat.

Rosalie gave a desperate wriggle, managing to pull in a full breath.

"Run!" she cried. "Get help!"

Daphne hesitated for half a second before she recognized the futility of fighting. Nodding, she took off running.

Rosalie expected the armed man to chase after

Daphne, but instead he refocused on Rosalie. Apparently one prize was enough for them.

Fear seized Rosalie, squeezing her insides tighter than the arms of her captor. Until that moment, she had been driven more by instinct than conscious thought. But now the reality of her situation hit her. She was alone and at the mercy of bandits.

And Daphne—never the best when it came to a sense of direction—had run the wrong way.

"Where's the other one?" the second man asked. He had made it up off the ground and was approaching Rosalie and the other two with an ugly expression on his face. Given the blood trailing out of both his ears, Rosalie was glad Daphne had fled beyond reach before he recovered. Had she burst both his eardrums?

"This one is as good as the other," the first man grunted, surveying Rosalie with satisfaction. "He said to bring whoever's been frequenting the castle, and this one has walked out there two days in a row. She'll do."

Daphne's mouth dropped open. The men weren't bandits? Who were they working for? And what interest did their unknown master have in the castle?

The man who was holding her relaxed a little, freeing her lungs enough for normal speech.

"I don't have anything to do with the castle!" she said as fervently as possible. "You have the wrong person." She wasn't willing to go as far as naming Dimitri, but she had a strong desire not to meet this leader of theirs.

"I'm just a local," she added. "I live nearby, that's why you've seen me." She drew another breath. "And I have three brothers. They'll be looking for me." It was a bit of a stretch but hopefully had enough ring of truth.

The men hesitated for a moment, exchanging looks. But the first man eventually shook his head. "We'll let him work that out. If he wants to let you go, he's free to do so. We did our part." He chuckled as if he didn't think it likely Rosalie would be freed.

Filled with fresh desperation, she kicked backward while simultaneously biting hard on the closest stretch of arm. Her captor grunted, giving her a vicious squeeze that once again robbed her of breath. While she was still trying to suck in enough air, he hoisted her over his shoulder like a sack of grain.

By the time Rosalie's head had stopped spinning, they were well into the trees. She watched the trunks and leaves flash past, queasy from the mode of travel.

If she waited for the right moment, she might be able to wiggle her way free. But she was as likely to fall on her head as her feet, and even if it worked perfectly, how far would she get with three men chasing her?

As much as she hated to give in, it seemed like her best chance was in waiting to speak to their leader. Perhaps she could find a way to reason with him. And in the meantime, the road was now clear for Daphne to turn around and head back toward Rosalie's home and Thebarton. Her brothers might not be the threatening presence she had claimed, but they could gather a group to search for her.

She wasn't sure if she was pleased or disappointed when the men turned into a hidden clearing among the trees. On the one hand, the further away she was, the harder it would be for the townsfolk to find her. On the other, it was too soon. She wasn't sure if Daphne would even have reached her mother and brothers yet.

When her captor dumped her onto her feet, it took a moment for Rosalie's head to stop spinning and her sense of balance to return. As soon as it had, she looked around, taking in the clearing in one glance. Her heart immediately dropped.

Five more men were gathered there, their attention on the new arrivals. She had been hoping it was only the first three and their absent leader. If a rescue party did set out from Thebarton, would they bring enough men? She didn't want her brothers to end up in the same desperate situation she was already in.

She had barely absorbed the situation before one of the men approached her with a length of rope, clearly meaning to secure her hands. She considered struggling, but if escape had been a poor chance before, it was even more so now. Better to pretend compliance.

She passively allowed him to bind her wrists, even holding her arms steady. But while she attempted to look as relaxed as possible, she was actually straining her arms apart, creating a small amount of room between her hands to provide wriggle room later.

The strategy seemed to work since the man binding her paid little attention to the task, his attention on the man with the ruptured eardrums. Those in the clearing had been quick to notice the blood on the side of the injured man's face, and they seemed to find it humorous that he had been hurt bringing in such a harmless-looking target. Rosalie could only be glad the man in front of her was more interested in jeering at his companion than tying her knots tight.

As soon as he'd finished, he moved away, and Rosalie straightened, taking a longer look at the clearing. She needed to work out which one was the leader so she could plead her case directly to him. Before she could identify him, however, one of the men pushed his way forward.

"Rosalie!" The man hurried to her side, his expression horrified.

Every word of her prepared speech fled her mind, replaced with empty shock.

"Jace?" She hated how small and tentative she sounded. Her thoughts had stalled, though. How could Jace be here with these men?

Jace's eyes dropped to the rope around her wrists, and he grimaced. Throwing a dirty look over his shoulder at the gathered men, he reached out a hand to her.

"Are you all right?" His hand gently cupped her cheek before pushing back her hair. His voice dropped lower. "I missed you."

Rosalie stiffened, finally finding her voice.

"How can you say that after what you did?" she hissed.

He pulled back slightly, looking pained. "I know the situation must have looked bad. But I thought you, at least, would trust me."

Rosalie's initial shock had given way to pain and anger, but even so, his final sentence made her pause. She wasn't proud to admit it, but her traitorous heart had lurched at the initial sight of him. She wasn't as impervious to him as she had thought. Was it possible she had misunderstood what happened the year before and misjudged him? Was he somehow a victim of these men just as she was?

She had claimed she loved him enough to plan a life with him. Had her love been so hollow that she had assumed the worst at the first opportunity without giving him the benefit of the doubt?

Jace must have read the hesitation in her voice because he stepped closer again, his hands dropping to hers as if he might undo her ties.

"You're as beautiful as ever," he murmured, and again her heart lurched.

But this time it continued dropping, reaching her stomach and setting off a wave of nausea. She was no longer the inexperienced, impressionable girl she had been when they first met. He was standing freely in her captor's midst while she was trussed up like a fowl on its way to the oven. She hadn't misunderstood anything.

His words might have been designed to make a girl's heart flutter, but she could see now what she should have seen from the start—the warmth didn't reach his eyes. There was a coldness to his features and expression that was more obvious after meeting Dimitri. They might look similar, but Jace's eyes were a flat brown that offered no depth to his supposed concern. She had known Dimitri for two days, but she had already seen more true concern in his hazel gaze than she could see now from the man who had claimed to love her. If she could detect any emotion in Jace's eyes, it was detached amusement.

She leaned forward, her gaze locked with his as she closed the already small distance between them. Holding herself in place, she waited to see if his hands were actually going to untie her. As expected, however, he merely continued to clasp her fingers. Everything was an act—just as it had been a year ago.

She spat in his face, leaning back with satisfaction as he reeled away, sputtering in shock. His mask immediately slipped, revealing the cold anger and calculation beneath.

"You're going to regret that," he said, regaining his cool. "We could have done this the nice way."

"I'm done believing anything you say," Rosalie ground out. Better to face the situation head-on than be taken in for a second time and lose all faith in herself.

Jace turned to one of the men who had abducted her. "Why did you bring *her*?" he snapped. "I told you to find whoever is frequenting that castle after all these years." His tone was commanding, and none of the men protested at his attitude, despite the gap in their ages. "I've already squeezed her for all she's worth."

Shock rocked Rosalie for the second time. She barely even heard his insult in the face of the bigger revelation. Jace wasn't just here with these men—he was the leader she had been searching for. He had been the one to send them after her.

Except it was clear he hadn't been targeting her specifically. His surprise at seeing her had been genuine, even if his words hadn't been.

"Aye, and that she is," the man replied, standing firm. "She was the one we saw hanging around the castle."

Rosalie noted there was no mention of the girl who had escaped, and she was relieved for Daphne's sake as well as her own. Perhaps, when Daphne managed to fetch help, her rescuers would take Jace by surprise.

A new man stepped into the clearing, cutting off Jace's response to his underling.

"There's someone coming," the new arrival said tersely.

Rosalie frowned. Even by the most optimistic measuring, it was too soon for a rescue team to have arrived at Daphne's fetching. But from the reaction of Jace and his men, they weren't expecting any more allies.

Hope blossomed inside her. She didn't know what distraction was approaching, but if she was prepared, she might be able to seize the chance to escape.

She squeezed her wrists together and started subtly working one of her hands out of the loose binding. When her opportunity came, she was going to be ready.

CHAPTER 6
DIMITRI

Dimitri gazed around the entryway of the castle. It didn't smell musty anymore, but it was still an unappealing space. Or perhaps it was the silence and solitude that rendered it so.

He needed to find his pack and prepare the last of his food supplies, but it was hard to muster much care for his next meal. Rosalie and Daphne had spoken as if food would magically appear on his plate, but if that was within the manor's capacity, it had yet to extend him such treatment. If he wanted to eat, he needed to provide the food himself, and that meant replenishing his supplies. He would need to walk into Thebarton the next day.

His pulse quickened at the idea that he might run into Rosalie again, but his need was legitimate. He was nearly out of food. And the walk would provide some activity in the day, at least. He felt no desire to spend an entire day alone in the manor.

He was still lingering in the entryway, lost in thought

and reluctant to venture further into the empty building, when he heard footsteps. Someone was approaching the manor, and they were coming at a flat sprint.

He hurried back to the door, pulling it open and stepping outside in time to meet Daphne on the front steps. Her expression transformed at the sight of him, her relief palpable. But she bent over, gasping too hard for speech.

"What is it?" He hurried down to her, alarm coursing through him. "Where's Rosalie?" He looked past her, but there was no sight of the other girl.

What could have happened to propel Daphne across the border of the manor grounds—and at such speed? None of the possibilities that presented themselves were pleasant.

"Is it Rosalie?" he asked again, barely holding in his impatience as Daphne struggled to regain her breath. "Is she injured? Does she need help getting home?"

"Abducted," Daphne panted out at last, making his blood freeze. "Three men attacked me. She fought them, and they seized her instead." Her face crumpled. "I didn't see where they took her."

"You did the right thing," Dimitri assured her, his hand already on the hilt of his sword. He hadn't made the mistake of leaving it behind that morning, which meant there would be no need for even a moment's delay. "If they'd taken you too, no one would know about it. Can you show me where the attack happened?"

He hesitated and shook his head. "No, you're too exhausted. Can you describe it for me?"

Daphne looked like she wanted to protest, but since her breathing still hadn't normalized, she couldn't do so.

"It was right after the third bend," she panted out. "They came from the trees to the east."

"Thank you!" he said. "You go inside and rest. Take the door to the left of the entryway. There's a sitting room with a banked fire and provisions—such as they are. I'll bring Rosalie back here when I find her."

Daphne blinked but didn't argue. Rosalie might not want to enter the manor grounds, but he didn't know what state she would be in, and the manor was the closest building to where she'd been taken.

He was determined not to think of the possibility that she might be badly injured or dead. Thoughts like that would only get in the way of what needed to be done. If it turned out she needed a doctor, he would deal with that when the time came.

Running down his drive, he forced himself to moderate his pace. It was difficult, but he couldn't afford to sprint as Daphne had done and end up too exhausted to continue. He had further to go than she'd had.

It took far too long to reach the third bend, but at last he saw it ahead of him. Putting on an extra burst of speed, he rounded the curve and slowed to a stop. Daphne had definitely said the third one, but he could see nothing unusual to indicate the struggle that must have happened there.

However, closer inspection revealed marks in the dirt beneath his feet that indicated more than passing footsteps. Something had happened in that spot, just as Daphne had claimed.

Hurrying to the trees on his left, he examined the greenery closest to the road. While he was far from an expert tracker, he had learned the basics from some of the older members of the mountain community, and he had often hunted large game through the trees on the mountain slope. It was easy to pick up the signs of the men he was pursuing—clearly they had made no effort to hide their passage.

He stepped past the tree line and paused. Should he be going to Thebarton first and gathering more men to accompany him? He only hesitated for a moment, though. Going into the town and searching for men would take far too much time. Who knew what harm might come to Rosalie in the meantime?

Daphne had said there were three men, and it was unlikely they were as well-trained with the sword as Dimitri. His closest neighbor on the mountain had been a retired weapons master, and Dimitri's mother had done all his laundry and cooking.

He picked up the pace, not moving as fast through the trees as he had on the road but still making good time. He only slowed whenever he lost his quarry's path, searching around each time until he found it again.

"Over here! Help!"

Dimitri tensed at the cry, spinning to stare into the trees. The voice had sounded a little odd, but the words had been clear. Whoever had taken Rosalie must have abducted others as well.

He tried to follow the voice, straining to hear any further calls or sounds of movement. An explosion of birds from a nearby tree made him startle, but he could see no sign of any people. Did he dare call out?

Just as he was about to risk it, he heard another cry.

"This way! We're over here!"

The voice sounded the same, but it was coming from back in the direction of his original trail. He hurried after it. How had the abductors made it past him without him seeing or hearing anything?

"Just a bit further!" the voice called again, this time leading him south.

He dashed through the trees, ears and eyes alert, but he could see none of the signs that had been guiding him so far. He finally slowed, frustrated. The voice had sounded close, so he should have reached them by now. Something was off.

"Are you there?" he risked calling out. There was nothing but silence.

His lips tightened. He didn't like to turn his back on someone in need, but he could see no sign of a fresh trail, and he had already lost valuable time. There was no way to follow a voice that had gone silent, and meanwhile he still had a clear path to follow in the other direction.

He retraced his steps until he saw evidence of the abductors' movements again. With a last glance back at the quiet forest, he resumed his earlier path.

After some distance, he heard voices again. He slowed to a crawl. The voices were different this time—rather than one person calling out, it was the low murmur of an exchange. And the sounds were coming from in front of him—right where the trail was leading.

He had finally caught up with them, and he would be wise to approach with caution. Drawing his sword, he held it ready as he crept closer. The voices had fallen quiet, but he had locked their location in his mind.

He slipped behind a large bush, carefully looking around it into a clearing. The leaves obstructed his view, however, and he hadn't located Rosalie when a voice spoke again, louder this time.

"Visitors are always welcome," it drawled. "But we do prefer them to come in the front door. Won't you join us?"

Dimitri froze. Were they talking to him?

"Come, come, don't be shy!" the man added after the silence stretched on.

There was cold amusement in the tone, and Dimitri didn't like the sound. But there was little point in lurking behind a bush if they knew he was there. Better to face the situation and see if he could brazen it out. He had his sword and his wits—and from the reaction of the few townsfolk he'd met, his position as owner of the manor gave him some standing in the region. He just hoped that was enough to master whatever situation he found in the clearing.

He slipped the blade back into its scabbard and strolled around the bush, forcing his face into impassive lines.

His first impression was of a small crowd of men—too many men. His fingers twitched toward the hilt of his sword, but he kept his arm at his side and his face calm.

His one advantage was that they looked as unpleasantly surprised to see him as he was unpleasantly surprised at their number.

His eyes locked on a man standing slightly in front of the others. He was young—Dimitri's age at a guess—but even so, Dimitri had the distinct impression he was their leader.

"You're not welcome in my woods," Dimitri told the man.

He used the same voice of command and authority that his mother had successfully deployed against his younger self. From his study of the manor's deed, he didn't really have any claim to this particular stretch of trees, but he was hoping these men wouldn't know that.

"If you're looking to cause trouble, you can do it elsewhere."

The leader's eyebrows rose. "Your woods, do you say? Don't tell me you're the prince from the castle." A small smile played around his lips, making Dimitri stiffen. "How very interesting."

The man stepped swiftly to one side, revealing Rosalie. Rope dangled from one of her wrists, suggesting she had been bound and subsequently freed. If it had been an escape attempt, she hadn't gotten far, however. A tall man stood behind her, one hand clasped around her waist to hold her in place and the other hand clamped over her mouth to keep her silent.

Her wide eyes were fixed on Dimitri, but their expression was shocked rather than pained, and she didn't appear to be injured. Even so, fury ripped through him at the sight of her restrained and silenced.

Without conscious intention, he drew his sword from its scabbard. Striding across the clearing, he took the leader by surprise, gripping the front of his shirt and holding the sharp edge of his blade to the man's throat.

"Let her go. Now." The words came out hard and cutting as ice.

The other men surged forward, but the leader's stance remained relaxed. He waved a hand for his men to stay back, his eyes fixed on Dimitri.

"How very, very interesting," he murmured, sending a chill down Dimitri's spine.

The leader's eyes flicked to one of the men hovering close by.

"It looks like you did a good job after all," he said to his underling. His voice rose in volume as he addressed the man holding Rosalie behind him. "Do let our lovely guest go. There's no need for restraints among friends."

"Sir?" the man asked, clearly confused. Whatever the leader was doing, it wasn't what his men expected.

"I think my words were clear," the leader said in a tone that made the man instantly release Rosalie, leaping away from her as if burned.

She whirled on him immediately and kicked his shin. He winced but didn't retaliate, and despite the situation, Dimitri couldn't help a small smile. He regretted it when he looked back at the leader, though. The man's eyes were on Dimitri, and his smile had grown.

"Very interesting," he murmured again. "Quite delightful, really."

He raised his brows, his eyes dropping to indicate the sword. Reluctantly Dimitri released him, stepping back. But he kept his eyes on the man and his blade ready.

He half-expected the leader to order an attack. But the man's smile remained in place as he straightened his shirt.

Rosalie tried to stalk past him with her nose in the air, but he stepped smoothly into her path. Dimitri's hand tightened on his hilt, and he started forward. But the man made no move to seize her, and Rosalie stopped. She could have sidestepped him easily enough, but she chose to face him, making Dimitri still. He couldn't interpret the expression she was wearing, and a sliver of unease crept down his spine.

"And I thought your usefulness was past," the man purred. "But look who came running to rescue you."

She remained silent, radiating an anger that Dimitri could feel from several steps away. The leader appeared unaffected, however, responding to his own comment.

"Why, it's none other than the new prince of the castle!" His smile widened further. "I'm not sure why I'm surprised. You are the youngest daughter of a merchant, after all."

Dimitri's brows tightened even further. What was the man implying?

The leader continued, using a voice that made Dimitri want to rip him away from Rosalie. "I think you're going to be very useful indeed. You must excuse my momentary discourtesy earlier. I meant no harm by it, of course. But if you need comforting, I'm sure your prince will be happy to oblige." He chuckled once.

"He isn't my prince," Rosalie said, her voice as stiff as her stance.

Her response hit Dimitri hard. Why did he feel like he was the outsider in this interaction? Who was this man? And more importantly, who was he to Rosalie?

"And yet he came running to save you," the man replied, still with a laugh in his voice. "He doesn't seem to be able to control his emotions where you're concerned either." He laughed outright, making Dimitri feel as if he'd been stripped bare, failing at a very important task in the process.

"None of it matters," Rosalie said. "I have no intention of ever seeing you again, Jace. You heard Dimitri. You're not welcome here."

The man reached out a single finger and ran it down her cheek. "What a pity," he whispered. "I did enjoy our time together, Rosalie."

A sequence of emotions flashed across Rosalie's face as Dimitri's chest tightened. Was this Jace the man who had hurt Rosalie in the past? The one Dimitri had wanted to find and set straight? And now he had abducted her?

Dimitri stepped forward, no clear plan in his mind but unable to remain still and watch Jace taunt her. But Rosalie reacted more quickly than he could. Slapping Jace's hand away, she stuck her nose back in the air and marched around him.

When her eyes met Dimitri's, he tried to rein in the

emotion on display, but he wasn't fast enough. Her expression softened in response.

"Come on," she muttered as she passed him. "We should get out of here before they change their minds about the letting us go part."

Once again, he smiled despite the situation. There was something so irrepressibly Rosalie about her. It relieved him to see it after her interaction with the man from her past.

He glanced back at Jace once, reluctant to let him go so easily. But the other men had closed ranks behind their leader, and Dimitri knew Rosalie was right. This wasn't the moment to call Jace to account for whatever he had done in the past.

Instead, Dimitri fell into step behind Rosalie, guarding her from the rear until they could gain some distance from her abductors.

Rosalie didn't appear to take note of the signs he had tracked through the trees, but she must have had a good sense of direction because she led them unerringly back the way they had come. Dimitri trailed behind with frequent glances back to make sure they weren't being followed. As far as he could tell, they weren't.

They had nearly made it back to the road—still moving in silence—when he heard the mysterious voice again.

"This way!" it called. "Over here!"

He stopped instantly. It had sounded close that time, as if the other captives were mere steps away. He looked around, but just like on the previous occasions he could see no sign of anyone. And there had been no indication back in the clearing that Jace was holding other captives.

Rosalie continued forward as if she hadn't heard the cry, only stopping when she no longer heard his footsteps behind. She swung around to stare at him.

"Did you hear that?" he murmured quietly in case there were more of Jace's men somewhere near.

Rosalie strode back to him, rolling her eyes. "Really?" She propped both hands on her hips.

Dimitri frowned, but he couldn't ignore the voice. Not now that Rosalie was free, and there was no urgent need for him to keep moving.

"I heard them on my way to you as well," he murmured. "It sounds like someone is in trouble."

Rosalie regarded him silently for a moment before sighing and indicating for him to follow her. She crept toward a nearby tree, stopping only when she reached its trunk. Tipping her head back she stared directly upward, pointing into the canopy.

Dimitri crowded beside her and stared upward as well, bemused. A brightly colored bird—some kind of parrot, he guessed—sat on a branch, the foliage concealing its position.

As they stood there, the bird opened its beak.

"Over here! Right here!" it called in such startlingly clean tones that Dimitri fell back a step.

"It was a bird?" he gasped. "I was hearing a bird?" It was hard to absorb. He had noticed the voice sounded a little strange, but he had never doubted it was human.

"What is a parrot even doing here? Don't they usually live in jungles?"

Rosalie shook her head. "You really don't know anything about Glandore, do you? They might not have lived here originally, but they're everywhere now. And absolute nuisances, the lot of them." She glared up at the bird as if it was the one who had abducted her. "It's all because of the Legacy, of course. The original Beast's castle had invisible servants who used the parrots to talk for them. So now we're all blessed with these pests. Not only can they talk, but they have a knack for saying the most disconcerting thing in any given situation. We can thank the Legacy for that, too, I assume."

Dimitri grimaced. He had delayed finding Rosalie because of one of those birds. It wouldn't have happened if not for his ignorance, and it was only luck that those extra minutes hadn't meant dire consequences for her.

Rosalie stared at him. "You really don't have any idea what you're doing, do you? But you still refuse to leave! Surely you must see the necessity of it now. As long as you stay in this castle, your mere presence puts us all in danger. You're worse than useless."

She stalked off, heading toward the road again, and Dimitri followed. Despite his self-condemnation, her words felt excessive.

"I did come rushing to rescue you," he pointed out. "I didn't do it for the sake of your gratitude, but surely it's worth something, at least?"

"Gratitude?!" Rosalie stared at him. "Do you seriously think you helped me back there? I know you were busy playing the gallant hero, but surely you noticed they let us go!"

Dimitri frowned. Given the numbers they had been facing, he had been grateful for the easy escape, but clearly he was missing something significant.

"I did notice, yes," he said slowly.

"And did you think they were doing that out of the goodness of their hearts?" Rosalie fixed him with a withering look.

Dimitri considered his words carefully. "It looked like you had some sort of...history with their leader. Jace, you called him?"

Rosalie instantly stiffened. "Jace doesn't do anything unless it benefits him. Thanks to your heroics, he now believes there's a connection between us, and he intends to turn that into a payday for him and his men. I'm never going to be able to shake him off now. Who knows what he'll do next!"

"But at least you're free," Dimitri said quietly. Whatever Rosalie thought, he saw a great deal of good in that.

Rosalie shook her head impatiently. "If you hadn't shown up, I would have convinced him that his men had grabbed the wrong person. They were looking for someone connected to the castle, and now they think that person is me."

Dimitri's brows snapped together. "Those men were after me?"

"No, I don't think they wanted you. I think they wanted..." She grimaced, seeming to have trouble finishing the sentence. "They must have been monitoring the transformation of the castle grounds," she said at last with a sigh. "They know you're in residence, and they wanted leverage against you."

Dimitri swallowed. "They wanted to use you against me?"

Rosalie shrugged. "I'm guessing that was their original plan. They intended to take you for whatever they could. But now he thinks the Legacy is pushing us together, and that if he lets it play out a little further, there will be a great deal more to take."

She stopped just inside the tree line, turning to look at him. "Those men back there want you to become a Beast because then the Legacy will fill your castle with gold, jewels, and other valuables. They intend to take that wealth, and they don't care what state they leave you in afterward. Is that clear enough for you? Before that little scene back there, there was someone who wanted to rob you. Now there's someone who wants to see you cursed for life."

"At least they're not still holding you, though," Dimitri said stubbornly.

Rosalie stared at him, mouth agape. "Are you determined to ignore all good sense?"

Yet again, Dimitri's lips twitched up despite himself. Rosalie's eyes flashed in response, and he quickly straightened his face.

"I can see I'm extremely deficient," he said gravely. "May I suggest we discuss it further once we've reassured your friend of your safety?"

Rosalie seemed to accept his words, but the moment

he stepped onto the road and turned northward, she called after him.

"Stop!" She marched to his side. "Where are you going? You can't think I'm going with you to your castle! That's the last place I intend to go. I'm going back home."

"Daphne's waiting for us at the manor," Dimitri said apologetically. "She was exhausted from sprinting all the way to fetch me, so I left her to rest and recover and said I would bring you to her there. It's closer than town, you see, and I wasn't sure what state you'd be in."

"You left her there alone?" Rosalie's eyes widened. "Anything could have happened to her!"

"She was inside," he offered. "I'm sure she won't have picked any roses."

Rosalie groaned. "Why did she run to you of all people?"

"She behaved very sensibly," Dimitri said. "I was the closest source of help. I'm relieved she came to me."

Rosalie narrowed her eyes. "You would be. Just think how all the girls in town will swoon."

Dimitri frowned, but Rosalie had already turned in the direction of the castle with an air of resignation.

"I'm going to fetch Daphne and that's all. Once I know she's safe, we're going home. We've both suffered enough from the Legacy today."

CHAPTER 7
ROSALIE

Rosalie walked as quickly as she could toward the castle. She didn't want to admit it to Dimitri, but the events of the day were catching up with her. Her legs trembled from a combination of exhaustion and weakness after the stress of her capture.

She couldn't slow down, though. Daphne—who hated running—had apparently sprinted all the way to the castle to get help for Rosalie. And she was currently sitting alone, probably terrified for Rosalie—not to mention shaken from her own attempted abduction. With the Legacy running amok at the castle, Rosalie couldn't just abandon her friend. For the sake of Daphne, Rosalie could manage to get in and out of the castle once without touching a rose.

Dimitri wisely remained silent for the short walk, and the distance passed quickly. But at the edge of the manor grounds, Rosalie stopped. Despite the recent dramatic events, it had only been a short time since she had last stood in the same spot. And yet the garden had already changed. Before, the beautiful, glowing roses had all been a rich scarlet. Now the deep red was interspersed with gold. Not yellow or a light peach, but actual gold.

Rosalie gulped. She had seen every possible natural hue of rose, but she had never seen golden roses before. What had prompted the fresh burst of power from the Legacy?

Dimitri stopped beside her. "Are you really that worried about the roses? You don't seem the type to be entranced."

Rosalie glared up at him. "And you are? You nearly picked one the first day yourself, remember! And you're the last person the Legacy wants to target. So just think how strong it's going to be for me!" The last words were almost a wail.

Dimitri moved suddenly, sweeping Rosalie into his arms and cradling her against his chest. Rosalie gasped in shock, instinctively throwing her arms around his neck to anchor herself in place.

He grinned down at her. "If you're so worried, I'll help you. I'll carry you into the manor, and you won't have to set foot in the grounds. I'll be sure to keep a tight hold and not let you lunge for any of the roses we pass."

He was laughing at her, but there was kindness behind the expression. She stared up into his eyes—now disconcertingly close. Her heart rate picked up despite her lack of motion, her gaze locked with his. At this distance she could see even more differences between Jace's eyes and his. Dimitri's were not only a lighter hazel but contained flecks of gold that amplified the warmth radiating from them.

Her heart picked up further. He was holding her as if she weighed nothing, his grip firm and light. If he bent his head just a little...

She wrenched her eyes away, turning her head slightly to break the moment between them. Her traitorous heart needed to go back to its usual rhythm. She had fallen for a pretty face once before, and she wasn't going to do it again.

Dimitri stepped off the road, carrying her up the long drive.

Rosalie's eyes immediately latched onto one of the new golden roses. Seeing it from closer range, it looked as if it were truly made of gold, the last of the sun's rays bouncing off it and making it shine.

What price would such a perfect golden rose fetch? Glandorians were used to roses, but not ones like these. If she took just one, she could cure her family's financial woes. They might even be able to move back into town again. All she needed to do was wriggle down and pick one. Just one. It would be—

She gasped and shut her eyes tight, turning her face into Dimitri's chest as if he could shield her from the Legacy. His muscles jumped, his arms tightening momentarily, but mercifully he said nothing. As humiliating as it was, she apparently did need him to carry her.

After what felt like several endless minutes, she cracked her eyes open and risked peeking toward the castle. She breathed a sigh of relief when she saw they were nearly there.

"Aren't you getting tired?" she asked, breaking the silence between them. She flushed slightly. "I'm not exactly light."

He laughed. "You're extremely light to me."

She gave him a disapproving look. "I'm not interested in empty flattery."

"I wouldn't dream of it," he reassured her, although the amusement was back in his eyes. "But I didn't mean it as a comment on your size. Carrying you really is easy, but I think that's because of the Legacy—or at least the effects of it."

"Why would the Legacy make me lighter?" Rosalie asked doubtfully.

"I don't think it made you lighter; I think it made me stronger. Remember how I said that the Legacy weighed me down while I was growing up in the mountains? I've been waiting for the sense of lightness to wear off as I adjust to life here, but I'm not sure it's going to. I didn't just carry that weight for a year or two—it was for all my growing years. I think my muscles—maybe even my lungs—grew stronger because of it."

Rosalie's eyes widened as he carried her up the front steps of the manor and used his shoulder to push the unlatched door wide. What he was saying actually made sense, and it made her feel a little better about using him like a beast of burden.

He put her gently down on her feet, and she pretended she didn't feel cold and a little bereft when he stepped away from her, taking his strength and warmth with him. She looked briskly around the large entryway, turning her focus back where it belonged.

"Where's Daphne? Shouldn't she have heard us arrive? How far into the castle did you send her?"

Dimitri frowned. "Only into the sitting room. It's that door there." He pointed at a door on their left.

Fresh fear gripped Rosalie. Had something happened to her friend, alone in this enchanted castle?

She hurried toward the indicated door, bursting through into the room beyond. It was a long room, lined with windows on one side and a large fireplace on the other. A banked fire smoldered in the middle of the grate, giving the room a warmth that the entryway had lacked.

Along with the fire, the sitting room contained a range of furniture, including at least two writing desks, several clusters of chairs, and a number of small tables. One of the sofas and several armchairs had been pulled into a close semi-circle in front of the fireplace, creating a cozier circle in the large room. Rosalie's eyes jumped straight to that space, but there was no sign of Daphne.

Rushing closer, Rosalie rounded the end of the sofa to find her friend laid out on its length. Dimitri gasped from behind her as Rosalie dropped to her knees beside Daphne.

"Is she all right?" Dimitri asked. "Is she under some kind of enchantment? I didn't think leaving her here would—"

"Relax." Rosalie rocked back on her heels. "She's just asleep."

"A...sleep?" Dimitri looked so astonished, Rosalie couldn't help bursting into laughter.

"Even...Even for Daphne this is a bit much," she got out between giggles. Her eyes were watering with a combination of mirth and the release of tension, and she struggled to suppress the laughter.

Daphne responded to the noise, yawning and opening her eyes. As soon as she saw Rosalie kneeling beside her, she sat bolt upright.

"You're back!" she cried. "Are you all right?" She leaned to the side, running her eyes over Rosalie from all angles, clearly looking for injuries.

"I was abducted, and you were *napping*!" Rosalie tried to glare at her friend, but she hadn't mastered the giggles that kept slipping out.

Daphne stretched, sitting upright again. "I paced for a good twenty minutes, you know!" She sounded indignant. "But then I realized that tiring myself out wasn't doing you any good, so I thought I'd sit down." She cast an affectionate look at the sofa. "It was very comfortable."

"Considering you can fall asleep on a fence post, I'm not in the least surprised you were unable to resist a sofa." Rosalie stood, holding out a hand to pull her friend up as well.

She didn't really feel any resentment toward Daphne for falling asleep. She was just relieved nothing untoward had happened to her.

"But are you really all right?" Daphne asked once she was standing. "Dimitri was able to rescue you?"

Rosalie's happy mood instantly vanished. "As to that...

I'll explain everything to you on the way home. We need to get away from here."

Daphne looked disappointed. "I was hoping the castle would produce something delicious to eat." She looked toward the nearest table hopefully. "It didn't happen for me on my own, but now that Dimitri is back..."

"Sorry," he said apologetically. "Nothing like that has happened for me either."

"So far," Rosalie said ominously. "But we'll be extremely fortunate if it remains that way."

Daphne frowned at her. "What do you mean?"

"Come on." Rosalie tugged on her arm. "Let's talk about it on the road. And don't think I've forgotten those moves you pulled on your attackers, either. Where did you learn those?"

"Oh that?" Daphne allowed herself to be reluctantly led out of the room and toward the castle's main door. "Our old neighbor in Oakden said I would be an outsider in Glandore and I would need to defend myself. So he taught me how."

"And you've been practicing all these years? You!?" Rosalie reached the front door and turned back to stare at her. "Why didn't you ever say anything?"

"Who knows what you would have wanted me to do?" Daphne yawned.

"I can guess," Dimitri said from behind them. "She would have wanted you to teach her, and then she would have tried to turn the two of you into a town defense patrol or something."

"Oh, I see you already know Rosalie well," Daphne said

placidly. "Even the idea of having to say no was exhausting, let alone the prospect of actually teaching her." She shuddered.

"Succeeding at saying no would have been impressive on its own," Dimitri said on a chuckle.

"Exactly." Daphne smiled at him while Rosalie narrowed her eyes.

Dimitri stepped toward her undaunted, however, arms extended. "Are you ready to go back to the road?"

Rosalie stepped backward. As much as she'd disliked needing his help, she'd been grateful for it on the way into the castle. But now she had Daphne, and she wasn't sure she could handle being held by Dimitri for a second time. Not so soon. She was already having enough trouble with her pesky emotions getting the wrong idea.

"That's all right," she said quickly. "Daphne will keep me in check, won't you, Daph?"

"Uh oh." Daphne's eyebrows rose. "That sounds alarming."

"I just need you to make sure I don't pick any roses on the way back up the drive."

Daphne's expression cleared. "Oh, that's all right then." She slipped her arm through Rosalie's and clamped down tight. "I won't let you go anywhere."

Dimitri gave them a skeptical look, disappointment lurking underneath. Rosalie's heart gave an odd lurch at seeing his reaction, only confirming she had made the right choice. Her heart was absolutely not allowed to jump at the idea that Dimitri had enjoyed holding her close.

"Don't worry," she told him. "You didn't see what

Daphne did to those men. She'll probably put me in a headlock if I try to escape."

Daphne laughed. "You've given me permission now. That means you can't be mad if I actually do it."

"If I try to make a break for the roses, you can do anything you need." Rosalie gave her friend a narrow look. "But only in that one case." Daphne was looking a bit too smug. She was still a better option than being carried by Dimitri, though.

The girls walked down the stairs in lockstep and had made it several yards up the drive before Rosalie looked suspiciously behind her. Dimitri was following them.

She pulled Daphne to a stop. "What are you doing?" she asked him over her shoulder, unwilling to turn around.

"I'm making sure you don't get abducted again on your way home," he said calmly.

"You're going to follow us all the way home?" Rosalie wanted to protest, but she couldn't stop her eyes dropping to the sword strapped to his waist.

"Yes, I am," he said gently, noting the direction of her gaze.

She flushed and looked forward again. She wanted to spurn his offer, but she was more shaken by her abduction than she cared to admit.

After a moment's hesitation, she stayed silent, pulling Daphne into motion.

"Thank you!" Daphne called back to Dimitri, apparently having no qualms about accepting his help. Which of course, she didn't. She was the one who had gone to him for help in the first place.

"What were you thinking running here?" Rosalie whispered, trying to keep her voice low enough that Dimitri wouldn't overhear. "You should have gone to Thebarton!"

"It was further away," Daphne said matter-of-factly. "And I had a feeling Dimitri would be able to handle it."

"Well, he didn't," Rosalie snapped, struggling to keep her voice lowered. "He made everything worse."

"Worse?" Daphne looked pointedly at Rosalie. "You're here, aren't you?"

Rosalie groaned. "It was Jace."

"Jace!?!" Daphne shrieked the name, and Rosalie looked hurriedly over her shoulder.

"Keep your voice down!"

"Jace!?!" Daphne repeated in a shocked whisper.

"Yes." Rosalie sighed and related the whole situation to Daphne, who was a suitably awe-filled audience.

"He really did that? And said that? Eww?" Daphne scrunched up her nose.

Rosalie nodded her hearty agreement, suddenly realizing they had reached the road without her even noticing. Relating the shocking story to Daphne had worked as an effective barrier to the Legacy's pull. She hadn't even noticed the roses.

She just appreciated that her friend wasn't saying "I told you so" at this fresh revelation of Jace's true nature. But Daphne had never said that, even though she had been the only one to doubt Jace from the beginning. Before Jace's betrayal, Rosalie had brushed her friend's dislike aside. Daphne had never warmed to anyone particularly, other than Rosalie, as if making friends was another thing she didn't have the energy for.

Daphne made an exception of friendship only for Rosalie which she claimed was because spurning Rosalie would have cost the same unwelcome level of effort as befriending anyone else. But Rosalie should have recognized there was more to Daphne's dislike of Jace. There was a difference between indifference and mistrust.

She had freely apologized to her friend after Jace's betrayal, and even then, Daphne had never said anything like "I told you so." And now she was being just as supportive in the wake of Jace's new perfidy as she had been after the initial disaster.

Daphne also immediately grasped the implications of Jace letting them go. Her previous approval of Dimitri seemed to dim, and she cast an uncertain look back at him, as if she was no longer sure about him trailing them home.

"Maybe I shouldn't have run to him," she murmured. "But I did, and he was genuinely worried for you. He went straight after you, and his arrival did lead to Jace letting you go. Maybe we should let him walk with us? I feel bad leaving him back there."

"Better he feels bad than the Legacy turns him into a Beast," Rosalie said firmly. She bit her lip. "I would have told him to stay behind but..."

"Yes, I agree." Daphne shivered, not needing Rosalie to put her reason into words. She peeped back at him again.

"Even so…" She hesitated. "Don't you think you're being too harsh on him?"

"Don't you think you're being too easy on him?" Rosalie asked back. "You're just assuming he rushed off to help me out of pure motives. But just look at his face. Men who look like Dimitri—especially ones with royal blood and their own castle—love to fill the role of noble hero. He was acting in service of his own ego, not me. Just wait until we find him at the inn regaling everyone with the story of his heroic rescue. Then you'll see."

"Maybe." Daphne drew the word out. "I still think you might be judging him harshly because he looks like Jace."

"Jace pretended to love me so he could embezzle my father's money—knowing full well that the Legacy would aid him in the task but that doing so would trigger it to ruin us completely. Even our house burned down!" Rosalie's voice rose at the end of her declaration, and she forced it back down. "I thought we were rid of him, at least, but here he is, back again and trying to trap me with the Legacy for a second time! I have good reason to be wary of anyone even remotely like him. I'm not saying Dimitri is working with Jace, I'm sure he's not. I'm not even saying Dimitri is the same as Jace. I'm just saying I have no room in my life for arrogant young men who are too focused on their own lives and apparent suffering to care about how much they're hurting the people around them."

Daphne sighed, but she didn't try to argue further, which was a relief to Rosalie. The afternoon had already dragged on far too long. She was exhausted, and if she didn't get home soon, her mother and brothers would have awkward questions.

As it was, it was getting dark by the time they arrived at her family's cottage, and all three of her brothers were in the small front yard.

"There you are!" Vernon exclaimed. He might be the middle brother, but he was usually the ringleader. "We were about to go looking for you."

"Here I am." Rosalie mustered as much cheerfulness as she was able. "And Daphne too. She's staying the night again."

All three boys exclaimed in approval, and this time Daphne didn't protest. Her parents were still out of town, so her other option was to spend the night in an empty house.

"But who are you?" Oscar asked, his gaze fixing on Dimitri who was lingering back, away from the gate. Oscar, as the youngest, rarely put himself forward. But he tended to notice things others didn't.

Rosalie bit back a groan. Didn't Dimitri have the courtesy to turn back as soon as they came in sight of her home?

"See!" she hissed at Daphne. "He's still lingering here to make sure he gets praised for saving me. But I have no intention of telling my brothers about that particular adventure!"

"Or maybe he just wants to see us safely inside," Daphne whispered back. "It's not like he knows what your brothers look like. They could have been Jace's men lurking in wait for you."

"Don't even say such a thing!" Rosalie whispered back furiously. "My brothers will never have anything to do with Jace again. And I know they all shot up last summer, but no one looking at them could think they were full-grown men!"

"I'm just saying, he might have had innocent motives," Daphne said, unruffled as always by her friend's fiery pronouncements.

Dimitri glanced uncertainly at Rosalie, reminding her that she had an audience. Her brothers already looked too curious at her whispered exchange with Daphne. She sighed.

"This is Dimitri," she said, resigned to the inevitable. "He was just escorting us home as there's been trouble on the roads recently." She added the last bit on the spur of the moment, hoping to give them a hint to be careful.

None of the boys appeared to notice the warning, however, latching onto the beginning of her words instead.

"Dimitri!" Vernon exclaimed. "You mean the new prince who's taken up residence at the manor? We heard about you in town! I'm Vernon." He pointed at the boy on his right. "That's Ralph." He pointed at the one on his left. "And that's Oscar." He directed a wounded look at his sister. "Why didn't you tell us you'd met him, Rosalie?"

"You weren't coming from the direction of Thebarton, though," Oscar said before she could answer. "Have you already been up to tour the manor? Will you take us through it, Dimitri? We've tried sneaking inside in the past

—just to have a look—but we couldn't get any of the doors or windows open."

"You what?!" Rosalie cried, horrified. "Hasn't this family had enough trouble already? I absolutely forbid you to go anywhere near the castle again." She swung around to face Dimitri who now lingered right by the gate. "Dimitri! Don't you dare let them onto the manor grounds, let alone into the castle!"

Dimitri gave the boys an apologetic look. "Sorry. You heard your sister. I can't help on that one, I'm afraid."

"Of course you'd take her side," Vernon muttered resentfully while Oscar looked curiously back and forth between Dimitri and Rosalie.

"Personally, I think she's right," Ralph said suddenly. "If there's a prince in that castle, none of our family should be anywhere near it." He directed a stern look at Rosalie. "And that includes you."

"I've been doing my best, believe me," Rosalie muttered, making Dimitri laugh under his breath.

"Do we have to keep standing out here?" Daphne asked plaintively, and all three boys instantly forgot about Dimitri.

But when Vernon had ushered her inside, Ralph close behind, Oscar paused to give a final look at Dimitri.

"Is it true the manor has already been transformed?" he asked. "Just because you arrived?"

Dimitri gave Rosalie an uncomfortable look. "I'm not entirely sure of the reason. But it's certainly improved since I got there. And the grounds have completely changed."

"They're...beautiful," Rosalie said quietly to her brother. "Far, far too beautiful. Don't let Vernon goad you into going anywhere near there. It's dangerous."

Oscar nodded seriously, seeming to understand the danger better than Vernon, if not as well as Ralph. Rosalie gave a sigh of relief. If Ralph and Oscar were united, they would manage to rein Vernon in.

Oscar still hesitated, however, his face slipping into a smirk as he looked between Rosalie and Dimitri. "It was interesting to meet you," he said. "I'll go inside now so you can bid each other farewell in private. Just the two of you, the garden, and three pairs of watchful brotherly eyes. Complete solitude in other words."

Dimitri laughed until he saw the faces of the other two boys pressed against the cottage's front window, watching them with grins on their faces and mischief in their eyes. His chuckle died, his expression changing to one of mild unease.

"Watch all you want," Rosalie said haughtily to Oscar. "If you can keep your eyes off Daphne long enough, that is."

"Touché, dear sister," he said with a mocking salute. "I am struck dead."

With a laughing glance at Dimitri, he finally strolled inside after the other boys, leaving Rosalie seething in his wake. She wanted to storm after him and hammer some sense into his brain. She had no interest in being alone with Dimitri, and if Oscar had any sense, he wouldn't be encouraging the man.

But common courtesy stopped her from abandoning

Dimitri to rush after her brothers. Regardless of his motivations, he had come to her rescue and provided shelter for Daphne. He had even walked them both home.

"Thank you," she said reluctantly. "For rescuing me. I'm sure you didn't realize the harm you were doing in coming after me." She acquitted him of ill intent in that regard, at least.

"You're welcome." Dimitri gave such a low bow that Rosalie flushed. Was he mocking her? She supposed it had been a halfhearted apology at best.

She tried again. "I appreciate you walking us home. I'm not usually so weak-hearted, but after..." She trailed off. "Anyway, I really did appreciate it. Daphne did as well."

For this one service at least, she could thank him with good grace—even if he had lingered around for praise and acknowledgment at the end. At least he'd had the sense not to bring the abduction up to her brothers when she didn't mention it.

"I'm happy to provide that service any time you need," he said.

She raised both hands in alarm. "No, no! It would be better if we never saw each other again. Good night, and I hope you have a successful life."

She rushed inside and closed the door firmly behind her.

CHAPTER 8
DIMITRI

Three brothers! Dimitri mused as he walked slowly back to the castle. They'd looked close in age, too —to each other, if not to Rosalie. What would it be like to have three younger brothers? He'd always wanted siblings, but since he'd never known his father, that had been unlikely.

He would have loved to say yes to their request and give them a tour of the castle—even if he hadn't yet explored the entire thing himself. He could have used the opportunity to find out more about Rosalie.

But given the circumstances, he had to admit she was right. After everything that had happened—and given his own obvious ignorance—tempting the Legacy seemed like a foolhardy idea. He would have to make a different plan. One that would let him learn more about her without putting Rosalie or her family at risk.

With that intention in mind, he headed back to the town center the next day. When he walked past Rosalie's cottage, he kept his attention on the door and garden, but no one emerged.

Moments after reaching the central square, however, the door of the largest and most elaborate house opened. A young woman with a vaguely familiar face came skipping down the steps. It took him a moment to place her name.

Blythe, he remembered, just in time to greet her.

She giggled, affecting surprise at seeing him, although he'd seen the curtain inside the front window twitch as he'd stepped into the square. At least her enthusiasm made his role as a newcomer much easier.

He gave her what he hoped was a charming smile. "I don't suppose you'd be willing to assist me? I've come into Thebarton for supplies but don't know the best place to buy them."

"Oh, you'll want one of the general stores for that!" she said with enthusiasm. "My family owns several, and the largest and best is right on this square. Over there." She pointed at a building in the far corner, just distant enough that he hadn't noticed it previously.

"How perfect!" he said, relieved there was no chance of his getting lost. "And could you perhaps direct me toward a reputable inn as well—preferably one where the reputation comes from the excellence of their dining room? I have a strong hankering for a proper meal." His smile widened in anticipation. He had been eating travel rations for too many days.

"Oh you can't possibly eat at an inn alone on your first

proper visit into town!" Blythe cried. "You must come and eat the midday meal at our house!"

"I couldn't possibly intrude," Dimitri said, a little alarmed.

"Oh, nonsense." Blythe beamed at him. "I'm inviting you on my mama's behalf—I know she would absolutely insist. You can't disappoint her. And Papa will be glad to meet you too. He's been talking about how he really should visit and welcome you to the area."

Dimitri relaxed at the news that her parents would be at the meal as well. If her father really was determined to meet him, it would be better to acquiesce and get the introduction out of the way. He wasn't ready for a stream of house callers at the manor.

"Very well, then." He gave a shallow bow. "I thank you for your hospitality."

She giggled and took his arm, dragging him toward her front door. He allowed himself to be tugged along but extracted his arm as soon as they were inside.

True to Blythe's words, an older woman appeared and welcomed him enthusiastically. She looked startlingly similar to her daughter and seemed alike in thought as well. She seconded her daughter's invitation heartily, and the last of Dimitri's misgivings faded away.

Madam Foster was soon joined by her husband who added his own welcome. Before Dimitri knew it, he was sitting down to an impressive spread in a large formal dining room.

Dimitri had grown up in a small two-bedroom cottage, and he couldn't help being impressed at both the room and the food. Although there were many rooms at the manor that were larger and more impressive, they still had an empty, abandoned air. He was a long way from hosting dinner parties in any of them.

The elder Fosters were unlike the adults he had grown up around in the mountains. Their affectations were exaggerated, and they had an obvious taste for luxury at odds with the mountain community's austere lifestyle. But beneath the surface mannerisms, they seemed genuinely warmhearted. He even caught glimpses of the shrewd business minds that had propelled them to their place as the richest family in Thebarton.

At only one point did awkwardness descend on the table. Despite Dimitri's attempts at subtlety, his first reference to Rosalie's family elicited an immediate negative response. He hadn't expected his hosts' closed hostility or their rapid attempts to change the subject. He couldn't think why, but they almost seemed afraid, and he had no choice but to let the subject drop.

When they had finally finished all the courses, he excused himself. All three of them escorted him to the door and lingered to wish him farewell.

"Let them know at the store that we sent you," Blythe's mother said. "They'll be sure to take extra care of you."

"Thank you, Madam." Dimitri bowed over her hand. "And thank you for an excellent meal. I can't remember the last time I enjoyed one so much."

She immediately went pink with pleasure and assured him she would pass on his compliment to her cook.

"And perhaps you could advise me, sir." Dimitri turned to Blythe's father. "I'm sure I'll be looking for a proper cooked meal again soon. Could you recommend Thebarton's best inn—at least in regards to their dining room?"

"You're always welcome here!" Blythe cried. "You could come every meal if you like! You don't want to be eating with just anybody at an inn."

Dimitri hesitated for a moment, unsure how to answer, and her father gave her a quelling look. She immediately blushed scarlet and stepped back.

"Excuse the enthusiasm of my daughter," he said. "Although of course we would be pleased to see you anytime. But for an excellent table, I can highly recommend the Mortar and Pestle. You must have passed it on your way in."

Dimitri nodded, relieved. He remembered the establishment because he'd noted its size on his way past. It was obviously well patronized by locals and visitors alike, and it was on his side of town as well. He could already envision Blythe's enthusiasm becoming a problem, and he was relieved he would be able to visit the inn without having to pass through the town square.

With more thanks, he tried to escape out the door, but Blythe's mother managed to seize his hands a final time. Dropping her voice, she murmured, "Please do excuse our Blythe. It's rare to have new residents in Thebarton—at least at our level. You'll understand."

She fixed him with a look, and he murmured something vague as he pulled his hand free. He didn't wish to be rude after their generous hospitality, but he couldn't help bristling at her words. He could only imagine Rosalie and her family were the sort of people they considered below their level.

When he finally escaped out into the square, he strode off toward the store Blythe had indicated. Her mother's final words reminded him of his first meeting with Blythe. Rosalie had interrupted them, and he thought he remembered a coldness in the greeting between her and the other girls, although he hadn't taken much note of it at the time.

Was she looked down on by the others? Was that all there was to the awkwardness of the Fosters when he had brought up Rosalie's family during the meal?

As usual, he had the distinct sensation he was missing a crucial piece of the puzzle—one that was familiar to everyone but him. He was almost tempted to forget the store and go straight to the Mortar and Pestle. But if he wanted to connect with other locals—old-timers who knew everything that had ever happened in the town—it was the wrong time. He was too late now for the midday crowd, and too early for the evening patrons. Besides, he really was in urgent need of supplies.

Reluctantly he accepted he would have to visit the Mortar and Pestle another time and instead loaded himself up with supplies from the store. Even without dropping the Foster name, the store clerk was cheerful and helpful, and he soon had as much as he could carry. It would be a heavy load on the return walk but worth it given how depleted his pack had become.

He was just grateful some Glandorian coin had been left among his mother's papers. He didn't know how much she had taken with her when she fled, but it must have been far more than he ever suspected. The remainder would be more than enough to sustain him for a while at least—hopefully for long enough to find some answers.

Thoughts of his mother consumed him as he walked back to the manor. Sometimes the newness of his experiences in Glandore made him forget all about her, but that only made the ache sharper when it inevitably reappeared. Worse, he wasn't even sure if the pain came from grief at her loss or anger at what felt like her betrayal.

How could she have taken him away from his family and his heritage—choosing a life away from his birth Legacy without ever giving him a choice? She hadn't even told him the truth after he became an adult. Had she been afraid that if she told him, he would leave her alone to return to Glandore? He would never know now.

Back at the manor, he prowled restlessly through some of the rooms he had been ignoring. In a small sitting room hidden on the second floor, he was stopped short by a portrait that took his breath away. He had no memories of his mother so young, but she was easily recognizable.

The golden-haired, blue-eyed young woman twirling in a soft pink dress was beautiful. But even more, she looked radiantly happy. Had she been a mother already when it was painted, or had it been Dimitri who stole that glow from her eyes?

From her papers, and from the tapestry in the entryway, he knew that his royal blood and the inheritance of the manor came through his mother, not his father. He didn't know a thing about his father's background. His mother had spoken of him in soft, wistful tones, but the only actual information she had imparted was his name—Jerome.

His mother, however, had been an only child who had inherited the manor on her own mother's death and who was in line to be the sole inheritor of her father's vast wealth. But she had left it all behind and run away.

She had left behind everyone except Dimitri, and in taking him, she had cut him off from everything she had rejected. He wished he could have just one more day with her so he could ask her why—one more chance to understand the parts of her she'd always kept hidden.

He stood in front of the portrait for a long time, gazing up at his mother when she must have been about his own age. It was both healing and painful to see her in the glow of life and youth. The mother he remembered was reserved, her stoicism tinged with melancholy, and her smiles short-lived.

When he finally tore himself away, he couldn't go tamely back to the fire burning in the front sitting room. Driven now, he continued to roam—poking his nose into dining rooms, sitting rooms, a ballroom, and bedroom after bedroom. All were furnished and free of dust, as if the inhabitants had left only the day before.

But something about the quality of the air convinced him the manor had been empty for many years. The Legacy's enchantment could cover a great deal, but it couldn't disguise everything. It was in the process of rehabilitating the manor, but the building had been empty a long time.

When he poked his head into yet another bedroom, he

paused, sensing something different about this one. The rooms he had seen previously had all been elegantly decorated, but most of them had felt lifeless—like guest rooms, not someone's private chambers. But this room had a different air.

The curtains around the four-poster bed were a soft filmy pink that reminded him of something. As he stepped into the room, he realized what it was—the dress his mother had been wearing in the portrait.

The chairs were all decorated in pink as well—the first room he had seen with that color scheme. He crossed over to the dressing table, running his fingers lightly along the fancy collection of brushes, combs, and bottles. They were made of gold and crystal and inlaid porcelain, but they sat in neat, untouched rows, as if his mother hadn't even considered taking any of them. They certainly would have had no place in her simple mountain life.

He picked up the book lying on the small table beside the bed. A history of Glandore. It seemed unexpected reading for his mother, but then it hadn't been the choice of the middle-aged woman he remembered but of the smiling young woman in the portrait. A young woman who was a stranger to him.

He flipped through the pages and realized it was a romanticized account of the original Beast and the woman who had freed him with her love. Apparently his mother had once believed in fairy tale love.

He set the book down abruptly, his throat clogging. Clearing it, he stepped to the window, glancing down at the grounds below. He had spent little time in the grounds at the rear of the manor, but they were full of the same splendid growth as the front. The Legacy's efforts were lavish, extending far beyond the stretch of garden that might lure in an unwary passerby.

He turned away from the window, his eye falling on the mantelpiece above the cold fireplace. He stiffened. A letter was propped up there, the paper crisp and fresh, looking like it had been left yesterday. But he wasn't fooled. He didn't need to open it to know it had been sitting there decades longer than that.

CHAPTER 9

DIMITRI

nly one word was written on the outside of the envelope.

Father

The letters were formed in a familiar, elegant cursive script. Dimitri had learned to read and write from a more mature version of that hand.

In a daze, his feet carried him across the room, and his hand reached for the letter. Only after it was in his hand did it occur to him to wonder if he should open it. But its intended recipient—his grandfather—had left this place long ago, leaving it behind. Either disaster had befallen him the moment his daughter disappeared, or else he had read it and carefully placed it back where he had found it. Had he intended for Dimitri to find it one day?

With trembling fingers, Dimitri opened it, retrieving

two tightly written pages. His eyes hurriedly scanned the words:

Father,

I have crept back in here to leave this note for you. I already know from the housekeeper that you visit my room every day. So do not feel bad. Even if your final words to me were harsh, I know you miss me, and the love you have for me is deep.

But I cannot return to you. Although you thought you were doing what was best for me, you have destroyed my chance at happiness. You were convinced Jerome's love was false, but it's you that made it so—however unwittingly you acted on that front.

You can see now why I hid from you and married in secret. I intended to return eventually —my family with me—but when you tracked me down and stripped away my inheritance, I lost everything. You couldn't take the manor itself since I received that from Mother, but you know its income is bound in a trust. You left Jerome and me with nothing.

Given your words at the time, you probably think our love is at fault. You said if our love was true, we could live on love. But how can love defeat the Legacy? Your actions have turned it against us, and now there is no hope for me.

You obviously didn't consider what happened to the original rich daughters when they lost their dowries and all their family's wealth. Their suitors abandoned them, and now the Legacy has betrayed me by forcing Jerome down the same path.

My beloved Jerome has been torn from me only a year after the birth of our darling Dimitri. I know Jerome loved him—loved me. I know his true self loves us still.

The hand became shaky at that point, and tear spots dotted the bottom of the paper. Dimitri's heart squeezed, but he turned to the next page and read on.

The Legacy has forced him away. It has forced him to abandon us and has placed a false veneer of sneering disdain and hatred over the true feelings that dwell in his heart. He claims he has no use for me or for Dimitri, but I know those are the words the Legacy is putting in his mouth. But its power is too strong for me.

I could not free him from its clutches, and now he is gone despite all my pleadings. I have even heard word from afar that it has forced him into courting another. I suppose it is all too easy for the Legacy to cast aside a secret wife.

I cannot bear this place without him by my side. And I will not allow my beautiful, perfect baby boy to remain within the Legacy's clutches. If I cannot free Jerome, at least I can free Dimitri.

You will not see me again. But know that while the pain of your actions means we will never see each other again in this life, I will always hold my love for you in my heart. I know you did the best you could for me after Mother's death and indeed you lavished much on me in our years together. I wish you nothing but health and happiness.

Your loving daughter

Dimitri staggered to the nearest chair and collapsed into it. He had wanted answers—had wanted to understand his mother—and this one letter had allowed him to do so. Despite the melancholy of her manner, he had never guessed at the depth of the pain she had kept locked inside. He had never considered what lurked behind her words when she'd called him her whole world.

His gaze wandered back to the book on her bedside table. If there had been a fire in the fireplace, he would have dashed the volume into the flames. She had lain in that bed and read those words and allowed herself to be caught up in a fantasy. She had fed the dream instead of reality and allowed it to blind her to all sense. She had ignored the warnings of those who loved her and the wisdom of those older and more experienced, convinced she understood both love and the Legacy better than them.

Dimitri was only just learning about the Legacy at twenty-one years old, but already he understood the delusion behind her words. The Legacy manipulated physical objects, like the roses and the manor, and it could sometimes influence small actions—like beguiling someone into picking a rose. He had experienced that himself. But every account agreed that while it manipulated circumstances, it had no power over what people did with the situations it created. It couldn't manufacture love, and neither could it strip it away. It didn't force words into someone's mouth.

It hadn't been the Legacy that had betrayed his mother, it had been his father. He had used words of love to lure a young girl away from her family and friends. He had married her in secret, and then when her income was cut off and her future inheritance withdrawn, he had abandoned both her and their child.

Dimitri's hand tightened slowly into a fist. The rustle of paper made him stop, however, and he smoothed the letter back out before he crushed it completely.

His mother had never given him details about his father or what had happened to him, but she had always spoken of his love for the two of them, speaking as if he had still been alive. For most of his life, Dimitri had believed he was dead anyway. He had concocted a story where his father's death had driven his mother into the mountains and put the sadness into her eyes. He had thought she spoke of his father as if he was still with them in order to ease the pain. But a small part of him had held onto hope that his father was still alive after all, and that in returning to Glandore, he might finally meet him.

That hope had proven true—his father was likely alive —but the desire behind it was gone. After reading the letter, he no longer had any desire to meet him. He could only be grateful such a man had given up the chance to have influence in his life. For all the tragedy of her delusion, he would rather have his mother's loyal heart than his father's fickle cruelty.

But what of his grandfather? Dimitri didn't have children of his own, so he could only imagine the pain his grandfather must have felt on reading the letter. Had he tried to track down his daughter and baby grandson? Had he wished to know Dimitri?

Dimitri had his answer in the tapestry that held the family tree. His grandfather had disapproved of Jerome enough to disinherit his only daughter, so his son-in-law did not appear on the family record. But Dimitri's name had been carefully stitched in below his mother.

But where was his grandfather now? Two decades had passed, so Dimitri had to accept the possibility he was dead.

He read the letter again more slowly, and it hurt just as

much the second time. At least he now knew why his mother had not only left Glandore but had hidden any knowledge of its Legacy from him. However misguided she had been, she had thought she was protecting her son from a malevolent and all-powerful force.

She had ultimately failed, however. While the Legacy wasn't what she had painted it as, it still had the power to cause harm, and he was more enmeshed in it now than he had ever been as a baby. His mother hadn't fit the criteria necessary to attract any serious amount of its power—she had already been married before she lost her fortune, making her belief in the Legacy's involvement even more nonsensical. But ever since Dimitri's return, he fit the Legacy's requirements far too closely.

He didn't regret returning—he couldn't regret it now that he'd found the letter. He had suspected the manor of holding answers, and he had been right. But he wasn't the only one caught up in his current situation, and he couldn't allow his choice to turn someone else into a victim. He needed to find out what was fueling Rosalie's excessive fear so he could work out how to shield her.

He leaped to his feet, ready to rush back into town. But darkness had almost fallen, and armed criminals lurked near the road. He would have to wait for the next day, however little he felt like patience.

As he prepared to sleep on the sofa in the sitting room, as he had on the previous nights, he decided it was time to choose a proper bed. There was no point heading into Thebarton too early, so he would spend the morning establishing himself in the home he had inherited. For a start, he would choose the most convenient of the bedchambers and make it his own.

By the time he walked into Thebarton the next day, he had spent enough hours working to have earned a meal at the Mortar and Pestle. The Legacy's enchantment had allowed him to avoid scrubbing, but there had still been furniture to shift as well as countless trips up and down the stairs. In the end, he had readied not only a bedchamber for himself, but a small dining room and a smaller sitting room as well.

The Mortar and Pestle was positioned on the main road into town, but closer to the town's edge than to the central square. Since it was well-positioned for passing travelers, it had a large, enclosed yard and substantial stables. A carriage had arrived just before Dimitri, the driver calling for a change of horses to be brought along with some refreshments. Its arrival set off a flurry of activity, and Dimitri had to skirt the chaos in the center of the yard as he approached one of the inn's doors.

Stepping through, he entered a calmer atmosphere. But when he followed the hallway into a large, open dining room, the noise levels picked back up. Apparently, plenty of the locals had come to enjoy the fare produced by the inn's cook. Dimitri had clearly been directed well by the Fosters. Not only was the dining room popular, but the number of families present indicated it was a respectable establishment.

He had intended to come early but had ended up becoming absorbed in his morning's task and was later than he had planned. Most of the inn's patrons had nearly finished their meals. Even so, he was only standing inside the room a matter of seconds before a middle-aged man bustled toward him. From his clothing and bearing, Dimitri guessed him to be the innkeeper.

The man bowed quickly, bouncing back up with a beaming smile. "You honor us with your presence, sir!" he said with enthusiasm.

Dimitri blinked in silence, taken aback.

"You'll be wanting a meal, of course!" the man continued, undaunted. "I'm sure you've heard of the excellence of our kitchen!"

"Y—yes, I have," Dimitri said.

"Of course, of course." The man finally seemed to notice Dimitri's confusion. "I forgot to introduce myself!" he cried. "I'm Otis, innkeeper here, as my father was before me and his father before him. Thebarton runs in my veins, you know. It's a prosperous town and large in size, but I still pride myself on knowing every face within it." His chest puffed out. "You mustn't be surprised at me recognizing you, Your Lordship."

"Just Dimitri," Dimitri said quickly. "Please."

His response seemed to please Otis, who attempted to lead him to an attractive table near a large window. Dimitri hung back.

"Actually," he said, "since I'm here alone, I was hoping to eat at the bar." He would learn nothing sitting in state by himself. It was the old-timers at the bar who had drawn him to the inn in the first place.

Otis's eyebrows shot up, but he recovered a moment later, his beaming smile returning. "Of course, of course!

I've heard you're a modest young man, as every young man should be. This way! This way!"

He ushered Dimitri toward the empty end of the bar, but Dimitri pretended not to notice, taking an empty seat beside an older man who was nursing a tankard with one hand and making short work of a large plate with the other.

Otis made no protest at Dimitri's choice of seat and had soon taken his order and disappeared into the depths of the inn. Dimitri remained silent, however, not trying to engage his neighbor in conversation. He had learned from the older men of the mountains that he would learn more by keeping quiet than by rushing in with questions.

Sure enough, when a few minutes of silence had passed, the man beside him spoke.

"Ye can't go wrong with a meal at the Mortar and Pestle," he said.

Dimitri murmured agreement before returning his eyes to the bar in front of him and nearly jolting off his seat. When had his plate of food appeared? He must have been more distracted than he'd realized not to notice Otis's return.

The enticing aroma of the food wafted up to his nose, and his stomach rumbled in response. The man chuckled, and Dimitri smiled.

"I'm very much looking forward to trying the food," he said. "I'm a newcomer to Thebarton, so it's my first time here."

The older man barked out a laugh. "Aye, aye. We all know who you are, princeling."

Dimitri winced. "I'm really not a prince."

"Oh, aye, aye." The man chuckled, apparently finding Dimitri's protests amusing. "I heard you were a good sort." He took several more bites before adding, "I'm Wyatt."

"Is there anyone in Thebarton who hasn't heard of me already?" Dimitri asked ruefully.

The mountain community had helped each other when necessary, but many of the inhabitants had been solitary folk. He hadn't anticipated how quickly the gossip would spread, especially in a town the size of Thebarton.

"Anyone not heard that the old lord's heir has finally returned? Not likely!" Wyatt grinned.

Dimitri wondered who had first told Wyatt and how many people Wyatt had subsequently passed the news on to. He couldn't regret the man's apparently garrulous nature, however. Not when he hoped to make use of it himself.

"I hope I may soon meet more of Thebarton's residents," he said. "I've not yet had the chance to spend much time in town."

"So you really do mean to stay?" Wyatt regarded him keenly as he waited for an answer.

"For the time being," Dimitri said after a slight hesitation, Rosalie's entreaties playing through his mind. "I have no other plans."

That seemed to satisfy Wyatt who nodded wisely. "Right shame it was to see such a fine estate going to ruin. I haven't been out there myself, but I hear you've turned it around quickly." He glanced sideways at Dimitri while he shoveled in another mouthful.

Dimitri grimaced. "I'm not sure I can take any credit for that. It seems the Legacy approves of my arrival."

Wyatt laughed. "Aye, indeed. I haven't heard tell of golden roses in this region since my grandfather's day."

"I can only hope the Legacy doesn't cause the locals any trouble," Dimitri said with a frown. "The manor's roses seem uncommonly attractive, and I understand matters might become...complicated if someone were to pluck one."

"You have more to lose than us, now, don't you," Wyatt said, as cheerful as ever. "Might want to get onto building a high wall round that manor of yours." He laughed at his own joke.

Dimitri considered how to turn the conversation in more informative directions.

"I dined with the Fosters yesterday," he said. "I understand they're one of Thebarton's most prominent families."

It wouldn't do to mention Rosalie too quickly. He had no desire to indicate his interest in her to either the gossips of the town or the Legacy itself. And while he wanted more information about her family's past, he needed to balance that against the secondary purpose of his excursion. He intended to show both Jace and the Legacy that if they were determined to link him with a young lady, there were plenty of options besides Rosalie.

"The Fosters?" Wyatt took a moment to chew a large piece of meat. "Aye, I suppose they're prominent enough nowadays. Top family, you might say. Seem to know it, too, if what they've done to their house is anything to go by." He sounded displeased about that for some reason.

"You disapprove?" Dimitri asked, trying to remember if there had been anything peculiar about the Foster's home. It had been rather ostentatious, but he hadn't thought it offensively so.

"In general, he's a careful one, Foster," Wyatt said. "But he's got a soft spot for his wife, and she doesn't always have the best sense when it comes to fancy displays. He indulges her, which is admirable as far as it goes, but he should know better about the house."

"I'm sorry, I'm not sure I follow." Dimitri was getting sick of conversations that made little sense to him.

"Well, everyone knows the risk, don't they?" Wyatt stabbed a round of cooked carrot. "The fancier the home, the more liable it is to burn down without warning."

Dimitri's eyes widened. He could only assume this was another quirk of the Glandorian Legacy. He did remember something about a house burning down in the original history, and he'd seen a burned-out husk on the town square as well. He'd assumed the fire must have been fresh, but perhaps the locals feared tempting the Legacy by rebuilding on the spot.

"Just look at Clifford," Wyatt continued. "He was always careful to keep his home modest in style, even if it was the largest and finest in town. And look at what happened to it anyway!"

"Is that the burned building on the square?" Dimitri asked. "How long ago did it burn?"

"Aye, that's the one. Burned down only last year. Clifford and his family used to live there before they lost everything." Wyatt shook his head. "A real shame that was. They were a fine first family for Thebarton, always generous to a fault and welcoming." He speared a hunk of potato. "They had more claim to the position than those Fosters, too. Clifford's merchant network was a good sight larger than any other business in town, including Foster's." He sighed heavily. "Clifford did everything he could to stay out of the Legacy's notice, too. But it was all for naught in the end. Determined to grab 'em, it was."

"Because he was a merchant?" Dimitri asked tentatively, fascinated by the story despite his original intentions for the conversation.

Wyatt nodded, warming to the tale. "Like I said, he was real careful because of it, but the Legacy can be tricksy." He leaned closer. "His wife had three girls, you know. Another man might have wanted a son to follow in his footsteps, but Clifford doted on those girls and said he wasn't taking any chances. Stopped with just the girls." Wyatt nodded approvingly. "Very sensible."

"You mean because of the danger of being a merchant with an equal number of sons and daughters?" Dimitri clarified, remembering something he'd read.

Wyatt grunted an affirmative. "Dangerous business that is, as we all know. Why the Legacy decided the total number don't matter, just that there be equal boys and girls, I don't know. Right illogical if you ask me, but there's no use thinking the Legacy should be reasonable. Doesn't have a brain to think, let alone reason. Not as if it's sentient." He laughed again at his own humor.

"So he only had three daughters, but the Legacy caused his house to burn down anyway?" Dimitri asked, feeling stirrings of alarm. Up until now the Legacy had seemed more odd than villainous—despite Rosalie's exaggerated fear and his mother's delusional conclusions.

"No, no, it started before that." Wyatt leaned closer. "Clifford and his wife intended to stop, but it don't always work out like we intend, do it?" He winked, but Dimitri wasn't sure what he was implying.

"Fell pregnant again several years later!" Wyatt explained impatiently when Dimitri remained blank. "And if the pregnancy wasn't the Legacy's work, the outcome was."

"The outcome?" Dimitri asked, still mystified.

"Triplets!" Wyatt proclaimed, clearly enjoying having a new audience for a tale the whole town must know. "And boys, the lot of them! Three sons to match the three daughters in one fell swoop."

"Triplet boys?" Dimitri asked slowly, a cold trickle of dread seeping down his spine.

"Aye! Three daughters and three sons. Any family with that number would be at risk, but doubly so given he was a merchant. O' course being a merchant is why the Legacy forced them into it in the first place." Wyatt shook his head sadly. "Not much poor Clifford could do after that. He held on for a good long while, but the end was inevitable."

"Inevitable that his house would burn down?" Dimitri asked. He wanted to ask the names of Clifford's children, but he already knew the answer. He had thought Rosalie's younger brothers looked close in age.

"Oh, that was only the start—or perhaps I should say the end." Wyatt pushed back his plate and turned more fully toward Dimitri, settling in for the story. "The one mercy was that he got his two older daughters safely married before the Legacy struck. Pretty girls they both were, and kindhearted too. Although the youngest is the true beauty—as youngests usually are." He shook his head. "But at least her sisters were settled and gone from Thebarton—and generous bequests settled on their new families—before it happened."

Wyatt's words gave Dimitri a stirring of hope that Wyatt wasn't talking about Rosalie and her family.

"I suppose Clifford and his remaining children went to live with the older daughters after their home burned down, then?" he asked, trying to hide his strong interest in the answer.

But Wyatt shook his head. "Didn't want to risk turning the Legacy's attention in their direction. And didn't want to leave Thebarton, neither. As I said earlier, he's a fine man is Clifford. Always did right by Thebarton, though he used to have the funds to move somewhere grander. Afterward he had to move his family to a cottage just outside of town. Hardly big enough for three thirteen-year-old lads that one, let alone a grown daughter as well." He sighed and shook his head again.

"And what about Clifford himself?" Dimitri asked.

"Travelin' last I heard. He's home whenever he can be, but he's gone for long stretches. Has to do himself what he once paid others for." Wyatt heaved a sigh and took a long drink. "Used to employ plenty around Thebarton, so it wasn't just Clifford who lost out when it all happened."

"What exactly did happen?" Dimitri asked, having to remind himself to keep eating. He was too absorbed in his companion's words to think of his food, despite the enjoyable flavor.

"He's a careful man, Clifford," Wyatt said. "But he has a weakness when it comes to his children. And it was Mistress Rosalie that brought the trouble. Not," he said firmly, "that anyone blames her, mind." His expression turned dark. "There are some who know how to use the Legacy to their advantage, and there are some whose situations make them vulnerable to it. Youngest daughter of a merchant with equal sons as daughters." He shook his head. "What hope did she have?"

"What happened to her?" Dimitri asked, trying to keep the urgency from his voice.

"A newcomer arrived in town," Wyatt said dramatically, clearly still enjoying his role of storyteller, despite the sad nature of the tale. "Mighty pretty he was. Mighty pretty." He paused and peered at Dimitri before bursting into hearty guffaws. "Much like yourself, come to think of it. Could be his twin! I hope you haven't come here to bamboozle Thebarton's young ladies." Given his humor, he clearly thought the manor's owner was above such behavior. And he didn't seem to have considered the possibility that Dimitri was merely impersonating the missing heir.

Then Dimitri remembered Rosalie and Daphne's

conversation. Obviously, they weren't the only ones who considered the state of the manor's garden to be convincing evidence of his claim on the estate.

"What was the newcomer's name?" Dimitri asked, although he had an unpleasant inkling he knew it. He had already met a young man with similar coloring to himself and a history with Rosalie.

"Jace." Wyatt practically spit the name, and Dimitri's heart sank the rest of the way.

"Pleasant young man he seemed," Wyatt continued after a moment. "Had a few conversations with him myself. And very taken he seemed with young Mistress Rosalie. Everyone noted it, and no one was surprised. Some thought she was a bit young, but then so was he. And she was both beautiful and wealthy, so it was natural enough she might catch any young man's eye. Plenty of the boys here liked her too, but knowing someone from the cradle don't give them a lot of allure." He gave a heavy sigh. "Can't be surprised she was beguiled by a newcomer."

The story kept getting worse, but Dimitri had to know how it ended. "What did he do?"

"Courted her, o' course," Wyatt said. "Won her over easily enough as well. Her father wouldn't let her get married right away—said she had to be at least eighteen for that." He nodded approval of Clifford's principles. "But he did find the boy a position in his business. Said the boy would be family soon enough and made him a clerk." He sighed. "Pity. Great pity."

"Why?" Dimitri asked.

"Turned out the only part of Mistress Rosalie that appealed to Jace was her wealth. That, and the fact she was the youngest daughter of a merchant with equal sons as daughters. He knew her family situation meant the Legacy's bamboozling ways would aid him. Like I said, Clifford was a careful one, but he counted that Jace as one of the family, and the Legacy helped obscure his theft."

"He cheated the family's business?" Dimitri asked, in a tight voice.

"Aye. Cleaned out everything he could get his hands on. Left them with nothing but what they had in their house. But once he cheated them, it triggered the rest of that particular sequence of the Legacy. Their house burned down the day after they discovered his treachery."

"And Jace?" Dimitri asked, although he already knew the answer. He had clearly not been apprehended for his crime.

"Slipped away before anyone even realized. Abandoned Mistress Rosalie and left her family with next to nothing. Didn't dim her spirits any, though," he added in an admiring tone.

Dimitri looked down, noting distantly that his hand was fisted so tightly around the handle of his fork that his knuckles had turned white. It was a good thing he hadn't known the whole story two days before, or he might not have managed to restrain himself around Jace.

But while he hadn't known Jace's history, he knew the story had a new chapter unknown to Wyatt. After everything Jace had already done to Rosalie, he had dared to return and abduct her. And having done so, he had talked to her as if...

Dimitri drew a long breath, attempting to calm himself. If he dwelt on how Jace had acted toward Rosalie, and what he had said to her, he might say or do something inappropriate for the dining room of the Mortar and Pestle.

As it was, he was struggling to hide the strength of his reaction from Wyatt and any other curious observers in the room. He was even tempted to warn Wyatt and the rest of the town of Jace's return. The man was clearly dangerous.

But he hesitated to do so without consulting Rosalie. She knew both Jace and the townsfolk better than he did, and it was her story far more than his. If she hadn't told anyone about her abduction—and he had to assume Wyatt would have mentioned it if word had spread through the town—she must have a good reason for staying quiet.

But while his reason told him to stay silent and calm, his emotions weren't so easy to tame. His reaction was more complicated than fury on Rosalie's behalf, as incensed as he felt for her. The story Wyatt had spun sounded far too similar to another story he had just learned—one from two decades before. His emotions were still raw from learning his mother's history, and his feelings surged against the barriers he imposed on them.

Already Dimitri had read his mother's letter enough times to memorize its contents, and her history sounded startlingly similar to Rosalie's. Both had been approached by young men interested in their family's wealth. Their supposed suitors had taken advantage of their youth and inexperience to fool them with lies of love, and then both had been abandoned when they were no longer useful.

But the stories diverged there. Rosalie's suitor had shown his true colors before they were actually married—a fact for which Dimitri felt great relief—but he had destroyed her family's wealth, livelihood, and even home. And he had already seen enough of Rosalie's character to know she must blame herself for her family's downfall.

His mother's family, on the other hand, had been untouched. She had even written of the underlying love that existed between her and her father despite their quarrel. If she had wished to return home to her wealthy and powerful family, she could have done so. The tapestry was a legacy to the fact that both she and Dimitri would have been welcomed.

And yet his mother had been the one to crumple beneath her pain. Despite her worse situation, Rosalie had shown a strength of character his mother had lacked. She hadn't shielded herself from the harsh truth by choosing a path of self-deception. She hadn't run from the situation either. She was still in Thebarton, still fighting for her family. And she was no longer susceptible to a 'pretty young man' as Wyatt put it.

Dimitri had already sensed how different Rosalie was from his mother and the others of their mountain community. But now he had proof of it. And his desire to protect Rosalie from any further tricks of the Legacy had only grown.

A rush of chatter from the doorway drew his attention. Many of the patrons of the midday meal had dispersed already, but in their place had come those looking for afternoon tea and cakes as well. A mob of young ladies had arrived, including several vaguely familiar faces and one whose name he could place—Blythe.

He stood, leaving the remains of his meal uneaten. He had succeeded at his first purpose of the day, and now he had a chance to address his second one.

CHAPTER 10
ROSALIE

Rosalie trudged in from the cottage's back garden, a heavy basket over her arm. She had managed to scrounge a full load, but she had picked the garden bare doing so. Her brothers had assured her they had already stripped the last of the harvest, but she had known better than to trust the thoroughness of their search.

"I managed to gather a little more, Mother," she called as she entered the cottage.

The five of them had already started the task of preserving as much of the produce as possible for the coming winter, and she knew her mother had been concerned about it stretching far enough. They worked hard to cover as much of the family's consumption as possible since her mother hated to draw from their meager stash of coin to cover the shortfall. Her father worked hard—leaving for long stretches of time—and all their coin was hard-earned.

"Good job," her mother called absentmindedly, her head bent over the stove top. She was preparing the midday meal, and Rosalie was disappointed to see she was alone.

"Where are the boys?" she asked, stowing the supplies she had gathered and setting the table for the midday meal with brisk, efficient movements.

"Hunting in the woods." Her mother lifted the pot off the heat.

Rosalie nodded, relieved. At least they were doing something useful. With any luck, they'd find substantial game and could be given the task of preserving it for the coming months.

But her approval waned when all three boys trooped in a minute later. Not only were their hands empty, but their boots were suspiciously free of mud.

Her eyes narrowed, and she nearly asked if they had been wasting their time in town when they were supposed to be hunting. But something in their demeanor stayed her tongue. Whatever mood hung over them, it was far stronger than the sheepishness she might have expected if they had been entertaining themselves instead of working.

All three appeared so downcast that she wondered if they were sickening. Vernon, in particular, looked as if he wouldn't be able to keep down the food. She couldn't imagine anything but extreme nausea interfering with his appetite.

She remained silent, watching the triplets closely as they all gathered around the table. As she had feared, all three of them only picked at the meal, a far cry from their usual ravenous hunger. But it was more than just a lack of appetite. Something was definitely weighing them down, and given their tension, she feared it was more than physical illness. It was a wonder their mother hadn't noticed.

Rosalie added her mother to her mental list of people to worry about. It wasn't like her to be so unaware of abnormal behavior from her children. She must be beyond exhausted.

If it had only been her and her brothers at table, Rosalie would have immediately demanded answers. But for their mother's sake, she remained silent. As soon as they had cleared away the meal, however, she suggested her mother take the opportunity for a small nap.

It took earnest entreaties from all four of her children for her mother to agree. Rosalie was glad to see her go, although the triplets' enthusiasm for the idea only increased her suspicion of them.

"Just a few minutes," her mother said, hesitating in the door of the bedroom she shared with Rosalie. "Your father often manages a small rest at this time of day if he doesn't have a full day of travel. Perhaps I can meet with him."

Rosalie's smile tightened, but she pushed back the feeling. She hoped her mother did manage to get news from her father. In Glandore, a couple with a close emotional connection—who trusted each other completely—could meet in their dreams. It was the only thing that had made the forced separation endurable for her parents.

But thinking of dream meetings made Rosalie think of Jace, and memories of him were especially unwelcome now he had returned. She had once hoped to meet him each night when she closed her eyes, and the foolishness of it made her mouth sour. During their short betrothal she had worried about the absence of any meetings, but she had allowed herself to be convinced by his reassurances. He had told her it was a connection that would come after their wedding, and foolishly she had believed him. The look he gave her when he said it—sometimes accompanied by a stolen kiss—had always made her blush, stealing away any further words of protests and replacing them with happy dreams of the future.

Why hadn't she recognized the warning signs?

Pushing aside thoughts of her betrothal—she had enough present troubles without dwelling on the past—she firmly shut the door to the cottage's one bedroom. When her father was away, Rosalie slept in the wide bed with her mother, moving to a pallet in front of the stove when he was home.

Her brothers slept in the cottage's loft, and as soon as she heard her mother's even breathing through the door, she silently indicated for the boys to climb the ladder. They obeyed without protest or question—yet another indication of just how badly something was wrong.

She followed after Oscar, barely managing to squeeze into the small space beside their lanky frames. The simple pallets they slept on barely fit as it was, and the four of them ended up cross-legged in a circle on top of them. As soon as Rosalie was settled, she directed a stern glare at each of them.

"Well?" she demanded in a hushed tone that was no less demanding for its volume. "Out with it! What's going on?"

Ralph and Oscar both looked to Vernon, who immediately hung his head.

"He was only trying to help," Ralph offered when Vernon didn't immediately speak.

"And we knew about it, so we're as much to blame," Oscar added loyally.

Rosalie's stomach lurched. Just how much trouble had they gotten into that Vernon was afraid to confess it to her?

"Come on," she said in a much softer tone, "you can tell me. It won't get any easier by delaying. Whatever it is, we'll find a way to work it out."

Vernon seemed to recognize the truth in her words because he took a deep breath and spoke. "I really was only trying to help. Whenever Father is back, we see how worried he looks, and we hear the whispers between him and Mother. Father works hard, but it's difficult to make money when you have nothing to invest at the start. So we thought..."

He glanced at his brothers before taking another breath. "We thought we could help by providing some initial investment money."

Rosalie gasped. "Please don't tell me you stole it!"

"What? No!"

"Of course not!"

"Never!"

Her brothers' indignant denials overlapped, soothing the worst of her fears.

"Keep your voices down," she reminded them, and they all instantly subsided. She looked from one to the other, her momentary relief drying up. "So what did you do?" she said. "Because I know you don't have any money."

"I borrowed it," Vernon said in a rush.

Rosalie's mouth dropped open. "You did what?"

"I borrowed it," Vernon repeated more quietly, not able to meet her eyes.

"There's no way the bank loaned you money," Rosalie said shortly. "Putting aside your age, I know Father already tried. More than once. Every local in Thebarton knows Father has an excellent head for business and sound judgment, but the bank wouldn't risk it—not once the Legacy started working against us."

"I...I didn't go to the bank," Vernon confessed. "It was a private loan. I figured once Father turned it into profit, we could easily pay it back."

"A moneylender? But the interest!" Rosalie cried before clapping her hand over her mouth and glancing down the ladder. She lowered her voice. "How could you have gotten a loan? Even moneylenders know better than to make deals with minors." She ran a hand over her eyes. "If you somehow did, well, you'll just have to give the money straight back."

Thank goodness the boys had been eaten up with guilt over their foolish action. Since they'd confessed to her so promptly, she could march them into Thebarton to repay the money before any significant interest had accumulated.

"I'm afraid it's too late for that," Ralph said gloomily.

"If we could repay it, we already would have," Oscar added.

"What do you mean?" Rosalie asked sharply. "Where is the money?"

"I told them it was Father borrowing the money," Vernon said in a rush. "I forged his signature and everything."

"And they believed that?" Rosalie asked, incredulous.

Vernon nodded, his expression utterly miserable. "I think they thought Father was too proud to go himself."

"But not too proud to send a child in his place?" Rosalie asked with increasing wrath.

"Vernon went to them last time Father was home," Oscar said. "The lie wouldn't have worked if Father was away at the time, so it had to be then."

Rosalie turned furious eyes on Vernon, and Oscar continued in a rush.

"Don't blame everything on Vernon! He told us what he'd done, and we both approved. The three of us took the money to Father together, so we're all at fault."

"You already gave Father the money?" Rosalie asked in dismay. "But why would he accept it? Where did he think you got it? Don't try to tell me he condoned what you'd done because I won't believe it!"

"We told him it was our pocket money," Vernon said. "You know how lavishly he and Mother used to provide for us all. We told him that since we never wanted for anything, the three of us had been saving our pocket money for years."

"And he believed that?" Rosalie stared at him in astonishment. "I never saw any of you receive a coin without immediately spending it on sweets!"

"You know that." Vernon's head drooped even lower. "And Mother knows that. But Father was always at the office when we spent it."

"He was touched," Ralph said in a clogged voice. "Kept checking we didn't want to spend it on ourselves. He felt bad about taking it, but he also understood that it would benefit us all if he could use it to build a new business."

"Wait," Rosalie said, fresh horror washing over her. "How long ago was this? Last time he was here, he was so down because of that promising new business venture that went wrong—the one that fell apart just before he started receiving profit. Are you telling me he'd invested your borrowed money in that?"

All three boys remained silent, their faces pictures of misery.

Rosalie's hands flew to her mouth. "The three of you were so upset about it," she whispered, "and he was so apologetic. But I thought you were just disappointed that we weren't going to get our old life back after all. It never occurred to me..."

"He apologized to us over and over," Oscar said in a small voice. "But we knew it wasn't his fault."

"I never should have borrowed it," Vernon murmured. "I realized it then, but it was too late to undo my mistake."

"Why didn't you say anything at the time?" Rosalie asked. "Why didn't Father say anything to Mother or me?" She stilled. "Does he still not know the truth about the money?"

All three boys shook their heads.

"How could we tell him when he was already so down?" Vernon asked. "I borrowed the money, so it's my responsibility." He glanced at his brothers. "We figured something would happen to allow us to repay it on our own."

Rosalie shook her head. Apparently the many disasters that had befallen their family still weren't enough to overcome the boundless optimism of youthful boys.

"How have you been paying the interest?" she asked. "Don't tell me the lender has been kindly waiving it because I won't believe you."

The three of them exchanged guilty looks.

"We're much better hunters than you and Mother think," Oscar admitted. "We've been selling some of the game we catch in town. We've always managed to scratch together enough for the interest, but we haven't been able to pay off any of the principal."

Rosalie's head spun. She could imagine just how it had been. Kindly townsfolk must have been purchasing the game and thinking they were helping Clifford's family in the process. After all her and her mother's hard work to make sure the family was self-sufficient, they had been relying on the kindness of others without even realizing.

She drew a deep breath, reminding herself that her brothers were still young. They had made a mistake, but the real villain was the one who had loaned them the money without checking with their father directly. And her brothers clearly felt bad enough without facing her wrath as well.

Her thoughts faltered. If the situation had been ongoing for months, what had happened to make them finally confess it? Had the forest been bare of game lately? Did they need help with the next interest payment? She wasn't sure where she could find extra coin, but if they needed it, she would have to find a way.

"So why are you telling me this now?" she asked, wishing she didn't have to hear the answer.

"We didn't want to tell you," Vernon said. "But telling Mother seemed worse. Besides, you really ought to know, given..." He faltered, and an uncomfortable presentiment filled Rosalie.

"What is it?" she asked. "Tell me quickly!"

"It's Jace," Vernon said quietly, watching her closely.

She went cold all over. She had known Jace was going to do something terrible, she just hadn't expected it to involve her brothers.

"What has he done?" she asked harshly.

Three pairs of eyes stared at her.

"Did you already know he was back?" Oscar asked, astonished.

"Unfortunately, yes," Rosalie sighed.

They waited for her to say more, but she stayed quiet. There was no way she was disclosing what Jace had done to her brothers of all people. They'd just demonstrated that they couldn't be trusted to make sensible choices, and the last thing she needed was them vowing to track Jace down and kill him.

"Why didn't you tell us he was in Thebarton?" Vernon asked, indignation in his tone.

She raised her eyebrows, and he immediately subsided, his cheeks flushing.

"So what does Jace have to do with any of this?" she asked.

"This morning we went to pay the latest interest installment like usual," Vernon said. "But the man who lent us the money refused the payment. He said he'd sold our debt."

Rosalie clapped a hand to her mouth, her meal turning over in her belly.

"He sold your debt to Jace? How did Jace even know about it?"

Vernon shrugged, none of the boys disputing her assumption. It was true, then. Her brothers owed Jace money. Possibly a lot of money. She needed to ask them the total, but she couldn't bring herself to do it yet.

"Our original moneylender told us to go see our new creditor and pay him the interest," Ralph said. "We didn't know who it was at that stage, so you can imagine our astonishment when we found Jace waiting for us."

"We tried to give him the coins, but he refused to take them," Vernon said.

"He refused your money?" Rosalie wasn't foolish enough to be relieved. Jace clearly had some terrible purpose for her brothers and their debt.

"Actually he demanded more," Vernon said. "He said the initial loan period has passed."

"Which is true," Oscar interjected. "But the original lender was quite happy to keep receiving interest."

"I bet he was," Rosalie muttered.

"So now Jace is demanding we pay back the whole loan immediately," Ralph finished. "He says he's giving us three days, and if we can't produce the money, he'll have the guards call in the debt. Which of course means they'll arrest us since we can't produce money we don't have."

Rosalie frowned. "Surely that's a bluff? Jace would never go to the guards. Not after what he did to us. He's a cheat and a liar, and the whole town hates him."

"Obviously, he didn't buy the debt in his own name," Oscar said with distaste. "He seems to have followers now, and officially, it's all been done through one of them. Jace's friend will be the one to go to the guards if it comes to that, and we'll have no evidence he's connected to Jace."

Rosalie had already seen Jace's new followers with her own eyes, so she could easily believe he had someone to stand in his stead. Their family's stolen money was enough to buy a lot of loyalty.

"They can only arrest me," Vernon said staunchly. "I was the one who borrowed the money, so I'm the only one they can lock away."

"Actually," Rosalie said in a hollow voice, "you weren't the one to borrow the money. Not officially. It's Father's name on the papers Jace purchased. He's the one the guards will come for."

All three of the boys' eyes widened, and if it was possible for them to look more sick, they did so. It clearly hadn't occurred to them that their father would be the one arrested in their stead.

"I'll...I'll tell them it was me!" Vernon said. "I'll swear it and insist they take me instead."

Rosalie gave him a withering look. "Do you really think Father would allow that? Or the guard would listen? They won't drag off a minor when an adult's signature is on the debt."

Vernon swallowed. He knew as well as she did that their father would take full responsibility to shield his son. And the Legacy would help him do so. When it came to a bargain, the Legacy loved substitution. A father for a son would suit it perfectly.

"I didn't...I didn't mean for Father to have to..."

"No," Rosalie said poisonously. "It's clear you didn't think from start to end of this whole affair! And now we're all in trouble. If Father can no longer work, we won't be able to pay the rent on even this tiny cottage. He may be arrested, but we'll be on the streets." She paused, letting that fully sink in before she added, "Not that we can allow Father to be arrested, obviously. We'll have to find a way to escape the situation in the next three days."

The simplest option—however unpalatable—was to find enough money. As much as she hated paying a single coin to Jace, she would do it to save her family. And if they couldn't find the money, they would have to think of another way to avoid Jace's scheme. The alternative was unthinkable.

All three boys perked up at her assurance, and their change of mood settled over her shoulders like lead. They thought she had the answer, but she had nothing, and what if she couldn't find a way?

She shook the thought off. She would find a solution. She had to. There simply wasn't any other option.

But something about the story still gave her pause.

"But why is he doing this?" she wondered aloud. "Jace has already taken everything our family had. Why is he targeting you?" She had been sure Jace's new target was Dimitri, and compared to his potential, the triplet's debt was spare change.

"Well..." Vernon exchanged a look with his brothers putting her instantly on the alert.

"Well, what?" she asked with narrowed eyes. "If I'm going to help you out of this, I need to know everything."

"Jace did say he'd forgive the debt," Vernon said slowly. "I just had to do one small thing for him."

"Don't do it," Rosalie said instantly.

Whatever it was, it wasn't worth it. She didn't need to hear any more to know that. If Jace wanted something from Vernon, it was only a way to entrap them all further.

But that didn't mean she wasn't curious.

She sighed. "Go on, then. Tell me what he wants. Why did he buy your debt?"

"He wants me to pick one of the manor's roses. He said if I picked one rose—any rose—and brought it to him, he'd forgive the whole debt."

"You haven't done it, have you?" Rosalie cried,

alarmed. "That's not a small thing he's asking! Surely you realize that?"

"Of course we do," Ralph said waspishly. "Why do you think we came to you instead of going to the manor? Now that Dimitri's in residence, we might unleash all sorts of trouble by picking a rose."

"He would likely end up a Beast for one." Rosalie felt sick again. "We are not going to get our family out of trouble by throwing someone else into it. And that's without considering what bargain the Legacy would extract in exchange for your theft."

"If I could guarantee it was me who paid the price, I would do it in a heartbeat," Vernon said dejectedly. "But..." He didn't need to say any more. All four of them knew how the Legacy loved substitution—and in such a direct parallel to the original history, the Legacy would exert a staggering amount of power.

"We have to find another way," Rosalie said. "Show me the original contract you signed, and I'll work out what to do."

She sounded a great deal more confident than she felt, but it was better than betraying her fear.

CHAPTER 11
ROSALIE

Her mother was still napping when Rosalie slipped quietly out of the house. Her brothers had wanted to accompany her, but she'd been firm in turning them down. She didn't think they would be an asset in the difficult conversation she needed to have.

But Vernon dashed out of the house and caught her at the gate. "You swear you aren't going to confront Jace?" He watched her face closely as he waited for her answer.

"I have no intention of doing anything so foolhardy," she said firmly, barely repressing a shiver.

She still hadn't told the triplets about her earlier encounter with Jace, but she wasn't desperate enough to seek out a second meeting. She hoped she never saw him again. Just remembering how she had once longed for his embrace made her feel queasy.

"Very well, then," Vernon said reluctantly.

Rosalie managed a smile at his obvious concern. "You

don't need to act as if I'm heading out to face a pack of wolves alone. I'm only going into Thebarton to explore our options. Relax. I will be well, I promise."

But as soon as she'd stepped onto the road, her smile fell away. It was true that her destination offered her no danger, but that didn't make it pleasant. There was no time for her to be squeamish or to worry about her pride, however. If the question had to be asked, it was better to do so immediately. That way there would still be time to explore other options if...

She shook her head. No. She couldn't think about failure. The Fosters had to be receptive to her request. If her family sold every item they still owned, down to her parents' bed, they still couldn't come up with the needed funds on their own.

Half an hour later, Rosalie stood in front of Blythe's parents, struggling to keep her head high and any tears from falling. She would have dropped to her knees and wept if she thought it would do any good, but she could already read on their faces that it wouldn't. And if that was the case, she preferred to hold on to the shreds of her dignity.

"I see." She thrust her hands into the folds of her skirt so they wouldn't see them trembling. "Thank you for your time. I'm sorry to have appeared unannounced with such a request."

Madam Foster's face immediately crumpled. She dabbed at her eyes with a lace handkerchief.

"No, no, my dear!" she exclaimed. "It's us who are sorry." She glanced at her husband. "The whole of

Thebarton feels for your family in your tragic situation. And clearly your young brother was taken advantage of."

"Foolhardy!" Foster barked out, earning a disapproving look from his wife.

"No, no," he amended quickly, "I don't mean the boy. He has his youth to excuse him. I mean whichever fool loaned him the money. A risky business."

Rosalie bit her lip to prevent herself from replying sharply. She knew it would do no good. Far too many people thought as the Fosters did—as if the attention of the Legacy was a disease that might be catching for anyone who did business with her family. It was the reason her father had made so little headway, having to take on only low profit or high difficulty trades.

"I must request your discretion," Rosalie said. "I wouldn't wish others to know about Vernon's misstep."

"Of course, my dear," Madam Foster said quickly. "We won't breathe a word."

"Naturally, naturally," her husband murmured, clearly ready for the conversation to end.

Rosalie got herself out of the room with as much grace as she could muster, but she hadn't made it to the front door when a breathy voice called for her to wait. She paused as Blythe dashed down the staircase toward her, clearly in a hurry.

She came to a stop in front of Rosalie.

"I'm sorry about my parents," she said in a rush. "They're just afraid."

Rosalie nodded, not sure what to say.

"I was listening at the door," Blythe continued shamelessly, "and I couldn't do nothing. I know it won't be enough, but—" She hesitated and thrust out a small leather pouch.

"You can have my allowance," she finished in a rush. "I haven't spent any of it this quarter."

Rosalie stared at her, still silent, too caught off guard to think of a reply.

"The Legacy can't mistake this for an investment, right?" Blythe asked anxiously. "It's just a gift between friends. So you mustn't pay it back."

Rosalie was finally shaken from her stupor. "That's very kind of you, Blythe," she said, truly touched. "But I couldn't possibly take your money. As you said, it's not enough to cover the debt, so I'll have to find another solution anyway. There's no reason you should go without for months—or risk angering your parents—when it wouldn't solve the problem."

"Oh." Blythe slowly withdrew the pouch, looking crestfallen. "I just..."

Rosalie watched her curiously. Did she feel guilty for taking the place that had once been Rosalie's? Whatever the motivation it was a kind gesture.

"Thank you," Rosalie said sincerely. "I truly appreciate the offer."

Blythe perked up, smiling back. "I'm about to go for tea and cake at the Mortar and Pestle," she said.

Rosalie waited, unsure why Blythe was sharing her schedule. It seemed an abrupt change of topic after her kind gesture. And even more puzzling was the mixture of pleasure, superiority, and underlying uncertainty in the look Blythe had fixed on Rosalie.

"If you'd like to come," Blythe finished, clearly thrown off by Rosalie's confusion.

"Oh." Rosalie blinked. That explained Blythe's expression.

Despite her compassion, she couldn't help enjoying having Rosalie in a position of humility before her. Although Blythe had taken Rosalie's social position with their peers, Rosalie herself had never acted with subservience toward her. She had refused to carve a new place in the group by fawning over Blythe. Instead, she had held her head high, acting as if she couldn't feel the pain of being so easily discarded. It was that stubbornness and pride that had sparked Blythe's animosity toward her.

Clearly those feelings remained, and yet Blythe had still offered Rosalie her whole allowance. Rosalie shook her head. She could acknowledge that she herself was both stubborn and prideful as well as brave and resilient. So it shouldn't be astonishing to find that Blythe could act out of true compassion and kindness while still enjoying having Rosalie in a position of humble submission.

"Thank you for the invitation," Rosalie said. "But I'm afraid I have other matters to occupy my afternoon."

"Oh, of course." Blythe looked genuinely disappointed, and Rosalie could imagine how much she would have enjoyed gliding into the Mortar and Pestle with Rosalie trailing meekly in her wake.

"Enjoy your afternoon," Rosalie murmured and let herself out of the house.

Despite her talk of other plans, she still had to work out what those plans were. So she let her feet direct her as she walked through the town. She couldn't go straight home and report her failure to her brothers. She had to think of a new plan first. Better yet if she could actually enact that new plan.

The Fosters were the richest family in Thebarton and the most likely to be able to afford a personal loan with a long repayment period. There were others who might be able to manage it, but Rosalie didn't hold out much hope after her reception by the Fosters. She didn't want to ask for assistance all over town if everyone would feel the same fear.

The townsfolk had been generous with small gifts—food from their gardens, game from the woods, outgrown clothes and shoes for the boys—but it was clear they thought of those in the same way Blythe did. A loan was another matter—it skirted too close to an investment.

Daphne would want to help, of course. But she didn't have that kind of money herself. She might be able to convince her parents to give the loan—and Rosalie was almost desperate enough to let her try—except her parents were out of town and would be until after the payment deadline. So Rosalie was saved from imposing on her most loyal friend in order to rescue her brothers.

Rosalie groaned and rubbed her eyes. Her thoughts were going around in circles with no new solutions presenting themselves.

Desperation seized her. She thought she'd left her pride behind at the Fosters' threshold, but she hadn't fully let it go. She shouldn't have rejected Blythe's offer. The money might not be enough to cover the loan, but it was a start. Rosalie couldn't afford to reject any help.

Turning her steps toward the Mortar and Pestle caused physical pain, but she forced herself to do it anyway. If she went to Blythe now—in front of all her old friends—Blythe would reinstate the offer. Even if she'd thought better of it already, she would be too pleased at seeing Rosalie humbled to refuse.

It was possible she was wronging Blythe in thinking that way. Blythe might be just as willing to accept Rosalie's change of heart if she approached her alone. But this way was both safer and faster. It would ensure Rosalie didn't go home to her brothers empty-handed.

Having made the decision, she increased her pace, giving proper attention to her surroundings for the first time. While her mind had been busy, her feet had led her deep into the town. She had some way to go to make it back to the central square, let alone the Mortar and Pestle. She increased her speed even further, impatient to get the coming ordeal over with. But she'd only made it a block before she noticed footsteps behind her.

Glancing back, she saw two unfamiliar men walking several lengths behind her. She sped up, and they did the same, maintaining the same distance.

Rosalie told herself it was a coincidence, but her racing heart was unconvinced. She tried harder. Thebarton was a large town, and she didn't know the face of everyone who lived there. It was the afternoon, and bright sun was shining down on her. Why would someone even be following her anyway?

Still, she hurried even faster, stopping just short of a run. The men behind her increased their pace again.

Rosalie looked around desperately for help, but she had wandered into a quiet part of town far from the stores and workshops where people gathered during working hours. She debated breaking into a full run. Would such an obvious action provoke the men into seizing her?

The terror from two days ago swept over her. Blind panic crept in as the memories of her abduction stole her remaining rationality. She had to get away before it happened again.

She broke into a run but only made it two steps before she ran headlong into a man stepping out from a narrow side street. He seized her arm, and before she could scream or even process what was happening, he dragged her into the alley.

Her new assailant pushed her against the brick wall of one of the buildings. Keeping his grip on her upper arm, he pressed his other hand over her mouth. Rosalie's breath heaved, and her eyes widened as she stared into a familiar face. Jace.

She had been terrified almost out of her wits a moment ago, but seeing Jace steadied her. She was still trapped and alone, but the rising fury burned off the unreasoning fog. She was still afraid, but she was also angry, and her ability to think had returned.

She reached up and pried his hand off her mouth.

"What are you doing?" she spat at him. "Are you seriously trying to abduct me in the middle of Thebarton?"

Jace smiled, the expression filling her with disgust. "Abduct you? No, of course not! I let you walk away, remember?"

Rosalie remained silent, fuming. She remembered it all too well.

Jace let go of her arm, but he leaned his left hand against the wall beside her, creating a makeshift barrier between her and the main street beyond. "I just want to talk," he said plaintively.

Rosalie could have pushed him away and run, but she hadn't forgotten the men behind her. They must have been Jace's men, and they were probably still lurking on the main street. Now that she was no longer ruled by unthinking fear, she didn't want to act hastily.

Jace wanted something, but she didn't think it was to harm her—not immediately anyway. Her pride wanted to turn her back on him and stalk away, but her family's situation was desperate enough that she needed to hear what he had to say. If she was going to find a way out, she needed as much information as possible.

"Spit it out, then," she said coldly.

"I'm hurt." Jace pretended to look wounded. "You always liked talking to me in the past." He gave a self-satisfied smile that made Rosalie want to kick some sense into her past self. Or perhaps just kick him.

"Talk now or I'm leaving," she growled.

Jace smirked but dropped the playacting.

"I just wanted to make sure you got my message," he said.

Rosalie's glare turned even icier. "Next time, if you have something to say to me, say it yourself. Don't send a message through my brothers. They're only children."

Jace chuckled. "I don't think they'd agree with that assessment. Don't you remember being thirteen?" His face twisted. "They've always been remarkably annoying youths, though." He looked back at her, and his face hardened. "Don't imagine I'll go easy on them because of their age. In three days I either receive that money, or..." He reached out and took a lock of her wavy hair, winding it around his finger. "Or a rose. I'm sure that charming suitor of yours will be more than happy to oblige your brother for a single rose."

Rosalie stiffened, shoving against his chest so forcefully that he lost his balance and staggered back. She shook out her skirts, brushing herself off and giving him a disdainful look.

"You'll have what is owed you, don't worry about that."

She stalked away, as she had wanted to do earlier, careful not to look behind her. Jace's low laugh floated after her.

"Oh, I'm sure I will. I always get what is owed me."

CHAPTER 12
ROSALIE

Rosalie hurried down the main street, surreptitiously glancing around as she tried to regulate her pace. She could no longer see the men from earlier, but it was harder to shake the creeping sensation of being watched. She suspected it would take a long time to disappear.

When she finally reached the central square, she caught sight of Daphne's door opening. Dashing the final steps, she threw herself at her friend and grabbed one of her arms.

"Daphne, you have to come with me," she said, desperate for a companion.

Daphne regarded her with an expression that was part suspicion, part concern. "I'll come with you, of course, but where are we going?" Her eyes narrowed further. "It isn't far, is it?"

Despite everything, Rosalie laughed. She had thought it would take a long time to feel normal again, but apparently her friend's presence was enough. Very little fazed Daphne.

"Don't worry, I'm only going to the Mortar and Pestle," Rosalie assured her.

Daphne relaxed. "That's all right, then." Her brow creased. "But why are you going there? Afternoon tea and cake isn't really your style." She looked at her friend more closely. "Is something wrong? You look a little odd. Even for you."

"Even for me?" Rosalie started to protest but cut herself off. "Never mind all that. I'm all right. I'm going there to find Blythe. I need..." She hesitated. "I need to ask her something."

"You need to ask *Blythe* something?" Daphne's eyebrows rose, but Rosalie didn't explain, and Daphne didn't press her.

Rosalie wasn't ready to tell Daphne about being accosted by Jace—not when that would mean telling the whole tale of her brother's sorry mess as well. Daphne would find out soon enough, but Rosalie was still trying to recover her equilibrium before facing Blythe.

"Do we have to go so fast?" Daphne complained, but Rosalie continued to propel them both forward at speed.

She couldn't slow down. Having Daphne beside her helped, but she'd feel even better when they were off the open street. She hated knowing the eyes of Jace or his men might be on her at any moment.

They dodged a carriage leaving the inn and wove around another one arriving, finally reaching the sanctuary of the door. Rosalie thrust it open and nearly tumbled inside, out of breath.

The midday crowd inside the dining room had dispersed, but as usual there was still a smattering of clients visiting for the Mortar and Pestle's famous cakes. A chorus of giggles drew her eyes to a particularly large cluster of people. They had pulled several small tables together, allowing Blythe to hold court at the center of the group. But while Rosalie had expected to see Blythe, she hadn't expected the person sitting at her side.

Rosalie stood rooted to the spot, staring at Dimitri. What was he doing at the Mortar and Pestle of all places? After all her warnings, he was not only brazenly wandering around Thebarton, but he had stopped to flirt with Blythe and her friends. It was just like the first time she'd seen him in the square.

Her hands balled into fists as fresh anger swept over her. The emotion sprang up easily, already lurking just below the surface after her encounter with Jace.

Was Dimitri determined to flaunt the Legacy at every turn? Even if her words hadn't been enough alone, he had seen Jace and his men for himself. He had to know the danger he was in. And yet here he was, leaving the castle unguarded while he wiled his time away flirting. Did he truly care so little about the people of Thebarton?

Rosalie instantly deflated. Of course he didn't care. She had known Dimitri was ignorant and self-absorbed from the beginning. If she had briefly forgotten his true nature, that was her foolishness. She had no reason to be so disappointed at seeing him there.

The last time they had seen each other, she had allowed herself to soften toward him. His escort home had made her feel safe, and she had thanked him sincerely. While she had hoped to never see him again, she had been glad they could part with goodwill on both sides. But assuming that was their final farewell had been foolish.

Dimitri clearly had no intention of doing anything as sensible as leaving. She shouldn't have allowed herself to weaken toward him just because his arms were strong, and his eyes danced with gold when he smiled at her.

She straightened her back, lifting her chin.

"Oh look, it's Dimitri," Daphne said, apparently oblivious to Rosalie's internal turmoil. "And he's with Blythe. Perfect."

She tugged Rosalie in their direction. For once Rosalie was the one trailing reluctantly behind. But she couldn't allow herself to be scared off by Dimitri's presence.

"Rosalie!" Blythe cried in affected delight. "You came after all. And you brought Daphne as well. How lovely." She turned to her friends. "Rosalie came by to see my parents earlier, so of course I invited her to join us."

Rosalie stiffened, but Blythe said no more about Rosalie's purpose at the Fosters' home. She supposed it would have been too much to expect her not to mention it at all. As long as Blythe kept quiet about the details, it didn't matter.

Blythe's friends all exclaimed at her generosity and warm heart. But Blythe's attention remained fixed on Rosalie as she gestured toward Dimitri, her smile smug.

"This is Dimitri," she said as if they hadn't all met in

the square previously. "He's from the manor, of course. When he dined with us, we recommended the meals here, and he wasted no time in visiting."

She finally glanced around the rest of the group, basking in the effect of her words. Her friends all responded with the expected mixture of admiration and jealousy at this indication of her apparent closeness with the manor's heir.

Rosalie felt only exhaustion. She had no energy for unnecessary drama. In the past, she would have scorned Blythe for such obvious tactics. But her most recent interactions with her had given her fresh insight. Blythe wasn't a heartless person, she was an insecure one. She wanted to lead the group, but she wasn't sure she could do so on her own merits.

And Rosalie suspected the other girls weren't as heartless as she had previously thought either. The Fosters' fear of the Legacy had been stronger than Rosalie had expected, so maybe that was true of her old friends as well. Maybe they had once valued her friendship, after all, but their fear—or that of their parents—had proven stronger than their loyalty. After everything that had happened to her family, she could hardly blame them.

She shook her head, her eyes catching on Dimitri. Her mouth went instantly dry. He was staring at her as if he hadn't taken his eyes from her since the moment she'd appeared. And his gaze held an intensity she hadn't seen before. Her pulse started racing, all weariness forgotten. Apparently, her treacherous body was determined not to listen to her protestations about his character. Was it the same weakness that had led her to fall for Jace?

Daphne looked curiously between them, and Rosalie tried to ignore her. Instead, she reached for her earlier indignation, directing a glare at Dimitri.

His brow creased, his expression turning confused. Did he really not know he was at fault? How could he be so persistently oblivious?

Blythe cleared her throat ostentatiously, drawing Rosalie's attention.

"We've just been discussing the improvements at the manor," she said with a smile.

"We're all eager to see its magnificence," Sable added. "We've been telling him he has to host a gathering there soon. Don't you both agree?"

Rosalie's eyes flew back to Dimitri's, horrified. He couldn't be serious in encouraging such nonsense! There was no way he could hold a party at the castle without someone succumbing and picking a rose.

Before she could protest, however, two older couples approached. Rosalie recognized them vaguely, but their attention was on Dimitri.

"A pleasure to see you here, sir," one of the men said, shaking Dimitri's hand. Apparently they had already met.

The others chimed in, and Blythe swelled with importance. "Won't you join our group?" she asked sweetly, indicating the remaining seats. "I'm sure Dimitri can be prevailed on to stay a little longer. We've just been telling him how everyone in town is eager to meet him."

The man cleared his throat before murmuring,

"Indeed." After an exchange of glances, the older couples joined the group.

Rosalie tried to remember any of their names and failed. She did remember the women were sisters, but they had only moved to Thebarton six months ago, and Rosalie had been too wrapped up in her family's daily survival to pay much attention.

All four of them looked askance at Rosalie, and she almost flinched. Were they wondering why she was standing awkwardly beside the seated group, or did they recognize her and not want to associate with her, however fleetingly?

Impatience rose inside her as she reluctantly took a seat alongside Daphne. She hadn't come to the inn to exchange empty pleasantries with strangers. But the more people who joined the group, the more difficult it became to raise the issue of the money with Blythe. And she couldn't just leave either—not until she found a way to get a word with Dimitri. Otherwise, he was going to catapult half the town into disaster.

She rubbed her temples. When she looked up, Dimitri was watching her, concern in his eyes. She frowned at him. He didn't have the right to look worried about her when he was half the cause of her stress.

"We hear the manor has already come a long way," one of the men said, rubbing his hands together. "A good thing in my opinion. Never liked having a derelict property so close to town."

His wife nodded agreement, but the other man looked less enthusiastic.

"I hear there's some significant power at work." He looked at Dimitri from under thick brows. "Worth being careful."

Dimitri finally pulled his eyes from Rosalie, nodding solemnly as he looked between the men. "I believe my family's estate can be an asset to this region again. The Legacy is a danger, certainly, but I don't believe it's an insurmountable one. I intend to be cautious."

The first man leaned back, lacing his hands over his stomach. "Fine words, sir, fine words."

Rosalie wasn't sure if she should laugh or cry. Dimitri thought he was being cautious?

"All of Thebarton was sorry to see your grandfather go." Blythe slid her chair a little closer to Dimitri. "That was before my time, of course, but my parents have mentioned it more than once."

She didn't notice the way he stiffened slightly, but Rosalie did. What did Dimitri know about his grandfather's history? Anything?

"My parents have mentioned it as well," Rosalie said softly. "When he announced he was packing up his household and moving to the capital, both my father and grandfather tried to talk him out of it. But he has distant relations there and wanted to be near them. It was around the time I was born, I believe. My father has met with him a few times when he traveled to the capital on business, but he hasn't been back there for over five years, so we haven't heard any updates recently."

Her words made both the older couples shift uncomfortably, and even some of the young women exchanged awkward looks. But Rosalie hadn't brought up her father's old business lightly. Dimitri had the right to know what had happened to his grandfather.

She could have done without the look he gave her in response, however. The warm glow of gratitude on his face confused her traitorous heart into strange behavior.

Her impulsive words had been motivated by compassion, but it occurred to her belatedly that if Dimitri's grandfather was still alive, he might be a motivating factor for Dimitri to leave. She had the impression the old man couldn't be much more than five and sixty, so there was no reason to think he wouldn't be living in the capital still. She straightened and fixed Dimitri with a hopeful look.

But he had turned his attention back to Blythe, helping her to another slice of cake while she smiled importantly. It turned Rosalie's stomach to see his excessive solicitude, as if he had nothing more to worry about than pretty girls and tasty food.

The rest of the group—even the older couples—responded by shifting their positions subtly, centering themselves on Blythe and Dimitri and edging Rosalie out. After everything that had happened in the last few hours, tears welled in her eyes.

She fought them back. Apparently, she was only welcome in public in Thebarton if she stayed quiet and didn't draw attention to herself. No one liked their merry gathering spoiled by reminders of what had happened to Rosalie and her family—and what could happen to any of them.

She was only sorry Daphne was being tarred with the

same brush. She glanced at her friend to check if she was equally hurt and nearly let out a watery chuckle. Daphne clearly wasn't bothered by any of them because she had put her head on the table and gone to sleep.

A serving girl who worked for Otis came forward with a fresh tray of cake. As she walked toward them, her appearance shimmered and stuttered strangely before her legs and one arm disappeared completely. The rest of her body steadied, but Rosalie could see the dining room through the places where her missing limbs should have been. Her progress didn't falter, however, and neither did the tray she carried with the invisible hand.

"Drat," the girl said, frowning down at herself.

Dimitri looked up and gave a shout of surprise. Surging to his feet, he stared at her, apparently speechless.

Several of the girls burst into giggles at his response, but Rosalie shook her head. How could he be cautious with the manor when he knew so little about the Legacy? She glanced sideways at his astonished face, and her expression softened. Despite herself, she had to admit there was something endearing about his shock.

"It's been worse than usual today," the girl said apologetically. "Otis lost both arms a couple of hours ago, and they're stubbornly refusing to come back. You can't imagine how disconcerting it is. He's already dropped two glasses because of it."

"Otis...lost his arms?" Dimitri asked, his eyes bulging.

The giggles erupted all over again while the serving maid regarded Dimitri with concern.

"He's quite all right, sir. His wife insisted he let her

clean it up, so he didn't cut himself on the broken glass. She hasn't done any serving today, so she's still perfectly visible."

Even Blythe was looking at Dimitri oddly, and Rosalie realized no one else knew the details of his background or his ignorance of the Legacy.

"Relax," she said. "It's just the Legacy. Servers have a disconcerting tendency to turn partially invisible. It always rights itself eventually."

Dimitri turned startled eyes on her while everyone else remained silent. They didn't understand the interaction, but they didn't want to ask questions when Rosalie was one of the speakers.

The serving girl was oblivious to it all, though.

"I once went completely invisible for a whole day!" she declared. "About a year ago it was." She suddenly caught on to the group's discomfort. Glancing sideways at Rosalie, she placed the tray on the table and quickly hurried away.

Rosalie winced. She knew why the Legacy's power had been swirling through Thebarton at an increased strength a year ago. And so did everyone else at the table. Except for perhaps, Dimitri—which was precisely the problem.

"Why would the Legacy make Otis's arms disappear?" Dimitri asked in a strangled voice.

"Because of the invisible servants from the original Beast's castle, of course, silly." Blythe swatted playfully at his arm. "Didn't it ever happen to the servers where you used to live?"

Everyone looked at him expectantly, and he winced,

glancing toward Rosalie and Daphne. Neither of them spoke to expose his past, though, and he shrugged.

"No, it didn't," he said. "I've never seen that before."

"How lovely to live somewhere entirely out of the Legacy's notice," one of the older women said. "Although I would miss the roses."

"You'd best get used to it now you're here," her husband warned Dimitri. "Any help you get up at the manor will probably spend half their lives transparent." He and the other man guffawed, but Rosalie winced.

"Will you be hiring staff soon?" one of the women asked, clearly fishing for gossip.

"I'm not sure." Dimitri sounded dazed, and Rosalie suspected he hadn't given the matter a moment's thought. With the power of the Legacy saturating the manor, he wouldn't be feeling the lack of servants.

"You'll need to hire someone before the party," Sable said enthusiastically. "My mother always hires extra help when she's hosting a large group."

The older couples looked interested at the mention of a party, and Sable explained the plan they were attempting to foist on Dimitri. To Rosalie's dismay, none of them expressed their disapproval of the scheme. The whole town seemed so excited by the manor's renewal that they were determined to ignore the danger. Or did it not matter to them as long as they weren't the ones who paid the price?

She tried to catch Dimitri's eye, but he avoided her gaze. He had transferred his attentions from Blythe to Sable, and Blythe was pouting slightly as a result. She was still playing hostess, though, offering the older couples more cake and cutting the slices herself.

"Maybe we should leave," Daphne murmured in Rosalie's ear, having just woken up. "It doesn't seem like a good moment to get a word with Blythe."

Rosalie started. She had entirely forgotten about her original reason for coming to the Mortar and Pestle. Drat Dimitri! How could she have forgotten about her brother's predicament, even for a moment?

"I'm sorry, I won't be able to host any visitors for some time," Dimitri said, bringing her attention snapping back to him. He was speaking to everyone, but he was looking at her, his expression mischievous and his eyes alight with suppressed laughter. "Rosalie might slaughter me if I did."

Blythe choked on the sip of tea she had just taken.

"See," he continued, gesturing toward Rosalie. "If looks could cut, I would be bleeding all over this elegant dining room."

Everyone swiveled to look at her, and she glared at him harder.

One of the older men snorted. "The lad has a point," he murmured to his wife.

"But whatever for?" the woman whispered back. "Why is she glaring at him like that?"

"Rosalie doesn't want to see anyone hurt by the Legacy," Daphne said protectively. "That garden is dangerous. I've been in Glandore for years now, and I've never seen roses like that before."

"The inside of the manor isn't even that impressive,"

Rosalie hurried to add. "It hasn't been affected by the Legacy nearly as much as the grounds."

"You've been inside?" Blythe asked, her voice sharp.

Rosalie winced, realizing her mistake. Now they were all looking between her and Dimitri.

His brow furrowed, as if he was unhappy with her words. Did he dislike being openly associated with her? She stuffed down the hurt that tried to unfurl inside her at that thought. Considering how strongly she'd fought any connection between them, she could hardly blame him for feeling the same way.

"I'm not ready to host visitors in the usual way," Dimitri replied to Blythe on her behalf. "But of course I stand ready to assist those who find themselves in need on the road."

Alarm shot through Rosalie, and she tried to send him a warning with her eyes. She didn't want Dimitri spilling the events of two days ago in such a public setting. The situation with Jace had become a great deal more complicated since then, and the last thing she needed was for it to become more complicated still.

He shot her the briefest glance, and she suspected his expression was meant to convey reassurance. She was not reassured.

But thankfully he said no more on the topic. Some of the girls were probably assuming she had faked an illness or injury to force her way in, but it was better than their being informed of the truth.

"I would love to repay your hospitality by hosting you and your parents for a meal," he told Blythe. "But I think it would be wise if I delay having visitors until the situation has...settled."

Blythe glowed at being singled out, while the other girls all looked disappointed. They had clearly been looking forward to the prospect of both a lavish party and a chance to poke around inside the manor.

Dimitri stood, moving some of the tea supplies to the small table in front of the older couples. He chatted quietly with them, arranging the supplies so they were within easy reach. As he did so, Blythe held court with her friends, assuring them that when she did visit the manor, she would take note of everything she saw and bring back a detailed report.

Dimitri moved with charm and ease, making it look entirely natural when, as a result of rearranging the supplies, he took a new seat. A seat beside Rosalie.

"What are you doing at an inn?" she hissed at him. One visit to town, and he was already talking about hosting people at the manor.

"I told you the Legacy isn't providing my meals. So I came here to eat, of course." He kept his face relaxed and his eyes on the main conversation, although she could hear the teasing note in his voice.

She made a huffing noise of frustration, and he flicked a brief glance sideways at her, his quiet voice becoming more serious.

"I'm here to protect you, Rosalie."

Rosalie stared at him, speechless. He thought he was protecting her? From what? Attack from an unruly selection of cake slices? Scalding from hot tea?

She glanced at Daphne, ready to share her exasperation, only to find her friend had gone back to sleep. Of course she had.

Rosalie sighed. She had come here to ask for the money Blythe had offered—preferably without revealing too much to Blythe's friends. And she still needed to find an opportunity to do that. But it was difficult to think with Dimitri so close.

He was so very...tall. Yes, he was tall and solid and far too commanding a presence. He pulled people toward him when what he needed to do was to keep them all away.

Jace had drawn people to him too. Rosalie squeezed her eyes shut, trying not to think of Jace. She was balanced precariously in the grip of too many strong emotions, and if she didn't hold herself carefully, she would be lost into the abyss.

Clearly Daphne was right, and it wasn't the moment to talk to Blythe. That meant she should focus on Dimitri.

She had tried to be subtle so as not to provoke Blythe and had already failed. Dimitri was doing a better job, though. It didn't look like anyone had noticed their side conversation. Perhaps he didn't want to ruffle his flirtation with Blythe by being seen talking to Rosalie.

Fresh irritation swept through her, washing away her sense of caution.

"Do you really mean to ignore all my warnings?" she asked heatedly, her voice at normal volume. "Even after everything that's happened?" She gave him a significant look.

"I'm not ignoring your warnings," he protested. "I'm here to—"

"Do not say you're here to protect me," Rosalie hissed through her teeth.

Dimitri frowned, his eyes jumping from her face to the rest of the group. She followed his gaze and instantly flushed. The main conversation had died, and everyone was staring at the two of them.

Dimitri immediately rose to his feet, smiling at the gathered company before gazing at her with impersonal concern.

"I'm sorry to hear you're feeling so weary, Mistress Rosalie. I would be happy to see you safely back to your family."

She blinked at him in stupefaction. She wasn't entirely sure which of them had lost touch with reality.

Blythe looked uneasily between them before focusing her gaze on Rosalie. "If you're not feeling well, Rosalie, I'd be happy to walk with you."

She glanced at Sable who quickly echoed the sentiment.

Dimitri took Blythe's hand and bowed over it. "You are gracious as always." He looked up at her with laughing eyes, and she snatched her hand away with a giggle. "But I won't have any of you tiring yourselves out. Since my home is located in the same direction as Mistress Rosalie's, it won't be out of my way at all."

He moved swiftly, guiding Rosalie to her feet in one smooth movement, and placing a hand on the small of her back. Before either she or Blythe could protest, he had her halfway out of the dining room.

Rosalie glanced over her shoulder as he propelled her forward. Despite his quick action, Blythe had also stood and looked as if she meant to follow after them. Her attempt was thwarted, however, by Daphne, who had woken up just in time to throw herself into Blythe's arms in a fit of tears.

Rosalie narrowed her eyes. Once again, Daphne had woken from her apparent nap at an awfully convenient time. But when Rosalie caught the look of horror on Blythe's face, she couldn't help laughing silently as she was swept out of the room. She had no idea what excuse Daphne would use for her sudden devastation, but her friend was surprisingly resourceful for someone who spent so much time asleep.

As soon as they were out of the dining hall, she opened her mouth to chastise Dimitri. But before she could do so, he made a sudden turn, propelling her with him so abruptly that she lost her breath. By the time she had caught both her breath and her bearings, her back was against the wall in a dark recess at the far end of the inn's corridor.

Dimitri lingered outside the recess, peering up and down to make certain there was no one within earshot. But she only managed one breath before he stepped in with her, apparently satisfied they were alone.

Rosalie's breath caught, her eyes widening as she found herself face to face with him inside the small space.

He stilled, his eyes locked on hers, and the same surprise showing on his face as she felt on hers.

A band constricted around Rosalie's chest. For the second time that afternoon, she found herself in unexpected proximity with a young man's handsome face. But Jace had invaded her space on purpose, and it had felt exactly like the unwelcome invasion it was. Being close to him had evoked fear, repulsion, and anger.

Dimitri, however, seemed as surprised as she was to find their faces only inches apart in the small, dark space. And his presence made her feel...

Her heartbeat rose to a staggering crescendo as she tried to complete the thought. What, exactly, did such close proximity to Dimitri make her feel? She could sense his warmth—although they weren't actually touching—and the earlier intensity had returned to his gaze. Against her will, her eyes dropped to his mouth, positioned just above hers.

The emotions within her whirled, the tangled mix of the last few days almost overwhelming her. The traumatic encounters with Jace twined together with the sense of safety and strength she had felt when Dimitri carried her in his arms.

She was teetering on the edge of losing control entirely. And she had no idea what she would do if that happened. Slap him? Kiss him? Run away crying? Each possibility was more horrifying than the last.

With extreme self-control, she forced her eyes to focus on his. As soon as she did, he spoke.

"What's wrong, Rosalie? Something's been bothering you since you walked in the door."

CHAPTER 13
DIMITRI

Rosalie blinked in response to his words as if she didn't understand the question, although it had been straightforward enough. She licked her lips, and his stomach tightened.

He stepped hurriedly back, hitting the other side of the recess and putting as much room as possible between them in the cramped space. It wasn't an ideal setting, but it had been the only option that presented itself. His one thought had been to find somewhere out of sight from Blythe and the other girls.

When Rosalie remained silent, he repeated the question.

"Something is clearly bothering you. It was obvious as soon as you walked into the inn. Won't you please tell me what it is?"

The new knowledge about her history was burning inside him. He wanted to let it all spill out—especially the connection with his mother's story. Most of all, he wanted to tell her that he would find a way to protect and shield her.

But he didn't say any of it. He was too afraid of scaring her off. As it was, she looked as if she was teetering on the edge of flight.

"Why don't you explain first?" she flung at him, some of her usual fire returning. "What did serving cake and flirting have to do with protecting me?"

"You noticed the flirting?" he asked, pleased.

He was used to turning his charms on the mostly older inhabitants of the mountain community, so he hadn't been sure he was doing it right with Blythe and her friends. Especially given his attempts to spread his attention between so many ladies.

Rosalie's mouth gaped open. "Of course I noticed! It would have been difficult not to."

Dimitri lowered his voice, although it was hardly necessary given their secluded location. "Do you think he had any spies in there?"

He waited expectantly, but Rosalie merely stared at him as if he'd lost his mind entirely. Hadn't she understood his plan?

She spoke carefully, as if afraid a louder tone might startle him. "Do I think there are any spies in Otis's dining room? I can't imagine it's likely."

Disappointment filled Dimitri. Perhaps he had overestimated Jace.

"Do you think the Legacy noticed, at least?" he asked.

"The Legacy?" Her brows rose. "Since it doesn't have eyes or a conscious mind, it wasn't watching you as such.

But if you're asking whether you attracted its power by having tea and cakes, I can't imagine—" She stopped herself abruptly, frowning. "Our server did go invisible. And Otis as well, apparently. Was just your presence enough to do that?" She tipped her head to the side slightly, regarding him quizzically.

He barely held back a smile in response. It was a relief to see her no longer looking as if she was either going to collapse or run, but he didn't think she would appreciate any levity. She already thought he wasn't taking the situation seriously enough.

"What exactly were you trying to do in there?" she asked. "Did you want to attract the notice of the Legacy?"

"I was flirting with girls who aren't you," he said. "You keep saying that my being here puts you in danger. And now that I know you're the youngest daughter of a merchant with two sisters and three brothers, I can understand why you're anxious."

"Well, obviously," she said impatiently.

"It wasn't obvious to me," he said indignantly. "I didn't know anything about your family! You just kept insisting that I was pulling you into disaster."

Rosalie opened her mouth to argue only to slowly close it again, a guilty expression on her face.

"Did you really not know?" she murmured in a small voice. "I'm so used to everyone knowing about my family and what happened to us."

"Well, I know now," he said, voice as gentle as he could make it. He hesitated, his eyes focused on her face. "And I know a few other things besides. I'm still not willing to leave, but I'm doing my best to distract both Jace and the Legacy away from you."

Rosalie's mouth dropped open. "That's what you were doing?"

Dimitri sighed. "I guess I wasn't doing a good job if even you didn't pick up on it."

Rosalie closed her eyes briefly before opening them and spearing him with a look he couldn't interpret.

"I don't think you understand how big a threat Jace is. He's already making moves against us, so I don't think he cares who you're flirting with. I can't predict how the Legacy will react, but Jace, at least, won't be so easily distracted." Her eyes lost their focus for a moment, and she shivered.

"What does that mean?" Dimitri asked, concern filling him. She still hadn't told him what had been bothering her all afternoon.

He gripped both her arms, allowing some of his worry to fill his voice. "What is it, Rosalie? What has he done? Have you seen him again?"

She stared back at him, seeming momentarily bereft of words.

"Rosalie?" he prompted, and she blinked, breaking eye contact.

"It doesn't matter," she muttered. She shook off his hands, and he reluctantly let them drop.

"It matters to me," he said firmly. "Please tell me. You say Jace is a bigger threat than I realize—convince me!"

As he had hoped, that proved an irresistible lure. The

light in her eyes fired up again, and she immediately responded.

"He's already taken steps to entrap my family. He's not going to change his mind because he heard rumors you were flirting with Blythe!"

"Your family?" Dimitri's hand strayed to the hilt of his sword before he realized what he was doing. "What has Jace done to your family?" The words came out as a growl, but he didn't try to take them back.

Rosalie grimaced, realizing the trap she'd fallen into.

"Look," she said. "This doesn't have anything to do with you. You should just stay out of it."

His eyebrows rose. "Nothing to do with me? Isn't my coming here the cause of all this? Of course it has to do with me."

Rosalie groaned. "Fine! My brothers did something very foolish and got themselves into debt. Somehow Jace found out and has bought the debt. He's threatening to have them arrested unless they can repay the full amount in three days—which we can't."

"What?" Dimitri's anger rose. "Why?"

Hadn't Jace already hurt Rosalie's family enough? What did he stand to gain by such behavior?

Rosalie slumped, her voice dropping so low he could barely hear it. "He's told them he'll forgive them the entire debt if they bring him a rose from your garden."

Dimitri's muscles tightened, his hand clenching on the sword hilt. He'd been right. It did have to do with him. A thought occurred to him, and his brows lowered.

"And your brothers were the ones to tell you about Jace's demands? He didn't accost you again?"

Rosalie shifted uncomfortably, an expression that looked too much like fear flitting across her face.

"We had...words on my way here."

"I think I need to have *words* with Jace," Dimitri growled.

Rosalie's hand flew to grasp his right arm, making his muscles jump.

"No, no!" she cried. "You mustn't go looking for him. That will only make everything worse."

Logically, Dimitri knew she was right. Jace had a whole gang of men, for one thing, while he was alone. But it was still hard to beat back the anger pulsing through him. Ever since he had arrived at the manor, it felt as if his life had become a game. He was sick of being a pawn in the middle of the board while shadowy figures chose the moves. If this was what it meant to live in Glandore, then perhaps his mother had been right about the Legacy.

Except running away hadn't been a solution either. There had to be another way. A way for them to be the players instead of the played.

A thought hit him with enough force that he gasped aloud.

"What?" Rosalie asked.

He gripped one of her arms again, hardly even noticing the gesture as excitement coursed through him.

"What if we do what Jace wants?" he asked.

Rosalie stared at him with a look that said her patience was running out.

"You think we should just allow ourselves to be victimized by the Legacy so Jace can profit?" she asked.

Dimitri shook his head. "No, the opposite. I want us to stop being victims. You've spent your whole life fighting against the path the Legacy is trying to force on you. But what if we do the opposite? What if we embrace it? The historical merchant's daughter and her family had a happy ending, remember."

"I've already told you that we don't get to pick which parts of the story the Legacy creates," she said impatiently.

"So we force it to give us the part we want," he said, his excitement unquenched.

Her eyebrows rose skeptically. "And how do we do that?"

"I know the Legacy usually pushes parts of the story in different places at different times. But you keep saying how close our situations are to the original history. What if we follow the story so closely that it forces the Legacy to keep going all the way through to the happy ending?"

"Except for the part where Jace steals everything the Legacy gives us," Rosalie said tartly, clearly not taking his idea seriously—yet.

"I said we should do what Jace wants, not that we should tell him we did it."

"And the distinction is...?"

"Once your brother picks a rose and sends you in his place, the Legacy should transform the castle as magnificently as it did the grounds. Didn't the original story include limitless gold and jewels? Your brothers can keep the rose and use some of the gold to pay Jace back instead. They don't have to tell him where it came from. We can keep the whole thing a secret until we get to the happy ending. Once we're free from the Legacy, I'll use our newfound wealth to make sure Jace finally faces justice for his crimes."

"You do know following the Legacy's path will involve you turning into a Beast, right?" Rosalie asked. "You're not worried we might fail and you'll end up stuck as a Beast forever?"

Dimitri gave her a cocky smile. "We won't fail."

Rosalie snorted. "Are you really that confident that if you can get me to move into the manor, I'll fall in love with you?"

Dimitri blinked. He hadn't been thinking anything of the sort. He hadn't even properly thought through the fact that his plan would involve them both living at the manor. But now that she'd said it, it was all he could think about.

"Really?" Rosalie asked when he didn't immediately respond.

He cleared his throat. "Everything I've read says the Legacy doesn't affect emotions. So how can it know what you feel? The important thing is what you do. Think of it like acting out a play. And once we've reached the end— with me restored to my usual form and your family enjoying even greater wealth and prosperity than before— you can go back to finding me infuriating."

He hoped she wouldn't. Surely there was a chance she might change her mind about him by then? It didn't seem like the right time to suggest the possibility, though.

Rosalie didn't reply, and hope filled him. Was she actually going to listen to him for once?

"I can't let you take that risk for us," she said, but there was enough reluctance in her voice to continue fueling his hope. "A lot would hinge on us keeping it secret. If Jace found out, we might both be in danger."

"From the sound of it, you and your brothers are already in danger," Dimitri said. "And if you are, I probably am too. Do you have the impression Jace is going to give up?"

Rosalie was silent for another long minute, worrying at her lip the entire time, her eyes fixed on a point behind his head as she thought.

She finally spoke. "If we wanted to follow the story as closely as possible, it would have to be my brother picking the rose, like you said. I couldn't do it myself. But I'm not willing to drag them any further into this than they already have been. What if the Legacy does something unpredictable? It wouldn't be the first time. They might end up trapped instead of me. That's not a risk I'm willing to take."

Dimitri grimaced. Her brothers had been the ones to get themselves into debt, and Rosalie didn't seem to question that she should take a risk to help them. Couldn't her brothers take a small risk to fix the problem they'd created? She seemed willing to let Dimitri take a bigger one.

He made no attempt to argue the point with her, though. Rosalie was protective of her brothers, and it was something he admired about her. If she didn't feel the same way about him, that was a good thing. She was willing to take any level of risk herself, and he would far rather she saw him as an equal and a partner than as a child who needed to be shielded.

He tried to think of another approach instead, unwilling to let the idea die. The more he thought about it, the more enamored he became with having Rosalie's company at the manor. He was less excited about becoming a Beast. But that was a shadowy possibility, so foreign that it was easy to ignore. Rosalie was in front of him, a mixture of solidity and enticing, flickering flame. What was a shadowy possibility compared to that? But it would come to nothing if he couldn't find a solution that didn't involve her brothers.

"I'll do it," a third voice said.

They both turned to see Daphne standing beside them. They had been so absorbed in their interaction that they hadn't heard her approach.

Rosalie immediately stepped out of the recess. Her cheeks were faintly flushed, and Dimitri had to fight down a flush of his own. It wasn't as if they had been doing anything scandalous. They had merely been talking.

"You can't be serious, Daph," Rosalie said, reminding Dimitri of what really mattered.

"Why not?" Daphne asked, regarding them both calmly. "You need someone else to pluck the rose so you can be the substitute. Given how much the Legacy loves substitutes, I think that part should go smoothly. But if there is a problem..." She shrugged. "I'm not as perfect a fit as you, Rosalie, but I could do a better job of seeing the ruse through than any of your brothers." She chuckled softly, and Rosalie joined in reluctantly.

Dimitri couldn't muster up any amusement at the idea, however. His reaction to the idea of Daphne taking Rosalie's place had been swift and violent, and he was still working to conceal it.

He wasn't sure if he'd succeeded. Rosalie seemed oblivious, but Daphne gave him a look that was a little too knowing for his comfort.

"It won't happen, though," she said, directing her words more in his direction than her friend's. "I don't think it matters much who picks that rose. There's no way the Legacy will resist the allure of swapping in Rosalie."

"And that is exactly what I've been so worried about ever since those roses appeared," Rosalie grumbled.

"Precisely." Daphne smiled smugly at her. "So you don't have any excuses left."

Rosalie's eyes widened a little as she realized she'd backed herself into a corner.

"Do you really think this is wise, Daphne?" she asked in a low voice, worrying at her lip again as she waited for a reply. "Am I being reckless to even consider it?"

Despite her offered support, Daphne apparently took the question seriously because she took a moment to consider before answering.

"I think this is your chance, and you shouldn't miss taking it. If this goes well, it would turn everything around for both you and your family. Surely that's worth some risk." Her mouth twisted. "Especially considering the situation you're in with Jace."

"Daphne!" Rosalie cried. "How long were you listening?"

"Since I got away from Blythe and worked out where you two had gone," Daphne said unapologetically. She gave Rosalie a look. "If Dimitri could work out something was wrong with you, did you think I would miss it?"

Rosalie didn't respond to that, looking from her friend to Dimitri instead.

"So we're really going to do this?" she asked in a soft voice.

The two of them looked at each other before both nodding.

"And you're sure about helping me like this?" Rosalie asked, looking at him as if she wasn't quite convinced he had selfless motives.

And if he was honest, she was right. His motives weren't entirely selfless. He wanted to get to know her better, and he had his own reasons for wanting to protect her. He felt as if he owed it to his mother to try. Only hours ago he had promised himself he would do whatever it took to protect Rosalie, and what better opportunity would he have?

None of those answers were right for the moment, however. She needed to be reminded that he had as much to lose from the Legacy as she did. Possibly more.

"I have no desire to end up as a Beast forever," he said. "Doing this is my way to escape from the Legacy as well."

From all the possible truthful answers, he seemed to have picked the right one, because her brow cleared.

"Shall we head to the manor now, then?" Rosalie

asked. In typical fashion, having made up her mind, she wanted to act on the decision immediately.

"Right now?" Daphne wilted, her expression turning pained.

Dimitri might have thought she was regretting her offer to help, but he had seen enough of her to know better. It was the necessity of walking out to the manor that she found distasteful.

"Of course we have to do it now!" Rosalie said. "If you were eavesdropping on our conversation, then you know that we only have three days. Less now!" She glanced toward the closest window, as if she could measure the hours passing by the day's light. "We don't know how long the Legacy might take to start transforming the castle."

"If the grounds are anything to go by, it won't take long," Daphne said. "But I suppose it makes sense for me to pick the rose this evening." She looked at Dimitri. "Make sure that when you threaten me, you say that I have to come back the next morning to be slaughtered."

"Come back to be what?" Dimitri asked, alarmed.

Rosalie frowned. "Don't you know your part? I thought you'd been studying the history."

"I guess I hadn't really considered that part of it," Dimitri said, realizing belatedly just how little he'd thought through a number of aspects of the plan. He wasn't going to pull back, though.

"I suppose it would be a good idea to modify it, just in case the Legacy doesn't allow a substitution," Daphne said thoughtfully. "You should tell me that I can either be slaughtered on the spot, or I can come back the next day to remain as your prisoner. And that the only way for me to escape is if I bring another young maiden in my place."

"Since I'm not eighty years old, I might not use the words 'young maiden,'" Dimitri said.

"Stop quibbling," Rosalie said. "I've noticed that's a habit of yours. It doesn't matter what exact words you use, just follow the general idea. Otherwise the whole plan will fail and who knows what catastrophic effect that will have!"

"So, no pressure?" Dimitri quipped with a grin.

"Don't make me regret trusting you," Rosalie said warningly, and he could see enough genuine uncertainty in her gaze to immediately drop the smile.

"Don't worry," he said seriously. "I won't make a mistake."

She regarded him for a moment before nodding. "In that case, let's not waste any more time."

CHAPTER 14
ROSALIE

Rosalie still wasn't sure she wasn't being wildly reckless. She had been foolish beyond limit once before in a bid to escape the Legacy. But the circumstances were more urgent in this case, and she didn't see any other option.

Having made the decision, she refused to second-guess herself, speed walking toward the manor at such a rate that Daphne complained a total of eight times. But Rosalie felt as if she were about to explode out of her skin, and the only thing she could think to do was keep moving. If she stopped, she was afraid she might implode completely. At least once the rose had been taken, there would be no possibility of turning back, and hopefully her nerves would relax.

She couldn't even look at Dimitri. After everything that Jace had done, she was putting her fate in the hands of a handsome newcomer again. But at least this time they were natural allies. Dimitri hadn't come up with the plan to save Rosalie—he had done it to save himself. Rosalie just hoped she could complete her part well enough that he was guaranteed to recover his normal form. If he was stuck as a Beast forever while her family lived in wealth and prosperity, she would never have another peaceful day.

Having rushed to the castle, she regretted her speed as soon as the grounds appeared. But she pushed her worries aside. She had a way to save her brothers and father, and she wasn't going to turn away from it.

"You'd better go and hide among the trees," Rosalie said to Dimitri. "Then you can emerge when Daphne picks the rose."

She leaned toward Daphne and lowered her voice. "If we really have to pick one, you might as well pick one of the gold ones."

Dimitri chuckled under his breath, and she glared at him. There was nothing funny about the situation.

Daphne, at least, didn't seem to find anything odd in her statement. "That's a good idea. Even if everything else goes wrong, I might be able to sell it for enough to pay Vernon's debt."

Rosalie nodded before cocking her head to the side in sudden confusion. "Did I ever say it was Vernon who borrowed the money?"

One side of Daphne's mouth twitched upward. "It wasn't hard to guess. Have Ralph or Oscar ever been the ones to get them into trouble?"

"They follow willingly enough," Rosalie grumbled, but she didn't disagree. Sometimes she didn't know if she wanted to protect her brothers or wring their necks herself.

"You'd better move back a bit, Rosalie," Daphne said. "If you're going to be the substitute, you can't be involved in this part."

Rosalie reluctantly nodded her agreement and walked back to the far side of the road. She hoped it was far enough because she couldn't bring herself to go out of sight completely. The important thing was that she not trespass on the manor's grounds.

As soon as Dimitri disappeared from sight, Daphne sent Rosalie one last inquiring look. When Rosalie nodded at her, she stepped off the road.

Rosalie held her breath, but of course nothing happened just because Daphne had walked onto the manor grounds. Rosalie had done that herself without anything dramatic happening.

She resumed breathing but soon had to force herself to stop biting her lip before she gave herself an injury. At least Daphne didn't walk far before she stopped in front of a rose plant. She was taking pity on Rosalie and staying in sight. Or perhaps the Legacy's roses had managed to enchant her that quickly.

The bush she had selected was growing a mix of red and gold roses. As promised, she plucked the largest of the glowing golden ones. Holding it in her hand, she stared down at it for a moment before looking around the garden.

There was no one in sight, and Rosalie's heart sank. Had something gone wrong already?

But she had barely finished the thought when Dimitri strode into sight. He struck a pose, hand on his sword hilt, and glared toward Daphne.

A slightly hysterical giggle worked its way up Rosalie's throat. He looked like an overly dramatic actor in a traveling play. She only hoped the Legacy was easily manipulated.

"Who dares to steal what is mine?" he bellowed.

Daphne dropped back a step, clearly more affected than Rosalie. Was she feigning the startled response? If so, she was a much better actor than Dimitri.

"I'm sorry." Her voice was quieter than his, and Rosalie could only just catch it. "I took it for a friend of mine who is in great need. Surely you can spare one rose?"

"If you wish to take something of mine, you must pay the price," Dimitri said before visibly hesitating over the next line. He finally sighed and continued. "I can either slay you where you stand, or else you can return tomorrow and agree to be my prisoner here."

"Oh no!" Daphne cried, warming to his overly dramatic style. "I could not do so! I only sought to help a friend. She is far more beautiful than I and has a kinder heart as well." She began to fake sob into her hands.

"In that case, your friend may choose to save you if she wills it. If she comes willingly in your place, you'll be free."

Daphne looked up, her face covered in instant smiles. "Oh excellent! Thank you!"

Dimitri frowned at her while Rosalie glared from afar. She shouldn't have sounded so eager—no matter how relieved she was that Dimitri had gotten his lines right.

"I mean," Daphne added quickly, "I couldn't possibly sacrifice another in my stead."

"Either you or she must come willingly tomorrow," Dimitri said in an even sterner voice. "Otherwise I will find you in your home."

"Very well," Daphne said with the appropriate quaver in her voice, although Rosalie suspected it was covering laughter.

She sighed. At least it wasn't Vernon in Daphne's place. He would have turned it into a true farce.

Daphne turned, the golden rose gripped firmly in her hand, and ran back to the road. Dimitri stood watching her until the two girls were reunited. Then he spoke a final word.

"Tomorrow!" he called loudly, but his eyes were on Rosalie, not Daphne.

"Oh thank goodness, we made it through." Daphne thrust the flower toward Rosalie. "I thought for sure I was going to break down into giggles at the end. I was nervous at the beginning, but Dimitri was just too much." The suppressed giggles burst out.

Rosalie backed away from the offered rose. "I can't take that. You should keep it safe. In case..."

Daphne pressed the rose into her hand. "I claimed that I stole it for you, remember? You're supposed to take it. Just leave it hidden in your house somewhere. If I need it, I'll find it."

Rosalie reluctantly accepted it, tucking it into the small satchel at her hip before turning in the direction of home. It was better to have it out of sight, just in case Jace turned up unexpectedly.

She hadn't made it more than a few steps, however, when she stopped, frowning toward the manor grounds.

"Is it just me," she asked, "or have the grounds already changed?"

"Changed?" Daphne stared in the direction of the garden. "It looks just as lush to me."

"I don't mean anything physical," Rosalie said slowly. "More the...feel of it. Doesn't it seem different?"

Daphne blinked several times, gazing up and down the gardens where they bordered the road for a long stretch.

"It's not glowing quite like it did before," she admitted after a minute.

"And you don't feel drawn to it, right?" Rosalie asked. "The pull to pick one of the roses is gone."

"That's a good thing, isn't it?" Daphne asked. "It means the plan is working."

Rosalie sighed. "Just as long as Jace doesn't notice."

She led the rest of the way home, lost in thought. She did feel less like bursting out of her skin now that it was done, but that didn't mean she felt comfortable either. She was going to have to come up with an excuse for her mother and brothers to explain her upcoming absence. It didn't help that she didn't know how long the Legacy would require her to stay at the manor.

"You'll have to tell them you're staying with me," Daphne said, correctly guessing the trajectory of her thoughts. "I had a letter from Mother today. Father has injured his ankle, so they won't be able to travel home for several weeks. So you can tell your mother that I don't want to be alone for so long. Given how small the cottage is, they'll understand if you come to my house instead of me coming to you."

"Daphne!" Rosalie cried, dismayed. "Why didn't you say something? Is he all right?"

"He's fine," Daphne said. "It's a straightforward injury, and he should make a full recovery. I was actually on my way to tell you when you showed up in the square. But you looked terrified, so it didn't seem the right moment to bring it up."

Rosalie stopped outside the cottage gate. "I hope you know that you can always tell me anything. It doesn't matter what chaos is going on in my life, I still want to hear about what's happening with you!"

"I know you do, friend." Daphne smiled at her warmly. "To be honest, I forgot about it myself in the middle of everything else going on. I've never taken part in some-thing so thrilling."

"That's because you don't spend enough time around my brothers." Rosalie marched toward her front door, bracing herself to face them.

Usually her brothers swarmed Daphne the moment she appeared, so it spoke to the depths of their concern and guilt that they shrank into themselves instead. When they turned to their sister with pathetically hopeful expressions, her heart softened.

She glanced around for their mother, and her brothers instantly understood her caution.

"She's out the back," Oscar said quietly. "In the garden."

"You can stop worrying," Rosalie murmured quietly when she confirmed they were alone. "I've found a way to get the money we need. I should have it for you by tomorrow evening. Or the next day at the latest." She hoped she wasn't wrong about how quickly the Legacy would move.

"You have? How? Where is it coming from?" Vernon grabbed her arm, his eyes locked on her face. Ralph leaned in as well, although he looked too relieved to speak.

"I can't tell you that," Rosalie said.

Vernon's brows immediately lowered. "Why not? You haven't done something terrible, have you?"

"Of course she hasn't." Daphne stepped forward and wound her arm through Rosalie's, smiling beatifically at the boys.

Vernon immediately nodded in silent acceptance of her reassurance. Rosalie rolled her eyes. If she had said the same thing, he would have refused to believe her and kept pressing her for answers.

With the buoyancy of youth, the boys recovered almost instantly in response to her news. They fell over each other to show off their cooking to Daphne, who largely ignored them. She did, however, wink at Rosalie.

Rosalie grinned back at her friend, relieved to have Daphne at her side. Everything would have been harder without her.

They waited until the whole family, plus Daphne, were

seated around the table for the meal before Daphne passed on the news about her father.

"Oh no, I'm sorry to hear that." Rosalie's mother's voice was laced with genuine concern. Not only was Daphne like another daughter to her, but her family had been the only ones to offer to take them in during the immediate aftermath of the fire. She viewed them all as family. "Is there anything we can do?"

"Actually," Daphne said, "I was hoping you might loan Rosalie to me. I've already been alone in my house for days, and I don't fancy being alone for weeks more. Do you think she could come and stay with me?"

"You could come here," Oscar said eagerly, earning a repressive look from their mother.

"You can't ask poor Daphne to squeeze in here!" she said before smiling at Daphne. "Of course Rosalie should stay with you. It's the least we can do after everything your family has done for us." She reached out and squeezed both Daphne's and Rosalie's hands.

Rosalie looked away, blinking furiously to fight back the moisture gathering in her eyes. She didn't want to deceive her mother, even in the mildest way. But they couldn't risk telling more people about their attempted ruse. If her family knew, they would just try to stop her, and it was too late for that.

The boys would probably be dramatic and claim she was sacrificing herself for them when she was only going off to live in luxury for a few weeks. At least, that was what she was telling herself. It was easier to focus on the luxury of life at the manor than to think about who would be sharing it with her.

Rosalie moved through the rest of the evening in a daze, helping her mother clean the dishes and tidy the kitchen, only pausing from time to time to chase her brothers away from Daphne who was barely staying awake. They were like bees to Daphne's flower, but Rosalie was willing to take the stings as she swatted them away. She couldn't even stay annoyed at them for long when she knew she would be leaving in the morning.

Squeezed into bed that night between Daphne and her mother, Rosalie listened to the steady rhythm of their breathing and wondered if she'd made a terrible mistake. Dimitri had said the Legacy didn't create love—or any other emotion. It just manipulated situations and created oddities.

But sometimes, when the memory of her past foolishness was hardest to bear, Rosalie wondered how anyone could be sure. What if they were wrong, and the Legacy could create emotions? Maybe it hadn't been her fault she had fallen so quickly and foolishly in love with Jace. Maybe the Legacy had made her do it.

Although she usually shook off such thoughts with the light of morning, she was susceptible to them again in the dark of night, especially as she contemplated the task before her. Could it be true? And if it was, what would happen when she moved into the manor? Would the Legacy force her into false feelings of love just so history could repeat itself? Was she about to make a fool of herself for yet another handsome face?

CHAPTER 15

DIMITRI

It was hard to turn around and walk away from the two girls. At least they had each other, while he was left alone with nothing to do but wait. He had no other option, though. If they were going to follow the story, they had to leave at least a little time for the substitution to be arranged.

As he walked back to the manor, he felt hot and itchy all over. His mental discomfort seemed to be leaching into his body, making him want to break into a run.

He pulled at his collar, dislodging the snowy white scarf he had carefully arranged before heading for the Mortar and Pestle. At least he would be sleeping in a proper bed that night after his efforts of the morning—a morning that felt impossibly distant.

He scratched at his back through his vest, irritated. Wasn't it enough for his mind to be in turmoil? Did he have to be so uncomfortable as well?

His fingers tried to reach the spot through the material, but there seemed to be something in the way. Did he have something stuck under his shirt? If some leaves from the garden had slipped down his collar that would explain the discomfort.

Pulling the ends of his shirt loose, he reached up his back for the itchiest spot. Yelping, he pulled his hand free. It didn't feel like a leaf. It felt like—

He touched his back again, swallowing hard when he felt the same furry sensation. Slowly his eyes dropped to his other hand.

Instead of a yelp, he gave a bellow. His once familiar hand was barely recognizable. The hair of his arm had grown so wildly long that it was bursting from the cuff of his shirt and obscuring most of the back of his hand.

Forgetting propriety completely, he pulled up his shirt to gaze with horror at his stomach. It wasn't just his arm or his back. He was covered in hair.

He broke into a run, racing for the manor door and a mirror. At least he could still move freely. He should be grateful he felt no urge to drop to all fours and lope along like a wolf. Or was that just because the transformation was incomplete?

He'd known their plan involved him turning into a fabled Beast. But the descriptions he'd read in books had been both vague and varied, so he'd had no clear idea of what to expect. And for some nonsensical reason, he hadn't expected it to happen so soon.

Everyone who turned into a Beast must have a different experience—like the different punishments the Legacy enacted for leaving the kingdom's borders. He only hoped the Legacy would continue to go easy on him.

Standing in front of the mirror, it was hard to muster relief, however. His body hair had grown so long it more closely resembled fur than hair, and his facial hair now obscured everything except his eyes. He didn't recognize himself at all, and if he attempted to venture into Thebarton, he would likely be chased away by fearful townsfolk. He wouldn't even be able to blame them. No one who saw him could mistake what had happened, and if they feared to associate with Rosalie's family, they would fear him even more.

"I should have gotten more supplies," he said aloud to the mirror. "I didn't think this through very well."

Perhaps they could request help from Daphne if they needed it. She wasn't likely to abandon Rosalie after going so far to help them.

With that mildly reassuring thought, he had to pull together an evening meal for himself and then attempt to sleep. The task seemed impossible, despite his comfortable new bed, but eventually he succumbed to slumber. As he drifted off, it was with thoughts of the next day's work. He would need to prepare a second bedchamber now that the manor was getting another inhabitant.

He was awake just after dawn and glad for an activity to fill his time. But when he got to the bedchamber he had chosen for Rosalie, he was left silent and staring. The manor had been keeping itself clean since his arrival, but it had now raised its efforts to a whole different level.

The room before him looked just as personalized as his

mother's had done, but it also gave off a fresh feeling, as if it had been prepared only hours before. Gone were the neutral colors he remembered previously, and in their place was deep purple with hints of gold. A room ready for royalty.

Fresh cut flowers filled the air with fragrance, and every possible luxury of furniture was positioned in the optimal way. Even the sheets on the four-poster bed looked and smelled fresh, as if someone had been busily changing them overnight.

He didn't need to do any work for Rosalie's arrival after all. But while the Legacy had done a better job than he could have, its efforts left him at a loose end. Part of him wanted to explore any other overnight changes to the manor, but another part of him was afraid of what he might find. It was one thing for the Legacy to pour power into his garden, or to keep the building free of dust, but he wasn't sure he liked the idea of it flowing freely through his home.

He took a further step into the room instead and caught a glimpse of himself in the mirror over the dressing table. Recoiling in shock, he nearly collided with the open door. Had he grown even more hair while he was sleeping? It looked matted now, and he recognized nothing of his old self except his height.

He turned quickly away from the reflection, deciding he could face the rest of the castle after all. But he had barely reached the top of the main staircase when a loud knock rang through the entryway, echoing from the double doors directly beneath him.

Someone had already arrived. Given his current appearance, he could only hope it was Rosalie.

He raced down the stairs only to pause with his hand on the latch. What would Rosalie think when she saw his new appearance?

When he had imagined her moving in, he had conveniently forgotten the state he would be in. Now that the moment had come, he hesitated to open the doors. Part of him resisted the idea of her seeing him as a Beast.

But the thought was pure foolishness. He couldn't avoid the meeting, and it didn't matter anyway. Rosalie had never seemed to like his face, so what did it matter if it had changed beyond recognition?

He pulled the doors open with one swift heave, and Daphne stepped inside. His heart immediately sank. Had Rosalie gotten cold feet in the night?

The thought was inconceivable. Had something happened to her then?

He barely had a chance to feel a flash of concern before Rosalie followed Daphne inside.

"I'm the one who asked for the rose," she said. "I'm here to take my friend's place."

Relief filled Dimitri, and he nearly forgot his line. But both girls were looking at him expectantly, so he managed to stumble over it.

"Do you come willingly?"

"I do," she said. "Even if I am to die, I'll remain gladly in place of my friend."

No sooner had she finished the sentence than a series of loud bangs sounded outside. All three of them jumped, and Rosalie and Dimitri both ran for the open doorway.

Outside, a series of bright fireworks in brilliant colors exploded across the sky, the deafening cracks continuing.

"What a waste," Daphne said from behind them, peering up at the sky over Rosalie's shoulder. "There's no point having fireworks in the daytime."

"At least we know the Legacy accepted the exchange." Dimitri looked down at Rosalie with a smile. So far everything was going according to plan.

"This is a disaster!" Rosalie hissed through her teeth, flattening his pleasure. "How do we make them stop?"

"Do we need to?" Dimitri asked as a final bang rang out and silence fell. He smiled. "Look, it obeyed your command."

"It doesn't matter," she said, almost on a wail. "Any fireworks is too many. I don't know where Jace is holed up with his men, but I'm guessing it was close enough to hear those!"

Dimitri paled as he finally realized what she had grasped immediately. Everything wasn't going to plan at all. Their whole strategy hinged on keeping his transformation a secret from Jace, but the Legacy had just made a very loud and public announcement.

"He can't know where it came from or what it signified," Daphne said. "Not for sure."

"Perhaps not." Tension radiated from Rosalie's shoulders. "But we'd better be prepared for him to come looking."

Dimitri's stomach tightened. He had already decided

never to step outside without his sword, but that didn't feel like enough. He needed to start wearing it inside the castle as well.

"Who knows," he said, trying to sound cheerful. "Maybe they'll take one look at me and run in horror."

Both girls turned to him and blinked, seeming to take in his new appearance for the first time. But there was only one reaction he cared about. His eyes stayed fixed on Rosalie.

CHAPTER 16
ROSALIE

Rosalie had been so focused on getting her lines right and successfully completing the substitution that she had barely even noticed Dimitri beyond his basic presence.

But now that she was properly looking at him, shock coursed through her. It wasn't that he was hideous—she had actually been fearing worse. His basic form remained the same as far as she could tell, he was just covered in so much hair that he looked entirely different. Even his clothes fit awkwardly.

It would have been worse if he'd had darker hair, she decided. It would have made the effect more startling. As it was, the most unnerving aspect was the inhuman air that now hung about him like a pall. Before she had looked at him and seen Jace. Now she looked at him and saw the Legacy.

She wasn't sure which was worse.

"The Legacy really does move quickly," Daphne said in choked tones.

Rosalie glanced at her suspiciously. Was she *laughing*? She owed Daphne a lot, but it seemed a little inconsiderate in the circumstances.

"Don't look at me like that, Rosalie," Daphne said primly. "I think it's an improvement."

Rosalie ignored her nonsense, focusing on the important point. "If the Legacy is moving quickly, that's a good thing." She looked around the entryway before turning back to Dimitri. "Have you noticed changes inside the manor yet? I can't see any in here, but I don't remember its old appearance that clearly."

He raised an eyebrow, gesturing up and down his body, finishing with his face. "No comment about this? Really?"

Rosalie frowned at him. "Yes, yes, it's a good thing the Legacy is moving so quickly. We already said that."

Dimitri laughed. "I suppose I should take that as a compliment. You aren't regretting your promise to come here? No inclination to run screaming?"

Rosalie gave a single, huffed laugh. "Have I given you the impression I'm that chicken-hearted? You would have to look a lot worse to scare me off."

"I don't think you could look frightful enough to scare Rosalie off," Daphne said. "That's why it's a good thing it's her, not me."

Rosalie gave her a chiding look. "You're far braver than you pretend to be, Daphne."

"Am I?" her friend asked in mild surprise, but Rosalie could see the laughter dancing in her eyes.

Most people looked at Daphne and saw only the excessive napping. They missed her dry humor, but Rosalie had known her too long to be taken in. Daphne was far more astute than she pretended to be.

Rosalie had tried calling her out on it, but Daphne claimed it wasn't worth the effort of convincing anyone. She seemed to like being underestimated.

"There isn't much change in here." Dimitri ran his eyes over the lofty entryway. "Everything seems brighter than yesterday, though, and I'm pretty sure that gilt edging wasn't there." He pointed at the doorframe and the stone of the mantelpiece. "But it's more noticeable elsewhere. I only had time to look in one bedchamber before you arrived, but the difference was startling."

He glanced at Rosalie with an expression she couldn't read. It was harder to read his face now that most of his features were obscured.

"It's the bedchamber I thought would work best for you," he said. "Apparently the Legacy thought so too."

"Why don't we check there first?" Rosalie suggested. "If the Legacy has transformed it with me in mind, we might find valuables there that Daphne can use."

She turned expectantly to Dimitri, and he made no protest, leading the way toward the stairs. He still seemed dazed from their cavalier acceptance of his new appearance, although she couldn't imagine why. They had all known he was going to change.

Rosalie frowned as she trailed behind him. Had

Dimitri not really believed their warnings about becoming a Beast? Or had he misunderstood what it would mean? She felt sorry if so, but it was too late for regrets now.

Dimitri turned left at the top of the stairs, passing several doors before stopping outside a closed one. He opened it with a flourish, stepping back to reveal the room beyond.

Rosalie gasped. She didn't know where to look first.

"It's gorgeous," she breathed, stepping inside.

"A room for a princess," Daphne agreed, giving the bed a longing look.

"No napping!" Rosalie told her sternly. "We need to find something you can sell. I'm relying on you to help the boys end their dealings with Jace as quickly as possible."

Daphne sighed but nodded. She looked around the room, her eyes fastening on the dressing table. Her eyebrows rose.

"That might do." She moved toward it, her fingers trailing across the top of the items laid out.

Rosalie glanced over and saw a row of gold-backed brushes, mirrors, and combs beside several exquisite crystal bottles with golden lids.

"Those weren't there yesterday," Dimitri said unnecessarily.

Rosalie's eyes strayed over to the wardrobe. Crossing to it, she pulled the doors wide. She had been half-expecting to find it full, but she still gasped at the array of dresses. Each was made in a more exquisite material than the last, decorated with gems or pearls, and all appeared to be her size.

She looked over her shoulder at Daphne. "One of these would do it, don't you think?"

The two girls held eye contact for a moment and then both broke into helpless giggles.

"Is there something funny?" Dimitri asked in confused tones.

"Sorry." Rosalie wiped the moisture from her eyes, trying to catch her breath. "It's just a bit overwhelming. The theory doesn't quite prepare you for the reality."

"Tell me about it," Dimitri muttered, making Rosalie feel instantly guilty.

She eyed him, still lurking in the doorway, and wondered why he didn't join them. But a glance from his position to the rest of the room gave her the answer. He was hanging back away from the dressing table and its mirror. Her guilt deepened. She was delighting in beautiful dresses while he was wearing the form of a Beast. She should focus on what needed to be done and not get lost in the Legacy's creations.

She looked back at the wardrobe. "What do you think would be best to sell, Daphne? These dresses must be worth a fortune given the jewels sewn into them, but the mirror and brush set would be easier to sell quickly. Even if they were just melted down for the gold, it might be enough."

"Uh...I don't think that will be necessary," Daphne said in a strangled voice.

Rosalie looked up but couldn't find her for a moment. She finally spotted her in a small, empty dressing room in the far corner of the room.

Her tone was enough to bring Dimitri into the room, the mirror apparently forgotten, and the two of them rushed to Daphne's side. They found her kneeling in front of a small, open leather trunk which was the only item in the room.

She looked up at them, eyes wide. No one spoke for a moment as they both stared at the contents of the chest.

It was full of coins. An entire chest full of coins.

"Well then," Rosalie said at last. "I guess you won't need to sell anything."

"How much do you think is in here?" Daphne whispered, but neither of them answered. Rosalie couldn't even make a guess.

"This is exactly why Jace wanted to push us into this farce," she said instead. "If we want any hope of keeping this a secret, that chest needs to stay right where it is. Sorry, Daph, but I think you should only take enough to pay off the debt. We'll have to pretend that we found a way to scrape the amount together. Jace can't be sure what those fireworks meant, and we need to keep him guessing."

Daphne nodded and produced a leather pouch. Rosalie helped her count out the exact amount of the debt, watching as she tucked it away in her dress.

"You'll coach Vernon on what to say?" she asked anxiously.

"Don't worry," Daphne said with more earnestness than was her usual wont. "I'll make sure it goes well. You focus on this." She gestured vaguely around at the room, the chest, and Dimitri. "Once it's over, your father will have all the investment money he needs."

"And your family as well," Rosalie said. "We'll share it between all of us."

They all stared back at the coins for a moment before Rosalie shut the lid firmly. It would be better to forget about the gold for the moment. There were still too many things that had to happen before she could claim any more of them.

"If the coins are staying here, then we need to find a different bed chamber for you," Dimitri said.

"But this one is so beautiful!" Rosalie protested. "Why should I move?"

"You said it yourself." He was frowning. "That chest is what Jace wants. If he realizes what's happened and comes after the gold, I don't want you anywhere near it."

"You're planning to just let him take it?" Rosalie cried. "If Jace is going to come for this chest, then we should have someone guarding it!"

"No amount of coins is worth you getting hurt—or, worse, killed," he said so earnestly that Rosalie's heart stuttered.

She ignored the sensation, her stubbornness growing stronger.

"I'm not standing aside so he can just waltz in and claim it," she said before softening a little. "Don't worry, I'll lock the door."

She produced the key she had found on the bedside table. "I'll keep the door locked whether I'm in here or not."

Dimitri hesitated before visibly capitulating. He sighed, but she ignored it. She appreciated his concern, but she hadn't come to the manor so he could order her around. The sooner he accepted that, the easier time they'd have together.

"Do you really think Jace will send his men to invade the manor?" Daphne sounded almost as concerned as Dimitri.

"I think it's a possibility we have to be prepared for," Dimitri said. "I'm hoping the Legacy will make them nervous enough to take a cautious approach. But I wouldn't want to bet my life on it—or Rosalie's."

"No." Daphne shivered.

"You have what you need," Rosalie said to her. "You should hurry back now." She pressed her lips together. All the talk of Jace was making her nervous. "I'm sorry you have to go by yourself. I wish I could walk you back..."

Daphne shook her head firmly. "Don't worry about me. You know you can't leave or it will ruin everything. You're supposed to be a prisoner, remember?" She gave Rosalie a stern look.

"Yes, ma'am," Rosalie said meekly, making Daphne laugh and throw a glance at Dimitri.

"Don't expect this mood to last long," she told him.

He laughed. "Don't worry. I have no unrealistic expectations."

Rosalie narrowed her eyes at both of them, putting her hands on Daphne's back and propelling her friend from the room. "Come on! No need to waste any more time in chit chat."

Daphne allowed herself to be pushed out of the manor, only pausing on the front step to look back. Her expression turned serious.

"I meant it when I said not to worry. Vernon will have paid Jace back by the end of the day. I'll make sure of it."

Rosalie nodded, knowing that when it came to things that really mattered, Daphne was completely trustworthy.

"What if Jace seizes you on the road?" Dimitri asked, less easily soothed. "He might be heading this way after those fireworks."

Rosalie's fear returned. She should have thought of that possibility.

"Don't worry," Daphne repeated. "I organized for someone to meet me and walk me back."

"You did?" Rosalie stared at her. "Who?"

"Be careful! And try to enjoy yourselves!" Daphne called hurriedly, rushing down the stairs with a cheery wave and disappearing down the drive.

Rosalie blinked after her. Did Daphne have a suitor she'd never mentioned? Why would she be keeping him a secret if so?

It was too late to get anything out of Daphne, though. Rosalie's curiosity would have to wait until Daphne's return—whenever that might be. Rosalie hoped Daphne would come back to deliver both an update and supplies at some point, but they hadn't actually made a fixed arrangement.

Realizing what Daphne's departure meant, Rosalie turned slowly to face Dimitri. They were alone.

"So," she said awkwardly. "What now?"

"I can carry your case up to your room." He picked it up and looked at her expectantly.

Rosalie nodded. She had abandoned the case in the entryway at the first firework and promptly forgotten all about it.

She followed Dimitri up the stairs for the second time, wondering why she was suddenly so tongue-tied. It wasn't like her.

"That's my room." Dimitri gestured at the second closed door on the left as they passed it.

Rosalie looked from his door to hers, only two doors down.

"That's your room? Right there?" she asked, glad her voice didn't squeak.

He paused with his hand on her doorknob and looked back. Once again, she couldn't read his expression.

"I thought you might be uncomfortable being in the room right next to me," he said. "But I don't think it's safe for us to be too far apart. This way if anything happens overnight, we should be able to hear each other calling." He paused. "Just in case. I'm sure nothing will happen."

He was clearly afraid something would happen, despite his words. Rosalie just wasn't sure if he was trying to reassure himself or her. She couldn't blame him for his anxiety, however. She had been too worried about her brothers and the debt to put much thought into what would happen after it was paid, and it was dawning on her that she hadn't sufficiently considered all the risks.

Dimitri put her case down just inside the door. "I'll leave you to get settled. Did you need anything else?"

He looked hopeful, but Rosalie quickly shook her head. She needed some space to think.

"I packed myself some food for today," she said, "since I wasn't sure about the state of your supplies. But I suppose we should meet for the evening meal."

Was Dimitri disappointed? It was hard to tell, and he didn't say anything either way.

"The shared evening meal seemed like a big feature of the original history," he said, "so that would probably be wise." He looked around the elaborately decorated and furnished room. "If this room is anything to go by, we may not have to worry about supplies."

Rosalie's eyes lit up. "Ooh! I hadn't even thought of that!"

What sort of delicious meals could they expect from the Legacy's power? Would they be even better than the ones at the Mortar and Pestle?

Suddenly the evening meal seemed too far away. She glanced at her case, remembering the unexciting food she had packed for the midday meal. But she didn't suggest they alter the arrangement. Since her brothers' confession the afternoon before, everything had been moving at breakneck pace. She needed a few hours to catch her breath and make a plan, and Dimitri's presence was unsettling in a way she couldn't define.

"So I'll see you this evening, then," he said, and she nodded.

When the door finally closed, she collapsed onto the bed with a sigh. She had meant to only lie down for a moment, but the mattress was deliciously soft—without being too soft—and the pillow was like floating on a cloud. Before she knew it, she was waking from a nap.

"Goodness!" She yawned and stretched, forcing herself off the bed. "I'm turning into Daphne."

Thank goodness she hadn't let her friend trial any of the beds in the manor. She never would have managed to pry her away from the place.

She ate the unappetizing food she'd brought and unpacked her things slowly. It seemed unnecessary given all the luxuries the room had already supplied, but she didn't know what else to do. And besides, there were some items you didn't want supplied by a magical entity—whether it had consciousness or not.

When she had everything arranged and rearranged to her liking, she peered out the large window at the lush gardens behind the manor. She would have liked to explore them, but she guessed Dimitri would disapprove.

Sighing, she turned back to the room and noticed a book she could have sworn hadn't been on the bedside table earlier. She picked it up, exclaiming in delight at the beautiful gold foil and edging.

It was a book of Sovaran tales, and she opened it with interest. She had heard a lot about Oakden from Daphne, but she knew far less about Sovar. But ever since Avery had been past with her cart full of Sovaran glass wonders, Rosalie had been wanting to learn more about the neighboring kingdom.

The chair beside the window proved as comfortable as the bed, and before she knew it the sun was sinking below the trees, sending shadows stretching across the floor.

Rosalie stretched, glad it was finally time to leave the room.

She hurried out, not bothering to close the curtains or light the fire. She would worry about those details later.

She did remember to lock the door, however.

Rosalie hurried down the stairs, only to stand uncertainly in the entryway. Perhaps she should have spent the afternoon touring the castle instead of reading. At the very least she should have asked directions to the dining room. As it was, she only knew the locations of their two bedchambers and the large sitting room to her right.

"Ready to eat?" Dimitri asked from behind her, and for once the sound of his voice was welcome to her ears.

She spun to face him, smiling at his outrageously shaggy appearance. She was adjusting to it far quicker than she had expected.

"I checked the kitchen earlier this afternoon." He rubbed his hands together. "Fresh supplies had appeared, and there was already a pot boiling on the stove. I think we're in for a treat."

Rosalie grinned back, accepting the exaggerated arm he offered her.

"Thank you, My Lord," she said primly, and he smiled down at her.

She smiled back, noting that his eyes were still visible. They, at least, hadn't changed at all.

"Remember, you mustn't be too agreeable," he chided as he led her through a door located behind the stairs.

She frowned up at him, the expression melting away when she saw his eyes were laughing at her.

"Ah, that's right," she said. "I mustn't forget my role."

"I've chosen a smaller dining room for us," he said apologetically as he let go of her arm to open a door and usher her through. "The main one is enormous. The idea of eating there on my own felt ridiculous and would only be slightly less so with two of us."

"This is just perfect." Rosalie looked around the cozy room with approval.

A fire danced in the hearth, driving off the autumn chill from the evening air, and a sturdy walnut dining table took up most of the room. It might be the manor's smaller dining room, but the table was still larger than the one she ate around in the cottage with her whole family.

Dimitri bowed her into a chair to the right of the table's head before taking the seat at the head for himself. Their positions reminded Rosalie that he was hosting her in his home, and she resolved to be more polite in future—except when acting a role for the Legacy, of course.

The door behind them opened, and two plates floated into the room, their contents hidden by domed silver covers. Rosalie blinked in surprise. Would she ever adjust to the power the Legacy was throwing at the manor?

She restrained her impatience as the plate gently floated down to its place in front of her. When both plates were in place, she and Dimitri looked at each other, grinning as they pulled off the covers in unison.

Rosalie stared down at the plate's contents.

"It's not exactly what I was expecting," Dimitri said after an extended silence. He prodded at a soggy, boiled carrot.

Rosalie couldn't have agreed more. She had been expecting a delicious feast, but the food on her plate looked barely edible.

"Maybe the Legacy is just out of practice?" Dimitri suggested hopefully.

Rosalie snorted. "I'm not sure that's reassuring."

"I'm just clinging to the hope it might get better." Dimitri popped a piece of meat in his mouth and chewed it with a cheery expression.

Rosalie narrowed her eyes as she assessed his face. She was getting a little better at reading his emotions, even without access to his chiseled features. But she wasn't sure if the meat was truly the more appetizing portion of the meal or if he was just putting a good face on the situation.

Her frown deepened. He was probably trying to fool her into tasting it herself.

He returned her suspicious look with an encouraging one. "That's just the right look! Why don't you flip the table next?"

Rosalie almost choked on the bite she'd finally put in her mouth. When she recovered, she shook her head. "You want me to flip the table over soggy vegetables?"

He grinned widely—a disconcerting expression on his new face. "Make sure the Legacy knows just how furious you are about being imprisoned here. We need somewhere to go, after all. Think how much it will be touched when you go from flipping the table to laughing with me."

Rosalie raised an eyebrow. "And how long will that take?"

"Oh...two or three days? I'm a very charming fellow, you know, despite the fur."

Rosalie snorted.

"You keep telling yourself that," she muttered. But she had to admit, he'd been nothing but considerate since she'd arrived at the manor. She had even been a little charmed when he'd jokingly held out his arm to lead her through to the meal.

She shook herself, her fears from the night before returning to her mind. She couldn't allow the Legacy's tricks to affect her emotions.

CHAPTER 17
DIMITRI

Somehow Rosalie seemed much less put off by his new appearance than Dimitri had feared. He had been sorry to spend the day alone after her arrival, but at least their meal together had gone well, despite the disappointing food.

It gave him courage to take action first thing the next morning. He didn't want to let another whole day pass him by. So as soon as he'd finished a breakfast tray in his room, he dressed and presented himself at her door.

She answered his knock quickly, a smile on her face. She was also dressed for the day with a tray of empty dishes behind her.

"You woke to breakfast too?" he asked.

She nodded and laughed. "It was much more appetizing than last night's meal, thankfully." She glanced at the banked fire in her grate. "The Legacy really is amazing. I came back yesterday evening to find the curtains pulled and a fire blazing. Even the bedcovers were pulled back. It's a pity it can't seem to cook."

"Let us take hope from the breakfast," Dimitri said. "We may yet get an edible evening meal." He hesitated, afraid she would refuse his next request. But she seemed in a brighter mood than the day before, so he forged on. "I wondered if you'd like to explore the grounds with me. It's a beautiful day, and we don't know how many more of those we'll get with winter approaching."

"Oh yes!" Rosalie said immediately. "I was gazing longingly out my window yesterday, but I didn't think you'd approve of me exploring on my own."

Relief filled Dimitri. She wasn't going to be entirely reckless, then. He'd found it hard to sleep knowing she had the chest of coins in the room with her. Every night sound and creak of the manor had sent him starting awake.

But he had still woken with energy for the day. Having company in the manor made all the difference. Waking two doors down from Rosalie had felt entirely different from waking alone in the vast building.

He led Rosalie out a back door, exiting directly into the vast grounds that stretched behind the building, out of sight of the road.

"I've never been back here," Rosalie said softly, gazing around with wide eyes.

The excessive abundance of roses was missing from the back gardens, presumably because they would do no good for luring travelers. But rose bushes were still dotted around in picturesque locations, perfectly balanced with the sculpted greenery and the well-placed trees. Like the trees in the front, the ones before them were all in both full bloom and full fruit, and Dimitri plucked a mandarin from one they passed and presented it to her.

She peeled it slowly, popping the portions into her mouth one at a time and making a humming noise that warmed his insides.

"I grew up in Glandore," she said, "but I still can't help marveling at this garden. Our harvests are plentiful, but we don't usually see so much fruit on the cusp of winter."

"Then imagine how I feel!" Dimitri turned to look back at the manor. "I know the Legacy is causing us significant problems." He glanced sideways at her. "And it has caused your family greater ones still. But it's useful for some things. The manor is larger than I expected and seems to have been abandoned for a long time. Without the Legacy, I would have neither the ability nor the funds to restore it."

"Do you think your grandfather knew the Legacy would preserve it when he left?" Rosalie asked, gazing at the building alongside him.

How had his grandfather felt when he left it for the last time? The emotions overwhelmed Dimitri, and he looked at the ground.

"I think he was probably in too much pain to care," he said. "I think he just needed to get away from the memories."

Rosalie fell silent at his raw answer. He wanted to tell her the full story, wanted to share everything he had found. But he was nervous about her reaction. Surely she would notice the parallels between his mother's story and her own.

"Oh look!" she cried, pointing at a stunningly crafted statue tucked away in a hidden nook of the garden.

He followed her over to examine it, the moment for sharing past. Now that it was gone, he couldn't decide if he was glad or regretful that he'd missed the opportunity.

Rosalie bent over to examine a detail on the statue, obscuring her face. He still heard her, however, as she muttered, "Coward!"

"Excuse me?" He flushed despite the protest. How had she known about the fear that was holding him back?

"Cowardly lobster! Errant noodle! Loitering peacock!" The voice spoke again, and this time it was obvious the speaker wasn't Rosalie. He should have recognized its avian nature at the first word.

Rosalie straightened and scowled toward the nearest tree. "Every history book they read us as children said the talking birds were a delight and a solace to the merchant's daughter during her time in the Beast's castle. They were basically her friends. So was it the history books that got it wrong or the Legacy? Because the ones we have are nothing but nuisances."

"Get lost!" she called into the tree.

"Blasted spinster!" the bird squawked back.

Rosalie propped her hands on her hips, facing off against the bird with narrowed eyes.

"Recalcitrant canary!"

"Mediocre chucklehead!"

"Pea-brained pigeon!"

"Colossal gadabout!" It flapped its wings as if particularly pleased with that effort.

Dimitri looked at Rosalie with wide eyes, but she burst into laughter.

"It's a game I like to play with them," she told him before calling to the parrot. "Be off with you now. Poor Dimitri isn't used to you ridiculous creatures."

The bird fluffed itself up, making a call that sounded disconcertingly like a chuckle.

"Yes, yes, I know you're very pleased with yourself," Rosalie said. "But we're trying to enjoy a nice morning here."

"*Very* nice," the bird said with another cackle. "But nicer for him or for you?"

Rosalie flushed, her mouth dropping open and her eyes darting everywhere but Dimitri.

"They really are a nuisance," she muttered.

"They can actually converse?" Dimitri asked, staring at the parrot who had begun preening.

Rosalie also looked up at the bird. "I often exchange insults with them, but a response that complex is new. It must be from the strength of the Legacy here." She frowned thoughtfully, whatever discomfort she'd felt earlier forgotten. "I wonder if it really understands us or if it's just a trick of the Legacy?"

"Nasty girl!" the parrot called. "Lovely prince!"

Dimitri laughed. "It seems to like me more than you. Do you think that's because you insulted it, or does the Legacy like me better?"

"Hmm..." She looked at him with a teasing challenge

in her eyes. "How much did it improve your room?" She waited expectantly.

When Dimitri winced, she crowed triumphantly. "Ha! I knew it. Of course the Legacy likes me best."

She grinned at him, and he grinned back.

"Kiss!" the parrot called loudly. "Smoochy kiss!"

Rosalie gave an outraged growl and stalked toward the tree. "I'm going to pluck out all your feathers!" she yelled up at the bird, although Dimitri caught the flushed warmth in her cheeks.

He was still fighting back the flush in his own cheeks as she hiked up her skirts and gripped the lowest branch. By the time he realized she truly meant to climb the tree, she was already halfway up.

The bird watched her from one beady eye until she reached his branch. The moment her hand gripped it, he took wing, cackling down at her as she swung herself up to sit where he had been. She shook her fist at him as he flew away.

But she was smiling as she swung her legs, gazing across the garden from her elevated position.

"I didn't realize just how much land was attached to the manor," she called down to him. "It's beautiful."

He gazed up at her from the base of the tree. "Are you planning to stay up there?"

"Why?" She grinned down at him. "Will you bring me a pillow if I decide to sleep here?"

"No, I'll make a nest of them at the bottom for when you roll out."

She wrinkled her nose. "Spoilsport!"

"If you want to exchange insults, you'll need to call the parrot back." He held up his arms invitingly.

He had meant it half in jest, but to his surprise, she didn't hesitate. Sliding straight out of the tree, she dropped confidently into his waiting arms. He caught her around the thighs with ease, supporting her weight as he gazed up at her.

She quirked an eyebrow at him, and he quickly relaxed his hold, letting her slide down to land gently on the ground. For a second they stayed there, their bodies face-to-face and his arms wrapped around her.

He could feel the warmth of her like a burning furnace, and he wanted to tighten his hold and press her firmly against him. But the strange, uncomfortable feel of the hair that covered him made him let go and step back instead. No girl would want to be held close by someone the Legacy had turned into a Beast. And Rosalie in particular had an aversion to the Legacy. She hadn't been fond of him before, but she had to be even less so now that he was a constant reminder of it.

If he wasn't careful, he was going to forget that Rosalie was only playacting falling in love with him. She was there to save her family, and he couldn't cross the line.

He cleared his throat. "Shall we have a look at the orange orchard?"

Rosalie didn't respond immediately. She was regarding him strangely, as if surprised by her own thoughts—whatever they might be. He wished—intensely—that he could read them, just for a moment.

But it was probably for the best that he didn't know her reaction to his nearness.

He gestured in the direction of the orchard, and she started, nodding and averting her face. He walked beside her in silence, heading for the trees that stretched along the northern side of the manor. He wished they hadn't started on such poor terms—wished the Legacy hadn't gotten between them from the moment they met. If she could have met him as just Dimitri, not the man connected with the abandoned manor, would she have seen him differently?

His face was directed ahead, but all his focus was on the small frame of the woman beside him. Thanks to his concentration, he nearly missed the sound of hushed voices from the orchard ahead.

Whisking his arm around Rosalie's waist, he spun behind the last of the tall hedges in one smooth movement, pulling her with him. She looked up at him wide-eyed, but she didn't make a sound. Had she heard the intruders as well?

For a moment her nearness made his thoughts stutter and disappear, his whole focus on the soft feel of her waist and her eyes looking up at him. Then his ears caught another sound, snapping his attention back to the lurking danger.

He raised a finger to his lips, inclining his head in the direction of the orchard, but she was already nodding. They both went still, straining to hear more.

"This one is locked too," a man said with a quiet grunt. "That's the sixth locked window. How serious do you think Jace was about not leaving any sign we were here?"

"Given the potential payday?" a second man replied. "I'd say very serious."

The first man grunted again.

Dimitri met Rosalie's eyes and mouthed *scouts*. She nodded agreement. He tried to remember if he'd locked the door behind them. He was fairly sure he'd been distracted by Rosalie's presence and had forgotten.

"Maybe we should have come at night after all," the second man said.

"You think they wouldn't be locked then?" the first man asked sarcastically. "Now was our most likely chance of finding something open. Besides, the whole point is to get a glimpse of her so we can confirm to Jace that she's here."

The second man chuckled. "Getting a sight of the gold and jewels would do just as well, I'd say."

"I don't know," the first man said doubtfully. "If it was anyone else...but the boss is funny about that girl. I've heard they have a history, and you saw him with her."

Dimitri's arm tightened around Rosalie's waist, a reminder that he was still holding her. He wanted to grasp her tighter—to never let her go—but he forced himself to drop his arm.

His other hand had strayed to his sword hilt, but when he looked down at it, all he could see was the hair pouring out of his shirt cuff. There were only two men out there, and Dimitri was confident in his ability to deal with them in any ordinary situation. But if he confronted them, they would know in a glance that he had turned into a Beast. Jace would have all the information he needed.

Jace's men couldn't be allowed to see Rosalie either, since that was their purpose in lurking around the manor in the first place. But how could he scare the men off if neither of them could be seen?

A rustle of leaves beside them made him jump. A flash of color followed as a parrot fluttered its wings. It cocked its head and regarded them through one bright, beady eye.

Rosalie's eyes narrowed, and she glanced between the arguing intruders and the bird. When she looked at Dimitri, she raised her eyebrows in a silent question, a mischievous smile on her lips.

Unfortunately he had no idea what wild scheme she had in mind, so he could only stare back blankly. She moved away from him, tiptoeing toward the bird with a finger pressed to her lips.

It continued to regard her quietly, making Dimitri wonder if it really did understand. When she reached it, Rosalie pointed in the direction of the arguing men and then at her own throat.

"Will you help us, Sir Parrot?" she whispered. "Help us defend the castle from marauders! I'll lead them to the willow. Then it will be your turn."

The bird fluffed up its feathers and launched into the air. Dimitri sighed. He wasn't sure what use the parrot could have been anyway.

But when Rosalie crept back to his side, she was smiling. He smiled back instinctively, although he didn't know what she was so happy about.

"Come on," she whispered as she slid her hand into his and grasped it.

She didn't flinch at the feel of the strange hair covering him, and he gripped her back strongly. It had been years since anyone had held his hand, and his insides warmed at the contact. There was something about the gesture that conveyed affectionate trust, and while Rosalie might have done it without thought or meaning, his chest still leaped in response.

She tugged him after her, only stopping when they reached the end of the hedge furthest from the intruders. She gave him one last mischievous smile before raising her voice to call loudly.

"Come on!" she cried clearly, her voice ringing across the garden. "Let's go this way!"

The muted sound of the intruders instantly stopped.

Rosalie's hand tightened, and she pulled him past the edge of the hedge, running for a group of nearby bushes. She plunged into the middle of them with abandon, dragging him with her. Not worrying about the branches tearing at her dress or the leaves catching in her hair, she pulled them through to the other side.

"Can you hear them?" she whispered, and he strained to listen.

The men's voices had ceased, but he caught the crunch of their feet on the gravel as they attempted to creep beside the carefully trimmed hedge. He raised his eyebrows at Rosalie, and she nodded.

"Look at that statue!" she called loudly and pulled him out of the bush.

They made another mad dash across open ground, plunging into a small cluster of trees. The trunks grew close together, providing just enough protection to keep them out of sight. Rosalie looked up at him and clapped her free hand over her mouth, holding back a giggle.

He grinned, shaking his head. She really was irrepressible. Did she feel no fear?

"It was this way," one of the men said quietly from the edge of the bush. "Can you see a statue anywhere?"

"A fountain!" Rosalie called again, startling Dimitri. "Just past the willow!" She pointed through the trunks to an ancient willow. Its thick, trailing branches created a dense shield, although it didn't extend all the way to the ground.

"Your turn," she whispered in his ear, her breath sending shivers across his skin. "Hopefully the bird will do its job, and then you can scare them away. Just make sure you keep your face and hands out of sight." She shoved him in the direction of the willow.

He ran, trying to make as little noise as possible. He didn't quite understand her plan, but he grasped enough to conceal himself behind the willow's draping branches.

He could barely see anything through the trailing leaves, but he managed to make out two shapes approaching the willow slowly.

"Careful now," one of them murmured. "We don't want to be spotted."

"We just need to get a glimpse of her so we can be sure before we tell the boss she's here," the other man said. "If we report it wrong, he'll dock our pay for sure. There's no reason to be so worried. We haven't broken in anywhere. Even if they catch us, who's to say we're not locals come to have a poke around the beautiful garden?"

The other snorted, and Dimitri was tempted to do the same. From what he'd seen of Jace's men, none of them were the sort to stop and smell the roses, and he doubted anyone would be foolish enough to think it.

But what was Rosalie wanting him to do? And what did she think the bird was going to do?

A flash of color exploded from one of the willow's branches, flying toward the men in a rustle of fluttering green leaves.

"A beautiful willow!" it called in the disconcerting impression of Rosalie's voice that it had used when it called Dimitri a coward.

The closest man shouted, throwing up his hands to shield his face.

"A bird!" the other exclaimed in disgust. "Was it one of those wretched creatures the whole time?"

"Cluttered loafbrain!" the parrot screeched in its normal voice. "Scruffy porcupine! Bedraggled pincushion!" It added its chuckling cry as it circled their heads just out of reach.

"That filthy creature fooled us on purpose!" the first man howled.

Dimitri recognized his cue. He stepped forward, stopping just behind the willow's leaves. They still concealed his upper body, but his legs were left exposed. Thankfully, his boots and clothes concealed the changes to his body.

"I suggest you leave my garden immediately," he

growled loudly and slowly, letting the threat hang in the air.

Both men flinched violently, one giving a shout of surprise as he spun to see Dimitri lurking there, mostly out of view.

Dimitri drew his sword with a clear ringing noise, holding it in front of him so the blade pierced the leaves.

"If you don't want to go, I'd be more than happy to make you into an actual pincushion," he said, letting a thread of dark humor trace his words.

A light appeared behind the men, shining directly on the leaves in front of him. He nearly flinched, only just keeping his posture steady and his stance threatening. He didn't want to ruin the effect Rosalie had orchestrated.

"Leave now," he repeated. "And tell Jace that if he wants to see his men again, he should keep them off my land."

The mention of Jace was the final straw. The men looked at each other and without a word turned and fled. Dimitri stayed still, waiting. He didn't want to risk revealing himself too soon.

After several drawn out minutes, the parrot flew back into view. "All clear!" it called.

He stepped through the willow's leaves. Had the bird really assisted them in their plan? As impossible as it seemed, he couldn't deny the creature's involvement, so he called his thanks in its direction.

The bird dipped a wing and flew away.

Rosalie met him beside the willow, her eyes alight

with laughter and her cheeks flushed with triumph. Dimitri seized her hand, wrapping his fingers firmly around hers and pulling her along as he ran. She didn't protest, seizing her skirts in her other hand and keeping pace behind him.

He led her straight to the manor. Only when they were safely inside and the door was locked behind them did he let her hand go.

She laughed a little wildly. "That was fun!"

"Fun?" He stared at her.

"You should have seen their faces!" She grinned up at him, but when he didn't laugh back, she sighed. "It's not good they were here, though." Her nose scrunched, her eyes turning dark. "What do you think they'll tell Jace?"

"Not the truth, I'm guessing. You heard what they said about having their pay docked. I doubt they'll be admitting they were fooled by a bird and caught by me before they saw anything of significance. I'm hoping they'll tell him nothing has changed yet. It's a fairly safe lie. Even if Jace eventually learns the true state of affairs here, they can always claim the changes happened after their visit. Even we didn't know how quickly the Legacy would move at the beginning."

Rosalie nodded. "Jace spent months preparing everything before he robbed my family. He knows how to be patient."

Dimitri hated the shadow that crossed her eyes when she mentioned her and Jace's shared past. He hated that they shared anything at all.

"You were brilliant," she said, sending his thoughts in a much more pleasant direction. "You were a perfect mix of creepy and threatening. The sword showing through the leaves was already good, but when that light lit up the leaves and made your eyes flash, it was perfection! The rest of your face was in shadow, so you were terrifying without showing any hint of the Beast."

Her expression turned confused. "But where did the light come from?"

"It wasn't you?" He hadn't known how she'd done it, but he'd assumed it had to be her.

She shook her head.

"The Legacy, then?" he suggested.

"Do you really think the Legacy would help us put on a show for Jace's men?" Rosalie asked.

"What else could it have been?"

"True," Rosalie said slowly. "I just don't remember anything like that in the original history."

"You're more of an expert on the histories than me." Dimitri shrugged. "I'm just glad the Legacy has decided to help us instead of hindering us."

Rosalie bit her lip. "I suppose so. I just don't like anything I can't explain. It makes me nervous that we're missing something."

"They were the ones to miss something," Dimitri said. "I think we're allowed to be happy about that. Hopefully it's all turned out for the best, and we've bought ourselves some breathing room as far as Jace is concerned."

He meant his words, but he was also aware the

morning could have gone significantly worse. As enjoyable as their walk had been at the beginning, it wasn't a good idea to spend further time out in the open. And he certainly wasn't going to leave any doors unlocked again.

CHAPTER 18

ROSALIE

When Rosalie sank into her beautiful, soft bed that night, she had to admit that Dimitri handled himself well in a crisis. And when he had wrapped a protective arm around her, she had felt safe and sheltered, just like previously.

She wasn't accustomed to the feeling of safety. Even before her family's troubles, she had always been bracing herself for disaster. Ever since her brothers had been born, she had lived with fear of the Legacy as a constant backdrop.

But now the worst of the Legacy's threats had all occurred. And she was finding, to her surprise, that there was freedom in letting her old fears go. She had been so sure that Dimitri's arrival spelled fresh disaster, and yet she couldn't remember the last time she had felt so safe with someone.

Every time he saw a threat from Jace, he acted quickly and decisively. It was more reassuring than she'd expected. She spent her days doing everything in her power to shield her family from the consequences of her mistake, and she was exhausted. She didn't want to acknowledge it, but it was pleasant to share the burden of Jace with someone.

They had won a minor victory in the garden, but he was still a threat. She trusted that Daphne and the triplets would have paid the debt already, but she didn't trust Jace. She wished she had some certainty that it had all gone smoothly.

Although perhaps the scouts were a sign of the successful repayment. Had Jace sent them because he was suspicious about how Vernon had managed to repay the debt? Rosalie brightened. It was a comforting thought, and it made it easier to drift into sleep.

The next morning, she woke again to a breakfast tray on the small table beside her bed. It included a steaming mug of hot chocolate, and she hummed appreciatively as she sipped the sweet, creamy drink. It had been a long time since she had drunk chocolate.

She and Dimitri had reluctantly agreed they would need to stay out of the garden for the time being which meant she was limited to the inside of the manor. But the building was so large it didn't seem like much of a hardship. She was looking forward to a day of indoor exploration.

A steady knock sent her hurrying for her bedchamber door. She swung it open to find Dimitri smiling at her, just as he had on the previous morning.

"Would you like to explore the manor today?" he

asked. "I haven't had a chance to uncover all the changes myself yet."

"Yes, please!" she said promptly. She'd been planning to explore, but it made her feel better to have permission before she poked around someone else's home.

As they fell into step down the corridor, she realized how comfortable it already felt to walk beside him. He was so much taller than her, but they matched rhythms easily, as if they had been walking together for years.

She glanced sideways at him. He still had the strange Beast appearance the Legacy had given him, but she no longer saw the Legacy when she looked at him. And any similarity to Jace was entirely obscured. He had become merely Dimitri.

It was a comfortable feeling, but also oddly disquieting. She wasn't yet ready to explore it too closely.

They reached the entryway, and she turned away from the door that led to the sitting room she had already visited. The opposite wall held a similar door, so she crossed to it first, pulling it open ahead of Dimitri.

"Oh!" She stared at the room beyond. She'd been looking for a distraction, but she hadn't expected something so startling.

"This is new," Dimitri said wryly from behind her.

She nodded silently. That much seemed obvious.

They stood together in quiet admiration. Enormous windows ran along one of the walls, letting in plenty of light and allowing a view of the gardens at the front of the manor. It was a double story room, and the windows stretched from the ground to far above her head. Even though she'd never been inside the room before, Rosalie thought she would have noticed the windows from the outside if they'd existed previously.

"Was it a library before, at least?" she asked.

"It was." He stepped forward and ran his hand along a shelf. "But it didn't have nearly as many books. And it definitely didn't have the chairs."

Rosalie's eyes jumped over the various features of the room, unsure where to rest. The Legacy had filled seemingly endless rows of shelves with books. The entire wall opposite the windows was covered in them, ladders giving access to the higher shelves. But they weren't ordinary ladders. The wooden poles that made up the sides were made from living wood, leaves and roses sprouting along their lengths.

But the rose theme didn't end there. The remaining books were scattered across the center of the room in short, half-height shelves each grouped with a huddle of chairs and small tables. The tables held lamps that shed enticing light in a soft rose color, emanating from lamp covers shaped like roses. And most remarkable of all were the soft armchairs.

Shaped like an actual rose, they were made of layers of soft material resembling petals. Positioned at an angle, the center of the rose was hollowed out, allowing someone to nestle within its heart. If someone had taken an actual rose and opened the center so a tiny fairy could use it as a seat, it would have looked like a miniature version of the chairs scattered across the manor's library. Even the base was made of a single large green stem instead of four legs.

It sprouted from a flat circle that allowed it to support the necessary weight, although it still looked like an impossible piece of furniture to Rosalie.

"Do you think we can actually sit in them?" she whispered.

"I don't see why not. The Legacy made them for us, didn't it?"

She gave a small squeak and rushed to the closest one. Sliding in was easier than she had imagined, and as she sank into the center, she sighed in bliss.

"I thought lying on my pillow was like floating on a cloud," she said, "but I was wrong. *This* is like lying on a cloud."

"I didn't realize you had so much experience with clouds," Dimitri said dryly.

She ignored him, too delighted with the chair to let anything dampen her enthusiasm. "It's much more supportive than I imagined as well," she said. "I think I could read in this chair all day."

He smiled. "So you like to read?"

"No!" Rosalie said quickly, earning a surprised look.

She bit her lip, looking about at their surroundings. "Actually," she said in a rush, "I do like to read."

The statement came out defiantly, and she could see from Dimitri's expression that he was bemused. But he had no idea what it had cost her to say.

"I've always insisted I don't like to read," she told him softly. "But I still remember the thrill the first time I managed to puzzle out an entire page on my own. It was like unlocking the door to a broader, richer life. Except I was convinced I had to hand the key back. I told everyone I didn't care for reading and made myself avoid it as much as possible."

"But why?" he asked softly, clearly confused but recognizing what the confession meant to her.

"Because the original merchant's daughter loved to read. All the histories mention it. When her family lost everything, her sisters mourned their jewels and their dresses and their suitors, but the youngest mourned the loss of her father's books."

Dimitri regarded her steadily but silently, allowing her to rest for a moment with the words she'd spoken. She could have hugged him for it except she didn't want to get out of her chair.

"I'm sorry," he said sincerely, gingerly sliding into the chair across from hers.

Her mouth twitched at the sight of his fur-covered body—still dressed as impeccably as always but now enveloped in an enormous rose.

He looked down and grimaced. "It suits you better than me."

"You look charming," she assured him with a grin. "And thank you. I know I've been doing nothing but blame you since you arrived at the manor. But I do know none of this is actually your fault."

"Any more than it's your fault," he said quickly. "I resent that my mother raised me in ignorance, depriving me of family in order to keep me away from the Legacy. But at least it allowed me to grow up with the Legacy as nothing but an unseen weight on my shoulders. So much of your life has been shaped by your struggle against it. You were so busy not being the original merchant's daughter that you had little space left to be yourself. You deserve better, Rosalie. You deserve to be truthful about who you are."

She stared at him. He had understood exactly. No one had ever understood it as quickly and completely as he had. Was it because his life had also been shaped by the Legacy, although in the opposite way?

"Yes, exactly," she said softly. "But I'm sorry for what was done to you as well." She hesitated. "Have you found any answers in this library? Not about the Legacy but about your family, I mean?" It might be intrusive to ask, but she couldn't help herself.

"Actually, I did find something," he said. "But not in here. My mother left a letter for my grandfather when she departed for the mountains, and it was in her old room, waiting for me. I think he left it there for me to find."

"A letter?" Rosalie asked softly. She could see from his face how significant it was for him to share with her, and she wanted to tread carefully.

He drew two folded pieces of paper from his pocket, smoothing them out carefully. He didn't meet her eyes as he chuckled uncomfortably.

"I've started carrying it around with me which is foolish. I suppose I thought..." He trailed off, and she had no idea how to finish the sentence.

But when he held the papers out to her, she forgot everything else.

"Are you sure?" she asked before reaching for them.

When he nodded, she accepted both sheets and eagerly scanned the elegant cursive script. Her eyes widened as she read, and when she finished, she looked up at him in silence. He had already mentioned that the Legacy couldn't influence emotions or control actions, so he understood the reality behind his mother's words. He knew she had been delusional, clinging to a foolish belief to avoid facing her husband's betrayal.

Rosalie's hand trembled as she returned the letter to Dimitri. He carefully folded it again and replaced it in his pocket.

"She wasn't brave like you," he said in a rush. "She wasn't strong like you either. I know you would never run away like she did, but please..." His voice faltered. "Please don't think too badly of her."

He finally looked at her, and the pain in his eyes pierced her chest. He saw his mother's weaknesses with clear eyes, but he loved her regardless. Of course he did. And he had just lost her.

Part of Rosalie wanted to speak quick, glib reassurances. But he had just told her to be truthful about her own feelings, and she wanted to do that now with him.

"I do resent her a little," she said slowly. "I resent her on your behalf, and a little on my own. She chose to run from her own pain, but she caused others so much pain in the process—you, your grandfather, even me, someone who hadn't even been born when she wrote this letter. If she had remained and built a new life, you would never have become a prince living alone in a castle, and the

Legacy wouldn't have latched on to the two of us like it has."

"I'm sorry," he said hoarsely, but she shook her head.

"I wasn't finished. I resent her a little, but I understand her as well. Better than you seem to think." She leaned back and looked at the ceiling, fighting back tears. When she regained control, she looked at him again and forced a weak smile. "I know the temptation to excuse my own weaknesses rather than face the full force of them. It's a powerful temptation."

"But you don't give in to it," Dimitri said.

"Don't I?" Rosalie looked away, afraid of what he might see if he looked too deep inside her.

"No one's perfect, Rosalie," Dimitri said. "Everyone stumbles sometimes. But you had your heart broken, and you didn't run away and abandon your family. You're still here right now, fighting to free both yourself and them from the Legacy's grip."

"Your mother didn't abandon her whole family," Rosalie said. "She didn't flee only for her own sake. She left hoping to protect the family member most important to her."

"Protection that sat as heavily as a vest of stone," he said with a sigh. But she could read appreciation in his eyes. She hadn't excused his mother, but neither had she vilified her. It was the truth of Rosalie's feelings, and apparently it was enough for Dimitri.

"Thank you," he said softly, and she had to blink rapidly and tip her head back against the soft petals of her chair again.

When she finally mastered her emotions and looked back, Dimitri was gone. She sat alone in the library, ensconced in a giant rose, as the day's light waxed and waned. When she finally stood on her own feet again, something had shifted. She was no longer the merchant's youngest daughter, named for a rose. She was merely Rosalie.

Whether they succeeded or failed in the castle, the Legacy had run its course with her. Dimitri had spoken of a vest of stone, but she had worn the Legacy like shackles. But no longer. With Dimitri's help, she had stepped free of them.

The day's efforts might not have been physical, but she felt a tiredness in her limbs regardless. As she walked toward the door, she wished aloud that her bed chamber was on the other side. The thought of stairs seemed daunting.

Pulling the door open, she blinked at the sight of purple and gold. Had she somehow sleepwalked from the library to her room? She twisted around to peer behind her. She was still standing on the threshold of the library, as she had thought. But her bedchamber didn't open off the library. They weren't even on the same floor.

Cautiously she stepped through the impossible doorway, finding herself in her bedchamber, just as her eyes had promised. Looking back, she could still see the library, as if the two rooms were joined after all.

She closed the door, her hand moving stiffly as her mind struggled to grasp what was happening. Had she fallen asleep in the rose chair, and she was about to awaken from a dream?

She counted out five seconds before pulling the door back open. The corridor outside her room was there just as usual. She pinched herself, but she didn't seem to be asleep.

A slow smile spread over her face. "Now that," she said aloud, "is a very handy feature."

They continued to eat each evening meal together, and the food grew progressively better. Dimitri kept insisting he had been right about the Legacy needing practice, but Rosalie was unconvinced.

"I still think you're humanizing it too much," she protested as they ventured out to explore the manor for the third day in a row.

"Then how do you explain last night's scalloped potatoes?" he asked with the air of one delivering a winning argument.

"They *were* quite compelling." Rosalie hummed at the memory, and Dimitri laughed.

"Do you even realize you do that?" he asked.

"Do what?"

"Hum in appreciation of delicious food."

Rosalie flushed. "Do I?" No one had ever pointed it out before.

"Don't worry," he said. "It's charming."

She flushed and looked away. "What about that door over there?" she asked quickly. "Where does it go?"

Most of the rooms they had explored the day before had turned out to be bedchambers, but their patience had finally been rewarded with an incredible hothouse full of plants just as lush as the ones outside. It had been a happy find since the gardens were currently barred to them, and she was hoping for another equally exciting discovery.

Dimitri chuckled softly before giving the door a proper look. "You know," he said after a moment, "I can't remember. It must not have been something very memorable."

"But that was before." Rosalie's hand hovered over the handle, and she looked back at Dimitri, savoring the anticipation. "Who knows what marvel the Legacy has put in here now!"

He responded to her smiles as he always did, smiling back as if he couldn't help himself.

"Why don't you open it and find out?" he invited.

She turned the handle and pushed the door open, giving a dramatic flourish that died halfway as she saw the empty room on the other side.

"This is disappointing." She walked slowly inside anyway.

He followed, his brow creased. "I'm sure it wasn't empty before. I would have remembered that because there weren't any completely unfurnished rooms."

"So the Legacy emptied it?" Rosalie's interest returned. "Why would it do that unless it had some purpose for the space?"

She looked up and down the room again, finally

noticing one lone stack of furniture. But the padded chairs piled in one corner were hardly of interest. She examined the walls instead, frowning as she realized there were windows on both sides.

"Isn't that an internal wall?" She pointed at the row of windows that were covered with drawn curtains.

"Yes, you're right, it is," he said. "So where are those windows looking into?"

He pulled back the closest curtain, his hand still grasping it as he leaped back in startled astonishment. "What in the kingdoms?" he muttered.

"Is that...a theater?" Rosalie stepped up to the edge of the window and pressed her fingers against the glass.

Impossible as it seemed, the window appeared to reveal the inside of a lighted theater. The rows of padded seats were filled with audience members, but none of them appeared to notice the window behind them or the two people peering through it. She could only assume that was because none of it was real. It certainly looked real, however.

"Sitting here would feel just like attending the theater," she breathed. "How marvelous."

She ran down the wall, pulling back the curtains on the next interior window.

"An opera!" she cried, once she'd taken in the sight before her.

The high notes of the singer on stage rang through the room, the noise clashing with the actor who had begun the play's opening monologue in the first window. She moved on to the final set of curtains.

"An orchestra!" she called back to Dimitri as the sounds of the instruments mingled with the operatic singing and the declaiming actor who was still completing his monologue.

Dimitri clapped his hands to his head. "What a cacophony. I don't think you're supposed to open them all at once."

Rosalie grinned but obediently closed the curtains on the opera, cutting off the singing. Dimitri did the same for the play, leaving only a pleasant orchestral background to their conversation.

"It's a more marvelous entertainment room than anything I ever imagined!" Rosalie said.

"You've never heard of anything like it?" Dimitri asked. "If it's here now, there must have been something similar in the histories."

Rosalie hesitated, a distant memory sparking. "Actually," she said slowly. "I think I did read a mention of an entertainment room in the histories about the original Beast's castle. That part was full of nonsense about reflections on mirrors, so I didn't really pay much attention. I thought one of the original historians must have gotten fanciful, so I skipped right over it."

"You only used to pay attention to the bad bits, didn't you?" Dimitri accused.

"Not only the bad bits! Roses aren't bad, are they?"

"Certainly not to me." Dimitri smiled. "But you've never seemed taken with them."

Rosalie rolled her eyes. "It wasn't that I focused on the bad bits. I was interested in the relevant parts—the elements the Legacy kept recreating. I've never heard of it recreating an entertainment room like this."

"That does sound like you," Dimitri said. "Too practical for romance."

Rosalie looked away. She hadn't been too practical to fall for Jace and his deception.

"Let's watch the play," Dimitri said suddenly, pulling the curtain closed on the orchestra and moving down to open the first window.

He ushered her over to it, fetching two of the chairs from the stack in the corner. Rosalie watched him surreptitiously. Had he noticed and understood the dip in her mood?

It was kind of him to try to cheer her up if so. And even kinder to do it so subtly. Dimitri had been doing a lot of kind things since she came to the manor.

The play turned out to be even more entertaining than she'd hoped, and she laughed until her sides hurt. When it finished, they closed the curtain over the play's window and wandered from the room.

As they walked down yet another corridor, they fell into conversation. Ostensibly, they were still exploring, but they did little beyond poking their heads into the storage rooms, sitting rooms, and bed chambers they passed. Rosalie's main interest was the doors—she wanted to identify all the ones that could lead to more than one place, but so far she had only found three.

"What about your sisters?" Dimitri asked. "I don't think I've ever heard you talk about them."

"Violet and Heather?" Rosalie looked surprised. "Have I never mentioned them?"

"Certainly not by name." He hesitated. "Were they cruel to you?"

"Cruel? No, never!" Rosalie frowned before realizing the source of his misconception. "Oh, you're thinking of the merchant's family from the history. My sisters were nothing like the original older sisters. Violet and Heather were...like normal big sisters, I suppose."

"Since I don't have any siblings and grew up in a community with few children, I'm not sure I'm the best judge of normal."

She laughed. "There was an age gap between Heather and me, so I annoyed them a great deal. When I was very little, they doted on me, dressing me up and treating me like a live doll. But eventually I got old enough to protest such treatment and to have my own ideas about how we should play our games."

Dimitri grinned. He could no doubt imagine how Rosalie would have disliked being ordered around.

"But then Mother had the triplets, and my sisters soon realized I wasn't annoying at all," Rosalie said with smug satisfaction.

Dimitri laughed. "I can imagine."

"You probably can't." Rosalie's eyes had lost focus, and she could feel the fond smile on her face as they walked slowly down the latest corridor. "I don't think anyone can really be prepared for triplets until they experience them."

"So Violet and Heather were closer to each other than

to you. And now they've both married and moved to the same town?"

Rosalie nodded, refocusing on the conversation. "They married cousins, actually, and live next door to each other. I miss them sometimes, but I have Daphne, so I'm not lonely. Even when they still lived here, they tended to spend their time together, while I spent my time with Daphne. Since she's an only child, and her family lived so close, we basically became sisters."

"That would have made it easier when they moved," Dimitri murmured.

"Yes, I'm grateful they did move given how everything turned out," Rosalie said. "Actually, I think that's why I haven't mentioned them. Violet and Heather belong to my old life—when I was the daughter of the richest merchant in town and lived on the village square. They were never part of our current life in the cottage on the edge of town, so I'm rarely reminded of them." She looked down. "I wonder if they're hurt by that? We've been so busy trying to survive that I haven't really thought about it from their perspective."

"I'm sure they understand why you built a new life here instead of going to them," Dimitri said reassuringly. "They're probably grateful that you're protecting them from the Legacy. And I'm sure they're busy too. Do they have children of their own now?"

Rosalie brightened. "They do! And once this is all resolved, I'll be able to visit them again. Mother and Father will be so pleased."

"And your brothers, too, of course," Dimitri added

with a straight face. "I'm sure they would love to be swarmed with small children."

"Naturally," Rosalie agreed, equally seriously. "Once I move back home, I'm going to suggest Mother send them to our sisters for a couple of months to help with babysitting. Poor Violet and Heather must be exhausted, and the boys will only be underfoot while we're getting resettled."

A lamp sconce on the wall creaked abruptly—as random objects in the castle had a habit of doing. It distracted Rosalie enough that she only just caught the end of Dimitri's disturbed expression before he smoothed it out.

She frowned, trying to remember what she had said that might have bothered him. Was he concerned for her brothers?

"Don't worry," she said quickly. "I'm only joking. I wouldn't really do that. And I'm sure my sisters wouldn't want them even if we offered."

Dimitri smiled. "I don't know...It might do them some good after all the trouble they've caused."

"True," she said thoughtfully. "Maybe we should threaten it, at least. Just the possibility might be enough to scare them into line. And if it isn't, I'm sure Violet and Heather could put up with them for a week or two."

"Just make sure you don't mention that I had anything to do with the idea," he said, alarmed.

Rosalie laughed because it seemed entirely natural that Dimitri would remain a part of her and her family's life when she finally left the manor and returned home.

CHAPTER 19

DIMITRI

Dimitri woke to the same sense of anticipation that had greeted him every morning since Rosalie arrived at the manor. He hadn't dared hope he would get to spend all of every day with her. The original history had only talked about the Beast and the merchant's daughter sharing evening meals. But Rosalie always seemed so enthusiastic to see him, and he could never resist returning to find her each morning. And once he was by her side, he could never bring himself to leave just for the sake of the play they were enacting.

Being around Rosalie made him feel alive in a way he never had before. A future in Glandore was starting to feel real, and he had begun dreaming about how he would fill it.

Rosalie was still encouraging him to leave the manor, but for his own sake, not for the Legacy. She thought he should go to the capital to find his grandfather, and she had promised to get an address from her father. His heart had sunk the first time she mentioned it—he had thought they had moved past the issue of him leaving. But when she chatted away about the trip, various innocent comments made it clear she was assuming he would return. That realization changed his feelings, and he had become enthusiastic about the prospect of finding his grandfather. He was even eager to see the capital, at least once.

It was paradoxical to want to travel so far considering he could barely tear himself away from Rosalie for the night hours. But her energy was catching, and if he was going to plan a future, he needed first to establish his roots. He also needed to make sure his claim to the manor was secure.

Rosalie listened to him talk about his plans with almost as much enthusiasm as he felt. Her fire for life flowed out to everything she touched—she wasn't the type to selfishly hoard it away.

She was particularly enthused about his thoughts on how the manor could benefit the local region. She had suggestions of her own each time the topic came up, and he appreciated her input since she knew the area and its needs far better than he did. A banked fire seemed to have taken residence in his belly, giving off a warm glow whenever he thought about how well they worked as a team.

He stretched in bed for several minutes, thinking pleasantly about his plans for the day. The night before, over the evening meal, she had expressed interest in seeing the kitchen, and he had promised to take her in the morning. They had already explored the rest of the manor

—some sections many times over—but they hadn't ventured to the kitchen.

He had slept a little longer than normal, but he didn't think Rosalie would mind. She had stocked up on books from the library the day before, and he suspected she was happily reading while she ate her breakfast. Sure enough, when she came to her bedchamber door, he caught a glimpse of the teetering pile stacked on her bedside table.

"What?" she asked defiantly when she noticed the direction of his gaze. "I have to make up for lost time."

He laughed. "I'm not complaining. You can read as much as you like." He hesitated. "Did you want to keep reading now, or do you want to come see the kitchen?"

"The kitchen," she said without hesitation, making his heart warm. Had she realized she was choosing him?

They started walking together, the glow still filling him. "Before the Legacy started cooking for us, I'd barely worked out how to use half the items in the kitchen," he said. "It's clearly designed to be used by a team of people with far greater knowledge than me."

"Given the size of the main dining room, I'm not surprised," Rosalie said. "If they really used to have so many here for meals, they would have needed a huge team to feed them."

They descended the stairs, and Dimitri froze. The double front doors were always firmly closed, but now one of them was ajar. His hand went to the key in his pocket, but it was still there.

"Rosalie," he murmured, but she had already seen it too. She looked at him with wide eyes.

"Go back to your room and lock yourself in," he whispered, but she stubbornly shook her head.

"My room is the most dangerous place to be, remember?" She gave him a look that told him there was no chance he was winning the argument.

Quietly, he descended the remaining stairs. At the bottom, he paused, looking to all sides for any further sign of another person. There was none.

Walking swiftly across the large entryway, he examined the door. There was no indication of forced entry. If he didn't know better, he would suspect it of having been left open since the day before. But neither of them had used it since their adventure in the garden. It had been closed and locked the previous day, as it had been all the days before. At least as far as he knew.

He glanced at Rosalie. "You didn't open it this morning, did you? Or last night, perhaps?"

"I don't have a key." She patted her pocket. "All I have is the one for my room." She moved a step closer to him, her voice lowering as her eyes darted around the empty entryway. "Does that mean there's someone in here?"

"Possibly." He wanted to believe otherwise, but it was hard to come up with any other conclusion. "Either that or they already came and went." He looked at her more sharply. "Your room...?"

She shook her head. "Everything was normal in my room, and I didn't hear anything in the night."

"They still may have been and gone. There are other valuables to steal in the manor. We should..." He trailed off, not sure what to suggest.

It was a large building with an unnerving number of places where someone could be concealed. Even if they did a systematic search, they couldn't guarantee that the places they checked remained clear. An intruder could easily move around while they were searching somewhere else. Two people just weren't enough to effectively search the whole manor. And that was assuming they split up— something he wasn't willing to do.

"If it's an ordinary thief, they must surely have left by now," Rosalie said, showing remarkable calm given the situation. "They won't be looking for a confrontation. If it's Jace, on the other hand..." She frowned unhappily. "I don't think Jace will be cowering in a cupboard somewhere. He was brazen from the start, and his success with my family only seems to have made him more so."

"He's had a taste of wealth and power, and it's feeding his ego." Dimitri's hands balled into fists. He still felt angry every time he remembered the way Jace had looked at Rosalie, let alone the way he'd talked to her.

"So the question is," Rosalie said, "if you were Jace, where would you be?"

Dimitri suppressed his instinctive repulsion at the idea of thinking like Jace and forced himself to consider the matter objectively.

"The dining room," he concluded. "The main one."

Rosalie looked at him questioningly, and he shrugged. "You keep calling this a castle, but it isn't one, so we have no throne room. That enormous dining table seems like the closest equivalent."

Rosalie's nose wrinkled. "You think Jace is playing at

being lord of the manor? That sounds painfully accurate. Let's try there first."

She started in the direction of the dining hall, but he caught her arm, stopping her.

"Are you sure about this?" he asked. "You really want to confront him? We don't know how many men he has with him."

"What's the alternative? Lock ourselves in our rooms and never come out again? Abandon the manor and let him have everything?"

"We could go get help."

"Without even knowing for sure if he's here? Who would help us when he hasn't actually done anything to us yet?"

"You call abducting you nothing?" he asked hotly.

She shrugged. "He didn't hurt me, so we don't have any proof that ever happened. If we race into town and claim Jace is back, that he kidnapped me and now he's broken into the manor, it might bring people running. But if they then find that he's not here, it will make the whole story seem suspect. They'll think I'm jumping at shadows and exaggerating, and next time we ask for help, they'll be reluctant to come. We can't go and raise an army to defend the castle until we know for sure there's actually an invading force."

She grimaced. "I'm sure that's why Jace has been careful not to attract attention so far. He doesn't want to give us evidence until he's gotten what he wants and made it far away."

Dimitri frowned at her words. His gut feeling told him

that even if Jace got his hands on the gold, he wouldn't be that easy to shake off. But he didn't say it aloud.

"Maybe I should go on my own," he said instead. "We don't know how Jace will react if he sees you."

"If seeing me might put him off balance, that's a point of advantage to us. And even if not, it's better to have two than only one. So let's stop wasting time and find out who opened that door."

Dimitri hesitated a moment longer, frowning at the door. Should he lock it again or leave it ajar?

With a sigh he left it, turning to join Rosalie. If their intruder had reinforcements, he'd already had ample time to get them inside. Better to leave the exit open in case whoever it was decided to leave on their own. He would rather have half the castle pilfered than lock a threat inside with Rosalie.

They walked to the main dining room in tense silence. Neither of them had spent much time in the room since it contained little beside the enormous table and an equally long sideboard. They were both familiar with its location, however, and they entered the room at the same time.

"Well, well, well," an amused voice said slowly. "The master and mistress of the manor have finally arrived."

Jace lounged across the enormous carved chair at the head of the table, his leg flung across one of its arms. He clapped mockingly, his eyes sliding to Rosalie and their expression darkening slightly. "Someone's been keeping secrets, I see."

Dimitri stepped in front of Rosalie, one arm lifting

slightly in a shielding gesture. Jace's grin in response sent a shiver down Dimitri's back.

"I've been extraordinarily patient, don't you think?" Jace drawled. "But I thought it was time to have a look for myself. So kind of you to leave the door open for me."

Dimitri frowned. Jace had found the door open? That couldn't be right.

Jace stood in one swift motion, stepping toward them. Dimitri retreated further down the room, sweeping Rosalie behind him as he drew his sword.

Jace ignored the weapon, speaking to Rosalie over Dimitri's shoulder. "You're a resourceful girl, Rose."

Dimitri felt her shudder at the nickname.

"When your brothers brought me the coin, I didn't know what to think. But I see you did the sensible thing after all."

His eyes strayed to Dimitri, and he laughed. "It suits him, don't you think?"

"What are you doing here, Jace?" Rosalie asked coldly.

Dimitri didn't have to turn and look at her to picture the glare she was giving Jace. She had directed it at him often enough in the past.

"What am I doing here?" Jace affected surprise. "You were never a stupid girl, Rosalie." He paused and laughed again. "Not in most areas, anyway. Surely you've worked it out?" He cocked his head to the side and gave her a half smile. "Isn't that why you were keeping all this a secret?" He made a circular gesture to encompass both Rosalie's presence and Dimitri's changed form. "Don't tell me you've been enjoying yourself playing house with a Beast?"

Rosalie stiffened behind Dimitri but said nothing.

"You are trespassing here and are not welcome," Dimitri said coldly, keeping his blade steady. "Leave immediately, or I'll forcibly eject you."

"Trespassing?" Jace's eyebrows rose. "That's a heavy word between friends."

"We are not friends!" Rosalie said in an impassioned voice, but he ignored her.

"The door was open," Jace continued. "I merely came to give a neighborly visit to the newcomer in the region."

"I'm not receiving visitors currently," Dimitri said steadily. "I repeat: leave my property immediately. You are not welcome here."

Jace sighed dramatically, pressing his lips together in an expression of feigned disappointment. "If that's the way you insist it has to be."

He shook his head before looking up at them both with a cold gleam in his eyes. "I'm afraid I can't leave until you tell me where it is."

"I don't know what you're talking about," Rosalie said, but Dimitri could hear the tremor in her voice.

"Oh, I think you do," Jace murmured with a predatory smile. "The Legacy has clearly showered you with favor. Is it so terrible to ask that you share that largesse with your friends?"

Dimitri briefly considered giving him the chest of coins just to get rid of him. But it wasn't his to give. He had promised it to Rosalie to restore her family's fortune, and she showed no inclination to make the offer.

If he could have guaranteed Rosalie's safety by handing it over, he might have done it despite her disapproval. But he had a strong instinct that it would do quite the opposite. If Jace discovered how much wealth the Legacy was pouring on the manor, he would never be satisfied, and they'd never escape his attention.

Giving in to Jace's demands wasn't the answer. They had to take a stand and show him they weren't victims to be exploited.

He lunged forward, his movement abrupt enough to take both Rosalie and Jace by surprise. Rosalie screamed, muffling the sound with her hand, and Jace froze, a sword tip pressed against his neck.

He remained still as his eyes found Dimitri's, but he didn't look alarmed. Quite the opposite.

"You don't want to go doing that," he said softly. "You didn't think I came alone, did you?"

Dimitri hadn't thought that at first, but seeing Jace alone at the table had given him hope. His men must be off searching the manor, though.

Dimitri gritted his teeth. He had explored the new marvels of the manor with Rosalie, and in his mind those spaces belonged to the two of them. The thought of Jace's men rifling through those rooms made him surge forward slightly, his sword pressing tighter against Jace's throat until a single drop of blood ran down his neck.

Jace clicked his fingers in response, and a stream of men poured through the door of the dining room. They arrayed themselves in a wall of muscle behind Jace, several growling as they took in the scene.

"If he kills me," Jace said tightly, "kill them both."

Dimitri's sword tip wavered. He could disable Jace easily enough, but he couldn't handle the eight men he had with him. Not alone.

A hand tugged at the back of his vest. Rosalie was trying to draw him backward. He let her, and as soon as he had stepped away from Jace, she grabbed his free arm and ran.

He knew instantly where she was heading. Unlike Jace and his men, Rosalie knew the manor. Jace might think he had them trapped inside the dining room, but he didn't know about the second concealed door that led directly into the kitchen.

The two of them burst through into the cavernous kitchen, angry yells chasing behind them. They separated, Rosalie running down one side of the long island bench while he ran down the other. His eyes scanned the benches as he tried to find something to use against their pursuers.

A collection of knives might be of use to Rosalie, but he was better served by the longer reach of his sword. It wasn't a weapon he needed but something to block or confuse their pursuers long enough for them to escape.

Men began to fill the room, and Dimitri's eyes jumped to Rosalie. She was backed into the corner by the pantry— a dead end—and two of the men were bearing down on her. They had slowed their headlong approach, stalking their trapped prey at a more leisurely pace. And she was completely weaponless since the knives were all on his side.

Dimitri leaped forward, slamming his free hand onto the bench and vaulting over it. He slid along its length in a desperate bid to reach her before they did. But he wasn't going to make it.

A poker on the far side of the substantial fireplace speared into the midst of the banked fire. Red hot coals flicked upward, perfectly aimed at the first of the men approaching Rosalie.

Several of the coals made contact, and the whole kitchen froze. The shocked silence was broken by the man's outraged bellow, his fury quickly changing to cries of pain as the coals burned through to his skin.

Turning blindly, he ran straight into the brick corner of the fireplace. He collapsed to the ground, too dazed to keep screaming.

His companion, having barely escaped the coals himself, picked up a pitcher of water and dumped the entire contents over the injured man. His clothes sizzled, the beginning of smoldering flames extinguished, but the man gave no response. He was already unconscious.

Dimitri finally landed in front of Rosalie and dropped into a crouch, his sword raised defensively. The man with the pitcher took one look at the ugly expression on his unnatural face and backed away.

A shout from one of the other men drew his attention to the other side of the kitchen. Three of the men had been hurrying toward Dimitri's old position, but they were all now frozen. In front of them, the air was full of floating knives. One of the men stepped forward cautiously, and a knife responded. Drawing briefly back, it flew forward, aiming for his head. The man ducked, and the blade lodged in a breadbasket behind him.

The man gulped and stepped behind one of his comrades. Another knife drew back, and all three of them turned and fled. The remaining men followed their lead, all of them streaming from the room.

Jace watched his men flee from the doorway, but he made no attempt to stop them. Instead, he stepped back, allowing them to pass.

"The Legacy is protecting something!" he called, sounding excited. "Search the manor until you find it. A double portion to whoever brings me the item of greatest value."

The men responded enthusiastically, spilling out into the manor's corridors. Dimitri watched them go with dismay. Facing nine at once had been too much. But it would be equally difficult to handle them if they were spread throughout the manor.

"Don't worry," Rosalie murmured from behind him, sounding surprisingly pleased with the situation. "The Legacy is helping us, like you said. And we know this manor better than they do."

When he glanced back at her, the light in her eyes was almost feral.

"It's our turn to be the hunters," she said. "Let's see how much they like being the prey."

He grinned at her enthusiasm, even while he worried

for her safety. But the moment's inattention cost him. When he turned back to look at Jace, the man was gone.

Dimitri raced forward, leaping over the unconscious man and the coals and poker that were now scattered across the floor. He found the dining room empty, so he ran for the entryway, reaching it just in time to see Jace slipping out the front door.

"He's a coward," Rosalie said fiercely from just behind him. "As soon as he saw there was danger, he ran and left his men to take the risks for him."

"Unfortunately, he has plenty of men," Dimitri said.

"At least they're spread out now." Rosalie's determined expression made her look fierce. "They'll each want the reward for themselves, so they won't be searching in packs. We just need to hunt them all down, one by one."

Her eyes swung toward the open library door. She indicated it with an inclination of her head, raising her eyebrows at him. He nodded, moving silently toward the door.

She kept pace, leaning over to murmur in his ear. "Remember how the seats molded themselves around us?" She snorted quietly. "Actually you were perched so gingerly on the edge that you might not have felt it. It was a remarkable sensation, though. Since the Legacy is working with us, I think we should try to get one of them into a chair."

Dimitri wasn't sure a rose armchair was going to be enough to restrain one of Jace's mercenaries, but it might slow the man down enough for Dimitri to handle him. He nodded.

They snuck through the door, their eyes jumping around the room. Sure enough, one of the men was in there. He was walking down the shelves, sweeping books off with one arm and letting them cascade to the floor. But he was cursing as he did it, his other arm protecting his head from the books that were springing back up off the floor and launching themselves at him.

Rosalie snickered, and if he hadn't been wound so tautly, he would have joined her.

"The Legacy really doesn't like them," Rosalie muttered.

The man caught her words, twisting in their direction. His face tightened at the sight of them, and he drew a dagger from his belt.

Dimitri charged at the man, sword raised. He lunged forward as soon as he reached him, but the man dodged out of the way, slashing his knife toward Dimitri.

Dimitri barely spun out of the shorter blade's reach, bringing his sword up to catch its length. He danced backward, just out of the man's reach, finally remembering Rosalie's instructions. He was supposed to be maneuvering the man toward a chair.

The man followed him, growling in frustration at Dimitri's greater reach. Given his superior weapon and training, Dimitri was confident he could win their fight. But it might prove fatal for his assailant if it came to that, and he'd barely been in his manor a week. He didn't want to fill it with dead bodies.

Instead, he maneuvered them both toward a cluster of chairs. Sidestepping into the middle of the chairs, he brought the man with him. His enemy was too focused on Dimitri and his sword to even notice their surroundings.

As soon as he was positioned in front of a rose chair, Rosalie darted forward from out of Dimitri's line of sight. She ducked under the man's knife and shoved him hard in the chest. He flailed, losing his balance and waving his knife wildly through the air.

Dimitri shouted a warning and dropped his own sword, darting forward to seize Rosalie around the waist and pull her out of reach of the uncontrolled blade.

The back of the man's legs hit the chair, and he fell backward into it.

"Please," Rosalie whispered, ignoring Dimitri's hands around her waist, her eyes fixed on the man. "Please."

Dimitri watched, fascinated, as the chair folded itself around the man, molding to his shape just as Rosalie had claimed it did. But this time, it didn't stop there.

The man yelped in horror, his blade clattering to the ground as the chair swallowed him completely. When it stopped, only his head was showing, his terrified eyes staring at Dimitri and Rosalie from the center of a rose made of scarlet material and cushioning.

Rosalie collapsed into giggles as the muscles in the captive's neck strained. He was clearly trying to thrash around and free himself, but he was too firmly restrained to move.

Rosalie stopped laughing and spun around within the clasp of Dimitri's hands. Exuberance poured off her, and she threw her arms around his neck.

"See!" she crowed. "We can do this!"

Dimitri froze, his hands around her waist and her arms around his neck. He looked down at her, barely able to breathe.

She gave a soft gasp, her eyes dilating as she stared up at him.

The prisoner behind them groaned, and Dimitri cleared his throat, quickly dropping his arms from Rosalie. She stepped back just as quickly, looking away.

Dimitri stooped to retrieve his sword, looking toward the trapped man. "Don't worry," he said kindly. "We'll come back and release you once we've dealt with the others. You won't be rose food forever."

Rosalie laughed again, a little more breathily this time. "Where next?" she asked.

Dimitri frowned, considering. "If they're trying doors, someone is bound to have noticed our locked bedchamber doors and considered it significant."

Rosalie's eyes lit up. "In that case," she said, "why don't we surprise them?"

She hurried to the library door, closing it and waiting for several seconds.

"I'd like to go to my bedchamber," she muttered before pulling it quickly open again. When a purple and gold room was revealed on the other side, she grinned triumphantly over her shoulder at Dimitri.

He smiled back, showing his teeth. "Time to go hunting."

CHAPTER 20
ROSALIE

L ogically Rosalie knew she should feel afraid. But facing Jace and his men on her home turf, and with Dimitri by her side, was entirely different from facing Jace and his men alone in the woods. She was sick of feeling weak and pathetic where Jace was concerned. Even if he had already escaped, she was going to make sure she stripped him of his followers.

She waited for Dimitri to follow her through to her bedchamber and then carefully closed the door behind them, shutting off their view of the library. Once again she waited a few seconds, allowing the connection between her bedchamber and the library to be severed.

A scratching sound reached her ears, as if someone was in the corridor outside her room, attempting to pick the lock. She twisted the key to unlock the door from inside, seizing the handle and thrusting the door open with all the force she could muster.

It collided with something—or someone—on the

other side with a satisfying thud. She pulled it closed and thrust it open a second time, once again whacking whatever was on the other side. Something heavy fell to the floor, and she realized her mistake. The heavy bulk she had just felled was now lying across the doorway, blocking the door from opening.

She stepped back and let Dimitri put his shoulder against it, heaving it open inch by inch. He stopped as soon as there was room for them to slip through, and they both looked down at the groaning man lying on the floor. Blood poured from his nose.

Dimitri hauled the man up and used the rope from her curtains to bind his wrists and feet. When he'd finished, he shoved the man into the closest storage cupboard.

His efforts didn't go unnoticed, however. A second man was kneeling a short way down the corridor, making the same lock picking attempt on Dimitri's door. As Dimitri wrestled the bound man into the cupboard, the second man advanced toward them, growling.

Before he reached them, yet another man arrived, running forward with a yell to join the lock-picker.

Rosalie looked from Dimitri to her bed chamber door. "The library?" she asked.

He grinned and nodded.

She closed the door, the required pause allowing time for the two men to approach closer. Just before they reached attack range, she whispered, "The library, please," and pulled the door open.

She and Dimitri ran through, and the men barreled after them, not immediately noticing the strangeness of the room on the other side. But after they had sprinted several yards into the library, they slid to a stop, looking around in confusion.

Their trapped companion tried to call a warning, but the sight of him only dazed them further. As they stared at him, open-mouthed, Dimitri and Rosalie sprang forward in unison. Each of them shoved one of the men hard enough to send him staggering forward straight into one of the rose chairs. Within seconds, they had both been completely absorbed except for their heads.

"Thank you," Rosalie said aloud.

"I thought you said the Legacy couldn't hear us." Dimitri gave an amused shake of his head.

Rosalie shrugged. "It can't. But it still seems polite to say thank you."

She quickly tallied in her head. "That's five men down. Six if we count Jace." She looked at the two closest men. "He abandoned you all, you know. Ran for it as soon as it got dangerous."

The men shouted angrily at her, their voices overlapping, but she merely strode away. Dimitri followed her out of the library into the entryway, closing the door behind him and muffling the angry yells.

"They can shout at each other," Rosalie said. "There's no reason we have to listen to it." She tapped her cheek. "Five men down means there are still three to go. Any guesses where we might find them?"

"We could try there." Dimitri pointed across the entryway to the door that led into the sitting room. "I moved some of the furniture around when I first arrived, so it looks more lived in than most of the manor's rooms. That might have attracted their attention."

He led the way, and Rosalie was happy to follow behind, keeping his sword between her and anyone who might be in the room. At first it appeared to be empty, but neither of them let down their guard. They advanced several steps inside, and a man appeared from behind a sofa.

He must have been crouched down examining the wall because for a moment he looked as surprised by them as they were by his sudden appearance. He let out a loud yell, calling for back up, and Dimitri immediately started retreating.

Rosalie stayed behind him, the two of them backing slowly out of the room, their eyes on the man in front of them. But they had barely made it into the entryway when running footsteps pounded down the stairs. The remaining two men were answering their comrade's call.

The man inside called out again, and the other two advanced, herding Dimitri and Rosalie back toward the door they'd just exited. Dimitri tried to step sideways, out of their trap, but Rosalie stopped him with a hand on his sleeve.

Instead, she closed the sitting room door, her eyes on the advancing men as she counted out the seconds in her mind. They had approached close enough that Dimitri and Rosalie appeared trapped when she feigned a terrified squeak and opened the door again.

The two men grinned, clearly thinking Dimitri and Rosalie were about to retreat into the arms of their companion. But when the four of them spilled through the doorway, they weren't inside the sitting room, and there was no sign of the third man.

Jace's men frowned, staring at the empty room lined with closed curtains. Their confusion gave Rosalie and Dimitri the chance to dart around them and back out the door. They slammed it closed behind them, and Dimitri seized the handle. Leaning back with his weight, he held it closed and looked at Rosalie.

"What now?"

She pulled out a large metal ring, lined with keys. "Just hold them long enough for me to find the right one."

It took her several tries, but she managed to locate the right key and lock the men inside. Dimitri relaxed, letting go of the handle and retrieving his sword.

"At least they'll be well entertained while they're stuck there," he said, making Rosalie giggle. "But where did you get those?" He frowned at the keys.

"I found them on the floor of the kitchen."

They appeared to be the housekeeper's master set, so she had stuck them in her pocket, thinking they might come in useful. At the very least, she hadn't wanted Jace to end up with them.

"Good thinking," Dimitri said approvingly, and warmth filled her.

"One left to go," he added, and she turned for the main stairs. She had nearly forgotten about the man still inside the sitting room. He must have been confused when all the people and voices on the other side of his door suddenly disappeared.

They ran down the stairs together, catching sight of the man as he cautiously stepped out of the sitting room. He looked up at them, hurrying down the stairs alone, and his eyes widened. For a second he hesitated. But before either of them could reach him, he turned and sprinted out the open front door. Dimitri ran after him, but he stopped at the door, watching the man's flight.

"Straight down the drive," he said. "So I guess Jace will be getting one report after all."

Rosalie smiled with satisfaction. She had wanted to catch all Jace's men, but seven out of eight was a good result.

The silence around them deepened, and her satisfaction slowly faded. In the heat of their battle, she hadn't considered what came next.

"What do we do with them now?" she asked. "We can't leave them where they are, but if we free them, there will be too many for us to control."

"Two locked in the theater room," Dimitri said thoughtfully, giving an inventory aloud. "Three in the rose chairs. One upstairs in the storage closet with a broken nose. Plus the man in the kitchen."

Rosalie's eyes widened. "I'd forgotten about him. We should check what state he's in. He needs medical attention, but he wasn't actually secured. He might have woken up and moved elsewhere."

Dimitri stepped in front of her protectively, the move seeming to be an instinctive response to her words. A secret thrill ran through her. She liked having someone to take care of her. Ever since Jace, she'd been working tirelessly to make up to her family for her mistake. Her parents often protested that she worked too much, but the truth was that they needed her to help the family make ends meet. She hadn't realized how exhausted she was until she came to the manor and finally stopped.

They walked to the kitchen together, and as she had feared, they found no sign of the burned man there. They both scanned the littered debris on the kitchen floor with concern.

Rosalie caught sight of a glistening trail, as if something large and wet had been dragged along it. "Is that…"

She pointed to it, following it with her eyes to where it ended at the closed pantry door. Dimitri strode over and tried to pull the door open. It was locked.

He placed his ear against the door and was silent for a moment, listening. When he straightened and looked at her, his expression was amazed.

"I can hear quiet groaning. He must be locked inside."

Rosalie frowned. The Legacy had helped them in their moment of need, but dragging a man into a pantry and locking him in seemed beyond its capabilities.

"So they're all secured," she said slowly, unable to think how else the man could have gotten there. "But what next? Should I go into Thebarton to report them? I can say that a group of men broke into the manor, attacked us, and attempted to rob you. I'm sure the guards will agree to come back with me and arrest them."

"No," Dimitri said quickly and firmly. "Jace and one of his men escaped. They could be waiting for you on the road." He rubbed the back of his neck. "I'll have to go. But you should lock yourself in your room while I'm gone."

"You'll go?" Rosalie looked at him doubtfully.

Turning into a Beast didn't mean you'd done anything wrong, so it should evoke pity in the townsfolk, not suspicion. But they would be shocked. And they might blame him for bringing so much Legacy power to their town.

"I'm sure they'll be surprised to see me like this," Dimitri said, "but don't forget the fireworks. I'm sure many of them have guessed something is going on out here." He hesitated. "I'll return as quickly as I can, and I'll check all the outside doors are locked before I go. But please do consider locking yourself in your room." He looked at her pleadingly, and she capitulated.

"Fine," she said. "If you insist. I suppose I can wait in my room as easily as anywhere else."

She didn't want to admit how unnerved she was at the prospect of being left alone in a building full of captive men. But neither did she like the idea of abandoning it entirely and going with Dimitri. Who knew what might happen in their absence?

She waved him off from the front door before climbing the stairs to her room. Her ears strained for any untoward sound, but the manor remained silent. Whatever protests or struggles the captives were making, they didn't reach her on the main stairs.

"The rose chairs are really going to surprise the guards," she muttered to herself, her chuckle echoing down the corridor.

She slipped inside her room and tried to pull the door

closed behind her. It caught, but with several more tugs, she got it closed. Once she had locked it, she collapsed onto her bed with a sigh.

Would Jace attack Dimitri as he walked into town? Would the townsfolk attack him before they realized who he was? Now that he was gone, she wished she'd gone with him after all. He might need her protection.

"Don't worry so much. Dimitri is going to be fine," Daphne's voice said into the silence.

Rosalie started so violently she nearly fell off the bed. Peering around, she tried to see where Daphne's voice was coming from, but she could see no one.

"Daph?" she called cautiously, hoping the day's events hadn't caused her to start hearing things. "Where are you?"

"Right here," Daphne said, sounding as if she really was standing in the middle of the room. "I'm just invisible."

"You're what?" Rosalie leaped to her feet.

"Invisible," Daphne repeated calmly. "You can't possibly think the Legacy dragged a man into the pantry and locked him in, can you?"

Rosalie's mouth fell open. "That was you? But what... why...what were you doing there?"

"I've been here the whole time."

"The whole time?" Rosalie stared around the room, still half-wondering if her mind was playing tricks on her.

"Who do you think has been serving your meals and lighting your fires?" Daphne asked.

"I thought the Legacy..." Rosalie's voice trailed off as

she finally absorbed the enormity of what Daphne was saying. "Have you really been here ever since I arrived?"

"Well, a few hours after. I had to take the coins to the triplets and make sure they paid their debt."

Rosalie swallowed hard, her cheeks warming as she thought of some of her interactions with Dimitri. How many times had they had an invisible audience?

"Don't worry," Daphne said. "I haven't been trailing you everywhere. I've been taking a lot of naps."

"Naps?" Rosalie said faintly. She picked up the cold cup of tea still sitting half-drunk on her breakfast tray and took a swig, trying to calm herself.

"I can't say the same for your brothers, though," Daphne said thoughtfully.

Rosalie choked on her mouthful and succumbed to a violent fit of coughing. "The *triplets*?! Please tell me my brothers haven't been lurking around the castle invisible!"

"Who do you think cooked those vegetables the first day?" Rosalie could almost hear Daphne's nose wrinkling. "Oscar assured me they knew how to cook without assistance, but..."

"But why?" Rosalie wailed before a further thought occurred to her. "Wait! So you're saying the Legacy can't cook and light fires and send trays floating through the air? So that means it was you and the boys in the kitchen earlier? You were the ones to flick the coals and wave all those knives around?"

"Was that what they did?" Daphne asked interestedly. "The mess was impressive, but I thought their claims of heroism sounded a bit outlandish. I was in the library."

"Throwing the books," Rosalie said weakly, sinking back down onto the bed. So the Legacy had helped with the rose chairs, but it couldn't do nearly as much as they had thought.

"What about the fresh supplies?" she asked. "Was the Legacy producing the food?"

"That was us, too," Daphne said. "I think edible items might be beyond its capability. One of the boys has been walking into town every couple of days to buy fresh supplies."

"The door!" Rosalie sat bolt upright. "And the keys." She drew the master key ring from her pocket and Daphne sighed.

"I knew I shouldn't have given that to Ralph. He's too distracted to do things properly. Did he drop it?"

"Yes!" Rosalie cried indignantly. "And he also left the front door unlocked. Jace and his men walked right in."

Daphne was silent for a moment. "Well, that's unfortunate," she said at last.

"Unfortunate?" Rosalie asked incredulously.

"We all handled it, didn't we?" Rosalie could almost hear her shrug.

"I still don't understand how or why you're here, let alone my brothers," Rosalie said, still struggling to fathom the truth behind her time at the manor.

"It was Vernon's idea to come," Daphne said. "He guessed there would be enough Legacy power swirling around the manor to turn us completely invisible the whole time. The invisible servants was the only role left in our little play, you see, so it seemed like the only way we could be here."

"But why didn't you tell me?" Rosalie cried.

"We knew you'd never agree to us being involved if we asked," Daphne said simply. "So it seemed easier to just come and stay quiet."

"So you decided to endanger yourselves for no reason?" Rosalie asked heatedly.

"Vernon said it was our civic duty," Daphne said apologetically. "Because if we left you two alone, you'd be at risk of murdering Dimitri before the week was out."

Rosalie jumped up before sinking back onto the bed. "Of course I wouldn't have done anything of the sort," she said, but she sounded sulky even to her own ears.

"No, you've been getting along quite well," Daphne agreed, making Rosalie flush again. "I suppose it's because of how he looks now."

"You think I'm being nice to him because I feel guilty?" Rosalie asked.

"No, I think you misjudged him before because he was too handsome. I said from the start that he reminded you of Jace, remember? So you judged everything Dimitri did as if he had the same motivations as Jace. But now that Dimitri doesn't look like Jace at all, you're seeing him for who he really is."

Rosalie frowned. Had she really rushed to misjudge Dimitri purely because of his appearance? She was sure there had been more to it, but it was too much to process along with all the other revelations.

"Never mind that," she said. "What about Mother?

What must she be thinking with all four of us disappeared at once?"

"We came up with an explanation for that," Daphne said. "I went back the second day and told her the story you and I had come up with. She thinks you're laid up in my house with a mild but infectious ailment, and that I'm at your side nursing you since I've had it recently enough to be safe. Meanwhile the boys had already told her that they found work for a few weeks with food and board included. Every time one of them goes into town for supplies, they also pop in to see her and give her their 'daily wages' for her to keep safe. She agreed because she's hoping one or more of them will get an apprenticeship out of it."

"Daily wages and purchasing supplies," Rosalie said knowingly. "I suppose you've been using those master keys to raid the chest." She glanced at her dressing room.

A rustle of fabric and a dip in the cushion of one of the chairs indicated that Daphne had sat down.

"Yes, I figured it was necessary usage. Since I had the master key ring, it was no trouble getting through your locked door."

"How reassuring," Rosalie said dryly.

"The really interesting thing," Daphne said with unusual enthusiasm, "is that the chest refills itself. No matter how much I take out, it's always completely full when I open it again. So I've been burying pouches of coins all over the manor grounds."

Rosalie blinked at Daphne's apparently empty chair.

"Whatever for? If the coins in the chest are unlimited, that seems unnecessary."

"The Legacy's power isn't going to pour into this place forever," Daphne said, mild chiding in her voice. "At least I wouldn't think so. Once Dimitri turns back into a normal man again, it will probably fade as quickly as it appeared. In that case, the chest will stop replenishing, and we'll be left with whatever it's already produced. So I'm making it produce more."

"And you've been burying the pouches," Rosalie said with foreboding. "Please tell me you remember where they all are!"

"Of course!" Daphne said cheerfully, then paused. "Most of them anyway. I've been making notes. Very cryptic ones in case someone else finds my notebook."

"You remember *most* of them?" Rosalie stared hard at the dent in the cushion that indicated Daphne's position.

"Well, there was one afternoon when I buried four. But before I got back inside, the afternoon sun lulled me into taking a nap on a patch of grass. When I woke up, I couldn't remember my mental markers for any of them." Daphne related the tale without any audible sign of remorse.

Rosalie groaned. "So you're telling me that once we finally deal with Jace, we'll have treasure hunters from Thebarton digging up the manor gardens in an attempt to find the missing coins?"

Daphne was silent for a moment. "I didn't think of that," she finally admitted. "We'd better not tell anyone about them."

"Oh, so you haven't mentioned it to the triplets, then?" Rosalie asked with narrowed eyes.

"Well..." Daphne finally sounded guilty.

Rosalie sighed. "There's no hope for it. We'll have every youth under twenty sneaking out here after sundown every night. And even once they've all been found, the legend will no doubt live on—probably forever."

"I suppose I'd better apologize to Dimitri," Daphne said. "Do you think he would accept several pouches of coins as restitution?"

"He will no doubt be far more forbearing than you deserve," Rosalie said.

Her lip suddenly began to tremble, tears springing to her eyes. Fabric rustled as Daphne stood, and invisible arms wrapped around Rosalie.

"Are you really that upset about it?" her friend asked, sounding worried.

"No, of course not," Rosalie sobbed. "It's not that."

"What is it then?"

"Just...just everything."

"Oh." Daphne's soft word contained a depth of understanding. "I imagine it's normal to feel a bit emotional after everything that's just happened." She paused. "But don't worry. Dimitri will be fine. He'll be back here in no time, and then the guards will take Jace's men away with them. You'll be able to go back to how it was before."

Rosalie wanted to tell Daphne that she wasn't crying out of concern for Dimitri. But she wasn't entirely sure the words were true. She didn't even know why she was crying. Perhaps she just needed a release.

When the tears finally subsided, she sat on the bed next to Daphne. As soon as she had mopped up the mess that was her face, she peered at the empty air where Daphne was.

"That's really unnerving, you know," she said.

"Right?" Daphne agreed enthusiastically. "We're invisible to each other and ourselves, too, and it's horribly inconvenient. You try using your invisible arm to hand a pan full of food to an invisible person."

Rosalie snorted and suddenly realized Dimitri had been wrong. She smiled smugly. It hadn't been the Legacy that had needed practice with cooking but three young boys who always did their best to weasel out of their chores.

"I think I hear Dimitri and the guards," Daphne said.

Rosalie jumped up, moving toward the door before stopping. "We should stay out of sight!" she said. "No one in Thebarton knows we're caught up in all this, and it's probably best to keep it that way."

"That's not going to be a problem for me," Daphne said dryly, making Rosalie snort laugh at herself.

"No," she said. "I don't suppose it will be." Her mouth twisted. "But it means I should stay in here."

She paced up and down, ignoring Daphne's pleas to stop being so exhausting. By the time she finally heard the double front doors swing closed with an echoing thump, Daphne had gone quiet. Rosalie listened for a moment and then laughed.

Based on the sounds of her breathing, Daphne had finally succeeded in stealing a nap on Rosalie's cloud bed.

CHAPTER 21

DIMITRI

Rosalie ran down the stairs, and Dimitri's tense muscles finally relaxed. He'd guessed she was staying out of sight on purpose and carefully hadn't mentioned her to the guards. But he'd still been anxious to check on her and to see with his own eyes that nothing had happened to her in his absence.

The day had been a victory, but Jace and at least one of his men had escaped. And they didn't know how many other men he had out in the woods still.

Dimitri smiled up at Rosalie, giddy with relief. "You should have seen the guards' faces when they saw the men in the library."

She smiled in acknowledgment of his comment, but she was clearly distracted, skipping straight over a greeting to blurt out, "You won't believe what I just found out."

His brow wrinkled. "What do you mean? Did something happen while I was gone?"

"No, not exactly. It's just that I found out what's actually been going on in this castle the whole time!" She shook her head. "Do you remember the serving girl at the Mortar and Pestle?"

He blinked at the abrupt change of subject, trying to remember back to his day at the inn. It already seemed distant.

"Oh!" he said, finally realizing what she must mean. "The one with the invisible limbs?"

She nodded, her smile turning smug. "Turns out I was right, and the Legacy hasn't been practicing its cooking."

His eyes slowly narrowed, and he gave her a sideways look. "Why do I have a creeping feeling of great foreboding?"

"Because you're a very canny man," she said, trying to suppress a rueful grin. "It turns out we've had a collection of dedicated servants the entire time we've been here. They've just been invisible."

"Invisible servants?" His eyes widened. "Actual real people like the girl in the inn? But...who?"

She winced. "Brace yourself. It's Daphne and my brothers."

"Your brothers!" He paled. "Your brothers have been creeping around the manor watching us this whole time?"

"To be fair to them, I don't think much creeping was needed, given they're invisible."

"Is that supposed to make me feel better?" he demanded.

"It didn't make me feel better if that's any comfort."

She explained everything Daphne had told her about

why they'd done it and how they'd made it work. When she finished, he glanced toward the library.

"It sounds like we got lucky with those chairs. The Legacy wasn't helping us as much as we thought."

"No." She grimaced. "But it was helping us. So I suppose that's a good sign, at least."

"So it was one of them who shone the light in my eyes in the garden that time?" he suddenly demanded.

"Oh!" Rosalie's eyes widened. "I didn't even think of that one. Now I'm going to be second guessing everything that's happened. And I haven't even told you about the many pouches of coins buried in the garden."

"The what?" He rubbed his temples. "Do I even want to know?"

"That one?" She winced. "Probably not, to be honest." She looked around. "I haven't actually seen my brothers yet."

His eyebrows rose. "Seen them?"

She laughed. "You know what I mean. Sensed their presence? Talked to them? Felt the wind of their passing?"

He broke into helpless laughter at the last one. She watched him with a bemused expression.

"Sorry," he said when the last of his chuckles subsided. "It's been an intense day."

"I understand," she said softly.

Something passed over her face as she said it, and he wanted to ask if there was more to her comment. But he couldn't help glancing around the entryway before speaking. Were they really alone? How was he going to speak freely—let alone get changed or bathe!—if there might be invisible people lurking everywhere?

"Ralph!" Rosalie suddenly shouted, making him jump. "Vernon! Oscar! If any of you are there, you had better say something right now or else you'll never have a peaceful night's sleep again when I get home! I'll make sure your blankets never cover your feet, your shirts are always slightly damp, and every one of your socks has a hole. On a different toe. Some on two toes."

"Does that make it worse?" Dimitri whispered.

She nodded solemnly. "It means you can't ever get used to the feel of it."

He laughed. "I'm starting to appreciate not having an older sister."

A throat clearing from the edge of the room made them both swing around.

Rosalie's eyes narrowed. "Who is it?"

"Vernon."

"And Oscar," a second voice added quickly.

Quiet footsteps sounded, and then a third voice said, "What's this? Are we telling them now?"

"And there's Ralph." Rosalie sighed.

"Apparently Daphne told her everything," Vernon said in complaining tones. "And now she's making all sorts of dire threats."

"Short blankets. Holes in the socks," Oscar said woefully.

"Whatever for?" Ralph protested. "What did we do other than slave to make their food and light their fires?"

There was the sound of a whack, followed by an irritated cry. Dimitri had no idea who had whacked who, however.

"No more sneaking around!" Rosalie said sternly. "The Legacy might make you invisible, but that doesn't mean we want you lurking around unbeknownst to us. From now on, you announce yourself whenever you get near either of us. And let us know when you leave too."

She glared in the direction of the voices. "And don't you dare say you're leaving and then hang around and eavesdrop."

"To what?" Vernon asked disgustedly. "Do you think we want to listen to our sister flirting all day?"

"I was not!" Rosalie flushed bright scarlet.

"You can't blame us," Oscar said. "We're your *brothers*. Of course we don't want to hear it."

"But don't think we're going to leave you two completely alone," Vernon said heatedly. "Did you really think we'd send you off to live with a strange man on your own?"

"Dimitri isn't strange," Rosalie protested.

"He's a stranger to us," Ralph said. "Or, he was. I think we all know more about him than we want to now."

Dimitri drew back, his hands rising instinctively to cover his chest. Just how much had they seen?

"Relax." Vernon snorted. "We're in and out to tend your fire and deliver your breakfast tray as fast as humanly possible. And Daphne always did your room, beloved sister."

"Don't think you can flatter me into forgetting about

this," Rosalie said darkly. "How did you even know I was coming here?"

"You must have thought we were babies if you thought you could send Daphne to us with the debt money, and we'd just accept it without question," Vernon protested.

"So you forced her to tell you the truth?" Rosalie frowned. "I hope you weren't unkind."

"Force her?" said Ralph. "Hardly. We already knew all about it by then. She told us as soon as she got back from picking the rose."

Rosalie's mouth fell open. "All those times I had to chase you away from her that night? You were all plotting together? Talk about betrayal!"

"Yes, yes," Oscar said. "We know how touched you are to have four people who take such care of you."

"Touched?" The fire in Rosalie's eyes leaped into full flame, and Dimitri seized her arm to keep her from finding and whacking her brothers.

All three of the triplets laughed, however.

"Don't worry," Vernon said. "She'll hold it in. Just. She always does."

"You must have more patience than I realized," Dimitri said to Rosalie, making her laugh.

"Every time I think I'm going to erupt at them, one of them does something sweet." She sighed. "Even this was sweet in its own way."

"Oh good, so everything is all sorted?" Daphne asked from the top of the stairs.

"Once again your nap was perfectly timed, I see," Rosalie muttered.

"Now that they know we're here, does that mean they'll do their own cooking?" Vernon asked hopefully.

"Unfortunately, no," Daphne said. "They've been capable of cooking the whole time, but we all need to keep to our roles."

"We are capable of cooking," Rosalie said quickly. "So you can all go home now. We don't need servants to make this little play work."

"You want us to leave when the manor was just invaded by an army?" Vernon cried. "I saved you, remember!"

"So that was you three with the coal and the knives." Dimitri was reluctantly impressed. "It was quick thinking."

"Thank you," Vernon said smugly. "But we certainly won't be leaving."

Rosalie wilted, but Daphne spoke again.

"That's right. We're as much a part of this as you two. But we can't risk upsetting the play by stepping out of our assigned roles. If we stop acting as servants, we might turn visible, and that could mess up the whole thing. Your family will be left with a chest of gold, but what about poor Dimitri? Do you want him to be stuck as a Beast forever because the Legacy dropped him halfway through?"

"I wouldn't mind so much," Vernon muttered rebelliously. "Personally I think he looks better now than he did before."

"Like sister, like brother," Daphne murmured, making Dimitri look at Rosalie.

She didn't appear to have heard her friend—or she was pretending she hadn't. What had Daphne meant? Did she really think Rosalie preferred the way he looked now? Surely that was impossible. Although she had certainly been softer and warmer to him after his change than she had been before.

He frowned. Did that mean that when—hopefully, not if —he went back to his true form, she would go back to being constantly irritated by him? It was a disheartening thought, but he refused to believe it. Thinking that way was unfair to Rosalie and the connection they had forged over the last few days. She actually knew him now, and she wouldn't see him differently just because of his appearance. He hoped.

That night he made the rounds of every external door and window in the castle twice before he could sleep. And he made the same circuit as soon as he woke in the morning, checking that nothing had been disturbed. The morning and evening circuits became his ritual, and he confiscated the housekeeper's set of master keys, refusing to let the triplets touch them.

Once Rosalie explained that Ralph's distracted oversight had given Jace and his men access, they didn't even protest. Much.

But that was the only relief any of them got from the boys' complaints. Dimitri's concern over the possibility of their silent presence was soon replaced with a desperate desire for them to return to being quiet, unseen shadows.

Now that they weren't trying to hide their presence, they accompanied all their actions with an endless stream of commentary.

"I have now entered the room," Vernon said at the evening meal one week after Jace's attack. "I am gliding quietly and gracefully across the room like a true servant. No one would even notice my presence, but I wish you to be aware that all private, personal, and nauseating conversation should now cease."

The plate that had been floating through the air lowered onto the table in front of Dimitri.

"I am now serving the great and glorious master of the manor, known to his relations and close friends as the Beast."

"Some feel this is a rather pompous appellation, given he strikes fear in no one's heart," Oscar said. "However, everyone is too polite to mention that fact."

Vernon cleared his throat reprovingly, and Oscar's plate paused in midair. "I offer my most abject apologies. It is, I, Oscar, and I too have entered the room. I glide even more effectively than the most revered servant, Vernon. Some have been known to faint at the wonder of my silent gliding."

"If only it was silent," Dimitri muttered, poking listlessly at his food.

"Are you three ever going to stop that?" Rosalie asked as Oscar finally put her plate in front of her.

"Whatever do you mean?" Vernon asked in mock surprise. "We are only doing as instructed by our venerable masters. We wouldn't wish to do anything in a *sneaky* manner."

"Oh really?" Rosalie glared in their general directions. "So you're going to stick to the claim that the frog in my bed yesterday morning got there entirely by its own efforts."

"Perhaps it was a love gift," Oscar suggested innocently.

When Dimitri growled quietly, he quickly added, "From the Legacy. To its beloved Beast and merchant's daughter."

"At least Mother will be pleased to discover your improved cooking skills," Rosalie said sweetly. "Does she think you're working for a chef? If not, I'll be sure to let her know that you were given kitchen duties and are now experts. I'm sure her delight will be so great that she'll put you on meal duty for the next year."

"We scurry quickly from the room like the lowly servants that we are," Vernon said in a monotone, his voice growing gradually quieter as they both presumably sped from the room.

"I'm sorry about them." Rosalie sighed, but it turned into a hum when she took her first bite of the food. "But I'm honestly impressed Daphne's whipped them into shape so quickly with the cooking."

"She's a force to be reckoned with," Dimitri agreed. "When she wants to be. Which isn't often."

Rosalie laughed. "I see you've gotten to know her quickly. You're a good judge of character."

"Even if I want to pitch all three of your brothers into the closest river?"

"An understandable instinct," Rosalie said sympathetically. "But I'm afraid they can all swim."

"I was hoping it would carry them away." Dimitri took a bite and paused. "Or maybe not. This is better than anything I can make. Or my mother either, to be honest."

Rosalie gazed around the room. "I suppose she never learned to cook growing up in this manor. I wonder how many people worked here when she was a child."

"A great many," Dimitri said. "I've been looking through the records my grandfather left behind. He paid generously and had a long payroll. Whole families lived and worked here. It was as much their home as my family's." His voice dropped. "I wonder what happened to them."

"Maybe your grandfather took them with him?" Rosalie suggested. "Surely my parents would have mentioned it if his departure left whole families homeless and without work."

Dimitri sighed. "I hope so. But if not, I need to find them and make restitution."

Rosalie smiled. "You will. Once all this mess is sorted out, you'll be free to do even more of that. Perhaps some of them will even wish to return."

"I glide into the room with far more grace than your two previous servers," Ralph's voice announced. "If you could see me, you would weep at the beauty of my movements."

Rosalie groaned. "Not you, too."

"You'd weep buckets of joy," he said firmly.

"Get back to the kitchen," Daphne commanded from the doorway.

"Yes, ma'am!" he cried and departed in silence, his tray of rolls deposited between Dimitri and Rosalie.

Dimitri took one eagerly, but Rosalie stared toward Daphne.

"Ma'am? How did you manage that?"

"I've decided that I'm the housekeeper," she said tranquilly. "And any junior servants who fail to show the proper respect risk being turned off without a character."

Rosalie laughed. "You mean you're shamelessly exploiting the fact that all three boys think they're in love with you."

"I have to make some use of it," Daphne said serenely. "Who knows when they'll grow up enough to develop an interest in girls their own age."

She left the room to laughter from both Dimitri and Rosalie.

Two days later, Rosalie wandered through the conservatory with Dimitri, examining the plants.

"Do you think if you brought a pot from another kingdom—one that was already filled with dirt from that kingdom—that it would grow something other than roses?" she asked.

"Surely someone's tried that before," Dimitri said, distracted. He kept imagining his mother running through the conservatory as a girl. "If it worked, wouldn't you have heard about it?"

Rosalie sighed. "I suppose so."

"The most humble and respectful of your servants walks subtly into the room," Vernon boomed out, making Rosalie start so badly that she pulled several leaves off one of the potted trees. "This silent and considerate servant delicately places the tray of your midday meal upon this table."

Rosalie snorted. "You've never done anything delicately in your life."

"Since I am but a humble servant employed in this manor, I don't know what you mean," he said in dignified tones.

"That is an excellent point!" Dimitri exclaimed.

"It is?" Vernon and Rosalie asked in unison.

"You are currently employed by this manor, and as the master of this manor, I am offering triple pay to any servant who can complete his duties with a *reasonable* level of calm communication."

"Triple pay, you say?" Vernon asked in a normal voice. "In that case, please be informed that I'm leaving the conservatory to return to the kitchen. In thirty minutes, Ralph will be here to pick up your tray."

Several branches rustled as he brushed past them on his way out of the conservatory.

Rosalie blinked after him. "Why didn't one of us think of that a week and a half ago? Daphne made them fill a bath for me last night. It took them half an hour, and they didn't stop talking the entire time."

"At least you knew you were truly alone when you finally got in," Dimitri said.

"It was cold by then."

Dimitri laughed. "Sorry, I'm not laughing at you. I'm honestly impressed at their creativity. Maybe they'll end up as florid novelists."

"Don't say that! We'd be expected to read every one of their books."

"That would be taking family loyalty much too far. Surely the first few pages of each one would do?" He grinned at her, but Rosalie fell silent, her expression clouding, and he realized what he'd said.

He'd spoken casually of them as family because that was how he already thought of them. But once they finished play acting for the Legacy, he would have no official role in her life.

She and her brothers and Daphne would all move back to their actual homes, and he would be alone in the empty manor. It had been unpleasant before, but it was unimaginable now. He didn't want their ruse to end.

But perhaps she would consider returning. Perhaps she would be interested in helping him build a future for both himself and the manor.

She had started to walk away from him, distracted by some plants further down the conservatory, and his hand reached for her. His mouth opened to ask the question burning inside him.

But his eyes caught on his strange-looking hand, and he snapped his mouth closed again. He was still trapped inside an inhuman body, with no guarantee he would ever return to his true form. He couldn't ask Rosalie about a future together while his situation was still so uncertain. It wouldn't be fair to her.

And he especially couldn't do it while they were still acting for the Legacy. His impatience had nearly ruined everything.

He had lost himself in the false life they were living and forgotten all the reasons it needed to end. Not only did he need his true form back before he could speak his heart, but all of their safety might depend on it.

He had managed to slip away twice for updates from the local captain of the guard. The guards had questioned Jace's men, but the captives had failed to provide any useful information. Jace had already moved his camp, and so far he had eluded all attempts to discover his location.

Dimitri appreciated the guards' efforts, but he also suspected they hadn't been as thorough and diligent as he would have been in their place. He itched to search for Jace himself, but while they were enacting their piece of theater for the Legacy, he couldn't be gone from the manor for long periods.

And as long as Jace remained free, Dimitri didn't believe he would give up on the wealth hidden in the manor. He would remain interested in Dimitri and Rosalie, and that meant Rosalie wasn't safe.

They needed to end the false bubble they were living in and return to the world. Then he could find his grandfather and restore the manor properly—not by fixing the building but by filling it with people again. The person he most wanted there might not return, but some company would be better than none. And before all that, he would fund a guard force of his own—one he could use to hunt Jace until he was finally found.

Rosalie had to return to her family, and he had to regain his true shape.

Rosalie called out in delight from the other end of the conservatory, beckoning him over to see a peach rose.

"It's the first one I've seen at the manor that isn't red or gold." She grinned up at him.

He smiled back, bending over to look more closely.

Rosalie had to leave, and he had to wait to find out if she would ever return. But she didn't have to leave yet. A few more days wouldn't hurt.

CHAPTER 22
ROSALIE

The best part of the aftermath of Jace's invasion was that they were free to enjoy the grounds again. The days, and especially nights, were growing colder as winter approached, and Rosalie didn't want to waste the last of the sun. On sunny days, she spent as much time outside as possible, wandering the gardens or resting on the soft grass.

It was utterly delightful to finally rest after nearly a year of frenetic activity. Knowing her family would soon have the means to rebuild their fortune allowed her to finally set down the load she had been carrying. But as the days drew into weeks, she started to find the inactivity of her life at the enchanted manor difficult.

"How do you do this all day?" she asked Daphne as they lay side by side in the grass one late afternoon.

"Do what?" Daphne asked sleepily.

"Rest. I like it, but I also get...antsy."

Daphne chuckled, the sound a little groggy. "You

would. You always have to be doing something. It's easy, though. Just make resting your achievement for the day."

Rosalie laughed. "It was all right while we still had the manor to explore. And then I made that map of the gardens. But now I know every corner and cranny of this place. There's nothing left to do." She looked up at the sky, enjoying the pink and gold hue of sunset. "I'll miss it here when we leave, though."

"Mmmm," Daphne murmured, "yes. You'll miss the *house*."

Rosalie ignored her, sitting up. "I'm itching to know what Dimitri is up to. Confess—you know why he forbade us from going anywhere near the western courtyard this afternoon, don't you?"

The grass rustled as Daphne rolled over. "There's no use hassling me because I don't know anything."

A calculating look settled on Rosalie's face.

"There's no point asking your brothers, either," Daphne said. "If Dimitri didn't tell me, there's no way he told them."

Rosalie flopped back down. "That's true."

"You're too curious for your own good, that's your problem," Daphne said.

"And you're not curious enough! I don't know how you do it."

"It's easy." Daphne yawned. "Just put it out of your mind and have a nap instead."

"We're here," Oscar announced. "All of us. And with the requested food."

Rosalie sat up again. "Food? Are we having a picnic?"

"No idea," Vernon said cheerfully. "We just did what we were told."

"Quadruple pay today," Ralph added.

"I'm glad he's been paying them daily out of the replenishing chest," Daphne said. "They're going to be rich by the end of this."

But Rosalie wasn't distracted. "It's getting a little cold now the sun's gone down. Are you sure the picnic wasn't supposed to be at midday?"

Dimitri cleared his throat, drawing her attention. She scrambled to her feet. "Have you finished in the courtyard?" she asked eagerly. "Are we allowed to look now?"

He bowed low and gestured in the courtyard's direction.

"Allow me to escort you, my lady."

"Are we all supposed to come?" Daphne asked.

He smiled around vaguely. "Is everyone here? Excellent. Please follow me, everyone. And make sure you bring the food, boys."

"Yes, sir!" Vernon said promptly.

"We should be paying them quadruple pay every day," Rosalie said admiringly.

Dimitri smiled down at her. "If you'd like it, we can. It's not costing us anything after all."

"When you put it like that, you make us sound stingy!"

She turned the corner of the building and came to a stop, one of her invisible brothers colliding with her back. Dimitri steadied her, and she grinned up at him.

"A firepit? Outside? When the manor already has approximately thirty-seven thousand fireplaces?"

"You like it?" He grinned back. "Now we can stay out long enough to look at the stars. There were a lot of shooting stars last night, so I'm hoping for the same tonight."

In the hours he'd been gone, he had built a secure firepit, placing logs in a circle around it, presumably for seats.

"Is this something you used to do in the mountains?" Daphne asked, and he nodded.

"The mountain community didn't all gather often, but when we did, it was always around a bonfire."

Rosalie's expression softened. He hadn't just made them a firepit and prepared a picnic; he was sharing something of himself with them.

"It's a lovely present," she said quietly. "We appreciate it."

"Yes, I'm sure it's a present for all of us," Daphne murmured behind them before the rustle of her clothes moved away.

She and the boys quickly laid out the food the triplets had brought, along with plates and cutlery and even cups and flagons of drink.

"This really is a feast!" Rosalie was impressed.

Perhaps she shouldn't have been so impatient all afternoon. Surprises could be enjoyable.

She shared a log with Dimitri, and darkness slowly fell, alleviated only by the light from the manor windows and the flames of the fire in front of them. The darker it became, the less noticeable the others' invisibility was, and by the time she finished her plate, it wasn't noticeable at all.

The six of them talked and laughed, keeping Dimitri entertained with stories of the triplets' childhood, and even some early tales of Rosalie and Daphne's.

"Why do I feel like you were reluctantly dragged into every single one of those disasters?" he asked Daphne.

"Because you've met Rosalie," she replied.

They all laughed, and Vernon launched into another tale. In the darkness, their surroundings felt magical and secluded. Weariness crept over Rosalie, and she let her head rest on Dimitri's shoulder.

He tensed slightly but made no protest, soon relaxing again. Eventually the talk dwindled into silence, and they all sat, staring into the mesmerizing flames. Rosalie was used to watching a fire, but there was something different about seeing one beneath the stars.

"This is lovely," she breathed sleepily. "Maybe my true calling is to be a peddler and travel the kingdoms. I could sit under the stars with a fire like this every night."

"Except when it was raining," Ralph said. "Or snowing. Or blistering hot."

"Thank you for that injection of practicality," she said dryly. "I see you read my mood precisely."

"Yes," Dimitri said in a strangely formal tone. "I've noticed your mood lately. Is it that you're missing your mother? It's been a long time since you've seen her." He put heavy emphasis on the final sentence.

Rosalie pulled away from him, the light, sleepy feeling gone.

"It has been a while," Vernon said. "That illness excuse is wearing thin too. She's starting to be concerned that it's dragging on so long and has been talking about visiting you."

"Hush!" Daphne said, in an unusually sharp tone.

Obviously, her friend had understood the significance of Dimitri's words, even if her brothers hadn't. Some of Rosalie's pleasure in the evening picnic evaporated now that she realized it had been a farewell.

But Dimitri was still waiting for her answer, and there was only one she could give. She should be happy to give it, but she found she wasn't in the least.

"I have indeed missed my mother," she said, equally formally. "May I have permission to leave here to visit her?"

"Alas," Dimitri said. "I cannot refuse you, and yet I know now that I will die. For if you leave me, I will surely sicken and perish."

"I will not leave you, Beast," Rosalie said, wishing she could put more enthusiasm into her script. "I swear that if you let me go to see her, I will return to you."

"Do you mean it?" he asked, and his acting was perfect. The words sounded utterly sincere.

"I will be gone only a day," she promised, seeing no need to drag out that portion of the story. "I will stay with her one night, and when I arise the next morning, I will return immediately."

"Thank you," Dimitri said, and again he sounded as if he meant the words.

They all headed inside quickly after that, but Rosalie

lay awake in her soft, cloud-like bed for a long time. It was the last time she would lie in it, and she couldn't bring herself to reach for sleep. She should welcome the morning and their imminent freedom from the Legacy, but somehow in her weeks at the manor, her original goal had become blurry and distant. She hadn't felt trapped by the Legacy—not since that solitary day in the library—and ending her weeks in the manor no longer felt like the culmination of all her efforts.

CHAPTER 23

ROSALIE

Rosalie walked away from the manor the next day with a silent and invisible escort. In exchange for a pouch of coins each, the boys had agreed to escort her home in complete silence and to then return to watch over Dimitri.

"You have to go straight back to him," she told them when they reached the yard. "I don't want him on his own. If something goes wrong, and he starts to sicken early, you've promised to come and fetch me. Don't forget!"

"You're going to be gone for one day," Vernon said. "Relax."

She waved them off, listening for their departing footsteps before she went inside to find her mother. She was greeted with great delight and a long hug.

When her mother finally pulled back, she held her by both shoulders, gazing into her face.

"But Rosalie, you look so well!" she exclaimed. "I

expected you to look thin and haggard after such a long illness, but your skin is glowing."

Rosalie clapped both hands to her cheeks, her face flushing. "Is it? It wasn't a severe illness. I could still eat." She made a silent promise to tell her mother the truth as soon as she was able. She hated deceiving her.

Her mother talked almost nonstop from morning until mid-afternoon. It made it easier for Rosalie, who didn't want to make up stories about her supposed convalescence, but it also saddened her to realize how lonely her mother must have been. At least her loneliness was over now. Soon they would be able to bring their father home and end his long trips.

In the late afternoon, someone called from the front garden, bringing both women to their door. The unfamiliar postman waved a letter.

"For Madam Clifford?" he called, peering from one to the other.

"That's me." Rosalie's mother hurried outside and accepted the letter. She brought it back into the house, tearing it open as she walked. "Oh!" she cried when she saw the signature at the bottom. "It's from one of your brothers-in-law. No wonder I didn't recognize the messenger. He must have come all the way from their town. Why ever did he spend so much to have a courier deliver the letter directly?"

She scanned the letter's contents, her furrowed brow deepening as she read.

"What is it?" Rosalie asked in sudden dread. "Has something happened to Violet or Heather?"

"It's the children," her mother replied, folding the letter back up. "All of them are ill, and now both Violet and Heather have succumbed as well. My son-in-law has written to beg me to visit and lend my assistance."

She looked at Rosalie, fresh concern filling her eyes. "But you've just returned today! And your brothers are away. I can't leave you alone."

"Of course you can," Rosalie said. "We've had the whole day to catch up, and it sounds like my sisters need you far more than I do. If I get lonely, I'll ask Daphne to come and stay."

Her mother immediately relaxed. "Dear Daphne." She smiled. "She makes me feel as if I have four daughters."

Her smile fell away, and she looked sideways at Rosalie, clearly concerned for her slip of the tongue. Rosalie continued smiling back at her, despite her sudden sadness. Had she really been that sensitive about the Legacy that her family had feared mentioning the number of siblings in their family? As if Rosalie might have forgotten and been upset at the reminder?

Dimitri had been right. She had allowed her fear of the Legacy to rule her life.

"Go, Mother," she said. "And when you come back, all will be well here." Better than well, she hoped.

She assisted her mother to pack a small case and waved her off in the direction of Thebarton. The last coach between the towns would be leaving soon, and she didn't have any time to waste.

But once she was gone, a heavy silence descended on the cottage. It was tiny compared to the manor, but it felt huge in its emptiness. Rosalie went through the familiar routines of the evening mechanically, her thoughts with the inhabitants of the manor. She didn't mind cooking for herself, but she wished she had Dimitri to share the meal with her.

Just thinking of him sitting at the table beside her made her smile. She rested her elbows on the table and relived their night by the campfire. She had already forgiven him for planning such an elaborate farewell. It had been time, even if she hadn't wanted to admit it.

But she had only been gone for a day, and she missed him with a fierce ache. It wasn't only the manor she had grown to think of as hers, it was the manor's owner as well. The thought that he would be traveling to the capital while she returned to her old life was unbearable.

Rosalie herself had been the one to insist he needed to go, but she regretted her rash words now. Dimitri had only ever lived in a small, remote community, so Thebarton must have seemed grand by comparison. But once he experienced life in the capital that would change. Would his grandfather convince him to stay there? He might even try to plan a marriage for him, with a lady from his own station.

Dimitri had talked as if he planned to return, but he might change his mind once he saw the reality of the capital and its inhabitants. He and Rosalie had gotten along well, but in the capital he would surely meet many ladies more beautiful and more interesting than she was. Dimitri might only be impressed by her because he had no comparison.

Rosalie stood and paced in the small space available to her. When she had left for the manor, she had feared the Legacy might manipulate her emotions. But that fear had long since disappeared. Now that she truly knew Dimitri, it was obvious that no manipulation would be needed to make a girl fall in love with him.

She froze at her own thought. Is that what had happened to her? Had she fallen in love with him?

She didn't even have to think about the answer. Of course she had. The realization filled her with a buoyant feeling, but it remained anchored by a subtle churning in her gut. She had been swept away by her feelings once before and been hurt. Giving way to them again scared her.

She didn't fear that Dimitri would use her as Jace had. But that didn't mean her heart was safe. Dimitri had made her no promises, and he had been open about his intentions to leave. She could already see how much it would hurt when she lost him.

She pushed aside those thoughts for the moment and let the buoyant feeling fill her again. For now, it was enough to admit to herself that she had fallen in love with Dimitri.

Despite the revelations of the evening, pacing could only occupy her for so long. She wished she could return to the manor immediately, but she had said she would come back after she awoke in the morning, and she needed to fulfill her final role.

With no one to talk to, and no current projects underway, Rosalie climbed into her bed early. She had thought she would be sleeping beside her mother that night, but she was once again alone—just without her comfortable bed from the manor. She had feared she might find her old bed uncomfortable after enjoying the manor's comfort for so long, but after her lack of sleep the night before, she drifted off quickly, despite the poor quality of the mattress.

Her last thought as she fell asleep was that she would go straight to the manor as soon as she awoke. She wouldn't even risk eating breakfast beforehand.

A loud bang woke her several hours later while the sky outside was still dark. It took a moment for her scrambled wits to make sense of where she was. She sat up just as her bedroom door crashed open.

The form of a man stood silhouetted by a faint light, making it hard to see anything but a dark outline. She screamed, but the startled cry was short-lived. There was no point wasting her breath when there was no one close enough to hear a call for help.

She tried to stand, but in the seconds it took her to untangle herself from the sheets, he had reached the side of the bed. Before she even had a chance to fight, the man had ripped one of the blankets off the bed and wrapped it around her, immobilizing her. She tried to protest, but a sack was placed over her head, and she was hoisted efficiently over his shoulder.

He grunted something to someone nearby, and she realized he wasn't alone. Any attempt to fight him off and escape would be useless. She was only glad her mother was gone. She would have tried to fight the men and ended up hurt or taken as well.

She tried calling questions to her captor, but her muffled words were ignored, and she quickly desisted. From the length of time they traveled, and the sounds beneath the men's feet, they were taking her into the woods. Her heart sank. It was a more sophisticated abduction this time, but they were treading a familiar path. She had made a similar journey already, and she could guess who was waiting at the end of it.

When she was finally lowered to the ground, she could barely keep her feet. Half her muscles cramped in protest, and the blanket upset her balance. Someone unwound it, and the moment her hands were free, she ripped the sack off her head.

It took her eyes a moment to adjust, but when they did, her fears were confirmed.

"Jace!" she spat out, too furious for a complete sentence.

"Naturally," he said with what she had once thought was a charming smile. "Were you expecting another? I even sent a warning to your mother to make sure she was out of harm's way. You should be thanking me."

"My mother?" Rosalie groaned as she thought of the unfamiliar postman.

Her sisters were going to be very surprised when their mother turned up unannounced. But Rosalie couldn't be sorry she and her mother had fallen for the ruse. Her mother wouldn't have been able to stop the abduction alone.

"Only you would do something so foolish as abduct me a second time," she said, wishing the words weren't so hollow.

"Is it foolish?" Jace smiled again. "I thought it was inspired myself. You helped, of course."

She glowered at him, and he stepped closer. She wanted to step back, but she didn't want him to know she was afraid, so she held her ground.

"So convenient of you to have last night's meal outside," he said.

She stilled, the blood rushing from her face. Jace had been there? Watching them? She shivered.

"I hope I'm not one to make the same mistake twice," he said, clearly pleased with himself. "After my first failure, it was obvious that a great deal more reconnaissance was needed. And since the Legacy evidently disapproved of a frontal assault, I've had to resort to more...Legacy-approved methods, shall we say. As I said, inspired, in my opinion."

Rosalie's mind scrambled as she tried to work out what Jace might have overheard and how he might plan to use the information. Her hurried thoughts led her to one conclusion, and she swayed, her knees nearly giving way.

Jace closed the short distance between them, steadying her with a hand on one arm. She desperately wanted to shake him off, but at the same time she was afraid she really might collapse if she did.

Jace was right. Horribly, tragically right. She had made it too easy for him.

"Ah, I can see you already understand," he said. "Your quickness is one of your many virtues, my dear."

She was afraid if she opened her mouth to insult him, she might lose the previous night's meal on him instead. So she kept her mouth clamped shut.

"Since I've already been so very patient," he said, "I did appreciate you setting the time to a single day. We won't have to wait long."

Rosalie swallowed. Why hadn't she predicted Jace might do this and taken steps to prevent him? She had gone over the original history so many times in her mind that the outcome had seemed a certainty already. But Jace had so easily pulled her off course.

All he had to do was keep her here past the morning. She didn't know how quickly the Legacy would cause Dimitri to sicken and die, but based on its speed thus far, she didn't think it would take long.

Her stomach heaved.

"You needn't look so alarmed, Rose," Jace said, still holding her arm. "This is by far the neatest way, you know. And if you choose to be cooperative, there's no need for you to lose out."

"What is that supposed to mean?" she snapped, finally finding her voice again.

"That you can still be mistress of the manor when this is over. Once the Legacy deals with the current owner, there will be no one to fight me for either the manor or its riches. Who's to say I'm not a descendant of the old lord as much as Dimitri? No one in Thebarton has reason to know different. I certainly look the part."

Rosalie's hot repudiation of his claim didn't make it past her lips. Both she and Daphne had noted Dimitri's similarity to Jace the first time they had met him. It was possible Jace's claim might actually be believed. He might even be able to convince the guards that Dimitri had attacked his men over a family squabble turned sour rather than the other way around.

His biggest problem was Rosalie herself—her and her family and her friend. They were the ones he had originally cheated, and they were the only witnesses to what had really happened in the manor. If he wanted to live openly as a free man, he had to secure their compliance. Jace's oily smile took on a whole new meaning.

He let go of her arm, running his fingers lightly up its length. She shuddered in disgust, but he seemed to take it as a promising sign.

"I hope you haven't forgotten how well we dealt together once," he murmured in her ear. "I'll acknowledge that I used your family ill, but that can all be undone now. I can pay back every coin with the wealth from that manor and still have enough to keep us both in luxury for the rest of our lives. You can share it with me. You'll lose nothing."

His hand glided into her hair, his fingers twisting around a lock of it. "You liked me well enough once, I'm sure you can like me again. For myself, well..." His smile grew. "I said before that you were just as beautiful as ever, but I think I was wrong. You seem to get more beautiful each time I see you. A wife fit for the lord of a manor. I'm sure we can deal extremely well together once more."

Rosalie pulled back, not able to keep the disgust off

her face. Strategically, it would have been better to play along, but she couldn't bring herself to do it. And she suspected that no matter how cooperative she seemed, Jace wouldn't drop his guard until enough time had elapsed to doom Dimitri.

"I was sincere in what I said at our previous meeting," she said. "I hope I never see you again. I certainly won't be marrying you."

Jace's hand dropped, and his expression turned ugly. He laughed—a harsh mocking sound.

"I certainly hope you haven't been foolish for a second time and fallen for your Beast," he said. "I thought you knew better than to let the Legacy play you yet again."

Rosalie's stomach writhed to hear her own thoughts and fears echoed from his mouth. She raised her chin defiantly.

"Oh dear," he said. "You have." He patted her face condescendingly, and she flinched away from him. "Poor Rosalie. It seems all your loves are doomed to end in tragedy. But think on my words. It's too late for your lover, but it's not too late for you. You can still accept my offer. I'd much prefer to marry you and have you willingly revoke the charges against me than to be forced to dispose of all my accusers. Given the past connection between us, it will be a tricky thing to get rid of your whole family without raising suspicion. But I have faith in my ingenuity, so the decision is in your hands. I *will* be lord of that manor. With you," he said, pausing meaningfully, "or without you."

He turned to one of the men standing a respectful distance away.

"Tie her up." He jerked his chin toward a nearby tree.

Rosalie stepped hurriedly backward, but she stepped straight into the restraining grasp of someone behind her. Within moments, she was bound and secured to the tree Jace had indicated.

She sat there with her head high, determined not to cry. But as the first rays of dawn pierced the leaves, silent tears ran down her cheeks.

CHAPTER 24
DIMITRI

The hours passed slowly. Painfully slowly. It seemed like days, not hours, since Rosalie had left.

He had paid the triplets a pouch of gold each to stay with Rosalie the whole time she was gone, but he still worried constantly. He would have had her surrounded by a squad of armed guards if that wouldn't have risked disrupting the Legacy.

They were so close to the finish line, and Dimitri knew he only needed to endure for a few more hours, but it was still hard to bear. He roamed from room to room, but everything he saw reminded him of her. He hadn't been thinking of the future when he'd made memories of Rosalie in every room of the manor. Enduring her absence was going to be unbearable.

When it was time for the evening meal, his steps took him to the dining room. He wasn't there to eat—how could he sit down to a meal when Rosalie might be in danger?—but it was what the two of them had always done at that time.

"Are you well?" a kind voice asked, and he remembered with a start that he wasn't quite alone in the manor yet.

"Do you think Rosalie is well?" he asked and heard the rustle of Daphne moving closer in response.

A cool hand that he couldn't see was placed against his forehead. "I've been watching you today," she said. "You seem fevered. I thought the Legacy wasn't supposed to start attacking you until after Rosalie's appointed time away?"

Dimitri sank into a chair, placing his head in his hands. "I can't even tell any more," he said hoarsely, strangely glad to have someone to unburden himself to, even if he didn't know Daphne well. "All I can think about is Rosalie. I go straight from happy memories to terrifying images of her hurt and hurting—and then back again. My stomach is churning too much to eat, and I can't stay still for more than a minute at a time." He looked up, forgetting for a moment that he couldn't see her. "I'm exhausted, but there's no way I'm going to be able to sleep."

He looked back down at the table. "Do you think...do you think all that is the Legacy? Is it messing with my head—making me desperate without her because I'm a Beast and she's my merchant's daughter?"

With a soft sigh, Daphne pulled out the chair next to him and sat down.

"Does it matter what I think? What do you think? Do

you think the Legacy can reach into your mind and place thoughts there?"

Dimitri frowned. Did he think the feelings he had for Rosalie were false ones created by the Legacy?

He rejected the thought immediately. He had recognized Rosalie's fire from the first moment of their meeting, and she had followed that up by proving herself intelligent, brave, active, and kind.

"Of all people, Rosalie doesn't need the help of the Legacy to win people over," he said.

Daphne laughed. "There are some who might disagree with you, but I'm glad you see her that way."

"I don't love Rosalie because of the Legacy," he said, and Daphne gasped at the word love.

He hadn't meant to say it. It had slipped out naturally. Rosalie had worked her way too far into his heart to use any other word. But, even so, the intensity of the feelings that had been consuming him since her departure were another matter. He was less certain those were natural.

Despite her gasp, Daphne didn't comment at his choice of words, so after a pause, he continued.

"This reaction,"—he gestured toward himself—"I'm less sure about."

"I don't believe the Legacy can control your thoughts," Daphne said thoughtfully. "But in this situation, with all the power it's pouring into you two, I'm sure it can give you a fever. And the fever might be enough to induce the frenetic intensity."

She hesitated before adding softly, "It worries me,

though. If you're reacting this badly this quickly, you might go downhill very fast tomorrow."

"That doesn't matter," he said with utter faith. "Rosalie will come. She'll come and then the Legacy will reverse whatever it's done to make me sick."

"Yes," Daphne said, but he was glad he couldn't see her face because she didn't sound sure.

But he trusted Rosalie completely. Regardless of how she felt about him, she was too kindhearted to put him at risk. He also didn't think he'd imagined the connection that had grown up between them in their weeks together. Rosalie would return to him, at least for long enough to satisfy the Legacy.

Pain pierced him at the idea that afterward he might have to live without her. The prospect of day after day like the one he had just endured gave him his first insight into his mother's mindset. Could he trust himself to be more sensible than she had been in the same circumstances? He was no longer as sure as he used to be.

What would he do if he knew he had already seen Rosalie for the last time?

He drew a deep breath and leaped to his feet. He had to move. He had to move his body or something inside him would break. He paced the length of the room once, twice, three times and then headed for the door.

A pulling at his sleeve made him stop.

"I'm not sure constant motion is a good idea for the sickness," Daphne said. "You'll make the fever worse."

"I'm sorry." He looked apologetically down at where

he thought she must be. "But I have no choice. I *have* to move."

She gave another soft sigh. "Why do I have such a bad feeling about this?" she murmured.

"Don't worry." He gently removed his sleeve from her grasp. "It's part of the story, remember? Things have to look bleak right before everything is fixed."

"In the histories, yes," she said in a worried tone. "But remember there's no guarantee the Legacy will see the story all the way through. That's why we've had to be so careful to keep feeding it. You aren't the first ones to attempt this."

Her final line made him freeze with one foot already out the door. He turned back to stare in the direction of her voice.

"Excuse me?" he asked.

"Since the Legacy keeps the manor clean, I've had some spare time since I got here," she said. "I've been using some of it to do research in your library. You're not the first ones to try this. It's not surprising, really. It's unusual for circumstances to align as perfectly as they did in your case, but the Legacy is influencing details all over the kingdom, so it's bound to happen from time to time. And given the potential wealth on offer, some people have gone out of their way to help create the right scenario."

"And all those people tried to act out the whole story like we've done?" Dimitri asked.

"Not all of them. But some have tried it—either in an attempt to gain the wealth or to free themselves from the form of a Beast."

"Why didn't you say anything?" he asked.

"There's a reason it's not tried more often," she said softly. "Many of the attempts didn't end well. But I didn't discover that until after we'd begun, and there didn't seem much point telling everyone at that stage."

"I see." He wasn't sure what else to say. Even now— even knowing it might end in disaster—if he could go back, he would make the suggestion just the same.

"On a more positive note, you seem to have a very mild case in terms of your transformation," she said, clearly trying to lift his spirits. "I think that means the Legacy recognized you're more purehearted than most who make the attempt."

"Thank you?" he said, wondering what greater discomforts the other Beasts had suffered but glad he didn't know at the same time.

"And you said you love her," Daphne said softly. "I think that will help as well. It's not just playacting now. You really did fall in love." The silence lengthened, and she finally continued. "I know my friend. She'll return tomorrow...if she possibly can."

Dimitri's feet started moving again before he realized he was back in motion, carrying him out of the dining room and toward the entryway. *If she possibly can.* The words rang in his mind, repeated on a loop that threatened to drive him mad. He had been worried about Jace, but should he be worrying about the Legacy instead? Would it conspire against them to keep them apart?

He had trusted her brothers to watch over her, but

what could they do against the Legacy? He would just go and check on her...

He wrenched himself to a stop with his hand on the front door handle. The Legacy *was* working against them —it had sent a fever to confuse him. If he left the manor grounds, their story would be broken.

Rosalie was counting on him to do his part. He had to prove he was stronger than the Legacy's wiles. If it wanted to test their resolve, it wouldn't find him lacking.

"I will wait for you, Rosalie," he said, each word pulled out of him with great effort. Sweat beaded on his forehead as he pried his hand off the door, finger by finger.

When he succeeded, he felt as weary as if he'd fought and won a great battle. But the restlessness lodged beneath his skin wouldn't fade. He strode toward the stairs, beginning another circuit of the manor.

He had intended to at least lie down once night fell, even if he already knew sleep was unlikely. But the agony of inaction made it impossible. Instead, he paced the manor in the moonlight with the same confident steps he'd used during the day. He knew the building well enough now to need little light to guide him.

When dawn finally sent its creeping fingers over the horizon and through the windows, he could wait no longer.

He refused to let the Legacy break him, but Rosalie might arrive at any moment. If he couldn't go to her, he could at least ensure there wasn't a moment's delay to their meeting. He would pace the manor's gardens instead of its rooms.

But Rosalie didn't appear. Time had passed slowly the day before, but it was nothing to the agony of each tick of the clock after dawn. Every minute must surely be an hour, and every hour a time too long to fathom. The sun kept climbing, and he felt the same urge to move, but his body was no longer obeying his commands.

His arms and legs were weak, and he staggered more than walked. At one point he thought he heard someone calling his name with concern, but it wasn't her voice, and he couldn't make out the words.

Eventually he staggered hard enough to fall, and he couldn't get back up. A cool hand pressed against his forehead, but it wasn't her hand. He didn't have to open his eyes to know that.

He couldn't open his eyes. For the first time he realized deep in his bones that he might never open his eyes again. He hadn't broken, but the Legacy might still defeat them. *Many of the attempts hadn't ended well.*

CHAPTER 25

ROSALIE

The first light spearing through the canopy sent desperation flooding through Rosalie. She thrashed wildly, trying to free herself, no longer worrying about drawing attention in the process.

But the attempt was as unsuccessful as her more subtle efforts had been. She was secured too well. And because of her own lack of foresight, no one even knew she had been taken. By the time anyone came looking for her, it would be too late for Dimitri.

She thrashed again, unable to help herself. But it only twisted her binds tighter. Jace's men certainly weren't concerned by her efforts.

She forced herself to stop. Jace had far fewer men than before, but it didn't really matter if he had the current four or the previous eleven. They were still an insurmountable barrier to her escape. And apparently Jace had enough wealth—thanks to the money stolen from her family—to ensure they remained loyal despite their comrades' arrest.

Rosalie needed a way to call for help, but they were too far into the woods for a simple cry to have any hope of succeeding. If it had, they would have gagged her. If only her father weren't so far away. If only—

Her thoughts stuttered to a stop. Her father was far distant, but her mother still communicated with him. Rosalie had never managed it with Jace, but she understood why now. Her love for Dimitri was real in a way her girlish feelings for Jace had never been, so perhaps she could reach him in her sleep?

It was an enticing prospect, but an enormous barrier still remained. Before she could communicate with someone in her dreams, she had to be asleep.

She immediately squeezed her eyes shut. She could feel the exhaustion pulling at her limbs and fogging her mind, but even so, she had never felt less sleepy in her life.

Being snatched from her bed and carried through the woods blindfolded, confronting Jace, and then being tied to a tree had been difficult. But those trials were nothing compared to the battle before her. She had to force herself to fall asleep.

The rough bark at her back itched. The ties around her wrists burned, and the ones around her arms forced her into a position that made her muscles ache. Around her, the woods were stirring to life, animals calling in the distance. Nearby, however, one of Jace's men had stretched out on the ground and started snoring—a gasping, snorting sound that drilled into her skull.

And worse than all of that were her racing thoughts.

The more she thought about needing to fall asleep, the less sleepy she felt.

She tried focusing all her thoughts on her body, slowly working her way up from her toes to her head, as her mother had taught her as a child when she was too energized to sleep. But all it did now was remind her of every aching discomfort and stinging pain.

An image of Dimitri, ill and injured, felled by the Legacy, filled her mind. How much time had passed since first light? When would he begin to feel the effects of her absence?

Her fear sent her thoughts racing again, imagining every horrifying scenario. Forcibly she shut the thoughts down, turning her mind backward instead. The evening before, when she had felt lonely, she had relived their evening around the campfire. She forced herself to do the same again, disciplining every errant thought, and channeling her mind into recreating that enjoyable evening as vividly as possible.

She tasted the delicious food, felt the warmth of the flames, heard the laughter of her brothers and friend, and basked in the solid nearness of Dimitri at her side. And then he was no longer at her side. She was walking up the steps of the manor, but it looked different. It had become her old home in Thebarton's central square.

"Rosalie!" She spun around to see Daphne rushing toward her, concern etched into every line of her face.

"Daphne?" Rosalie peered at the square behind her friend, but her surroundings shifted and changed, their appearance both familiar and unfamiliar at once. "Are you really here, or is this just a dream?"

"Both," Daphne said promptly, her usual languor entirely absent. "Don't you recognize a communication dream? I've been searching for you for hours."

"Is that what this is? I've never had one before."

"You don't talk with your father?" Daphne was momentarily distracted.

"My mother does, but it's a connection that usually only works for those with a romantic attachment."

"Truly?" Daphne stared at her. "The lessons on the Glandore Legacy in Oakden were less detailed than yours must have been here. I only remember hearing you had to trust the person completely. The first time my parents had to travel for their work, I immediately started looking for them in my dreams. We've always been able to connect without a problem." She frowned. "Is that really a strange thing?"

"I suppose they did say that trust and love are the most important elements," Rosalie admitted. "But all the examples in books were married couples. My friends and I just assumed..." She shook her head. "I never tried to do it with a friend or my sisters. But it makes sense that if I can communicate with anyone, I can do it with you. You're more a sister to me than my actual sisters are. But if it's so easy, why have we never done it before?"

Daphne snorted. "We're neighbors or close enough. We see each other almost every day. What need have we ever had to communicate this way?"

"You're not invisible," Rosalie said, realizing how long

it had been since she'd seen her friend's face. "And you seem...different."

Daphne looked down at herself. "Of course I'm not invisible in my own dreams. And thank goodness for that or my parents would have realized something was going on by now. But never mind any of that." She seized Rosalie by both arms. "It must be well past dawn. I didn't get to sleep until the early morning which is the only reason I'm still sleeping now. But why are you asleep? I thought for sure you would be here the moment it was light."

Rosalie stared at her, noting again her uncharacteristic agitation. What if it wasn't part of the dream's strangeness...?

"What is it?" she asked. "Has something happened to Dimitri?"

"You need to get here quickly," Daphne said. "The Legacy has hit him hard. He was already feverish yesterday, and he hasn't been able to eat or sleep. He can't even rest. He's been pacing constantly since you left. His body is going to give out soon."

"What?" A cold chill ran down Rosalie's spine. "It wasn't supposed to start so early!"

"Everything will be all right as long as you get here soon," her friend said reassuringly. "You need to wake up and run straight over here."

"But I can't!" Rosalie wailed, tears spilling from her eyes. "Jace has me."

"WHAT?" Daphne stared at her. "What do you mean he has you?"

Rosalie explained what had happened, describing the

direction they had gone in the woods, and her best guess for how far they'd traveled.

"But where are your brothers?" Daphne asked. "Why haven't they rescued you? It shouldn't have been that hard to follow you and cut you free given they're INVISIBLE!"

Rosalie stared at her friend. She'd never seen Daphne so worked up, and the sight of her distress sent Rosalie's fear spiking. How bad was the situation for Daphne to lose her usual cool?

"I paid the triplets a pouch of gold each to walk me home and then return to watch over Dimitri," she said. "Aren't they with you?"

Daphne groaned. "And Dimitri paid them a pouch of gold each to walk you home and stay to watch over you. They must have decided that if they kept their distance from both of you, then they could keep both pouches. I can't believe they'd just abandon you like that, though! They knew how worried Dimitri was."

Rosalie closed her eyes, the whole situation now blindingly obvious.

"Our cottage isn't like the manor. Even invisible, they couldn't have hidden from me inside it. I would have tripped over them within minutes. So they probably decided to watch over me from outside. I'm sure they thought nothing would happen, and you know how deeply they sleep. They must have fallen asleep outside the cottage somewhere and slept through the entire abduction. They're probably still asleep right now."

"I am going to wake up in approximately one minute," Daphne said through her teeth, "and then I'm going down there to find them. And when I do, I'm going to wring their necks—all three of them at once."

"You can't do that without me there to watch," Rosalie objected, but her voice quavered slightly at the end.

"I'm going to find them," Daphne said, "and then the four of us will come find you. Given our invisibility, we should have you rescued in no time."

"No!" Rosalie shook her head frantically. "Send the triplets after me, but you need to go back to Dimitri." She held her friend's gaze, trying to communicate her seriousness. "You have to keep Dimitri alive until I get there, Daph. I'm relying on you."

Reluctantly Daphne nodded. "I'll do everything I can. I promise. But you need to hurry."

"I'll be waiting for the boys," Rosalie said. "You need to wake up and run."

She was thrown instantly out of the strange dreamscape. But she didn't regain proper consciousness. Instead, her surroundings formed again from one breath to the next, the nonsense of the jump feeling strangely logical in the way it does in dreams.

She was in the manor gardens, although they looked like no actual part of the manor grounds. But it didn't matter because she knew her location with unwavering certainty, as if it was as familiar as her own hand. She looked around, confused as to why she was alone. Was Daphne still asleep after all and waiting somewhere here for her? Or was Rosalie stuck wandering this strange dreamland until she found a way to wake herself?

"Y...You're here," the gravelly whisper was instantly recognizable despite its volume.

She turned slowly, both hopeful and afraid.

Dimitri stood before her, a smile in his eyes, although his face couldn't quite form the expression. She ran to him, fresh tears streaming down her cheeks as she collided with his chest.

He staggered backward, and she gasped an apology. But he had already steadied, his arms coming firmly around her. She rested her cheek against his chest, feeling the soft padding of his fur beneath the vest.

"At least the Legacy is letting me dream of you one last time," Dimitri said, his voice low and weak. "It's more than I expected."

Rosalie pulled back, her eyes flying to his face.

"This isn't a dream!" she cried. "Or, well, it is, but I'm really here. We're both asleep, and so we're together." She was making a muddle of the explanation. Hadn't he read about Glandore's sleep communication?

If he had, he didn't seem to remember the information. He was holding her tightly, but she was no longer sure if it was him holding her or her holding him up.

She wound her arms around him and held on tighter, struggling to keep him on his feet.

"Even if it is just a dream," he said, his words dropping so low she had to strain to hear them, "I'm glad I have the chance to tell you. I love you, Rosalie."

She gasped, momentarily struck silent, and his legs crumpled. His weight was more than she could hold, and he slid slowly to the ground, his eyes fluttering closed.

CHAPTER 26
ROSALIE

"No!" Rosalie shot into gasping wakefulness. "No, no, no!" She tipped her head back and closed her eyes.

But if it had been difficult to sleep before, it was impossible now. Dimitri had said he loved her. He had thought it was merely a dream, but she knew it had been the real him. And she hadn't been able to say it back.

But as little as she wanted to admit it, it didn't matter that she couldn't return to sleep. She hadn't been the one to cut their dream connection. Dimitri was no longer sleeping but truly unconscious.

Just unconscious, she told herself, refusing to think of anything else that might have severed the connection between them.

She slowly straightened and opened her eyes, still trying to calm her breathing. At least she had succeeded in getting a message out. Her brothers would be coming for her.

But she couldn't just sit and wait. Dimitri didn't have the time. She needed to do something to speed her brothers up and help them find her. She had to find a way to make enough noise that it would travel through the trees.

She considered her limited options. If she started screaming, she would quickly end up gagged, which would only make her situation worse. And if she acted too soon, her brothers wouldn't be close enough to hear, no matter what she did. Even if Daphne ran flat out, it would take her some minutes to reach and locate Rosalie's brothers—especially if they were invisible and asleep.

Assuming her brothers set out immediately to search for her, it would still take them some time to get deep enough into the trees to have a chance of hearing her. So as difficult as it was, the first thing she had to do was wait.

She marked off the minutes in her head, forcing herself to count steadily and not to rush. Focusing on the numbers actually helped, pushing the endless, rushing, consuming fears for Dimitri into the background.

While she counted, she felt around carefully with her foot until she located a small stone just within reach. It took a little maneuvering, but she positioned it in the perfect spot and waited as the minutes rolled out in her mind.

When she had finally counted enough, she flicked her foot upward in one swift movement. Thanks to the possession of three younger brothers, Rosalie had perfected a great many useless life skills. But on this occasion, being able to flick a stone with her foot with great accuracy turned out not to be as useless as she'd always imagined.

The stone sailed unerringly through the gold-toned early light of day and hit the snoring man in the side of the face. He grunted and shot upright, glaring around him.

"Who was that?" he bellowed, far louder than any shout Rosalie could have achieved.

"It was him!" she said quickly, inclining her head toward the second largest of Jace's men. He had been given the dawn shift and had been looking surly and grumpy ever since the snorer had handed the watch over to him and fallen asleep.

She expected him to deny it, and for both of them to quickly figure out who was really to blame. But it didn't matter if they turned on her. She didn't care who was being yelled at, just as long as they kept yelling.

But the accused man leered at the snorer. "At least we don't all have to listen to your racket now."

The snorer surged to his feet and crossed the clearing in several quick strides. His approach made the other man look nervous, but he didn't back down.

"I don't even know what your problem is," the man on watch said coldly. "I didn't do anything."

"What?" The snorer grabbed him by his collar. "You're going to blame the girl with her hands tied to a tree, are you?" His voice rose. "You think I'm a fool?"

The accused's temper overcame the last of his good sense, and he shouted back. "Biggest one I ever met!"

She wasn't sure who pulled their arm back first, but they both managed to land a punch. They fell back, the force of the blows pushing them away from each other. But with an ear-shattering bellow, the sleeper rushed forward again, and the two fell into a brawl.

The remaining two men had woken from all the noise, and they cheered the fighters on, calling encouragement to first one and then the other, laughing at the early morning spectacle. If Rosalie's brothers were anywhere in the area, they would surely hear the commotion.

The fight swung in her direction, and Rosalie pulled her legs up, bending her knees and scrunching her body into as small a space as her binds allowed. She had been even more successful at causing chaos than she had hoped, but she didn't want to be injured in the process.

The rope tying her to the tree shifted and pulled. She strained to see if someone was behind her, but the trunk blocked her view. She wanted to call out, but she didn't dare risk it in case it was her brothers. But could they really have made it all the way to her that quickly?

"Quiet for now," an unfamiliar female voice whispered. "This should only take a moment." The ropes vibrated, tugging back and forth. Were they being cut with a knife?

"Can you move?" the woman asked after a moment. "Once these are loose, we'll have to get out of here quickly. We might not have much time before they notice you're free."

Rosalie didn't know the identity of her rescuer, but she wasn't going to turn down assistance.

"I can run," she breathed. She hoped it was true.

She scanned the clearing for Jace, but there was no sign of him. He had stepped out just after dawn—either leaving for some unknown mission or else doing the day's necessaries at some distance from the rest of them. Hopefully he stayed away a bit longer.

With a final rasp, the tension in the ropes collapsed. They dropped loosely around her, setting her free. Rosalie whisked her feet under her, crouching for a moment and being sure nothing had gone to sleep.

As soon as she was certain she had control of her body, she sidled sideways around the curve of the tree trunk, still in a crouch. Every nerve was screaming at her to run, but she forced herself to move slowly and smoothly, trying to avoid anything that might draw the men's eyes.

The second she reached the other side of the trunk, two slender hands grasped her and pulled her into the trees. She stumbled after the woman, her body less coordinated than she would have liked after the cold, uncomfortable hours.

The two of them wove between tree trunks, trying to watch their steps and make no noise until the woman pointed at a particularly dense clump of bushes.

"There!" she said quietly and disappeared into the depths of the clump.

Rosalie hesitated only a moment before following. It was surprisingly roomy beyond the first layer of branches, and she finally relaxed enough to catch her breath, leaning over to brace herself on her knees.

"Are you all right?" the woman asked, her voice setting off a wisp of memory in Rosalie's mind.

Rosalie peered up at her. The day had already grown brighter, and even in the middle of the clump of bushes, she was able to see long wavy hair, so dark it was almost black, and full lips.

She straightened with a startled exclamation. "You're Avery! The peddler! But whatever are you doing here? Why did you rescue me?"

"I prefer roving merchant," the other young woman said with dignity, but her eyes were amused. "As to what I'm doing here...Originally I was passing through the woods. But that commotion would have attracted anyone's attention."

Rosalie grinned. "That was the idea."

She wanted to ask why Avery had been so far from any roads, but she didn't want to respond to a rescue with an inquisition.

"I'm glad it worked," she said instead. "Although you weren't the one I was hoping to alert."

Avery's eyebrows rose. "You did that on purpose? I'm impressed."

Rosalie flushed. Avery might not be much older than she was, but she had always admired the woman's independence and capability. Few people could endure the rigors of constant travel between the kingdoms.

"I'm sorry for getting in the way of your rescue," Avery said with a laugh. "Perhaps I shouldn't have gotten involved. But when I saw a group of angry men fighting each other and a lone girl tied to a tree, it didn't require a lot of discernment to work out whose side I was on."

"Thank you!" Rosalie said fervently. "I really do appreciate your intervention, and I don't want to seem ungrateful, but I have to leave quickly. There's a situation, and it's urgent. You see, I—"

"If it's urgent, don't waste any more time talking to me," Avery said. "But will you be all right? Do you need help?"

Rosalie shook her head. "Thank you, but it's something only I can do. I just have to get there quickly."

Avery nodded, not questioning her further, although her eyes were alight with curiosity.

Rosalie turned to leave but paused and looked back. "But what about you? Is your camp far away? What if Jace's men find you while they're searching for me?"

"Jace?" Avery frowned. "I heard about him last time I traveled through Thebarton. He's back?"

Rosalie sighed. "Unfortunately, yes. Those are his mercenaries." Her lip curled. "As you can see, he's put my family's money to good use."

Avery's eyes narrowed. "Don't worry about me. I can take care of myself. But..." She hesitated before drawing something from her boot and holding it out to Rosalie. "You should take this."

Rosalie responded instinctively, accepting the tiny dagger and its scabbard before she realized what she was holding. She looked from the miniature weapon to Avery.

"Thank you?" It came out more hesitantly than she'd intended.

Avery chuckled. "Don't worry, size is deceiving in the case of that little beauty. Plus it fits in your boot, which is very convenient!"

Rosalie slipped it into her boot as instructed, despite her continued confusion. She wasn't in the position to turn down a weapon, no matter how insufficient.

As she straightened, Avery murmured, "It was gifted to me by a talented Oakdenian herbalist."

Rosalie eyes widened. "Ohhh," she breathed, looking down at her boot.

In Oakden, they had herbs infused with their Legacy that could be used to make powerful sleeping potions. The potions were sold to doctors throughout the kingdoms and were highly prized. But she'd heard rumors that the herbs could be used to make a different type of substance —a more potent version that they rubbed on the blades of weapons. One prick was enough to send someone to sleep. Possession of the weapons gave the Oakdenian armed forces an advantage, and neither the herbs nor the weapons were ever traded to outside merchants.

"I can't take such a valuable gift!" she exclaimed. "What if you need it?"

"Don't worry. He gave me more than one." She winked. "He was extremely grateful."

"If you go around rescuing strangers in need, I'm not surprised!" Rosalie said. "But are you really sure—"

Avery held up a hand to silence her. "I hear something! If your mission is so urgent, you'd better go now or else we might end up trapped here for some time."

Rosalie's breath caught as she heard the voices a

beat behind Avery. She recognized Jace's tones among them, so he must have returned to the clearing. Obviously he had discovered what his men had failed to notice.

"Thank you," she murmured a final time and plunged through the branches, moving in the opposite direction to the voices.

She was running toward the distant road and the manor, but she had lingered too long. Almost immediately a shout of discovery went up. She risked a look back over her shoulder. One of Jace's men was pointing in her direction, the others turning to look.

Avery burst from the bushes behind her, emerging almost on top of the men. She let out a piercing scream of surprise.

Her unexpected appearance distracted Rosalie's pursuers, but Rosalie hesitated to use the opportunity to escape. She couldn't leave Avery to be captured in her stead.

As she faltered, Avery looked once in her direction and mouthed, "Go!" before sprinting off into the trees in the opposite direction, trailing several of the men behind her. She must have staged the entire thing to create a diversion for Rosalie.

Rosalie resumed her own flight, feeling the dagger in her boot as she ran. Avery was clearly equipped with far more tricks than Rosalie. If she believed she could protect herself, Rosalie believed it too.

Unfortunately, footsteps and shouts still followed Rosalie as she ran. The men must have split up to pursue both girls. She risked a glance behind her and saw Jace and two of his men on her tail.

She bit her lip and increased her pace, panting as she ran. She knew she couldn't keep up the headlong speed indefinitely. If she didn't find a way to evade them soon, they would catch her.

Hands grabbed her, jerking her body sideways between two tree trunks. Her forward momentum sent both her and her new attacker careening into a tree. They smashed against each other, and both fell to the ground.

A male voice groaned, but it sounded much younger than any of Jace's men. Rosalie jumped to her feet and groped around blindly, trying to find her brother and haul him to his feet. As she searched, she peered back toward her pursuers.

They were calling out in surprise at her sudden disappearance, increasing their speed in an attempt to reach her. As they neared her position, a length of rope sprang up from the detritus on the ground, held taut between two invisible posts. Jace's followers both ran into it at speed and were knocked off their feet.

They rolled on the ground, clutching their midriffs and groaning. Before either had a chance to recover, their bodies contorted, as if kicked by invisible feet.

Rosalie's hand finally found a collar, and she hauled her unnamed brother to his feet. Dragging him behind her, she raced toward the others.

"Stop!" she cried, and the two men on the ground stilled, both groaning even more deeply than before. "We don't have time for this."

Her eyes caught on Jace, lingering far back and watching his men with wide, horrified eyes. They didn't have time to deal with Jace either. He appeared terrified by the invisible attack, and she didn't think he would continue the pursuit alone. He was too much of a coward for that. She hated to leave him free, but she couldn't let anything else slow her down.

"We need to get to Dimitri," she said more quietly.

She started running again, not waiting to hear her brothers' assent. Thankfully, their footsteps kept pace with her, assuring her of their presence, although she couldn't see anyone.

One of the sets of footsteps veered close, and Vernon's voice sounded between puffs. "I'm sorry, Rosalie!" he sounded both guilty and angry, but she knew his anger was for himself and for Jace. "We meant to take it in turns keeping watch, but..."

"Save your breath for running," she managed between gasping breaths of her own. She didn't have the energy to either scold or forgive them when all her attention was focused on getting to Dimitri as quickly as possible.

Much to her dismay, her body couldn't keep pace with her will, and they had to alternate between walking and running. Each time she dropped to a walk, the lack of speed chafed so badly that she broke into a jog again as soon as she'd even slightly caught her breath. All she could think of was Dimitri collapsing in their shared dream.

Finally the road came into view. She staggered through the last of the trees and stood panting as she tried to orient herself. With a burst of joy, she realized she had emerged some distance north of where she had been taken. The land bordering the road to the west was already the manor grounds. They were nearly at the drive.

She took off jogging again before she had properly caught her breath, riding a new wave of energy as she left her brothers behind. As she turned down the drive and raced toward the house, she scanned the garden on either side. He had been outside in their dream, but she hadn't been able to see exactly where.

When she reached the manor without spotting him, she tried to push open the doors. They wouldn't budge. She knocked, but without much force. Somehow she already knew the manor was empty.

Hurrying back into the gardens, she hesitated, looking left, then right. She could see nothing to indicate which way she should go. Turning left at random, she moved at a half jog, peering between hedges and flower beds.

"Rosalie!" Daphne's voice called from behind a hedge, and Rosalie raced toward it.

She rounded the end of the hedge, and her eyes fell on Dimitri. She forgot all about Daphne at the sight of his unmoving body stretched out on the ground, his face gray.

She could see his still features clearly. His unnatural long hair was gone, and his original appearance had been restored. She was too late. She had been too slow. He was already dead.

"No!" She threw herself onto his unmoving chest.

She had tried so hard. It couldn't all be for nothing.

Dimitri couldn't be gone from her life without even a farewell. He was too full of life to be felled like this.

"He isn't dead!" Daphne's hurried words penetrated the haze of her grief. "Not yet. He's been holding on. Just."

As if triggered by her words, Rosalie felt the subtle rise and fall of his chest. The breath was labored, but it had happened. He really was alive.

She sat up, feeling foolish. If he was still alive then she needed to act quickly. But as she stared down at him, she saw his features for the first time in weeks. Her breath caught as his face blurred, and she saw another in its place.

Jace.

She shuddered, but she couldn't delay. No matter what tricks her mind was playing on her, she had to speak the words that would save Dimitri.

"Don't die, Beast," she croaked out, the words of her role tasting sour on her tongue. "I l..." She faltered. Pulling herself together, she tried again and got it out. "I love you."

Nothing happened.

She looked in the direction of Daphne's voice, desperate.

"I don't think it's enough to playact this part," her friend said. "I think you have to mean it."

Rosalie's stomach clenched. She had meant it. She loved Dimitri.

She looked at him again, still seeing Jace's face. She tried to shake away the effect, but while she had physically escaped from Jace, he still had poisonous hooks in her mind.

She trusted Dimitri, but she didn't trust herself. What did she know of her own heart or the hearts of others? She thought she loved him, but what if her supposed love was as hollow as her love for Jace had been? Had the Legacy seen the truth and rejected her confession?

After everything they'd done, she wasn't enough to save him. Pain tore through her middle. She had to try again.

But the words lodged in her throat. She had thrown off the shackles of being the merchant's third daughter, but she was still weighed down by her own mistakes. How could she ever trust herself after getting it so badly wrong?

Dimitri's eyes fluttered open, meeting hers. They were dull, their light almost extinguished, but they were also familiar. They were the eyes of both Beast Dimitri and regular Dimitri. He had looked at her with those eyes when he told her he loved her.

Staring into them, she no longer saw Jace or the reminder of her past weakness. The man in front of her wasn't a stronger, more vibrant, more handsome version of Jace. He was just Dimitri. And her love for him was real. The Legacy was wrong.

Dimitri had helped her walk away from the burden of the Legacy without expecting anything in return. He hadn't tricked or trapped her. He hadn't taken anything from her at all. He had merely offered to help her. He had literally put his life on the line and lay dying as a result.

She didn't love Dimitri because of the Legacy, as she

had loved Jace. She loved him in spite of it. She and Dimitri had met in their dreams when she had never been able to meet Jace. And while she might have misjudged Jace, she had learned many hard lessons in the year since he'd left. She was stronger and wiser than she had been then.

Daphne had been right all along. From the moment Rosalie met Dimitri, she had been attracted to him, and she had judged him as a result. After the pain of Jace's betrayal, she had acted just like the original merchant's daughter. The historical daughter had been unable to see past the Beast's form, forcing him to approach her in her dreams with his true face. Rosalie had been the opposite, only opening up to Dimitri when he gave up his true face and took the form of a Beast.

She gazed down at his strong features and allowed herself to feel the full force of the attraction she had been suppressing. She acknowledged that she loved him inside and out—his whole person. He didn't have to become someone else for her.

This was what the Legacy had been testing. It was the reason it had restored his true face before her confession. It wanted to know that she could see beyond his appearance despite her past hurt. And finally she had passed. They had completed the story the Legacy insisted on foisting on them.

She cupped Dimitri's face with both hands, watching as his eyes lit up in response.

"I love you," she murmured, tears dropping from her eyes to run down his cheeks. "I love your brave, determined heart, your clever mind, your thoughtfulness, your natural skill with people—even your strong arms. I loved you as the Beast, but I love you even more as a man. Being around you makes my heart beat uncomfortably fast. It always has. I'm sorry I tried to close my eyes and my heart to you."

The change was instantaneous. Even as she was speaking, his color returned, and the moment she spoke the final words, he surged upward. With one movement, he had her on his lap and his lips melded to hers.

She returned the embrace, and he wrapped her in his arms, cradling her close as he deepened the kiss. She closed her eyes and sank into it, kissing him back with an enthusiasm that matched her previous fear. His arms tightened around her in response, a low rumble sounding in his chest.

"I see we made it back in time," a nauseated voice said from above them.

Rosalie gasped and pulled away, but Dimitri's lips followed hers, a growling, wordless protest in his throat.

Daphne laughed, and Dimitri straightened with a resigned sigh. He kept his arms around Rosalie, though.

"Would all invisible people please take themselves off," he said, his eyes still on Rosalie. "Preferably somewhere very far away."

She blushed, her eyes dropping while her lips curled into a smile.

"Actually, we're not invisible anymore," Daphne said, making both of them finally look up.

Rosalie blushed further and scrambled up from

Dimitri's lap, although she didn't know why it made a difference. It wasn't as if she and Dimitri were the ones who'd been invisible.

Standing, she gazed around the garden, looking for any other obvious differences. It looked the same as far as she could tell, with plants growing in profusion everywhere.

She felt the difference inside her, though. They had done it. They had managed to beat the Legacy.

CHAPTER 27
DIMITRI

"So we really did succeed," Rosalie murmured, sounding like the events of the last few hours still hadn't sunk in.

She looked back at him, and he could barely restrain himself from taking her in his arms again. If only their blasted audience would truly disappear.

"I'm sorry I was late," Rosalie said softly. "Jace tried to stop me coming. He wanted to get rid of you so he could take the manor."

Dimitri shuddered. Despite his previous intention, he pulled her close, leaving one hand at her waist. He couldn't hold her properly, but he needed to feel the living, breathing warmth of her beside him.

"If he touched you..." he breathed darkly.

Jace had wanted to take his home and his new wealth, but he guessed the weasel had wanted to take Rosalie as well. He probably saw her as another prize to be claimed. But Rosalie had chosen Dimitri.

His breath caught as he relived her declaration. He had been lost in a dark haze, but her words had reached him, along with the feel of her tears on his face. He had wanted to tell her not to cry, but he hadn't been able to form the words until her confession suddenly revived him to full strength.

More than full strength. He could probably uproot mountains single-handedly from the force of her love and her safe return.

"I'm fine," she said quickly. "I really am. Avery helped me escape not too long after dawn. I've mentioned her before, do you remember? The peddler girl. And then the triplets showed up to help as well. So I had plenty of assistance."

"The triplets?" Dimitri's brow creased. "They weren't there when Jace came for you?"

"What matters," Oscar said quickly, "is that the two of you succeeded—with our help. And now we can all be free of the Legacy."

"Not completely free," Daphne said cheerfully. "There's still nothing but roses and hedges in this garden."

"Personally, I just want the kissing to stop." Vernon eyed Dimitri darkly. "No brother should have to watch an exhibition like that. I think my eyes were about to jump out of their sockets and run for the hills."

"*I* think you have some explaining to do," Dimitri said in a voice that made all three boys take a step backward. "And it sounds like you each have a pouch of gold to return to me as well."

Rosalie looked as if she expected them to protest, but

Dimitri knew better. He didn't know the details, but they had clearly behaved irresponsibly and allowed Rosalie to fall into danger. From their demeanor, they knew it too.

They all lowered their eyes, scuffing their feet and remaining silent. He was tempted to give them a few more pithy truths, but he stayed his tongue. They clearly knew their error and were feeling bad enough already.

Rosalie put her hand on his arm. "They've already apologized," she said quietly before turning a stern look of her own on them. "But they have *two* pouches of coins to return."

Dimitri raised an eyebrow, a general idea of what had happened starting to take shape. Maybe he would need a few follow up words with the triplets—later, at a more private moment. They weren't likely to be receptive while Daphne was present and listening.

"The details can wait for later," he said. "But what about Jace? Where is he now?"

Rosalie grimaced. "I have no idea. All I cared about was getting back to you as quickly as possible. We couldn't stay to deal with Jace because I was worried..."

She looked at him with a shade of her past fear lurking in her eyes, and it took great willpower not to take her in his arms and kiss the shadow away.

"Thank you," he said instead. "I appreciate that. But it does leave us with an...unfinished problem."

He glanced from Daphne to the triplets who were still lurking nearby with uncertain expressions.

"I'm very grateful you broke the enchantment when you did, but unfortunately it means we've lost our primary advantage. We no longer have any invisible forces."

"But Jace doesn't have many men either," Rosalie said. "He only had four left—at least from what I saw in the woods. And the triplets injured two of them. I don't think those two will be feeling well enough to fight anytime soon. So that just leaves Jace and two men. We outnumber him for once."

"But we also don't know where he is or what he's planning." Dimitri hesitated. "None of us believe this will be enough to make him give up, do we?"

All five of them shook their heads.

"He talks as if he thinks he's entitled to the manor and its wealth," Rosalie said regretfully. "I'm afraid he's more likely to be angry than resigned."

"Then we need to act quickly before he can hire more men," Dimitri smiled, feeling a violent satisfaction at finally being released to search for Jace himself. "That's twice now he's abducted you. I don't intend to leave him free to try it a third time."

A flash of color flew past, and a parrot landed on Rosalie's shoulder. She jerked backward in surprise, but it kept its grip.

"Intruders!" it squawked. "Foxes in the hen house! Locusts in the wheat!"

"We aren't intruders," Rosalie said in exasperation, but she was smiling fondly at the bird.

Dimitri frowned. "Are you sure it means us?"

An echoing bang rang across the garden—like a large door thudding closed. Dimitri didn't wait to see the others' reactions, taking off at full speed toward the manor doors. When he arrived, both of them were firmly closed.

He knew he had stumbled out of the doors at some point that morning, but he could barely remember it. All his memories from Rosalie's absence were hazy. He looked toward Daphne. She was frowning.

"I definitely locked it," she said. "You were too ill to think of it, so I took your key out of your pocket to do it." She held it out to him. "I'd already given the master key ring to Vernon, so I had to use your key instead."

"Why would you give the master ring to Vernon?" Rosalie demanded.

"Dimitri was staying here, and he already had a key," Daphne explained. "So since we were splitting up, I thought each group should have keys. Of course, that was when I thought the boys were actually going to be with you…"

Dimitri tried to turn the key Daphne had just given him in the lock. It didn't work.

He turned grimly to Vernon. "So where exactly is that second key ring?" he asked.

Vernon thrust his hands into his pockets only to go still, his face turning pale. He searched around more frantically but failed to produce any keys.

Rosalie groaned. "Were you the one who tackled me in the woods?"

"I didn't tackle you!" he protested. "I just pulled you out of harm's way."

"And we both fell," she said. "So I'm guessing that's when you lost the keys."

"Jace was there?" Dimitri asked, already knowing the answer.

Vernon nodded miserably. "I'm sorry."

"So Jace found the keys you'd dropped in the forest," Dimitri mused aloud. "He must have guessed what they were for and come straight here. And he conveniently found us all in the garden." He sighed. "So he's inside now, and he's left his key in the lock to stop us using ours. Honestly, it could be worse. At least we know where he is now. I wonder if he's thought to bar the other doors?"

"He might not have if he doesn't need long," Rosalie said. "His plan might be to wait until we circle the building trying other doors, and then he'll escape back out the front door with whatever he's stolen."

Dimitri glanced at her. He wasn't convinced Jace would be content with just stealing a few valuables. But even if he was, Dimitri didn't intend to let him get away with it.

"This way." He hurried along the front of the manor. "The door in the conservatory is closest. And Jace likely doesn't know about it, so I doubt he's secured it from the inside."

"I never noticed an outside door in the conservatory," Oscar said doubtfully. "Are you sure there's one there?"

"It's half size," Rosalie explained. "We think the gardeners used it to shovel soil and move plants in and out. So they wouldn't have to carry them as far, or trail dirt through the manor."

They reached the conservatory at a half run, taking only a moment to locate the door. Dimitri used his key to open it, dropping to his hands and knees and crawling through first.

It was a tight fit, and at one point he feared his clothes had been caught. But he managed to force his way into the glassed room. And he was the largest. If he'd made it through, the others would as well.

He didn't wait to watch them enter, crossing straight to the room's main door and easing it open. No one was visible in the corridor beyond, so he stepped through.

"Wait!" Rosalie hissed behind him, and he glanced back.

He wanted to rush ahead, to face the danger on his own. He hated the thought of Rosalie being at risk yet again. But they didn't even know where the danger was. Despite his impatience, it was safer for them all to stay together.

Daphne and the triplets crowded behind Rosalie, although he wasn't sure which boy was which. He had learned to tell them apart by their voices, and he was still getting used to who was who by appearance.

"We outnumber them," he said, "but they might be armed. No one do anything rash." He focused his words toward the boys, but after their latest mistakes they were too subdued to behave rashly.

He drew his sword, and Rosalie gave a start at the sight of it. He frowned. Was she afraid? She had never reacted to the weapon before.

But she didn't look fearful as she retrieved something

from her boot. When she straightened, she was holding the hilt of a miniature dagger, the blade still enclosed in an equally small scabbard. Apparently, the sight of his weapon had reminded her that she had one of her own. If something that tiny could even be considered a weapon.

She looked at him and gave a classic Rosalie smile. "I can explain it," she whispered, "or we can find Jace before he steals everything the Legacy gave us."

He grinned back. "I vote we find Jace."

He led them down the corridor, Rosalie following with Daphne at her side.

"Do you have one for me?" Daphne whispered behind him.

"Sorry, she only gave me one," Rosalie murmured back, spiking his curiosity.

He couldn't imagine why anyone would want a dagger so small it could do little damage. He preferred his sword steady in his hand any day.

The entryway seemed the best place to start, so he headed straight there. He was rewarded by the sight of three men descending the last of the main stairs. The one in front—Jace—carried a slim case, while the other two huffed with the shared weight of a closed chest.

Rosalie had been right. They'd gone straight for the locked rooms and were already trying to get out again.

Dimitri strode forward, standing in the middle of the entryway and meeting Jace's eyes.

"I already told you that you're not welcome here."

Jace laughed. "I don't know what you're talking about. I have a key." He held up the master key ring with one finger. "Do you really think the guards will appreciate being dragged into a family squabble?"

Rosalie joined Dimitri, and he had to squash the instinct to sweep her back, out of danger.

"I already told you that I won't let you get away with your lies!" she cried to Jace, her whole body quivering with fury.

Dimitri tensed. They were talking about something he didn't understand, and he hated the reminder of all the threats Jace had made to Rosalie. What had he said to her now?

"But I'm not lying." Jace's smug smile moved from Rosalie to Dimitri. "Can't you tell by looking at us?"

Rosalie's indignation faltered, her brow creasing as her eyes traveled between them. She didn't have to answer. He already knew she'd noticed a similarity between him and Jace. Even Wyatt had commented on it at the Mortar and Pestle.

Dimitri stared at Jace, trying to analyze his features objectively. He supposed he could see a similarity—in general coloring if nothing else. And their eyes were quite alike. But Jace lacked the straight nose that graced a number of portraits in the manor and which Dimitri also saw in his mirror.

"I don't care what you look like," Rosalie said, recovering her fire. "You're not a distant cousin of the old lord, and no one around here is going to believe nonsense like that. You're forgetting that everyone in Thebarton knows your true colors. And my family isn't going to retract our claim against you either."

"It's true that I'm no relative of the old lord," Jace said, admitting the truth with surprising alacrity. "But that doesn't mean I'm not a relative of Dimitri." His smile grew. "Why do you think I came to Thebarton in the first place? I found no sign of my brother back then, only a useless, derelict building. Happily I discovered you instead."

Dimitri fell back a step, grinding his teeth at Jace's revelation. His claim was a mockery of Dimitri's dream of finding his family. But he was certain that Jace, at least, believed his words were true.

Rosalie sucked in a breath, and Dimitri's field of vision darkened even further. Jace had come to Thebarton because of him. That meant Dimitri had been indirectly responsible for everything that had happened to Rosalie and her family.

"Brother?" she whispered.

It came out as a question, but he could already see the dawning acceptance on her face. The sight stung, although it shouldn't. They had both known his father was not an estimable man, so it was no surprise he didn't raise estimable men either.

Rosalie's hand gripped his arm, clearly trying to convey reassurance. He smiled down at her. He didn't like the idea of sharing blood with Jace, but if she thought he was shaken by the revelation, she didn't need to worry. He might not have any family around him at that moment, but he had been raised by family. He knew enough about what family meant to know that Jace was no family of his.

"Any blood we share isn't blood I claim," he said coldly

to Jace. He had already guessed what the connection must be. "You are no family of mine."

Jace's expression turned ugly. "I shouldn't be surprised. You're just like your mother, I see. The only family you're interested in are the rich and powerful ones." He spat on the stone floor of the entryway.

"Is that what your father told you?" Dimitri asked.

"Our father," Jace countered quickly, but Dimitri continued.

"If he said Mother abandoned him because he was poor, he lied. He was the one to leave her."

"If he did, it was the old lord's fault," Jace said bitterly. "He rejected our father first. He was so stingy—so determined to hold onto his wealth and not share it with anyone—that he turned his back on his own son-in-law. If our father left your mother, it's because your grandfather forced him into it."

"My grandfather shared his wealth with a great many people," Dimitri said calmly. "His objection to your father was due to his character, not his status. But where is your father now? If he feels he has a right to this place, why are you here instead of him?"

"He's dead." Jace said the word baldly and without feeling. "When I was a child, the old lord came searching for us—as if he hadn't done enough damage already. He revealed to everyone that my father already had a wife and child. When my mother discovered her marriage was invalid, she took ill. She was useless after that, and I'm fortunate I was old enough that Father took me with him when he left. My mother's family turned their backs on us, so he had no choice but to seek other funds."

"You mean he had to find someone new to cheat," Dimitri said bluntly.

Jace shrugged. "He cheated the wrong people eventually. He died several seasons back in a tavern brawl after he was caught cheating at cards. It was the old lord who reduced him to such straits, so it seemed fair I should come and claim something of his in exchange." He looked around the building. "It's just fortunate you turned up and inspired the Legacy to get involved. It was slim pickings before that. Whereas now..."

He opened the case in his hands and displayed the glittering jewels inside to Rosalie.

"I would have placed these around your neck with my own hands. You should have accepted my offer when you had the chance."

"I don't want anything from you," Rosalie said stiffly, but Dimitri could tell she was as awed by the jewels displayed inside the case as he was.

The lustrous gems were larger than any he'd ever seen, and the craftsmanship of the jewelry was of the highest quality. The one case contained a selection of necklaces, bracelets, rings, earrings, and tiaras, each piece beautiful enough to meet the approval of a queen. On his journey to the manor, he had seen storefronts proudly displaying much lower quality wares.

"Is this something you should store in the bottom of your wardrobe?" Jace asked chidingly. "You were wasting it anyway, so why not share with family?"

Rosalie grimaced at Dimitri and whispered, "I guess I should have checked the furniture in my chamber more closely."

He shook his head. Rosalie needed no adornment.

"Enough of this," he said wearily to Jace. "Put down what you've stolen and leave. I owe neither you nor your father anything. You want consideration for shared blood between us? Fine. If you walk out that door now and keep going—never returning to Thebarton nor coming near any of us again—I'll let you go. But this is your only chance."

The two men behind Jace shifted uncomfortably, sharing a glance. When they put down the chest, Dimitri hoped they might leave. But instead they drew weapons, one pulling out a sword and the other a knife. He tensed.

"I'm disappointed, brother," Jace murmured, his soft voice dangerous.

"And I, likewise," Dimitri replied.

He eased in front of Rosalie, his sword ready and legs poised to lunge. But Jace signaled to his men, and they lunged not toward Rosalie, but toward Daphne.

They moved quickly, reaching her before Dimitri could change direction and intervene. The knife wielder seized her from behind, holding his blade to her throat, while the one with the sword held back the outraged triplets.

"It doesn't do to get predictable," Jace said with a satisfied smile as his men retreated in his direction, dragging Daphne with them. "And now unless you want to see this woman dead, I recommend you put down your weapon, stand aside, and let us leave in peace. We'll call this a small gift between brothers. I'm sure no one would question such a thing."

Dimitri glanced sideways at Rosalie. She had one hand hidden in her skirts, hiding her tiny weapon, and she was staring at him with pleading eyes. What was she trying to communicate?

He didn't need to guess, though. There was no way Rosalie would risk her friend's life.

Reluctantly he put his sword down, and even more reluctantly he kicked it away when Jace indicated to do so. As he backed toward the side of the entryway, he swept Rosalie with him, keeping his attention on Jace.

He stopped after only a few steps, unwilling to go too far from Daphne. She had been silent since the moment of her capture, and her eyes were fixed on Rosalie as if urging her to do something.

His ears caught the tiniest whisper of steel against leather, and he tensed. Had Rosalie just drawn her minuscule dagger?

Jace walked back to the chest. He needed to carry it himself now that his men had their hands full. His distraction meant he missed the tense readiness in Rosalie's stance, and the way her eyes didn't leave Daphne's.

The two girls held each other's gaze for a moment before Daphne flicked her eyes in a half-formed nod.

Rosalie responded instantly. Stooping, she slid the naked dagger across the floor toward Daphne and her captor. At the exact moment she moved, Daphne began to wail, her body shaking with distress.

"She's going to faint!" Dimitri shouted, not sure

exactly what was happening but grasping that some sort of distraction was underway.

Jace and the swordsman both turned to look at Daphne as she swayed. The man holding her was struggling to support her weight while still keeping his blade in place. As she sagged sideways, he staggered with her, taking a step at the exact moment that Rosalie's spinning blade slid under his foot.

He stepped down on it, the force of his body's weight driving the razor-sharp blade through the leather of his sole. Dimitri expected to hear a shout as it pricked his foot, but instead he froze. For a second he stood there, motionless, and then his arms and legs relaxed, and he crashed to the floor.

The moment his knife arm loosened, Daphne slumped to the ground herself, sliding away from his blade in a much more graceful movement than his. As soon as she was free, Rosalie shouted, "Now!", and the entire entryway erupted into movement.

Dimitri threw himself across the room toward his sword, snatching it from the ground and spinning toward the remaining armed man. He brought up his blade just in time to meet the descending blade of his opponent in a deafening clang.

All three triplets surged toward Daphne, each attempting to grab her and rush her to safety.

"Not me!" she cried, pointing toward Jace. "Him!"

Dimitri parried again, blocking another thrust from his opponent and preventing him from moving toward the others. He had to keep the man contained, but it was a desperate struggle not to be distracted by the sight of Rosalie moving in the corner of his eye.

Like him, she had also dived for her blade, pulling it free of the downed man's boot. Dimitri still didn't understand what had happened to Daphne's captor, but clearly it was a more powerful weapon than he'd realized.

He blocked another attack from his opponent, responding with a lunge of his own that sent the man scurrying backward. The movement opened a clear path for Rosalie to run toward Jace and she did so, dagger outstretched.

Jace pulled a hidden knife from the back of his waistband, causing Dimitri to forget all about his own fight.

"Rosalie! Watch out!" he shouted.

The silver of a falling sword flashed in the corner of his eye, and he swung his own blade up wildly in defense. Leaping backward, he barely managed to escape the oncoming blade.

Frantic energy coursed through him as he regained his balance. He couldn't waste any more time on his own battle.

Lunging forward, his sword danced in a complicated series of movements. The final thrust disarmed his opponent, sending his blade flying. It landed with a clang, sliding across the floor until it hit the far wall.

Dimitri instantly spun toward Rosalie, braced to see her injured and bleeding. But instead, he saw a struggling mass of bodies and heard Jace screaming his anger.

In the chaos, the triplets had managed to get behind Jace. When he had drawn his knife on Rosalie, all three of them must have launched themselves at him. They had attached themselves to three of his limbs and were hanging there, weighing him down.

Jace was attempting to turn his knife against them, but since both of his arms were weighed down by the full force of a lanky thirteen-year-old, he was having little success.

Daphne rose to her feet, dusting herself off, and looked at Rosalie. "That's enough of that, don't you think?"

Rosalie nodded and darted toward Jace. He tried to swing for her, but the triplets held him back as Rosalie pricked the tip of the tiny dagger into his shoulder.

Like his underling, he froze for a second and then collapsed.

"It's poisoned?" Dimitri asked.

"Not poison, exactly." Daphne held out her hand for the weapon.

Rosalie handed it over, and Daphne turned it this way and that, examining it.

"A delicate piece," she said neutrally as she handed it back to Rosalie. "I'm filled with curiosity as to how you acquired it."

"Avery," Rosalie said as if the single name was enough to explain. And from Daphne's knowing laugh, perhaps it was.

Rosalie looked toward him. "It came from Oakden."

Dimitri's eyebrows rose into his hairline. A sleeping weapon. He should have thought of it at once. But since he had been focused on learning about Glandore, he had only seen the weapons mentioned once or twice in passing. He was definitely going to need the story of how it had come into Rosalie's possession.

"Well done," he said to the triplets, and all three of them swelled with pride, clearly relieved at having had the chance to redeem themselves.

Tramping boots outside interrupted their conversation. Dimitri stepped toward Rosalie, but the fleeing swordsman gave a loud cry of alarm from the front steps. The new arrivals weren't allies for Jace.

Dimitri strode over to the door.

"Guards," he reported to the rest of them.

Rosalie and the triplets looked as confused as he felt at the arrival of the unexpected visitors. But Daphne nodded placidly.

"I suppose they got my note," she said.

"You sent someone a note?" Rosalie asked. "How?"

"There wasn't time to send it. But after I roused the twins and directed them into the woods, I stayed just long enough to scribble a note for your mother. I left it in the house for when she returned, with instructions for her to send the guards to the manor. She must have found it."

Rosalie stared at her blankly. "But my mother left Thebarton to visit my sisters. It was a ruse from Jace, but even so, she couldn't have gotten there and back so quickly."

"Perhaps she realized it was a ruse for herself," Daphne suggested.

"That sounds like Mother," Vernon agreed.

Oscar, however, wasn't listening. He pointed at the

chest, now sitting abandoned on the entryway floor, its lid flung open.

"If the guards are coming, what are we going to do about that?" he asked. "I'm guessing we don't want to draw attention to it."

He was right, but it was a heavy chest, and they only had seconds before the guards arrived. Dimitri looked around blankly for something to throw over it, but Daphne was already moving.

Flipping it closed, she sank gracefully down beside it, crossing her arms over the lid. Laying her head on them as if they were a pillow, her eyes fluttered closed. Within seconds she was breathing steadily as if asleep. Her body and gown didn't entirely conceal the chest, but they obscured it enough to make it a barely noticeable piece of furniture.

The guards pushed open the door, loudly calling for Dimitri.

"We heard there was trouble," the captain said gruffly as he stepped inside. "And we found this gentleman fleeing the sce..." His voice trailed off as he caught sight of the two collapsed men.

"Thank you for your prompt attendance," Dimitri said formally. "Unfortunately, I've been attacked in my home at this early hour and have been forced to defend myself and my guests."

The guards filing in behind the captain exchanged surprised looks, but they responded readily, securing the sleeping men's hands just as they started to rouse.

"What are you doing?" Jace cried when he woke to find

his hands being tied behind him. All his usual charm evaporated as he babbled in panic. "It's all a misunderstanding. I'm family! I'm just visiting my family! I'm—"

The captain hauled him to his feet, shaking him by the collar until the flow of words ceased.

"Don't you try your bamboozling tricks on us," he said. "You're Jace, and we know you well enough in these parts. Plenty of guards have been spoiling to get their hands on you—and some of the townsfolk as well. So you'd best stop complaining and thank us instead. I warrant you'll be glad of our protection soon enough. There are some who would be happy to take the law into their own hands where you're concerned. Clifford employed plenty of people, so it wasn't only his family you ruined." He nodded respectfully toward Rosalie and her brothers, although he was clearly confused by their presence.

"And what about her? Is she one of the perpetrators?" another guard asked, pointing toward Daphne.

"Oh, no," Dimitri said quickly. "She's one of my guests."

The guard leaned over for a closer look. "Is she...sleeping?" He looked astonished for a moment before his face cleared. "Oh, it's only Daphne. Well, then, it looks like that's the lot of them. Sir?" He looked at his captain for instructions.

"If it's just the three of them, we'll be going," the captain said. When Dimitri nodded confirmation, he signaled to his guards. "Come on, men!"

They formed up around the two prisoners and marched them outside to join the third man. Dimitri,

Rosalie, and the triplets watched them go in silence. As soon as the sounds of their marching feet had disappeared down the drive, Daphne sat up and yawned. She blinked up at them and then glanced around the otherwise empty room.

"Is it all finished?" she asked.

Rosalie narrowed her eyes at her friend. "There is no way you were actually asleep just then. Admit it!"

"I'm an excellent sleeper," Daphne said primly. "You know that."

"Even the guards apparently know that," Dimitri murmured, earning himself a glare from Rosalie.

"Of course she was sleeping!" Ralph said loyally. "She's brilliant!"

Dimitri choked on his laugh, not entirely succeeding at keeping it in. All three triplets glared at him, their faces giving an unnerving impression of their older sister.

"I think," he said quickly, "that we should all repair to the kitchen and see about breakfast. What do you think, Rosalie?"

She wrapped both arms around his waist and gazed up at him with an expression that made it hard to breathe.

"I think that we're finally free of both the Legacy and Jace." Her face darkened. "But I'm sorry he turned out to be your brother. I hope you know—"

"I know," he said, wanting to see the dark look banished. "And I meant what I said to him. I don't consider him family." He ran his finger along the curve of her cheek, marveling at the softness of her skin.

"I think breakfast is a wonderful idea!" Vernon said loudly.

All three of the boys converged on Rosalie, prying her from Dimitri and propelling her in the direction of the kitchen. She looked helplessly back at him, but he shook his head and followed with Daphne.

"You get used to them eventually," she said consolingly.

"Like a hole in my sock?" he asked, and her lips twitched. He lowered his voice. "You can tell me—I won't tell anyone else. Were you really sleeping?"

"It was a tiring morning," she replied with a mischievous smile. "And a tiring night, come to think of it."

Dimitri instantly turned serious. "Thank you for everything you did. You were the one with me before Rosalie came, weren't you?"

She nodded. "Yes, but there's no need to thank me. I'm just grateful Rosalie found you. I've always worried about what will happen to her when I leave Glandore. But I'm not worried anymore."

Dimitri nodded his thanks for the compliment. There was no need for her to explain her intention to leave. He had endured life outside his birth kingdom, so he understood that she would eventually have to return to Oakden.

"Help!" Rosalie called from ahead of them. She was gripping the frame of the dining room door as the triplets attempted to push her through. "They're saying I have to do all the cooking to make up for their weeks of slavery."

Dimitri increased his pace to catch up with her.

"I'll help you," he said with a smile. "I don't mind cooking."

Cooking every day with Rosalie sounded like a dream come true. He only hoped they could work beside each other every day for the rest of their lives.

Her expression caught on his, and the laughter in her eyes softened to something more intimate. He stepped forward and pressed a kiss on her lips, the horrified protests of triplets echoing in his ears.

It was a swift kiss, a silent promise between them. They had helped each other defeat the Legacy, and together they would face whatever challenges came next.

Even if those challenges included an overabundance of younger brothers.

EPILOGUE

ROSALIE

"He's here!" Oscar burst into the room, panting from a recent sprint. "One of our friends saw his carriage passing the Mortar and Pestle."

"Already?" Rosalie's mother cried in dismay, looking around the disordered room. "But we haven't finished organizing yet!"

"Dimitri doesn't care about the cushions matching the curtains, Mother." Vernon entered the room with Ralph in tow. "We've told you that a hundred times."

"Maybe not," his mother sighed. "But I really wanted to have the house organized before he got here. He's used to living in the manor, remember! And now he's come from the capital. He must have been living in a fine house while he was there."

Rosalie ignored them, the joy inside her swelling until

she thought she might burst. He was back! Dimitri had finally returned.

She hurried toward the front door, leaving her brothers still arguing with her mother. She had also hoped they would finish the last touches on the house before Dimitri arrived. She had wanted to surprise him with it. He had seen the bones of her family's new house go up throughout the spring—new life in the ashes of the old. But it hadn't been habitable when he left at the start of the summer.

But now that he had arrived, she didn't care about any of that. She just wanted to see him.

She was nearly at the front door when a loud knock sounded through the hall. She ran the last few steps and threw open the door.

A flash of tan leather, white linen, golden-brown eyes, and fair hair was all she saw before Dimitri was inside the house and wrapping his arms around her. She sank into the strength and warmth of his embrace, tears pricking her eyes.

She had been the one to encourage him to go—she had known how important it was for him to find his roots. But she had still missed him intensely in the weeks of his absence. And though they had met often in their dreams, it wasn't the same as being together in person.

Sometimes, when she had been feeling particularly low, she had even felt a shadow of her old worries. Would Dimitri find the capital such a fascinating place that he never wanted to return to Thebarton?

But each time, she had shaken the fears aside. She

knew Dimitri and knew his heart for both her and his mother's manor. She had been confident he would return as planned, and now here he was.

"You're back," she laughed, tipping her head up to look at him. "You're early!"

He smiled down at her, his eyes devouring her face. "I missed you too much to linger on the road. I just wanted to be home."

Home. She let the word soak in.

"Do you like our new house?" she asked.

"House? Are we in a house?" His eyes twinkled down at her. "I can't see anything but you."

She laughed and poked his chest, forcing a small bit of space between them. "We worked far too hard on this house—half of Thebarton did!—for you not to notice it."

"It's very beautiful. The nicest house I ever saw." His eyes still hadn't left her face.

She laughed again. "I hope you'll do better than that with my mother. She's been working tirelessly to get it ready."

"I appreciate the warning," he said. "I'll be sure to compliment everything I see. I wouldn't want to disappoint your family."

As soon as he said the word family, he froze. When he let his arms drop and stepped back, she feared something was wrong. But his face was lit up, and he was smiling broadly as he glanced back through the open door.

"I can't believe I nearly forgot!" he exclaimed. "I was so excited to see you, I nearly forgot that I brought you a surprise."

"A surprise?" Rosalie followed his gaze and saw his carriage sitting in the square outside her house.

"I hope you're going to love it as much as I do," he said with the same boyish grin.

Running down the shallow steps, he pulled open the carriage door and stuck his head inside. Rosalie watched him with a furrowed brow, wondering what sort of item he might have brought her from the capital. After the wonders the Legacy had created in the manor, it was hard to think of anything worthy of so much excitement.

When he emerged again, he was holding only a slim mahogany cane. Rosalie frowned at it. Surely Dimitri didn't think she needed a cane?

A second head appeared behind him, this one covered in gray hair. A tall, slim man alighted, his stature straight despite the cane which he accepted from Dimitri.

Rosalie gasped, her hands flying to her mouth. The older man had the same straight nose as Dimitri. He had brought his grandfather to her.

She knew from their shared dreams that Dimitri had found his grandfather and been welcomed by him. But Dimitri hadn't breathed a word about bringing him back to Thebarton.

Dimitri strode back to her side. "Surprise!" He smiled down at her. "Grandfather was almost as eager to come home as I was."

"I had to meet the famous Rosalie." His grandfather's strong, clear tones were softened by the warmth in his eyes.

He ascended the stairs, the cane appearing more decorative than functional. In the doorway, he took Rosalie's hand and bent over it.

"It's a very great pleasure to meet you, my dear."

"And you," Rosalie returned, still trying to overcome her shock. "I didn't expect...We didn't dream...But of course you're most welcome! More than welcome!"

She smiled from him to Dimitri. She had wanted Dimitri back with her, but she had felt guilty for pulling him away from his newfound family. Now she had no shadow in her happiness.

The old lord turned to survey the town square. "It's good to be back," he murmured.

There was a hint of sadness in his voice, the weight of loss, but when he turned back to them, he was smiling.

"As soon as Dimitri told me he meant to return and make his home at the manor, I insisted he bring me back to Thebarton with him." His proud gaze lingered on his grandson. "It took me a while to convince him I really meant it, but I can be stubborn when I want to be."

"I'm so happy you came," Rosalie said impulsively. "It makes everything perfect."

"Does it?" The old man's lips twitched. "I can see why my grandson is so taken with you, Mistress Rosalie."

Rosalie's cheeks flushed as Dimitri laughed and put an arm around her.

"I think I drove Grandfather to distraction with my impatience on the journey."

His grandfather chuckled. "I remember what it is to be young."

"My lord!" The cry from Rosalie's father sounded both

surprised and pleased. "I didn't realize you were coming with Dimitri. What a pleasant surprise!"

"Clifford. A pleasure to see you again. It's been too long." Dimitri's grandfather shook hands with Rosalie's father, smiles on both their faces. "You can imagine my astonishment when my grandson told me he'd fallen in love with one of your daughters. It brought many memories back, and I fear I must have bored him with an old man's reminiscences." He turned to Rosalie. "Your grandfather was a fine man and a good friend. He did much for this town, and I was greatly saddened to hear of his loss."

"Thank you," she said softly.

"Dimitri! Welcome!" her mother called from the end of the corridor. She hurried forward only to stop in surprise as she caught sight of the unexpected guest.

"My lord!" She curtsied. "But what are you all doing in the doorway?" She turned a disapproving look on her husband. "You must come in! We have comfortable chairs and hot tea and scones."

She bustled them all down the hallway and into the main sitting room where the triplets were waiting. The boys attempted to swarm Dimitri but subsided at a warning look from their father.

After introductions were made on both sides, a serving woman appeared with an enormous tray bearing a tea pot, cups, and an assortment of food. She beamed at them all, seeming almost as happy as Rosalie's family.

The first thing Rosalie's father had done when his fortunes were restored was to rehire all those he had been forced to abandon. Some had already moved on to other jobs, but many were grateful to return to their old positions. As a result, Thebarton felt even more warmly toward Clifford and his family than they had done before.

But before any of them could avail themselves of the tray's goodies, the front door banged open, and footsteps hurried down the hall. Daphne burst in, wide-eyed.

"Am I too late?" she gasped.

"Daphne, were you running?" Rosalie asked in astonishment. "Is something wrong?"

"No, I just overslept." Daphne looked at Dimitri, not seeming in the least surprised by either his presence or his grandfather's. "Am I too late?"

"Too late for what? Dimitri's arrival?" As glad as Rosalie had been to see Dimitri again, she couldn't imagine his presence was enough to send her friend sprinting between their houses.

"Not my arrival," Dimitri said. "Something else. I sent her a note because it only seemed right that she should be here for this."

He slipped off the sofa and knelt in front of Rosalie.

"Rosalie, before I met you, I was alone in the world and knew nothing of my home kingdom. Now I have traveled throughout Glandore, and I have family beside me." He glanced at his grandfather who smiled encouragingly. "But none of that has changed how I feel about you. I want to build a new life and future at the manor, but I can't imagine that life without you at the center. I love you, Rosalie. Will you marry me?"

Tears streamed down Rosalie's face despite her wide smile.

"Of course I'll marry you!"

Dimitri stood, pulling her up with him and wrapping her in his arms.

"Thank you," he murmured into her hair.

They only had a moment to linger in the embrace before Rosalie's family swarmed them, creating a mass of hugs, tears, and happy exclamations. When they finally emerged, Dimitri's grandfather took his turn congratulating them.

"I'm sorry to saddle you with an old man like me," he told Rosalie. "But now that I've found my grandson again, I intend to stick close."

"Oh, please do!" she exclaimed. "It would make us both so happy." She smiled up at Dimitri. It made the moment complete that they could both have their family around them.

"I want to be married as soon as possible," Dimitri said, smiling back down at her. "I don't want us to be apart any longer."

"How about the last day of summer?" Rosalie's mother surprised her by asking.

"But that's only two weeks away," Rosalie gasped. "Can we really be ready by then?"

Her mother gave a satisfied grin. "I may have begun preparing a few things already. I had a feeling this was coming. There's been a lot of work involved in getting the house ready, but that isn't the only reason I've been so busy lately."

"Mother! I can't believe it!" Rosalie shook her head.

Her brothers edged closer, all grinning smugly.

"We've been helping," Vernon said.

"The three of you? And you managed to keep it a secret?" She stared at them, her astonishment real.

"We're fourteen now," Ralph said proudly. "Mother knows she can rely on us."

Rosalie caught her mother's quickly hidden smile and burst out laughing herself.

"You have my admiration and my thanks," she assured her offended brothers when her laughter subsided.

"Was I that obvious?" Dimitri asked ruefully.

Rosalie's father chuckled. "We were only surprised you didn't propose before you left."

Dimitri glanced at Rosalie. "I wanted Rosalie to know that it didn't matter where I traveled or who I met—my feelings about her weren't going to change."

Both of Rosalie's parents beamed approval of his words, and Rosalie's already full heart expanded even further.

"Thank you," she whispered to Dimitri. She was still getting used to being more open and vulnerable about her true self, and it meant a lot that he hadn't just dismissed her fears.

She turned away to surreptitiously wipe her eyes while the others broke off into several smaller conversations. When she had recovered, she gave Daphne a hug.

"I'm so glad you're here too, Daph," she said. "You know you're family as much as anyone else, right?"

Daphne smiled. "Of course. I did run, didn't I?"

Rosalie laughed, but while she feared she might float

away from the happiness filling her, Daphne seemed a little sad behind her smile.

"Are you sure everything is all right?" Rosalie asked, not wanting her situation to overshadow Daphne's, as it sometimes had in the past.

Daphne sighed. "I'm sorry. I didn't want to spoil any part of your big moment. I'm truly so happy for you, Rosalie. You're the only sister I have. I'm just sad that I have to leave."

"You're going? Already?" Rosalie felt some of her joy ebb.

She had always known Daphne would leave eventually. Daphne needed the chance to become her true self just as Rosalie had. And the only way for Daphne to step out from under the Legacy's weight was to return to Oakden. But Rosalie had convinced herself that it wouldn't be for a while yet.

"To be honest, I was originally planning to leave as soon as I turned eighteen," Daphne said. "But I couldn't leave with you and your family in such an awful situation."

"You stayed for me?" Fresh tears filled Rosalie's eyes.

Daphne gave her a gentle nudge with her shoulder. "Sisters, remember?" She cleared her throat before adding. "I thought I would stay another month or two, but I had a letter from my cousin, Olivia, yesterday. The Sovaran one. She's managed to get herself into a pickle which doesn't sound like her. Mother wants me to check on her, so I'm going to visit Sovar on my way through to Oakden. It means I need to leave earlier than I'd planned, though."

"But you'll stay for the wedding, at least?" Rosalie asked, alarmed. "It's only two weeks away."

Daphne nodded. "I wouldn't miss it. And I already brought the first flower for your bouquet." She held out a perfect golden rose.

"I was wondering what happened to that!" Rosalie took it from her, marveling at the rose's beauty. It must have been truly made of gold because it hadn't wilted or faded with time.

"I rescued it from the cottage before your move," Daphne said. "I was saving it for this."

"It's the only one left now," Rosalie said wistfully. "You were right about that. I visited the manor yesterday, and the gardens are still beautiful, but there's no sign of any golden roses. The rosebushes are all normal Glandorian ones. And the trees no longer flower and fruit at the same time."

"The real tragedy is the chest," Vernon said, intruding on their conversation. "It no longer refills. But at least the three of us have managed to dig up most of the pouches."

"We'll find the last two soon," Ralph assured Daphne earnestly.

She sighed. "No, the true tragedy is that the manor no longer cleans itself. There's already dust everywhere."

Rosalie shuddered. "That is a tragedy."

"In that case," Dimitri said, appearing at her side and winding an arm around her waist, "we'll just have to fill the manor with enough people to actually use and care for such a large building."

He looked down at her, waiting for her to nod her approval before he continued.

"Rosalie and I have spent many happy hours imagining a future for the manor. But one feature that never changed was that it should be full of people. It's far too large a home for just two of us—even if we employ an army of staff."

He turned to Rosalie's mother. "I know you've only just finished preparing this beautiful house, but I was wondering if you would consider moving to the manor with us after the wedding? Grandfather, you too." He looked at his grandfather, who nodded, his eyes glistening with suspicious moisture. "And I know you took several families with you when you moved to the capital. We're hoping some of them might like to return as well."

His grandfather drew a long breath, waiting a moment to speak. "Yes, Dimitri, I think they would. They've missed their home, just like I have." He looked to Rosalie. "But are you sure your bride agrees?"

Rosalie smiled. "We spent days exploring the manor when we were shut up there, and we came up with all sorts of dreams about what could be done with the building. Of course, it was just a theoretical exercise at that point, but Dimitri knows how I feel. We want to divide the manor into smaller apartments, while keeping the communal spaces like the kitchen, library, dining hall, and conservatory. We can live in community with each family still having their own space."

"If we all work together, we can finally put the land

attached to the manor to good use again," Dimitri said. "I'm hoping we can revitalize this whole region."

His eyes were shining as he said it, and Rosalie couldn't resist giving him a squeeze. She loved seeing Dimitri full of excitement and plans for the future—their future.

"I want Rosalie to invite anyone she wants to join us," Dimitri said. "Daphne, I know you have to leave, but your parents would be welcome if they liked."

"Thank you," Daphne said. "I'll ask them, and I hope they say yes. I've been worried about them being lonely after I'm gone."

"Oh yes, they must join us!" Rosalie's mother said. "I'll convince them if need be."

"So you'll come?" Rosalie asked, looking between her parents. "Even though you just rebuilt this house?"

"It's a lovely house, but it isn't as fine as the manor," her father said with a chuckle. "Seeing it restored has been enough for me. And I'm sure we'll have no trouble selling it now that there's to be so much new activity in the area."

"I want to be together with my family far more than I care about any house," her mother said. "I've already lost your sisters to distance, so I'm going to stick tight to you."

Rosalie gave a sniff and hurried over to hug her mother.

"You could invite Avery to join us as well, if you like," Dimitri said when she pulled back from her mother. "We owe her a lot."

"You found her?" Rosalie cried hopefully. She had commissioned Dimitri to search for news of the peddler.

She couldn't rest completely easy until she knew Avery had escaped from Jace's men unscathed.

"She wasn't in the city, so I didn't meet her personally," he said, "but there was plenty of talk about her. She has attracted some attention recently among Grandfather's circles."

"So she's well?" Rosalie clarified.

"I believe so."

"That's wonderful news!" She considered Dimitri's original suggestion. "If she comes through Thebarton again, we could make the offer. But I'm not sure Avery is someone who wants to settle down."

"I just hope we have some grandchildren soon," her mother said with a cheeky twinkle in her eye. "Enough to fill the manor."

"Mother!" Rosalie protested, rolling her eyes. "We're not even married yet! I want a few years before thinking about children."

"Just make sure you have a great many when the time comes," her mother said. "Given your history, you'll have to do the same as the royal family—make sure there's never one child left behind by having a large family."

"As long as there are no triplets," Rosalie said with a shudder. "One baby at a time will be plenty for me. And no botanical names!"

"Oh, but they're so beautiful," her mother said with a sigh. "Surely there wouldn't be any harm with something like Iris? Or Daisy?" She looked at Rosalie hopefully.

"Absolutely not," Rosalie said firmly.

Dimitri laughed, putting an arm around her and

pulling her close. "I'm surprised your parents don't call you Rose."

"We tried," her mother said with a sigh. "But even as a toddler, Rosalie wouldn't respond to it."

"Being Rosalie was bad enough," Rosalie muttered.

"I think it's a beautiful name." Dimitri pressed a kiss to the top of her head. "I've thought you were even more beautiful than a rose since the first time I saw you."

Rosalie's indignation melted. "I suppose it isn't such a terrible name," she murmured. "Not now anyway." Her eyes narrowed. "But no botanical names for our children!"

"Whatever you say, my Rose," Dimitri said, making her sputter and swat at him before she got a look at his face and collapsed into laughter.

When she regained her breath, he pulled her close again. The expression in his eyes had shifted, and she was at risk of turning breathless for an entirely different reason, swept away by the love and admiration she saw in his gaze.

"Two weeks until we're husband and wife," he murmured quietly. "I like the sound of that."

She rested her head against him and nodded agreement. It was a beautiful thought. She would marry Dimitri, and they would live in the manor—not as lord and lady but as the heart of a whole new community. And one day they would have children to join them—children who might live in a castle but who would never attract the Legacy's attention because they would have ordinary, boring names and a great many siblings.

She sighed happily. It sounded delightful.

NOTE FROM THE AUTHOR

I hope you enjoyed Rosalie and Dimitri's story! To read the story of Daphne's cousin in Sovar, continue the series with Legacy of Glass: A Cinderella Tale.

Or you can travel with Avery, the roving merchant, in her story, Ties of Legacy, which is part of Tethered Hearts, a multi-author series.

To be informed of my new releases, as well as new bonus shorts, please sign up to my mailing list at www.melaniecellier.com. At my website, you'll also find an array of free extra content for my various worlds.

Thank you for taking the time to read my book. I hope you enjoyed it. If you did, please spread the word! You could start by leaving a review on Amazon or Goodreads or Facebook or any other social media site. Your review would be very much appreciated and would make a big difference!

ACKNOWLEDGMENTS

It's always an equal mix of daunting and exciting to start a whole new story world. This is especially true when starting a new fairy tale world after spending a decade writing in my first one. I knew if I wanted to revisit some of the best-loved tales, it needed to be in a world with its own distinct life and flavor, while hopefully maintaining the same heart and fun of my original world. I hope that I've succeeded in that goal with Legacy of Roses. Given the stressful world situation that surrounds us all in 2024, I also set out to create a fun, cozy sort of world where readers can find quirky landscapes rather than stress. I hope I've succeeded in bringing readers that sort of diversion, and I want to sincerely thank every reader who was willing to give a new story world a try.

Of course I can't create a book alone, and thanks also need to go to all of those who helped in this book's creation. In some cases that was direct assistance, but in others it was helping me to keep going and my creativity to keep flowing. So thank you to my husband who fed me and generally kept me functional, and our little crew who bring daily love and delight. Thanks also to my author friends who help keep me sane. Shari, Kenley, Brittany, Aya, Kitty, Marina, Constance, and Alora—I appreciate all the author chats, the memes, the kdrama recommendations, the writing sprints, and the general friendship. You all make an awesome writing tribe!

In ways relating more directly to the book, I am thankful as always for my incredible team who work like a well-oiled machine to smooth over my inability to keep to a schedule. To Lyra for being an assistant extraordinaire and having endless patience with me forgetting things; to Mary for her developmental edit and encouragement which she does with grace and flexibility; to my dad and James for combing through my manuscripts for typos and other errors and for accepting my inability to remember certain grammar rules; and of course, to Karri, for designing a whole new series of stunning covers. I love the way you brought Rosalie and Dimitri to life. I also love the way Becca turned my scribbles into a gorgeous map that breathes life into the kingdoms of Legacy. I love looking at it while writing!

I also want to give a special thanks to my narrators, Esther—a familiar colleague at this point—and Nathaniel, a new one. I'm so excited to hear this book aloud and to be able to make it available to readers in all formats on release. I appreciate how fantastic you both were to work with as well as your excellent narration skills.

And a final thanks goes to God who extends me infinite patience and grace and whose creative well is always overflowing.

ABOUT THE AUTHOR

Melanie Cellier grew up on a staple diet of books, books and more books. And although she got older, she never stopped loving children's and young adult novels.

She always wanted to write one herself, but it took three careers and three different continents before she actually managed it.

She now feels incredibly fortunate to spend her time writing from her home in Adelaide, Australia where she keeps an eye out for koalas in her backyard. Her staple diet hasn't changed much, although she's added choc mint Rooibos tea and Chicken Crimpies to the list.

She writes young adult fantasy including books in her *Spoken Mage* world, her *Mage's Influence* world, and her various *Four Kingdoms* and *Kingdoms of Legacy* series that are made up of linked stand-alone stories that retell classic fairy tales.